The Best Science Fiction of the Year #12

At last, the eagerly awaited annual anthology of the best short fiction in the science fiction field is presented for your reading pleasure. Spanning the astounding themes, styles and ideas of today's finest science fiction writers, this collection features the finest short stories, novelettes and novellas in print today.

Books by Terry Carr

Fantasy Annual #4
Fantasy Annual #5
The Best Science Fiction of the Year #10
The Best Science Fiction of the Year #11
The Best Science Fiction of the Year #12

Published by TIMESCAPE BOOKS

THE BEST SCIENCE FICTION OF THE YEAR #12

TERRY CARR, EDITOR

A TIMESCAPE BOOK
PUBLISHED BY POCKET BOOKS NEW YORK

Another *Original* publication of TIMESCAPE BOOKS

A Timescape Book published by
POCKET BOOKS, a division of Simon & Schuster, Inc.
1230 Avenue of the Americas, New York, N.Y. 10020

ISBN: 0-671-46680-1

First Timescape Books printing July, 1983

10 9 8 7 6 5 4 3 2 1

POCKET and colophon are registered trademarks
of Simon & Schuster, Inc.

Use of the trademark TIMESCAPE is by exclusive license
from Gregory Benford, the trademark owner.

Printed in the U.S.A.

ACKNOWLEDGMENTS

"The Pope of the Chimps" by Robert Silverberg. Copyright © 1982 by Agberg Ltd./Robert Silverberg. From *Perpetual Light,* by permission of the author.

"Swarm" by Bruce Sterling. Copyright © 1982 by Mercury Press, Inc. From *Fantasy and Science Fiction,* April 1982, by permission of the author.

"Souls" by Joanna Russ. Copyright © 1981 by Mercury Press, Inc. From *Fantasy and Science Fiction,* January 1982, by permission of the author.

"Burning Chrome" by William Gibson. Copyright © 1982 by Omni Publications International, Ltd. From *Omni,* July 1982, by permission of the author.

"Farmer on the Dole" by Frederik Pohl. Copyright © 1982 by Omni Publications International, Ltd. From *Omni,* October 1982, by permission of the author.

"Meet Me at Apogee" by Bill Johnson. Copyright © 1982 by Davis Publications, Inc. From *Analog,* May 1982, by permission of the author.

"Sur" by Ursula K. Le Guin. Copyright © 1982 by Ursula K. Le Guin. From *The New Yorker,* February 1, 1982; this revised version from *The Compass Rose,* by permission of the author and her agent, Virginia Kidd.

"Understanding Human Behavior" by Thomas M. Disch. Copyright © 1981 by Mercury Press, Inc. From *Fantasy and Science Fiction,* February 1982, by permission of the author.

"Relativistic Effects" by Gregory Benford. Copyright © 1982 by Abbenford Associates. From *Perpetual Light,* by permission of the author.

"Firewatch" by Connie Willis. Copyright © 1982 by Davis Publications, Inc. From *Isaac Asimov's Science Fiction Magazine,* February 15, 1982, by permission of the author.

"The Wooing of Slowboat Sadie" by O. Niemand. Copyright © 1982 by Mercury Press, Inc. From *Fantasy and Science Fiction,* September 1982, by permission of the author.

"With the Original Cast" by Nancy Kress. Copyright © 1982 by Omni Publications International, Ltd. From *Omni,* May 1982, by permission of the author and her agent, Virginia Kidd.

"When the Fathers Go" by Bruce McAllister. Copyright © 1982 by Terry Carr. From *Universe 12,* by permission of the author.

Contents

INTRODUCTION

≈≈≈≈≈≈≈≈≈≈≈≈≈≈≈≈≈≈≈≈≈

Terry Carr

SCIENCE FICTION IS MORE POPULAR TODAY than it has ever been before, as you know if you pay any attention to lists of the highest grossing movies and best-selling books. The amounts of money to be earned by producers of even such spin-off items as video games and *Star Wars* T-shirts are often astonishing, proving that there is now a far greater number of people fascinated by space-ships and creatures with pointy ears or knobby three-fingered hands than anyone would have dreamed even a decade ago.

Science fiction has become a major part of popular culture, so much so that we now have to think twice when we see the word "alien"—more often than not, it doesn't refer to immigrants from other countries these days (unless you consider, say, Procyon IV to be another country).

Science fiction's success was fully certified when, in the December 1982 issue of *Harper's,* a poet named Arnold Klein published an article attacking it for being inane, unoriginal, one-dimensional and downright stupid. You may be sure that *Harper's* would not have published an article on this subject if science fiction weren't so popular that it is crowding other forms of literature off of publishers' lists, for though Klein's critical polemic at least was conscientious enough to consider such high-water sf achievements as *The Left Hand of Darkness* and *The Demolished Man* and Klein did admit that a few sf writers like Ursula K. Le Guin and Pamela Sargent are capable prose stylists, the overwhelming tone of his remarks was suspiciously like envy.

It's easy to sympathize with a writer of poetry for being annoyed by a genre whose popularity is making the publication of books of poetry even harder to achieve than it already was, especially since Klein truly does not seem to like science fiction; it must be extremely galling for him to see writers of what he considers junk making large amounts of money while he and his compeers continue to struggle. But I have a measure of cold comfort to offer Klein: most science fiction writers are still struggling too.

For every Robert A. Heinlein or Arthur C. Clarke who can make millions of dollars from science fiction there are dozens of skilled, thoughtful writers of sf who earn very little money from their efforts, who live on the edge of bankruptcy or support themselves primarily by taking non-literary jobs. The list of sf writers with major writing talent who cannot earn a living from science fiction is very long, and includes names that would astonish you.

The percentage of sf writers who are actually able to cash in on science fiction's wide popularity is astonishingly small, something less than 5% at an educated guess. There are complicated reasons for this, having to do with the economy, sociological attitudes and distribution among other things.

But what the situation means is that the overwhelming percentage of published science fiction is written by people who do it more for love than money. Anyone who, like Arnold Klein, dislikes science fiction as a genre will find that hard to comprehend, but I suspect that even he would realize that since most sf is written earnestly and honestly, the resulting stories are better than they would be if everyone in this field were getting rich from it.

And despite the minuscule financial rewards for most sf writers—and the fact that most beginning sf writers are fully aware of the situation—the science fiction field has more new writers entering it today than ever before. Many of them are very good and some of them will become best-selling writers in time, but meanwhile we as readers can enjoy the stories they are writing now, their serious attempts to equal and surpass the stories that attracted them to science fiction in the first place. At the same time, we continue to have before us the stories of established writers who have either made their reputations and perhaps considerable profit from their earlier work or who continue to write science fiction despite lack of fame and fortune because it's what they most want to do.

The present book of *The Best Science Ficton of the Year*

contains offerings from both old and new writers. Writers such as Silverberg, Le Guin and Pohl are among those who have made much money because their achievements have been widely appreciated, while William Gibson, Nancy Kress, and Bruce Sterling and others are newer writers whose names may be unfamiliar to you so far. What they all have in common is strong writing talent seriously applied—and the conscientious imagination of people who know that science fiction at its best can be stimulating and rewarding literature.

Presumably you agree with them, or you wouldn't have bought this book.

—TERRY CARR

THE POPE OF THE CHIMPS

≈≈≈≈≈≈≈≈≈≈≈≈≈≈≈≈≈≈≈≈

Robert Silverberg

Robert Silverberg's reputation is primarily that of a writer who explores serious, even painful, subjects in a coolly thoughtful style; his award-winning novella Born with the Dead *was a superb example of this. But Silverberg's imagination also has a humorous aspect and he enjoys taking a seemingly silly idea and treating it seriously. The notion that a group of chimpanzees might develop a religion based on that of the researchers studying their behavior, as in the following story, could have been frivolous and even silly in the hands of a lesser writer, but Silverberg plays it straight, with fascinating results.*

After a writing hiatus in the late 1970s, Robert Silverberg returned to science fiction recently with the very popular novel Lord Valentine's Castle. *Currently he has a sequel to it in progress.*

EARLY LAST MONTH VENDELMANS AND I WERE alone with the chimps in the compound when suddenly he said, "I'm going to faint." It was a sizzling May morning, but Vendelmans had never shown any sign of noticing unusual heat, let alone suffering from it. I was busy talking to Leo and Mimsy and Mimsy's daughter Muffin and I registered Vendelmans's remark without doing anything about it. When you're intensely into talking by sign language, as we are in the project, you sometimes tend not to pay a lot of attention to spoken words.

But then Leo began to sign the trouble sign at me and I turned around and saw Vendelmans down on his knees in the grass, white-faced, gasping, covered with sweat. A few of the chimpanzees who aren't as sensitive to humans as Leo is thought it was a game and began to pantomime him, knuckles to the ground and bodies going limp. "Sick—" Vendelmans said. "Feel—terrible—"

I called for help and Gonzo took his left arm and Kong took his right and somehow, big as he was, we managed to get him out of the compound and up the hill to headquarters. By then he was complaining about sharp pains in his back and under his arms, and I realized that it wasn't just heat prostration. Within a week the diagnosis was in.

Leukemia.

They put him on chemotherapy and hormones and after ten days he was back with the project, looking cocky. "They've stabilized it," he told everyone. "It's in remission and I might have ten or twenty years left, or even more. I'm going to carry on with my work."

But he was gaunt and pale, with a tremor in his hands, and it was a frightful thing to have him among us. He might have

6

been fooling himself, though I doubted it, but he wasn't fooling any of us: to us he was a *memento mori*, a walking death's-head-and-crossbones. That laymen think scientists are any more casual about such things than anyone else is something I blame Hollywood for. It is not easy to go about your daily work with a dying man at your side—or a dying man's wife, for Judy Vendelmans showed in her frightened eyes all the grief that Hal Vendelmans himself was repressing. She was going to lose a beloved husband unexpectedly soon and she hadn't had time to adjust to it, and her pain was impossible to ignore. Besides, the nature of Vendelmans's dyingness was particularly unsettling, because he had been so big and robust and outgoing, a true Rabelaisian figure, and somehow between one moment and the next he was transformed into a wraith. "The finger of God," Dave Yost said. "A quick flick of Zeus's pinkie and Hal shrivels like cellophane in a fireplace." Vendelmans was not yet forty.

The chimps suspected something too.

Some of them, such as Leo and Ramona, are fifth-generation signers, bred for alpha intelligence, and they pick up subtleties and nuances very well. "Almost human," visitors like to say of them. We dislike that tag, because the important thing about chimpanzees is that they *aren't* human, that they are an alien intelligent species; but yet I know what people mean. The brightest of the chimps saw right away that something was amiss with Vendelmans, and started making odd remarks. "Big one rotten banana," said Ramona to Mimsy while I was nearby. "He getting empty," Leo said to me as Vendelmans stumbled past us. Chimp metaphors never cease to amaze me. And Gonzo asked him outright: "You go away soon?"

"Go away" is not the chimp euphemism for death. So far as our animals know, no human being has ever died. Chimps die. Human beings "go away." We have kept things on that basis from the beginning, not intentionally at first, but such arrangements have a way of institutionalizing themselves. The first member of the group to die was Roger Nixon, in an automobile accident in the early years of the project, long before my time here, and apparently no one wanted to confuse or disturb the animals by explaining what had happened to him, so no explanations were offered. My second or third year here Tim Lippinger was killed in a skilift failure, and again it seemed easier not to go into details with them. And by the time of Will Bechstein's death in that helicopter crackup four years ago the policy was explicit: we chose not to regard his disappearance from the group as death, but mere "going away," as if he had only retired. The chimps do understand death, of course. They may even equate it with "going away," as Gonzo's question suggests. But if they do, they surely see human death as something quite different from chimpanzee death—a translation to another state of being, an ascent of a chariot of fire. Yost believes that they have no comprehension of human death at all, that they think we are immortal, that they think we are gods.

Vendelmans now no longer pretends that he isn't dying. The leukemia is plainly acute and he deteriorates physically from day to day. His original this-isn't-actually-happening attitude has been replaced by a kind of sullen angry acceptance. It is only the fourth week since the onset of the ailment and soon he'll have to enter the hospital.

And he wants to tell the chimps that he's going to die.

"They don't know that human beings can die," Yost said.

"Then it's time they found out," Vendelmans snapped. "Why perpetuate a load of mythological bullshit about us? Why let them think we're gods? Tell them outright that I'm going to die, the way old Egbert died and Salami and Mortimer."

"But they all died naturally," Jan Morton said.

"And I'm not dying naturally?"

She became terribly flustered. "Of old age, I mean. Their life-cycles clearly and understandably came to an end, and they died, and the chimps understood it. Whereas you—" She faltered.

"—am dying a monstrous and terrible death midway through my life," Vendelmans said, and started to break down, and recovered with a fierce effort, and Jan began to cry, and it was generally a bad scene, from which Vendelmans saved us by going on, "It should be of philosophical importance to the project to discover how the chimps react to a revaluation of the human metaphysic. We've ducked every chance we've had to help them understand the nature of mortality. Now I propose we use me to teach them that humans are subject to the same laws they are. That we are not gods."

"And that gods exist," said Yost, "who are capricious and unfathomable, and to whom we ourselves are as less than chimps."

Vendelmans shrugged. "They don't need to hear all that now. But it's time they understood what we are. Or rather, it's time that we learned how much they already understand. Use my death as a way of finding out. It's the first time they've been in the presence of a human who's actually in the process of dying. The other times one of us had died, it's always been in some sort of accident."

Burt Christensen said, "Hal, have you already told them anything about—"

"No," Vendelmans said. "Of course not. Not a word. But I see them talking to each other. They know."

We discussed it far into the night. The question needed careful examination because of the far-reaching consequences of any change we might make in the metaphysical givens of our animals. These chimps have lived in a closed environment here for decades, and the culture they have evolved is a product of what we have chosen to teach them, compounded by their own innate chimpness plus whatever we have unknowingly transmitted to them about ourselves or them. Any radical conceptual material we offer them must be weighed thoughtfully, because its effects will be irreversible, and those who succeed us in this community will be unforgiving if we do anything stupidly premature. If the plan is to observe a community of intelligent primates over a period of many human generations, studying the changes in their intellectual capacity as their linguistic skills increase, then we must at all times take care to let them find things out for themselves, rather than skewing our data by giving the chimps more than their current concept-processing abilities may be able to handle.

On the other hand, Vendelmans was dying right now, allowing us a dramatic opportunity to convey the concept of human mortality. We had at best a week or two to make use of that opportunity; then it might be years before the next chance.

"What are you worried about?" Vendelmans demanded.

Yost said, "Do you fear dying, Hal?"

"Dying makes me angry. I don't fear it; but I still have things to do, and I won't be able to do them. Why do you ask?"

"Because so far as we know the chimps see death—chimp death—as simply part of the great cycle of events, like the darkness that comes after the daylight. But human death is going to come as a revelation to them, a shock. And if they pick up from you any sense of fear or even anger over your dying, who knows what impact that will have on their way of thought?"

"Exactly. *Who knows?* I offer you a chance to find out!"

By a narrow margin, finally, we voted to let Hal Vendelmans share his death with the chimpanzees. Nearly all of us had reservations about that. But plainly Vendelmans was determined to have a useful death, a meaningful death; the only way he could face his fate at all was by contributing it like this to the project. And in the end I think most of us cast our votes his way purely out of our love for him.

We rearranged the schedules to give Vendelmans more contact with the animals. There are ten of us, fifty of them; each of us has a special field of inquiry—number theory, syntactical innovation, metaphysical exploration, semiotics, tool use, and so on—and we work with chimps of our own choice, subject, naturally, to the shifting patterns of subtribal bonding within the chimp community. But we agreed that Vendelmans would have to offer his revelations to the alpha intellegences—Leo, Ramona, Grimsky, Alice, and Attila—regardless of the current structure of the chimp/human dialogues. Leo, for instance, was involved in an ongoing interchange with Beth Rankin on the notion of the change of seasons. Beth more or less willingly gave up her time with Leo to Vendelmans, for Leo was essential in this. We learned long ago that anything important had to be imparted to the alphas first, and they will impart it to the others. A bright chimp knows more about teaching things to his duller cousins than the brightest human being.

The next morning Hal and Judy Vendelmans took Leo, Ramona, and Attila aside and held a long conversation with them. I was busy in a different part of the compound with Gonzo, Mimsy, Muffin, and Chump, but I glanced over occasionally to see what was going on. Hal looked radiant—

like Moses just down from the mountain after talking with God. Judy was trying to look radiant too, working at it, but her grief kept breaking through: once I saw her turn away from the chimps and press her knuckles to her teeth to hold it back.

Afterward Leo and Grimsky had a conference out by the oak grove. Yost and Charley Damiano watched it with binoculars, but they couldn't make much sense out of it. The chimps, when they sign to each other, use modified gestures much less precise than the ones they use with us; whether this marks the evolution of a special chimp-to-chimp argot designed not to be understood by us, or is simply a factor of chimp reliance on supplementary non-verbal ways of communicating, is something we still don't know, but the fact remains that we have trouble comprehending the sign language they use with each other, particularly the form the alphas use. Then, too, Leo and Grimsky kept wandering in and out of the trees, as if perhaps they knew we were watching them and didn't want us to eavesdrop. A little later in the day Ramona and Alice had the same sort of meeting. Now all five of our alphas must have been in on the revelation.

Somehow the news began to filter down to the rest of them.

We weren't able to observe actual concept transmission. We did notice that Vendelmans, the next day, began to get rather more attention than normal. Little troops of chimpanzees formed about him as he moved—slowly, and with obvious difficulty—about the compound. Gonzo and Chump, who had been bickering for months, suddenly were standing side by side staring intently at Vendelmans. Chicory, normally shy, went out of her way to engage him in a conversation—about the ripeness of the apples on the tree, Vendelmans reported. Anna Livia's young twins Shem and Shaun climbed up and sat on Vendelmans's shoulders.

"They want to find out what a dying god is really like," Yost said quietly.

"But look there," Jan Morton said.

Judy Vendelmans had an entourage too: Mimsy, Muffin, Claudius, Buster, and Kong. Staring in fascination, eyes wide, lips extended, some of them blowing little bubbles of saliva.

"Do they think she's dying too?" Beth wondered.

Yost shook his head. "Probably not. They can see there's nothing physically wrong with her. But they're picking up the sorrow-vibes, the death-vibes."

"Is there any reason to think they're aware that Hal is Judy's mate?" Christensen asked.

"It doesn't matter," Yost said. "They can see that she's upset. That interests them, even if they have no way of knowing why Judy would be more upset than any of the rest of us."

"More mysteries out yonder," I said, pointing into the meadow.

Grimsky was standing by himself out there, contemplating something. He is the oldest of the chimps, gray-haired, going bald, a deep thinker. He has been here almost from the beginning, more than thirty years, and very little has escaped his attention in that time.

Far off to the left, in the shade of the big beech tree, Leo stood similarly in solitary meditation. He is twenty, the alpha male of the community, the strongest and by far the most intelligent. It was eerie to see the two of them in their individual zones of isolation, like distant sentinels, like Easter Island statues, lost in private reveries.

"Philosophers," Yost murmured.

Yesterday Vendelmans returned to the hospital for good. Before he went, he made his farewells to each of the fifty chimpanzees, even the infants. In the past week he has altered markedly: he is only a shadow of himself, feeble, wasted. Judy says he'll live only another few weeks.

She has gone on leave and probably won't come back until after Hal's death. I wonder what the chimps will make of her "going away," and of her eventual return.

She said that Leo had asked her if she was dying too.

Perhaps things will get back to normal here now.

Christensen asked me this morning, "Have you noticed the way they seem to drag the notion of death into whatever conversation you're having with them these days?"

I nodded. "Mimsy asked me the other day if the moon dies when the sun comes up and the sun dies when the moon is out. It seemed like such a standard primitive metaphor that I didn't pick up on it at first. But Mimsy's too young for using metaphor that easily and she isn't particularly clever. The older ones must be talking about dying a lot, and it's filtering down."

"Chicory was doing subtraction with me," Christensen said. "She signed, *'You take five, two die, you have three.'* Later she turned it into a verb: *'Three die one equals two.'* "

Others reported similar things. Yet none of the animals were talking about Vendelmans and what was about to happen to him, nor were they asking any overt questions about death or dying. So far as we were able to perceive, they had displaced the whole thing into metaphorical diversions. That in itself indicated a powerful obsession. Like most obsessives, they were trying to hide the thing that most concerned them, and they probably thought they were doing a good job of it. It isn't their fault that we're able to guess what's going on in their minds. They are, after all—and we sometimes have to keep reminding ourselves of this—only chimpanzees.

They are holding meetings on the far side of the oak grove, where the little stream runs. Leo and Grimsky seem to do most of the talking, and the others gather around and sit very quietly as the speeches are made. The groups run from ten to thirty chimps at a time. We are unable to discover what they're discussing, though of course we have an idea. Whenever one of us approaches such a gathering, the chimps very casually drift off into three or four separate groups and look exceedingly innocent—"We just out for some fresh air, boss."

Charley Damiano wants to plant a bug in the grove. But how do you spy on a group that converses only in sign language? Cameras aren't as easily hidden as microphones.

We do our best with binoculars. But what little we've been able to observe has been mystifying. The chimp-to-chimp signs they use at these meetings are even more oblique and confusing than the ones we had seen earlier. It's as if they're holding their meetings in pig-latin, or doubletalk, or in some entirely new and private language.

Two technicians will come tomorrow to help us mount cameras in the grove.

Hal Vendelmans died last night. According to Judy, who phoned Dave Yost, it was very peaceful right at the end, an easy release. Yost and I broke the news to the alpha chimps just after breakfast. No euphemisms, just the straight news. Ramona made a few hooting sounds and looked as if she might cry, but she was the only one who seemed emotionally upset. Leo gave me a long deep look of what was almost certainly compassion, and then he hugged me very hard. Grimsky wandered away and seemed to be signing to himself in the new system. Now a meeting seems to be assembling in the oak grove, the first one in more than a week.

The cameras are in place. Even if we can't decipher the new signs, we can a least tape them and subject them to computer analysis until we begin to understand.

Now we've watched the first tapes of a grove meeting, but I can't say we know a lot more than we did before.

For one thing, they disabled two of the cameras right at the outset. Attila spotted them and sent Gonzo and Claudius up into the trees to yank them out. I suppose the remaining cameras went unnoticed; but by accident or deliberate diabolical craftiness, the chimps positioned themselves in such a way that none of the cameras had a clear angle. We did record a few statements from Leo and some give-and-take between Alice and Anna Livia. They spoke in a mixture of standard signs and the new ones, but, without a sense of the context, we've found it impossible to generate any sequence of meanings. Stray signs such as "shirt," "hat," "human," "change," and "banana fly," interspersed with undecipherable stuff, *seem* to be adding up to something, but no one is sure what. We observed no mention of Hal Vendelmans nor any direct references to death. We may be misleading ourselves entirely about the significance of all this.

Or perhaps not. We codified some of the new signs and this afternoon I asked Ramona what one of them meant. She fidgeted and hooted and looked uncomfortable—and not simply because I was asking her to do a tough abstract thing like giving a definition. She was worried. She looked around for Leo, and when she saw him she made that sign at him. He came bounding over and shoved Ramona away. Then he began to tell me how wise and good and gentle I am. He may be a genius, but even a genius chimp is still a chimp, and I told him I wasn't fooled by all his flattery. Then I asked *him* what the new sign meant.

"Jump high come again," Leo signed.

A simple chimpy phrase referring to fun and frolic? So I

thought at first, and so did many of my colleagues. But Dave
Yost said, "Then why was Ramona so evasive about defining it?"

"Defining isn't easy for them," Beth Rankin said.

"Ramona's one of the five brightest. She's capable of it.
Especially since the sign can be defined by use of four other
established signs, as Leo proceeded to do."

"What are you getting at, Dave?" I asked.

Yost said, " *'Jump high come again'* might be about a
game they like to play, but it could also be an eschatological
reference, sacred talk, a concise metaphorical way to speak
of death and resurrection, no?"

Mick Falkenburg snorted. "Jesus, Dave, of all the nutty
Jesuitical bullshit—"

"Is it?"

"It's possible sometimes to be too subtle in your analysis," Falkenburg said. "You're suggesting that these chimpanzees have a theology?"

"I'm suggesting that they may be in the process of evolving a religion," Yost replied.

Can it be?

Sometimes we lose our perspective with these animals, as
Mick indicated, and we overestimate their intelligence; but
just as often, I think, we underestimate them.

Jump high come again.

I wonder. Secret sacred talk? A chimpanzee theology?
Belief in life after death? A religion?

They know that human beings have a body of ritual and
belief that they call religion, though how much they really
comprehend about it is hard to tell. Dave Yost, in his
metaphysical discussions with Leo and some of the other
alphas, introduced the concept long ago. He drew a hierar-
chy that began with God and ran downward through human
beings and chimpanzees to dogs and cats and onward to
insects and frogs, by way of giving the chimps some sense of
the great chain of life. They had seen bugs and frogs and cats
and dogs, but they wanted Dave to show them God, and he
was forced to tell them that God is not actually tangible and
accessible, but lives high overhead although His essence
penetrates all things. I doubt that they grasped much of that.
Leo, whose nimble and probing intelligence is a constant
illumination to us, wanted Yost to explain how we talked to

God and how God talked to us, if He wasn't around to make signs, and Yost said we had a thing called religion, which was a system of communicating with God. And that was where he left it, a long while back.

Now we are on guard for any indications of a developing religious consciousness among our troop. Even the scoffers—Mick Falkenburg, Beth, to some degree, Charley Damiano—are paying close heed. After all, one of the underlying purposes of this project is to reach an understanding of how the first hominids managed to cross the intellectual boundary that we like to think separates the animals from humanity. We can't reconstruct a bunch of Australopithecines and study them; but we *can* watch chimpanzees who have been given the gift of language build a quasi-protohuman society, and it is the closest thing to traveling back in time that we are apt to achieve. Yost thinks, I think, Burt Christensen is beginning to think, that we have inadvertently kindled an awareness of the divine, of the numinous force that must be worshipped, by allowing them to see that their gods—us—can be struck down and slain by an even higher power.

The evidence so far is slim. The attention given Vendelmans and Judy; the solitary meditations of Leo and Grimsky; the large gathering in the grove; the greatly accelerated use of modified sign language in chimp-to-chimp talk at those gatherings; the potentially eschatological reference we think we see in the sign that Leo translated as *jump high come again*. That's it. To those of us who want to interpret that as the foundations of religion, it seems indicative of what we want to see; to the rest, it all looks like coincidence and fantasy. The problem is that we are dealing with non-human intelligence and we must take care not to impose our own thought-constructs. We can never be certain if we are operating from a value system anything like that of the chimps. The built-in ambiguities of the sign-language grammer we must use with them complicate the issue. Consider the phrase "banana fly" that Leo used in a speech—a sermon?—in the oak grove, and remember Ramona's reference to the sick Vendelmans as "rotten banana." If we take *fly* to be a verb, "banana fly" might be considered a metaphorical description of Vendelmans's ascent to heaven. If we take it to be a noun, Leo might have been talking about the Drosophila flies that feed on decaying fruit, a metaphor for the corruption of the flesh after death. On the other hand, he may simply have been making a comment about the current state of our garbage dump.

We have agreed for the moment not to engage the chimpanzees in any direct interrogation about any of this. The Heisenberg principle is eternally our rule here: the observer can too easily perturb the thing observed, so we must make only the most delicate of measurements. Even so, of course, our presence among the chimps is bound to have its impact, but we do what we can to minimize it by avoiding leading questions and watching in silence.

Two unusual things today. Taken each by each, they would be interesting without being significant; but if we use each to illuminate the other, we begin to see things in a strange new light, perhaps.

One thing is an increase in vocalizing, noticed by nearly everyone, among the chimps. We know that chimpanzees in the wild have a kind of rudimentary spoken language—a greeting-call, a defiance-call, the grunts that mean "I like the taste of this," the male chimp's territorial hoot, and such: nothing very complex, really not qualitatively much beyond the language of birds or dogs. They also have a fairly rich non-verbal language, a vocabulary of gestures and facial expressions; but it was not until the first experiments decades ago in teaching chimpanzees human sign language that any important linguistic capacity became apparent in them. Here at the research station the chimps communicate almost wholly in signs, as they have been trained to do for generations and as they have taught their young ones to do; they revert to hoots and grunts only in the most elemental situations. We ourselves communicate mainly in signs when we are talking to each other while working with the chimps, and even in our humans-only conferences we use signs as much as speech, from long habit. But suddenly the chimps are making sounds at each other. Odd sounds, unfamiliar sounds, weird clumsy imitations, one might say, of human speech. Nothing that we can understand, naturally: the chimpanzee larynx is simply incapable of duplicating the phonemes humans use. But these new grunts, these tortured blurts of sound, seem intended to mimic our speech. It was Damiano who showed us, as we were watching a tape of a grove session, how Attila was twisting his lips with his hands in what appeared unmistakably to be an attempt to make human sounds come out.

Why?

The second thing is that Leo has started wearing a shirt and a hat. There is nothing remarkable about a chimp in clothing; although we have never encouraged such anthropomorphization here, various animals have taken a fancy from time to time to some item of clothing, have begged it from its owner, and have worn it for a few days or even weeks. The novelty here is that the shirt and the hat belonged to Hal Vendelmans, and that Leo wears them only when the chimps are gathered in the oak grove, which Dave Yost has lately begun calling the "holy grove." Leo found them in the toolshed beyond the vegetable garden. The shirt is ten sizes too big, Vendelmans having been so brawny, but Leo ties the sleeves across his chest and lets the rest dangle down his back almost like a cloak.

What shall we make of this?

Jan is the specialist in chimp verbal processes. At the meeting tonight she said, "It sounds to me as if they're trying to duplicate the rhythms of human speech even though they can't reproduce the actual sounds. They're playing at being human."

"Talking the god-talk," said Dave Yost.

"What do you mean?" Jan asked.

"Chimps talk with their hands. Humans do too, when speaking with chimps, but when humans talk to humans they use their voices. Humans are gods to chimps, remember. Talking in the way the gods talk is one way of remaking yourself in the image of the gods, of putting on divine attributes."

"But that's nonsense," Jan said. "I can't possibly—"

"Wearing human clothing," I broke in excitedly, "would also be a kind of putting on divine attributes, in the most literal sense of the phrase. Especially if the clothes—"

"—had belonged to Hal Vendelmans," said Christensen.

"The dead god," Yost said.

We looked at each other in amazement.

Charley Damiano said, not in his usual skeptical way but in a kind of wonder, "Dave, are you hypothesizing that Leo functions as some sort of priest, that those are his sacred garments?"

"More than just a priest," Yost said. "A high priest, I think. A pope. The pope of the chimps."

Grimsky is suddenly looking very feeble. Yesterday we saw him moving slowly through the meadow by himself, making a long circuit of the grounds as far out as the pond and the little waterfall, then solemnly and ponderously staggering back to the meeting-place at the far side of the grove. Today he has been sitting quietly by the stream, occasionally rocking slowly back and forth, now and then dipping his feet in. I checked the records: he is 43 years old, well along for a chimp, although some have been known to live fifty years and more. Mick wanted to take him to the infirmary but we decided against it; if he is dying, and by all appearances he is, we ought to let him do it with dignity in his own way. Jan went down to the grove to visit him and reported that he shows no apparent signs of disease. His eyes are clear, his face feels cool. Age has withered him and his time is at hand. I feel an enormous sense of loss, for he has a keen intelligence, a long memory, a shrewd and thoughtful nature. He was the alpha male of the troop for many years, but a decade ago, when Leo came of age, Grimsky abdicated in his favor with no sign of a struggle. Behind Grimsky's grizzled forehead there must lie a wealth of subtle and mysterious perceptions, concepts, and insights about which we know practically nothing, and very soon all that will be lost. Let us hope he's managed to teach his wisdom to Leo and Attila and Alice and Ramona.

Today's oddity: a ritual distribution of meat.

Meat is not very important in the diet of chimps, but they do like to have some; as far back as I can remember Wednesday has been meat day here, when we give them a side of beef or some slabs of mutton or something of that sort. The procedure for dividing up the meat betrays the chimps' wild heritage, for the alpha males eat their fill first, while the others watch, and then the weaker males beg for a share and are allowed to move in to grab, and finally the females and young ones get the scraps. Today was meat day. Leo, as usual, helped himself first, but what happened after that was astounding. He let Attila feed, and then told Attila to offer some meat to Grimsky, who is even weaker today and brushed it aside. *Then Leo put on Vendelmans's hat* and began to parcel out scraps of meat to the others. One by one they came up to him in the current order of ranking and went through the standard begging maneuver, hand beneath chin, palm upward, and Leo gave each one a strip of meat.

"Like taking communion," Charley Damiano muttered. "With Leo the celebrant at the Mass."

Unless our assumptions are totally off base, there is a real religion going on here, perhaps created by Grimsky and under Leo's governance. And Hal Vendelmans's faded old blue work-hat is the tiara of the pope.

Beth Rankin woke me at dawn and said, "Come fast. They're doing something strange with old Grimsky."

I was up and dressed and awake in a hurry. We have a closed-circuit system now that pipes the events in the grove back to us, and we paused at the screen so that I could see what was going on. Grimsky sat on his knees at the edge of the stream, eyes closed, barely moving. Leo, wearing the hat, was beside him, elaborately tying Vendelmans's shirt over Grimsky's shoulders. A dozen or more of the other adult chimps were squatting in a semicircle in front of them.

Burt Christensen said, "What's going on? Is Leo making Grimsky the assistant pope?"

"I think Leo is giving Grimsky the last rites," I said.

What else could it have been? Leo wore the sacred headdress. He spoke at length using the new signs—the ecclesiastical language, the chimpanzee equivalent of Latin or Hebrew or Sanskrit—and as his oration went on and' on, the congregation replied periodically with outbursts of—I suppose—response and approval, some in signs, some with the grunting garbled pseudo-human sounds that Dave Yost thought was their version of god-talk. Throughout it all Grimsky was silent and remote, though occasionally he nodded or murmured or tapped both his shoulders in a gesture whose meaning was unknown to us. The ceremony went on for more than an hour. Then Grimsky leaned forward, and Kong and Chump took him by the arms and eased him down until he was lying with his cheek against the ground.

For two, three, five minutes all the chimpanzees were still. At last Leo came forward and removed his hat, setting it on the ground beside Grimsky, and with great delicacy he untied the shirt Grimsky wore. Grimsky did not move. Leo draped the shirt over his own shoulders and donned the hat again.

He turned to the watching chimps and signed, using the old signs that were completely intelligible to us, "Grimsky now be human being."

We stared at each other in awe and astonishment. A couple of us were sobbing. No one could speak.

The funeral ceremony seemed to be over. The chimps were dispersing. We saw Leo sauntering away, hat casually dangling from one hand, the shirt, in the other, trailing over the ground. Grimsky alone remained by the stream. We waited ten minutes and went down to the grove. Grimsky seemed to be sleeping very peacefully, but he was dead, and we gathered him up—Burt and I carried him; he seemed to weigh almost nothing—and took him back to the lab for the autopsy.

In mid-morning the sky darkened and lightning leaped across the hills to the north. There was a tremendous crack of thunder almost instantly and sudden tempestuous rain. Jan pointed to the meadow. The male chimps were doing a bizarre dance, roaring, swaying, slapping their feet against the ground, hammering their hands against the trunks of the trees, ripping off branches and flailing the earth with them. Grief? Terror? Joy at the translation of Grimsky to a divine state? Who could tell? I had never been frightened by our animals before—I knew them too well, I regarded them as little hairy cousins—but now they were terrifying creatures and this was a scene out of time's dawn, as Gonzo and Kong and Attila and Chump and Buster and Claudius and even Pope Leo himself went thrashing about in that horrendous rain, pounding out the steps of some unfathomable rite.

The lightning ceased and the rain moved southward as quickly as it had come, and the dancers went slinking away, each to his favorite tree. By noon the day was bright and warm and it was as though nothing out of the ordinary had happened.

Two days after Grimsky's death I was awakened again at dawn, this time by Mick Falkenburg. He shook my shoulder and yelled at me to wake up, and as I sat there blinking he said, "Chicory's dead! I was out for an early walk and I found her near the place where Grimsky died."

"Chicory? But she's only—"

"Eleven, twelve, something like that. I know."

I put my clothes on while Mick woke the others, and we went down to the stream. Chicory was sprawled out, but not peacefully—there was a dribble of blood at the corner of her mouth, her eyes were wide and horrified, her hands were curled into frozen talons. All about her in the moist soil of the streambank were footprints. I searched my memory for an instance of murder in the chimp community and could find nothing remotely like it—quarrels, yes, and lengthy feuds, and some ugly ambushes and battles, fairly violent, serious injuries now and then. But this had no precedent.

"Ritual murder," Yost murmured.

"Or a sacrifice, perhaps?" suggested Beth Rankin.

"Whatever it is," I said, "they're learning too fast. Recapitulating the whole evolution of religion, including the worst parts of it. We'll have to talk to Leo."

"Is that wise?" Yost asked.

"Why not?"

"We've kept hands off so far. If we want to see how this thing unfolds—"

"During the night," I said, "the Pope and the College of Cardinals ganged up on a gentle young female chimp and killed her. Right now they may be off somewhere sending Alice or Ramona or Anna Livia's twins to chimp heaven. I think we have to weigh the value of observing the evolution of chimp religion against the cost of losing irreplaceable members of a unique community. I say we call in Leo and tell him that it's wrong to kill."

"He knows that," said Yost. "He must. Chimps aren't murderous animals."

"Chicory's dead."

"And if they see it as a holy deed?" Yost demanded.

"Then one by one we'll lose our animals, and at the end we'll just have a couple of very saintly survivors. Do you want that?"

We spoke with Leo. Chimps can be sly and they can be manipulative, but even the best of them, and Leo is the Einstein of chimpanzees, does not seem to know how to lie. We asked him where Chicory was and Leo told us that Chicory was now a human being. I felt a chill at that. Grimsky was also a human being, said Leo. We asked him how he knew that they had become human and he said,

"They go where Vendelmans go. When human go away, he become god. When chimpanzee go away, he become human. Right?"

"No," we said.

The logic of the ape is not easy to refute. We told him that death comes to all living creatures, that it is natural and holy, but that only God could decide when it was going to happen. God, we said, calls His creatures to Himself one at a time. God had called Hal Vendelmans, God had called Grimsky, God would someday call Leo and all the rest here. But God had not yet called Chicory. Leo wanted to know what was wrong with sending Chicory to Him ahead of time. Did that not improve Chicory's condition? No, we replied. No, it only did harm to Chicory. Chicory would have been much happier living here with us than going to God so soon. Leo did not seem convinced. Chicory, he said, now could talk words with her mouth and wore shoes on her feet. He envied Chicory very much.

We told him that God would be angry if any more chimpanzees died. We told him that *we* would be angry. Killing chimpanzees was wrong, we said. It was not what God wanted Leo to be doing.

"Me talk to God, find out what God wants," Leo said.

We found Buster dead by the edge of the pond this morning, with indications of another ritual murder. Leo coolly stared us down and explained that God had given orders that all chimpanzees were to become human beings as quickly as possible, and this could only be achieved by the means employed on Chicory and Buster.

Leo is confined now in the punishment tank and we have suspended this week's meat distribution. Yost voted against both of those decisions, saying we ran the risk of giving Leo the aura of a religious martyr, which would enhance his already considerable power. But these killings have to stop. Leo knows, of course, that we are upset about them. But if he believes his path is the path of righteousness, nothing we say or do is going to change his mind.

Judy Vendelmans called today. She has put Hal's death fairly well behind her, misses the project, misses the chimps. As gently as I could, I told her what has been going on here.

She was silent a very long time—Chicory was one of her favorites, and Judy has had enough grief already to handle for one summer—but finally she said, "I think I know what can be done. I'll be on the noon flight tomorrow."

We found Mimsy dead in the usual way late this afternoon. Leo is still in the punishment tank—the third day. The congregation has found a way to carry out its rites without its leader. Mimsy's death left me stunned, but we are all deeply affected, virtually unable to proceed with our work. It may be necessary to break up the community entirely to save the animals. Perhaps we can send them to other research centers for a few months, three of them here, five there, until this thing subsides. But what if it doesn't subside? What if the dispersed animals convert others elsewhere to the creed of Leo?

The first thing Judy said when she arrived was, "Let Leo out. I want to talk to him."

We opened the tank. Leo stepped forth, uneasy, abashed, shading his eyes against the strong light. He glanced at me, at Yost, at Jan, as if wondering which one of us was going to scold him; and then he saw Judy and it was as though he had seen a ghost. He made a hollow rasping sound deep in his throat and backed away. Judy signed hello and stretched out her arms to him. Leo trembled. He was terrified. There was nothing unusual about one of us going on leave and returning after a month or two, but Leo must not have expected Judy ever to return, must in fact have imagined her gone to the same place her husband had gone, and the sight of her shook him. Judy understood all that, obviously, for she quickly made powerful use of it, signing to Leo, "I bring you message from Vendelmans."

"Tell tell tell!"

"Come walk with me," said Judy.

She took him by the hand and led him gently out of the punishment area and into the compound, and down the hill toward the meadow. I watched from the top of the hill, the tall slender woman and the compact, muscular chimpanzee close together, side by side, hand in hand, pausing now to talk, Judy signing and Leo replying in a flurry of gestures, then Judy again for a long time, a brief response from Leo, another cascade of signs from Judy, then Leo squatting, tugging at blades of grass, shaking his head, clapping hand to elbow in his expression of confusion, then to his chin, then taking Judy's hand. They were gone for nearly an hour. The other chimps did not dare approach them. Finally Judy and Leo, hand in hand, came quietly up the hill to headquarters again. Leo's eyes were shining and so were Judy's.

She said, "Everything will be all right now. That's so, isn't it, Leo?"

Leo said, "God is always right."

She made a dismissal sign and Leo went slowly down the hill. The moment he was out of sight, Judy turned away from us and cried a little, just a little; then she asked for a drink; and then she said, "It isn't easy, being God's messenger."

"What did you tell him?" I asked.

"That I had been in heaven visiting Hal. That Hal was looking down all the time and he was very proud of Leo, except for one thing: that Leo was sending too many chimpanzees to God too soon. I told him that God was not ready to receive Chicory and Buster and Mimsy, that they would have to be kept in storage cells for a long time, until their true time came, and that that was not good for them. I told him that Hal wanted Leo to know that God hoped he would stop sending chimpanzees. Then I gave Leo Hal's old wristwatch to wear when he conducts services, and Leo promised he would obey Hal's wishes. That was all. I suspect I've added a whole new layer of mythology to what's developing here, and I trust you won't be angry with me for doing it. I don't believe any more chimps will be killed. And I think I'd like another drink."

Later in the day we saw the chimps assembled by the stream. Leo held his arm aloft and sunlight blazed from the band of gold on his slim hairy wrist, and a great outcry of grunts in god-talk went up from the congregation and they danced before him, and then he donned the sacred hat and the sacred shirt and moved his arms eloquently in the secret sacred gestures of the holy sign language.

There have been no more killings. I think no more will occur. Perhaps after a time our chimps will lose interest in being religious, and go on to other pastimes. But not yet, not yet. The ceremonies continue, and grow ever more elaborate, and we are compiling volumes of extraordinary observations, and God looks down and is pleased. And Leo proudly wears the emblems of his papacy as he bestows his blessing on the worshippers in the holy grove.

SWARM

Bruce Sterling

A comparatively new author, Bruce Sterling is busily writing a series of stories set in a richly imagined future universe where human expansion into the stars is complicated by meeting alien races who are at a higher stage of development than ours. His sure command of science combines with vivid writing to produce outstanding stories, and eventually he plans to write a novel set in this imagined future. Meanwhile, here is "Swarm," the best of his stories so far.

Bruce Sterling is in his late twenties, married and lives in Texas. His first two novels were Involution Ocean *(1977) and* The Artificial Kid *(1980).*

"I WILL MISS YOUR CONVERSATION DURING THE rest of the voyage," the alien said.

Captain-doctor Simon Afriel folded his jeweled hands over his gold-embroidered waistcoat. "I regret it also, ensign," he said in the alien's own hissing language. "Our talks together have been very useful to me. I would have paid to learn so much, but you gave it freely."

"But that was only information," the alien said. He shrouded his bead-bright eyes behind thick nictitating membranes. "We Investors deal in energy, and precious metals. To prize and pursue mere knowledge is an immature racial trait." The alien lifted the long ribbed frill behind his pinhole-sized ears.

"No doubt you are right," Afriel said, despising him. "We humans are as children to other races, however; so a certain immaturity seems natural to us." Afriel pulled off his sunglasses to rub the bridge of his nose. The starship cabin was drenched in searing blue light, heavily ultraviolet. It was the light the Investors preferred, and they were not about to change it for one human passenger.

"You have not done badly," the alien said magnanimously. "You are the kind of race we like to do business with: young, eager, plastic, ready for a wide variety of goods and experiences. We would have contacted you much earlier, but your technology was still too feeble to afford us a profit."

"Things are different now," Afriel said. "We'll make you rich."

"Indeed," the Investor said. The frill behind his scaly head flickered rapidly, a sign of amusement. "Within two hundred years you will be wealthy enough to buy from us the secret of our star-flight. Or perhaps your Mechanist faction will discover the secret through research."

Afriel was annoyed. As a member of the Reshaped faction, he did not appreciate the reference to the rival Mechanists. "Don't put too much stock in mere technical expertise," he said. "Consider the aptitude for languages we Shapers have. It makes our faction a much better trading partner. To a Mechanist, all Investors look alike."

The alien hesitated. Afriel smiled. He had made an appeal to the alien's personal ambition with his last statement, and the hint had been taken. That was where the Mechanists always erred. They tried to treat all Investors equally, using the same programmed routines each time. They lacked imagination.

Something would have to be done about the Mechanists, Afriel thought. Something more permanent than the small but deadly confrontations between isolated ships in the Asteroid Belt and the ice-rich rings of Saturn. Both factions maneuvered constantly, looking for a decisive stroke, bribing away each other's best talent, practicing ambush, assassination, and industrial espionage.

Captain-doctor Simon Afriel was a past master at these pursuits. That was why the Reshaped faction had paid the millions of kilowatts necessary to buy his passage. Afriel held doctorates in biochemistry and alien linguistics, and a master's degree in magnetic weapons engineering. He was thirty-eight years old and had been Reshaped according to the state of the art at the time of his conception. His hormonal balance had been altered slightly to compensate for long periods spent in free-fall. He had no appendix. The structure of his heart had been redesigned for greater efficiency, and his large intestine had been altered to produce the vitamins normally made by intestinal bacteria. Genetic engineering and rigorous training in childhood had given him an intelligence quotient of one hundred and eighty. He was not the brightest of the agents of the Ring Council, but he was one of the most mentally stable and the best trusted.

"It seems a shame," the alien said, "that a human of your accomplishments should have to rot for two years in this miserable, profitless outpost."

"The years won't be wasted," Afriel said.

"But why have you chosen to study the Swarm? They can teach you nothing, since they cannot speak. They have no wish to trade, having no tools or technology. They are the only spacefaring race to be essentially without intelligence."

"That alone should make them worthy of study."

"Do you seek to imitate them, then? You would make monsters of yourselves." Again the ensign hesitated. "Perhaps you could do it. It would be bad for business, however."

There came a fluting burst of alien music over the ship's speakers, then a screeching fragment of Investor language. Most of it was too high-pitched for Afriel's ears to follow.

The alien stood, his jeweled skirt brushing the tips of his clawed, bird-like feet. "The Swarm's symbiote has arrived," he said.

"Thank you," Afriel said. When the ensign opened the cabin door, Afriel could smell the Swarm's representative; the creature's warm, yeasty scent had spread rapidly through the starship's recycled air.

Afriel quickly checked his appearance in a pocket mirror. He touched powder to his face and straightened the round velvet hat on his shoulder-length reddish-blond hair. His earlobes glittered with red impact-rubies, thick as his thumbs' ends, mined from the Asteroid Belt. His knee-length coat and waistcoat were of gold brocade; the shirt beneath was of dazzling fineness, woven with red-gold thread. He had dressed to impress the Investors, who expected and appreciated a prosperous look from their customers. How could he impress this new alien? Smell, perhaps. He freshened his perfume.

Beside the starship's secondary airlock, the Swarm's symbiote was chittering rapidly at the ship's commander. The commander was an old and sleepy Investor, twice the size of most of her crewmen. Her massive head was encrusted in a jeweled helmet. From within the helmet her clouded eyes glittered like cameras.

The symbiote lifted on its six posterior legs and gestured feebly with its four clawed forelimbs. The ship's artificial gravity, a third again as strong as Earth's, seemed to bother it. Its rudimentary eyes, dangling on stalks, were shut tight against the glare. It must be used to darkness, Afriel thought.

The commander answered the creature in its own language. Afriel grimaced, for he had hoped that the creature spoke Investor. Now he would have to learn another language, a language designed for a being without a tongue.

After another brief interchange the commander turned to Afriel. "The symbiote is not pleased with your arrival," she told Afriel in the Investor language. "There has apparently been some disturbance here involving humans, in the recent past. However, I have prevailed upon it to admit you to the Nest. The episode has been recorded. Payment for my diplomatic services will be arranged with your faction when I return to your native star system."

"I thank Your Authority," Afriel said. "Please convey to the symbiote my best personal wishes, and the harmlessness and humility of my intentions. . . ." He broke off short as the symbiote lunged toward him, biting him savagely in the calf of his left leg. Afriel jerked free and leapt backward in the heavy artificial gravity, going into a defensive position. The symbiote had ripped away a long shred of his pants leg; it now crouched quietly, eating it.

"It will convey your scent and composition to its nest-mates," said the commander. "This is necessary. Otherwise you would be classed as an invader, and the Swarm's warrior caste would kill you at once."

Afriel relaxed quickly and pressed his hand against the puncture wound to stop the bleeding. He hoped that none of the Investors had noticed his reflexive action. It would not mesh well with his story of being a harmless researcher.

"We will reopen the airlock soon," the commander said phlegmatically, leaning back on her thick reptilian tail. The symbiote continued to munch the shred of cloth. Afriel studied the creature's neckless segmented head. It had a mouth and nostrils; it had bulbous atrophied eyes on stalks; there were hinged slats that might be radio receivers, and two parallel ridges of clumped wriggling antennae, sprouting among three chitinous plates. Their function was unknown to him.

The airlock door opened. A rush of dense, smoky aroma entered the departure cabin. It seemed to bother the half-dozen Investors, who left rapidly. "We will return in six hundred and twelve of your days, as by our agreement," the commander said.

"I thank Your Authority," Afriel said.

"Good luck," the commander said in English. Afriel smiled.

The symbiote, with a sinuous wriggle of its segmented

body, crept into the airlock. Afriel followed it, The airlock door shut behind them. The creature said nothing to him but continued munching loudly. The second door opened, and the symbiote sprang through it, into a wide, round, stone tunnel. It vanished at once into the gloom.

Afriel put his sunglasses into a pocket of his jacket and pulled out a pair of infrared goggles. He strapped them to his head and stepped out of the airlock. The artificial gravity vanished, replaced by the almost imperceptible gravity of the Swarm's asteroid nest. Afriel smiled, comfortable for the first time in weeks. Most of his adult life had been spent in free-fall, in the Shaper's colonies in the rings of Saturn.

Squatting in a dark cavity in the side of the tunnel was a disk-headed, furred animal the size of an elephant. It was clearly visible in the infrared of its own body heat. Afriel could hear it breathing. It waited patiently until Afriel had launched himself past it, deeper into the tunnel. Then it took its place in the end of the tunnel, puffing itself up with air until its swollen head securely plugged the end of the corridor. Its multiple legs were firmly planted in sockets in the walls.

The Investor's ship had left. Afriel remained here, inside one of the millions of planetoids that circled the giant star Betelgeuse in a girdling ring with almost five times the mass of Jupiter. As a source of potential wealth it dwarfed the entire solar system, and it belonged, more or less, to the Swarm. At least, no other race had challenged them for it within the memory of the Investors.

Afriel peered up the corridor. It seemed deserted, and without other bodies to cast infrared heat, he could not see very far. Kicking against the wall, he floated hesitantly down the corridor.

He heard a human voice. "Doctor Afriel!"

"Doctor Mirny!" he called out. "This way!"

He first saw a pair of young symbiotes scuttling towards him, the tips of their clawed feet barely touching the walls. Behind them came a woman wearing goggles like his own. She was young, and attractive in the trim, anonymous way of the genetically reshaped.

She screeched something at the symbiotes in their own language, and they stopped, waiting. She coasted forward, and Afriel caught her arm, expertly stopping their momentum.

"You didn't bring any luggage?" she said anxiously.

He shook his head. "We got your warning before I was sent out. I have only the clothes I'm wearing and a few items in my pockets."

She looked at him critically. "Is that what people are wearing in the Rings these days? Things have changed more than I thought."

Afriel looked at his brocaded coat and laughed. "It's a matter of policy. The Investors are always readier to talk to a human who looks ready to do business on a large scale. All the Shaper's representatives dress like this these days. We've stolen a jump on the Mechanists; they still dress in those coveralls." He hesitated, not wanting to offend her. Galina Mirny's intelligence was rated at almost two hundred. Men and women that bright were sometimes flighty and unstable, likely to retreat into private fantasy worlds or become enmeshed in strange and impenetrable webs of plotting and rationalization. High intelligence was the strategy the Shapers had chosen in the struggle for cultural dominance, and they were obliged to stick to it, despite its occasional disadvantages. They had tried breeding the super-bright—those with quotients over two hundred—but so many had defected from the Shapers' colonies that the faction had stopped producing them.

"You wonder about my own clothing," Mirny said.

"It certainly has the appeal of novelty," Afriel said with a smile.

"It was woven from the fibers of a pupa's cocoon," she said. "My original wardrobe was eaten by a scavenger symbiote during the troubles last year. I usually go nude, but I didn't want to offend you by too great a show of intimacy."

Afriel shrugged. "I usually go nude myself in my own environment. If the temperature is constant, then clothes are useless, except for pockets. I have a few tools on my person, but most are of little importance. We're the Reshaped, our tools are here." He tapped his head. "If you can show me a safe place to put my clothes. . . ."

She shook her head. It was impossible to see her eyes for the goggles, which made her expression hard to read. "You've made your first mistake, doctor. There are no places of our own here. It was the same mistake the Mechanist agents made, the same one that almost killed me as well. There is no concept of privacy or property here. This is the

Nest. If you seize any part of it for yourself—to store equipment, to sleep in, whatever—then you become an intruder, an enemy. The two Mechanists—a man and a woman—tried to secure an unused chamber for their computer lab. Warriors broke down their door and devoured them. Scavengers ate all their equipment, glass, metal, and all.''

Afriel smiled coldly. "It must have cost them a fortune to ship all that material here."

Mirny shrugged. "They're wealthier than we are. Their machines, their mining. They meant to kill me, I think. Surreptitiously, so the warriors wouldn't be upset by a show of violence. They had a computer that was learning the language of the springtails faster than I could."

"But you survived," Afriel pointed out. "And your tapes and reports—especially the early ones, when you still had most of your equipment—were of tremendous interest. The Council is behind you all the way. You've become quite a celebrity in the Rings, during your absence."

"Yes, I expected as much," she said.

Afriel was nonplused. "If I found any deficiency in them," he said carefully, "it was in my own field, alien linguistics." He waved vaguely at the two symbiotes who accompanied her. "I assume you've made great progress in communicating with the symbiotes, since they seem to do all the talking for the Nest."

She looked at him with an unreadable expression and shrugged. "There are at least fifteen different kinds of symbiotes here. Those that accompany me are called the springtails, and they speak only for themselves. They are savages, doctor, who received attention from the Investors only because they can still talk. They were a space-going race at one time, but they've forgotten it. They discovered the Nest and they were absorbed, they became parasites." She tapped one of them on the head. "I tamed these two because I learned to steal and beg food better than they can. They stay with me now and protect me from the larger ones. They are jealous, you know. They have only been with the Nest for perhaps ten thousand years and are still uncertain of their position. They still think, and wonder sometimes. After ten thousand years there is still a little of that left to them."

"Savages," Afriel said. "I can well believe that. One of

them bit me while I was still aboard the starship. He left a lot to be desired as an ambassador."

"Yes, I warned him you were coming," said Mirny. "He didn't much like the idea, but I was able to bribe him with food. . . . I hope he didn't hurt you badly."

"A scratch," Afriel said. "I assume there's no chance of infection."

"I doubt it very much. Unless you brought your own bacteria with you."

"Hardly likely," Afriel said, offended. "I have no bacteria. And I wouldn't have brought microorganisms to an alien culture anyway."

Mirny looked away. "I thought you might have some of the special genetically altered ones. . . . I think we can go now. The springtail will have spread your scent by mouth-touching in the subsidiary chamber, ahead of us. It will be spread throughout the Nest in a few hours. Once it reaches the Queen, it will spread very quickly."

Placing her feet against the hard shell of one of the young springtails, she launched herself down the hall. Afriel followed her. The air was warm and he was beginning to sweat under his elaborate clothing, but his antiseptic sweat was odorless.

They exited into a vast chamber dug from the living rock. It was arched and oblong, eighty meters long and about twenty in diameter. It swarmed with members of the Nest.

There were hundreds of them. Most of them were workers, eight-legged and furred, the size of Great Danes. Here and there were members of the warrior caste, horse-sized furry monsters with heavy fanged heads the size and shape of overstuffed chairs.

A few meters away, two workers were carrying a member of the sensor caste, a being whose immense flattened head was attached to an atrophied body that was mostly lungs. The sensor had eyes and its furred chitin sprouted long coiled antennae that twitched feebly as the workers bore it along. The workers clung to the hollowed rock of the chamber walls with hooked and suckered feet.

A paddle-limbed monster with a hairless, faceless head came sculling past them, through the warm reeking air. The front of its head was a nightmare of sharp grinding jaws and blunt armored acid spouts. "A tunneler," Mirny said. "It can take us deeper into the Nest—come with me." She launched herself toward it and took a handhold on its furry, segmented back. Afriel followed her, joined by the two immature springtails, who clung to the thing's hide with their forelimbs. Afriel shuddered at the warm, greasy feel of its rank, damp fur. It continued to scull through the air, its eight fringed paddle feet catching the air like wings.

"There must be thousands of them," Afriel said.

"I said a hundred thousand in my last report, but that was before I had fully explored the Nest. Even now there are long stretches I haven't seen. They must number close to a quarter of a million. This asteroid is about the size of the Mechanists' biggest base—Ceres. It still has rich veins of carbonaceous material. It's far from mined out."

Afriel closed his eyes. If he were to lose his goggles, he would have to feel his way, blind, through these teeming, twitching, wriggling thousands. "The population's still expanding, then?"

"Definitely," she said. "In fact, the colony will launch a mating swarm soon. There are three dozen male and female alates in the chambers near the Queen. Once they're launched, they'll mate and start new Nests. I'll take you to see them presently." She hesitated. "We're entering one of the fungal gardens now."

One of the young springtails quietly shifted position. Grabbing the tunneler's fur with its forelimbs, it began to gnaw on the cuff of Afriel's pants. Afriel kicked it soundly, and it jerked back, retracting its eyestalks.

When he looked up again, he saw that they had entered a second chamber, much larger than the first. The walls around, overhead and below were buried under an explosive profusion of fungus. The most common types were swollen, barrel-like domes, multi-branched massed thickets, and spaghetti-like tangled extrusions, that moved very slightly in the faint and odorous breeze. Some of the barrels were surrounded by dim mists of exhaled spores.

"You see those caked-up piles beneath the fungus, its growth medium?" Mirny said.

"Yes."

"I'm not sure whether it is a plant form or just some kind of complex biochemical sludge," she said. "The point is that it grows in sunlight, on the outside of the asteroid. A food source that grows in naked space! Imagine what that would be worth, back in the Rings."

"There aren't words for its value," Afriel said.

"It's inedible by itself," she said. "I tried to eat a very small piece of it once. It was like trying to eat plastic."

"Have you eaten well, generally speaking?"

"Yes. Our biochemistry is quite similar to the Swarm's. The fungus itself is perfectly edible. The regurgitate is more nourishing, though. Internal fermentation in the worker hindgut adds to its nutritional value."

Afriel stared. "You grow used to it," Mirny said. "Later I'll teach you how to solicit food from the workers. It's a simple matter of reflex tapping—it's not controlled by pheromones, like most of their behavior." She brushed a long lock of clumped and dirty hair from the side of her face. "I hope the pheromonal samples I sent back were worth the cost of transportation."

"Oh, yes," said Afriel. "The chemistry of them was fascinating. We managed to synthesize most of the compounds. I was part of the research team myself." He hesitated. How far did he dare trust her? She had not been told about the experiment he and his superiors had planned. As far as Mirny knew, he was a simple, peaceful researcher, like herself. The Shapers' scientific community was suspicious of the minority involved in military work and espionage.

As an investment in the future, the Shapers had sent researchers to each of the nineteen alien races described to them by the Investors. This had cost the Shaper economy many gigawatts of precious energy and tons of rare metals and isotopes. In most cases, only two or three researchers could be sent; in seven cases, only one. For the Swarm, Galina Mirny had been chosen. She had gone peacefully, trusting in her intelligence and her good intentions to keep her alive and sane. Those who had sent her had not known whether her findings would be of any use or importance. They had only known that it was imperative that she be sent, even alone, even ill-equipped, before some other faction sent their own people and possibly discovered some technique or fact of overwhelming importance. And Dr. Mirny had indeed discovered such a situation. It had made her mission into a matter of Ring security. That was why Afriel had come.

"You synthesized the compounds?" she said. "Why?"

Afriel smiled disarmingly. "Just to prove to ourselves that we could do it, perhaps."

She shook her head. "No mind-games, Doctor Afriel, please. I came this far partly to escape from such things. Tell me the truth."

Afriel stared at her, regretting that the goggles meant he could not meet her eyes. "Very well," he said. "You should know, then, that I have been ordered by the Ring Council to carry out an experiment that may endanger both our lives."

Mirny was silent for a moment. "You're from Security, then?"

"My rank is captain."

"I knew it. . . . I knew it when those two Mechanists arrived. They were so polite, and so suspicious—I think they would have killed me at once if they hadn't hoped to bribe or torture some secret out of me. They scared the life out of me, Captain Afriel. . . . You scare me, too."

"We live in a frightening world, doctor. It's a matter of faction security."

"Everything's a matter of faction security with you lot," she said. "I shouldn't take you any farther, or show you anything more. This Nest, these creatures—they're not *intelligent,* captain. They can't think, they can't learn. They're innocent, primordially innocent. They have no knowledge of good and evil. They have no knowledge of *anything*. The last thing they need is to become pawns in a power struggle within some other race, light-years away."

The tunneler had turned into an exit from the fungal chambers and was paddling slowly along in the warm darkness. A group of creatures like gray, flattened basketballs floated by from the opposite direction. One of them settled on Afriel's sleeve, clinging with frail, whiplike tentacles. Afriel brushed it gently away, and it broke loose, emitting a stream of foul reddish droplets.

"Naturally I agree with you in principle, doctor," Afriel said smoothly. "But consider these Mechanists. Some of their extreme factions are already more than half machine. Do you expect humanitarian motives from them? They're cold, doctor—cold and soulless creatures who can cut a living man or woman to bits and never feel their pain. Most

of the other factions hate us. They think we've set ourselves
up as racist supermen because we won't interbreed, because
we've chosen the freedom to manipulate our own genes.
Would you rather that one of these cults do what we must
do, and use the results against us?"

"This is double-talk." She looked away. All around them
workers laden down with fungus, their jaws full and guts
stuffed with it, were spreading out into the Nest, scuttling
alongside them or disappearing into branch tunnels departing in every direction, including straight up and straight
down. Afriel saw a creature much like a worker, but with
only six legs, scuttle past in the opposite direction, overhead. It was a parasite-mimic. How long, he wondered, did it
take a creature to evolve to look like that?

"It's no wonder that we've had so many defectors, back in
the Rings," she said sadly. "If humanity is so stupid as to
work itself into a corner like you describe, then it's better to
have nothing to do with them. Better to live alone. Better not
to help the madness spread."

"That kind of talk will only get us all killed," Afriel said.
"We owe an allegiance to the faction that produced us."

"Tell my truly, captain," she said. "Haven't you ever felt
the urge to leave everything—everyone—all your duties and
constraints, and just go somewhere to think it all out? Your
whole world, and your part in it? We're trained so hard,
from childhood, and so much is demanded from us. Don't
you think it's made us lose sight of our goals, somehow?"

"We live in space," Afriel said flatly. "Space is an unnatural environment, and it takes an unnatural effort from unnatural people to prosper there. Our minds are our tools, and
philosophy has to come second. Naturally I've felt those
urges you mention. They're just another threat to guard
against. I believe in an ordered society. Technology has
unleashed tremendous forces that are ripping society apart.
Some one faction must arise from the struggle and integrate
things. We who are Reshaped have the wisdom and restraint
to do it humanely. They's why I do the work I do." He
hesitated. "I don't expect to see our day of triumph. I expect
to die in some brushfire conflict, or through assassination.
It's enough that I can foresee that day."

"But the arrogance of it, captain!" she said suddenly.
"The arrogance of your little life and its little sacrifice!
Consider the Swarm, if you really want your humane and

perfect order. Here it is! Where it's always warm and dark, and it smells good, and food is easy to get, and everything is endlessly and perfectly recycled. The only resources that are ever lost are the bodies of the mating swarms, and a little air from the airlocks when the workers go out to harvest. A Nest like this one could last unchanged for hundreds of thousands of years. Hundreds, of thousands, of years. Who, or what, will remember us and our stupid faction in even a thousand years?"

Afriel shook his head. "That's not a valid comparison. There is no such long view for us. In another thousand years we'll be machines, or gods." He felt the top of his head; his velvet cap was gone. No doubt something was eating it by now.

The tunneler took them even deeper into the honey-combed free-fall maze of the asteroid. They saw the pupal chambers, where pallid larvae twitched in swaddled silk; the main fungal gardens; the graveyard pits, where winged workers beat ceaselessly at the soupy air, feverishly hot from the heat of decomposition. Corrosive black fungus ate the bodies of the dead into coarse black powder, carried off by blackened workers themselves three-quarters dead.

Later they left the tunneler and floated on by themselves. The woman moved with the ease of long habit; Afriel followed her, colliding bruisingly with squeaking workers. There were thousands of them, clinging to ceiling, walls, and floor, clustering and scurrying at every conceivable angle.

Later still they visited the chamber of the winged princes and princesses, an echoing round vault where creatures forty meters long hung crooked-legged in midair. Their bodies were segmented and metallic, with organic rocket nozzles on their thoraxes, where wings might have been. Folded along their sleek backs were radar antennae on long sweeping booms. They looked more like interplanetary probes under construction than anything biological. Workers fed them ceaselessly. Their bulging spiracled abdomens were full of compressed oxygen.

Mirny begged a large chunk of fungus from a passing worker, deftly tapping its antennae and provoking a reflex action. She handed most of the fungus to the two springtails, which devoured it greedily and looked expectantly for more.

Afriel tucked his legs into a lotus position and began chewing with determination on the leathery fungus. It was tough, but tasted good, like smoked meat—a Terran delicacy he had tasted only once. The smell of smoke meant disaster in a Shaper's colony.

Mirny maintained a stony silence. "Food's no problem," Afriel said cheerfully. "Where do we sleep?"

She shrugged. "Anywhere. . . . there are unused niches and tunnels here and there. I suppose you'll want to see the Queen's chamber next."

"By all means."

"I'll have to get more fungus. The warriors are on guard there and have to be bribed with food."

She gathered an armful of fungus from another worker in the endless stream, and they exited through another tunnel. Afriel, already totally lost, was further confused in the maze of chambers and tunnels. At last they exited into an immense lightless cavern, bright with infrared heat from the Queen's monstrous body. It was the colony's central factory. The fact that it was made of warm and pulpy flesh did not conceal its essentially industrial nature. Tons of predigested fungal pap went into the slick blind jaws at one end. The rounded billows of soft flesh digested and processed it, squirming, sucking, and undulating, with loud, machinelike churnings and gurglings. Out of the other end came an endless conveyorlike blobbed stream of eggs, each one packed in a thick hormonal paste of lubrication. The workers avidly licked the eggs clean and bore them off to nurseries. Each egg was the size of a man's torso.

The process went on and on. There was no day or night here in the lightless center of the asteroid. There was no remnant of a diurnal rhythm in the genes of these creatures. The flow of production was as constant and even as the working of an automated mine.

"This is why I'm here," Afriel murmured in awe. "Just look at this, doctor. The Mechanists have computer-run mining machinery that is generations ahead of ours. But here—in the bowels of this nameless little world, is a genetically run technology that feeds itself, maintains itself, runs itself, efficiently, endlessly, mindlessly. It's the perfect organic tool. The faction that could make use of these tireless workers could make itself an industrial titan. And our knowledge of biochemistry is unsurpassed. We Shapers are just the ones to do it."

"How do you propose to do that?" Mirny asked with open

skepticism. "You would have to ship a fertilized queen all the way to the solar system. We could scarcely afford that, even if the Investors would let us, which they wouldn't."

"I don't need an entire colony," Afriel said patiently. "I only need the genetic information from one egg. Our laboratories back in the Rings could clone endless numbers of them."

"But the workers are useless without the rest of the colony to give them orders. They need the pheromones to trigger their behavior modes."

"Exactly," Afriel said. "As it so happens, I possess those pheromones in concentrated form. What I must do now is test them. I must prove that I can use them to make the workers do what I choose. Once I've proven it's possible, I'm authorized to smuggle the genetic information necessary back to the Rings. The Investors won't approve. There are, of course, moral questions involved, and they are not genetically advanced. But we can win their approval back with the profits we make. Best of all, we can beat the Mechanists at their own game."

"You've carried the pheromones here?" Mirny said. "Didn't the Investors suspect something when they found them?"

"Now it's you who has made an error," Afriel said calmly. "You assume that they are infallible. You are wrong. A race without curiosity will never explore every possibility, the way we Shapers did." Afriel pulled up his pants cuff and extended his right leg. "Consider this varicose vein along my shin. Circulatory problems of this sort are common among those who spend a lot of time in free-fall. This vein, however, has been blocked artificially, and its walls biochemically treated to reduce osmosis. Within the vein are ten separate colonies of genetically altered bacteria, each one specially to produce a different Swarm pheromone."

He smiled. "The Investors searched me very thoroughly, including x-rays. They insist, naturally, on knowing about everything transported aboard one of their ships. But the vein appears normal to x-rays, and the bacteria are trapped within compartments in the vein. They are indetectable. I have a small medical kit on my person. It includes a syringe. We can use it to extract the pheromones and test them. When the tests are finished—and I feel sure they will be successful, in fact I've staked my career on it—we can empty the vein and all its compartments. The bacteria will die on contact with the air. We can refill the vein with the yolk from a developing embryo. The cells may survive during the trip back, but even if they die, they won't rot. They'll never come in contact with bacteria that can decompose them. Back in the Rings, we can learn to activate and suppress different genes to produce the different castes, just as is done in nature. We'll have millions of workers, armies of warriors if need be, perhaps even organic rocketships, grown from altered alates. If this works, who do you think will remember me then, eh? Me and my arrogant little life and little sacrifice?"

She stared at him; even the bulky goggles could not hide her new respect and even fear. "You really mean to do it, then."

"I made the sacrifice of my time and energy. I expect results, doctor."

"But it's kidnapping. You're talking about breeding a slave race."

Afriel shrugged, with contempt. "You're juggling words, doctor. I'll cause this colony no harm. I may steal some of its workers' labor while they obey my own chemical orders, but that tiny minority won't be missed. I admit to the murder of one egg, but that is no more a crime than a human abortion. Can the theft of one strand of genetic material be called 'kidnapping'? I think not. As for the scandalous idea of a slave race—I reject it out of hand. These creatures are genetic robots. They will no more be slaves than are laser drills or bulldozers. At the very worst, they will be domestic animals."

Mirny considered the issue. It did not take her long. "It's true. It's not as if a common worker will be staring at the stars, pining for its freedom. They're just brainless neuters."

"Exactly, doctor."

"They simply work. Whether they work for us or the Swarm makes no difference to them."

"I see that you've seized on the beauty of the idea."

"And if it worked," Mirny said, "if it worked, our faction would profit astronomically."

Afriel smiled genuinely, unaware of the chilling sarcasm of his expression. "And the personal profit, doctor . . . the valuable expertise of the first to exploit the technique." He spoke gently, quietly. "Ever see a nitrogen snowfall on

Titan? I think a habitat of one's own there—large, much larger than anything possible before. . . . A genuine city, Galina, a place where a man can scrap the rules and discipline that madden him. . . ."

"Now it's you who are talking defection, captain-doctor."

Afriel was silent for a moment, then smiled with an effort. "Now you've ruined my perfect reverie," he said. "Besides, what I was describing was the well-earned retirement of a wealthy man, not some self-indulgent hermitage. . . . there's a clear but subtle difference." He hesitated. "In any case, may I conclude that you're with me in this project?"

She laughed and touched his arm. There was something uncanny about the small sound of her laugh, drowned by a great organic rumble from the Queen's monstrous intestines. . . . "Do you expect me to resist your arguments for two years? Better that I give in now and save us friction."

"Yes."

"After all, you won't do any harm to the colony. They'll never know anything has happened. And if their genetic line is successfully reproduced back home, there'll never be any reason for humanity to bother them again."

"True enough," said Afriel, though in the back of his mind he instantly thought of the fabulous wealth of Betelguese's asteroid system. A day would come, inevitably, when humanity would move to the stars en masse, in earnest. It would be well to know the ins and outs of every race that might become a rival.

"I'll help you as best I can," she said. There was a moment's silence. "Have you seen enough of this area?"

"Yes." They left the Queen's chamber.

"I didn't think I'd like you at first," she said candidly. "I think I like you better now. You seem to have a sense of humor that most Security people lack."

"It's not a sense of humor," Afriel said sadly. "It's a sense of irony disguised as one."

There were no days in the unending stream of hours that followed. There were only ragged periods of sleep, apart at first, later together, as they held each other in free-fall. The sexual feel of skin and body became an anchor to their common humanity, a divided, frayed humanity so many light-years away that the concept no longer had any meaning to them. Life in the warm and swarming tunnels was the here and now; the two of them were like germs in a bloodstream, moving ceaselessly with the pulsing ebb and flow. They tested the pheromones, one by one, as the hours stretched into months and time grew meaningless.

The pheromonal workings were complex, but not impossibly difficult. The first of the ten pheromone was a simple grouping stimulus, causing large numbers of workers to gather as the pheromone was spread from palp to palp. The workers then waited for further instructions; if none were forthcoming, they dispersed. To work effectively, the pheromones had to be given in a mix, or series, like computer commands; number one, grouping, for instance, together with the third pheromone, a transferral order, which caused the workers to empty any given chamber and move its effects to another. The ninth pheromone had the best industrial possibilities; it was a building order, causing the workers to gather tunnelers and dredgers and set them to work. Others were annoying; the tenth pheromone provoked grooming behavior, and the workers' furry palps stripped off the remaining rags of Afriel's clothing. The eighth pheromone sent the workers off to harvest material on the asteroid's surface, and in their eagerness to observe its effects the two explorers were almost trapped and swept off into space.

The two of them no longer feared the warrior caste. They knew that a dose of the sixth pheromone would send them scurrying off to defend the eggs, just as it sent the workers to tend them. Mirny and Afriel took advantage of this and secured their own chambers, dug by chemically hijacked workers and defended by a hijacked airlock guardian. They had their own fungal gardens to refresh the air, stocked with the fungus they liked best, and digested by a worker they kept drugged for their own food use. From constant stuffing and lack of exercise the worker had swollen up into its replete form and hung from one wall like a monstrous grape.

Afriel was tired. He had been without sleep recently for a long time; how long, he didn't know. His body rhythms had not adjusted as well as Mirny's, and he was prone to fits of depression and irritability that he had to repress with an effort. "The Investors will be back sometime," he said. "Sometime soon."

Mirny shrugged. "The Investors," she said, and followed

the remark with something in the language of the springtails, that he didn't catch. Despite his linguistic training, Afriel had never caught up with her in her use of the springtails' grating jargon. His training was almost a liability; the springtail language had decayed so much that it was a pidgin tongue, without rules or regularity. He knew enough to give them simple orders, and with his partial control of the warriors he had the power to back it up. The springtails were afraid of him, and the two juveniles that Mirny had tamed had grown into fat, overgrown tyrants that freely terrorized their elders. Afriel had been too busy to seriously study the springtails or the other symbiotes. There were too many practical matters at hand.

"If they come too soon, I won't be able to finish my latest study," she said in English.

Afriel pulled off his infrared goggles and knotted them tightly around his neck. "There's a limit, Galina," he said yawning. "You can only memorize so much data without equipment. We'll just have to wait quietly until we can get back. I hope the Investors aren't shocked when they see me. I lost a fortune with those clothes."

"It's been so dull since the mating swarm was launched. And we've had to stop the experiments to let your vein heal. If it weren't for the new growth in the alates' chamber, I'd be bored to death." She pushed greasy hair from her face with both hands. "Are you going to sleep?"

"Yes, if I can."

"You won't come with me? I keep telling you that this new growth is important. I think it's a new caste. It's definitely not an alate. It has eyes like an alate, but it's clinging to the wall."

"It's probably not a Swarm member at all, then," he said tiredly, humoring her. "It's probably a parasite, an alate mimic. Go on and see it, if you want to. I'll be here waiting for you."

He heard her leave. Without his infrareds on, the darkness was still not quite total; there was a very faint luminosity from the streaming, growing fungus in the chamber beyond. The stuffed worker replete moved slightly on the wall, rustling and gurgling. He fell asleep.

When he awoke, Mirny had not yet returned. He was not alarmed. First, he visited the original airlock tunnel, where the Investors had first left him. It was irrational—the Investors always fulfilled their contracts—but he feared that they would arrive someday, become impatient, and leave without him. The Investors would have to wait, of course. Mirny could keep them occupied in the short time it would take him to hurry to the nursery and rob a developing egg of its living cells. It was best that the egg be as fresh as possible.

Later he ate. He was munching fungus in one of the anterior chambers when Mirny's two tamed springtails found him. "What do you want?" he asked in their language.

"Food-giver no good," the larger one screeched, waving its forelegs in brainless agitation. "Not work, not sleep."

"Not move," the second one said. It added hopefully, "Eat it now?"

Afriel gave them some of his food. They ate it, seemingly more out of habit than real appetite, which alarmed him. "Take me to her," he told them.

The two springtails scurried off; he followed them easily, adroitly dodging and weaving through the crowds of workers. They led him several miles through the network, to the alates' chamber. There they stopped, confused. "Gone," the large one said.

The chamber was empty. Afriel had never seen it empty before, and it was very unusual for the Swarm to waste so much space. He felt dread. "Follow the food-giver," he said. "Follow smell."

The springtails snuffled without much enthusiasm along one wall; they knew he had no food and were reluctant to do anything without an immediate reward. At last one of them picked up the scent, or pretended to, and followed it up across the ceiling and into the mouth of a tunnel.

It was hard for Afriel to see much in the abandoned chamber; there was not enough infrared heat. He leapt upward after the springtail.

He heard the roar of a warrior and the springtail's choked-off screech. It came flying from the tunnel's mouth, a spray of clotted fluid bursting from its ruptured head. It tumbled end over end until it hit the far wall with a flaccid crunch. It was already dead.

The second springtail fled at once, screeching with grief and terror. Afriel landed on the lip of the tunnel, sinking into a crouch as his legs soaked up momentum. He could smell the acrid stench of the warrior's anger, a pheromone so thick that even a human could scent it. Dozens of other warriors would group here within minutes, or seconds. Behind the enraged warrior he could hear workers and tunnelers shifting and cementing rock.

He might be able to control one enraged warrior, but never two, or twenty. He launched himself from the chamber wall and out an exit.

He searched for the other springtail—he felt sure he could recognize it, it was so much bigger than the others—but he could not find it. With its keen sense of smell, it could easily hide from him if it wanted to.

Mirny did not return. Uncountable hours passed. He slept again. He returned to the alate's chambers; there were warriors on guard there, warriors that were not interested in food and opened their immense serrated fangs when he approached. They looked ready to rip him apart; the faint reek of aggressive pheromone hung about the place like a fog. He did not see any symbiotes of any kind on the warriors' bodies. There was one species, a thing like a huge tick, that clung only to warriors, but even the ticks were gone.

He returned to his chambers to wait and think. Mirny's body was not in the garbage pits. Of course, it was possible that something else might have eaten her. Should he extract the remaining pheromone from the spaces in the vein and try to break into the alate's chamber? He suspected that Mirny, or whatever was left of her, was somewhere in the tunnel where the springtail had been killed. He had never explored that tunnel himself. There were thousands of tunnels he had never explored.

He felt paralyzed by indecision and fear. If he were quiet, if he did nothing, the Investors might arrive at any moment. He could tell the Ring Council anything he wanted about Mirny's death; if he had the genetics with him, no one would quibble. He did not love her; he respected her, but not enough to give up his life, or his faction's investment. He had not thought of the Ring Council in a long time, and the thought sobered him. He would have to explain his decision. . . .

He was still in a brown study when he heard a whoosh of air as his living airlock deflated itself. Three warriors had come for him. There was no reek of anger about them. They moved slowly and carefully. He knew better than to try to resist. One of them seized him gently in its massive jaws and carried him off.

It took him to the alates' chamber and into the guarded tunnel. A new, large chamber had been excavated at the end of the tunnel. It was filled almost to bursting by a black-splattered white mass of flesh. In the center of the soft speckled mass were a mouth and two damp, shining eyes, on stalks. Long tendrils like conduits dangled, writhing, from a clumped ridge above the eyes. The tendrils ended in pink, fleshy plug-like clumps.

One of the tendrils had been thrust through Mirny's skull. Her body hung in midair, limp as wax. Her eyes were open, but blind.

Another tendril was plugged into the braincase of a mutated worker. The worker still had the pallid tinge of a larva; it was shrunken and deformed, and its mouth had the wrinkled look of a human mouth. There was a blob like a tongue in the mouth, and white ridges with human teeth. It had no eyes.

It spoke with Mirny's voice. "Captain-doctor Afriel. . . ."

"Galina. . . ."

"I have no such name. You may address me as Swarm."

Afriel vomited. The central mass was an immense head. Its brain almost filled the room.

It waited politely until Afriel had finished.

"I find myself awakened again," Swarm said dreamily. "I am pleased to see that it is no major emergency that concerns me. Instead it is a threat that has become almost routine." It hesitated delicately. Mirny's body moved slightly in midair; her breathing was inhumanly regular. The eyes opened and closed. "Another young race."

"What are you?"

"I am the Swarm. That is, I am one of its castes. I am a tool, an adaptation; my specialty is intelligence. I am not often needed. It is good to be needed again."

"Have you been here all along? Why didn't you greet us? We'd have dealt with you. We meant no harm."

The wet mouth on the end of the plug made laughing sounds. "Like yourself, I enjoy irony," it said. "It is a pretty trap you have found yourself in, captain-doctor. You meant to make the Swarm work for you and your race. You meant to breed us and study us and use us. It is an excellent plan, but one we hit upon long before your race evolved."

Stung by panic, Afriel's mind raced frantically. "You're an intelligent being," he said. "There's no reason to do us any harm. Let us talk together. We can help you."

"Yes," Swarm agreed. "You will be helpful. Your companion's memories tell me that this is one of those uncomfortable periods when galactic intelligence is rife. Intelligence is a great bother. It makes all kinds of trouble for us."

"What do you mean?"

"You are a young race and lay great stock by your own cleverness," Swarm said. "As usual, you fail to see that intelligence is not a survival trait."

Afriel wiped sweat from his face. "We've done well," he said. "We came to you, and peacefully. You didn't come to us."

"I refer to exactly that," Swarm said urbanely. "This urge to expand, to explore, to develop, is just what will make you extinct. You naively suppose that you can continue to feed your curiosity indefinitely. It is an old story, pursued by countless races before you. Within a thousand years—perhaps a little longer—your species will vanish."

"You intend to destroy us, then? I warn you it will not be an easy task—"

"Again you miss the point. Knowledge is power! Do you suppose that fragile little form of yours—your primitive legs, your ludicrous arms and hands, your tiny, scarcely wrinkled brain—can *contain* all that power? Certainly not! Already your race is flying to pieces under the impact of your own expertise. The original human form is becoming obsolete. Your own genes have been altered, and you, captain-doctor, are a crude experiment. In a hundred years you will be a Neanderthal. In a thousand years you will not even be a memory. Your race will go the same way as a thousand others."

"And what way is that?"

"I do not know." The thing on the end of the Swarm's arm made a chuckling sound. "They have passed beyond my ken. They have all discovered something, learned something, that has caused them to transcend my understanding. It may be that they even transcend *being*. At any rate, I cannot sense their presence anywhere. They seem to do nothing, they seem to interfere in nothing; for all intents and purposes, they seem to be dead. Vanished. They may have become gods, or ghosts. In either case, I have no wish to join them."

"So then—so then you have—"

"Intelligence is very much a two-edged sword, captain-doctor. It is useful only up to a point. It interferes with the business of living. Life, and intelligence, do not mix very well. They are not at all closely related, as you childishly assume."

"But you, then—you are a rational being—"

"I am a tool, as I said." The mutated device on the end of its arm made a sighing noise. "When you began your phero-monal experiments, the chemical imbalance became apparent to the Queen. It triggered certain genetic patterns within her body, and I was reborn. Chemical sabotage is a problem that can best be dealt with by intelligence. I am a brain replete, you see, specially designed to be far more intelligent than any young race. Within three days I was fully self-conscious. Within five days I had deciphered these markings on my body. They are the genetically encoded history of my race . . . within five days and two hours I recognized the problem at hand and knew what to do. I am now doing it. I am six days old."

"What is it you intend to do?"

"Your race is a very vigorous one. I expect it to be here, competing with us, within five hundred years. Perhaps much sooner. It will be necessary to make a thorough study of such a rival. I invite you to join our community on a permanent basis."

"What do you mean?"

"I invite you to become a symbiote. I have here a male and a female, whose genes are altered and therefore without defects. You make a perfect breeding pair. It will save me a great deal of trouble with cloning."

"You think I'll betray my race and deliver a slave species into your hands?"

"Your choice is simple, captain-doctor. Remain an intelligent, living being, or become a mindless puppet, like your partner. I have taken over all the functions of her nervous system; I can do the same to you."

"I can kill myself."

"That might be troublesome, because it would make me resort to developing a cloning technology. Technology, though I am capable of it, is painful to me. I am a genetic artifact; there are fail-safes within me that prevent me from taking over the Nest for my own uses. That would mean falling into the same trap of progress as other intelligent races. For similar reasons, my lifespan is limited. I will live for only a thousand years, until your race's brief flurry of energy is over and peace resumes once more."

"Only a thousand years?" Afriel laughed bitterly. "What then? You kill off my descendants, I assume, having no further use for them."

"No. We have not killed any of the fifteen other races we have taken for defensive study. It has not been necessary. Consider that small scavenger floating by your head, captain-doctor, that is feeding on your vomit. Five hundred million years ago its ancestors made the galaxy tremble. When they attacked us, we unleashed their own kind upon them. Of course, we altered our side, so that they were smarter, tougher, and, of course, totally loyal to us. Our Nests were the only world they knew, and they fought with a valor and inventiveness we never could have matched. . . . Should your race arrive to exploit us, we will naturally do the same."

"We humans are different."

"Of course."

"A thousand years here won't change us. You will die and our descendants will take over this Nest. We'll be running things, despite you, in a few generations. The darkness won't make any difference."

"Of course not. You don't need eyes here. You don't need anything."

"You'll allow me to stay alive? To teach them anything I want?"

"Certainly, captain-doctor. We are doing you a favor, in all truth. In a thousand years your descendants here will be the only remnants of the human race. We are generous with our immortality; we will take it upon ourselves to preserve you."

"You're wrong, Swarm. You're wrong about intelligence, and you're wrong about everything else. Maybe other races would crumble into parasitism, but we humans are different."

"Certainly. You'll do it, then?"

"Yes, I accept your challenge. And I will defeat you."

"Splendid. When the Investors return here, the springtails will say that they have killed you, and will tell them to never return. They will not return. The humans should be the next to arrive."

"If I don't defeat you, they will."

"Perhaps." Again it sighed. "I'm glad I don't have to absorb you. I would have missed your conversation."

SOULS

~~~~~~

Joanna Russ

Joanna Russ has been one of the most literarily accomplished sf writers for twenty years, winning a strong following with such stories as "My Dear Emily" and the award-winning "When It Changed," and half a dozen novels including Picnic on Paradise *and* The Female Man. *"Souls" is one of her strongest stories, a tale of a medieval saint who was much more than she seemed.*

This story, like Sterling's "Swarm," is one of a series (she says there will eventually be a book of them), but like all outstanding stories it is effective and moving by itself.

Deprived of other Banquet
I entertained myself—
                    —Emily Dickinson

THIS IS THE TALE OF THE ABBESS RADEGUNDE
and what happened when the Norsemen came. I tell it not as
it was told to me but as I saw it, for I was a child then and the
Abbess had made a pet and errand boy of me, although the
stern old Wardress, Cunigunt, who had outlived the previous
Abbess, said I was more in the Abbey than out of it and a
scandal. But the Abbess would only say mildly, "Dear
Cunigunt, a scandal at the age of seven?" which was turning
it off with a joke, for she knew how harsh and disliking my
new stepmother was to me and my father did not care and I
with no sisters or brothers. You must understand that joking
and calling people "dear" and "my dear" was only her
manner; she was in every way an unusual woman. The
previous Abbess, Herrade, had found that Radegunde, who
had been given to her to be fostered, had great gifts and so
sent the child south to be taught, and that has never happened here before. The story has it that the Abbess Herrade
found Radegunde seeming to read the great illuminated book
in the Abbess's study; the child had somehow pulled it off its
stand and was sitting on the floor with the volume in her lap,
sucking her thumb, and turning the pages with her other
hand just as if she were reading.

"Little two-years," said the Abbess Herrade, who was a
kind woman, "what are you doing?" She thought it amusing,
I suppose, that Radegunde should pretend to read this great

56

book, the largest and finest in the Abbey, which had many, many books more than any other nunnery or monastery I had ever heard of: a full forty then, as I remember. And then little Radegunde was doing the book no harm.

"Reading, Mother," said the little girl.

"Oh, reading?" said the Abbess, smiling. "Then tell me what you are reading," and she pointed to the page.

"This," said Radegunde, "is a great *D* with flowers and other beautiful things about it, which is to show that *Dominus,* our Lord God, is the greatest thing and the most beautiful and makes everything to grow and be beautiful, and then it goes on to say *Domine nobis pacem,* which means *Give peace to us, O Lord.*"

Then the Abbess began to be frightened but she said only, "Who showed you this?" thinking that Radegunde had heard someone read and tell the words or had been pestering the nuns on the sly.

"No one," said the child. "Shall I go on?" and she read page after page of the Latin, in each case telling what the words meant.

There is more to the story, but I will say only that after many prayers the Abbess Herrade sent her foster daughter far southwards, even to Poitiers, where Saint Radegunde had ruled an Abbey before, and some say even to Rome, and in these places Radegunde was taught all learning, for all learning there is in the world reamins in these places. Radegunde came back a grown woman and nursed the Abbess through her last illness and then became Abbess in her turn. They say that the great folk of the Church down there in the south wanted to keep her because she was such a prodigy of female piety and learning, there where life is safe and comfortable and less rude than it is here, but she said that the gray skies and flooding winters of her birthplace called to her very soul. She often told me the story when I was a child: how headstrong she had been and how defiant, and how she had sickened so desperately for her native land that they had sent her back, deciding that a rude life in the mud of a northern village would be a good cure for such a rebellious soul as hers.

"And so it was," she would say, patting my cheek or tweaking my ear. "See how humble I am now?" for you understand, all this about her rebellious girlhood, twenty years' back, was a kind of joke between us. "Don't you do

it," she would tell me and we would laugh together, I so
heartily at the very idea of my being a pious monk full of
learning that I would hold my sides and be unable to speak.

She was kind to everyone. She knew all the languages, not
only ours, but the Irish too and the tongues folk speak to the
north and south, and Latin and Greek also, and all the other
languages in the world, both to read and write. She knew
how to cure sickness, both the old women's way with herbs
or leeches and out of books also. And never was there a
more pious woman! Some speak ill of her now she's gone
and say she was too merry to be a good Abbess, but she
would say, "Merriment is God's flowers," and when the
winter wind blew her headdress awry and showed the gray
hair—which happened once; I was there and saw the
shocked faces of the Sisters with her—she merely tapped the
band back into place, smiling and saying, "Impudent wind!
Thou showest thou has power which is more than our silly
human power, for it is from God"—and this quite satisfied
the girls with her.

No one ever saw her angry. She was impatient sometimes,
but in a kindly way, as if her mind were elsewhere. It was in
Heaven, I used to think, for I have seen her pray for hours or
sink to her knees—right in the marsh!—to see the wild duck
fly south, her hands clasped and a kind of wild joy on her
face, only to rise a moment later, looking at the mud on her
habit and crying half-ruefully, half in laughter, "Oh, what
will Sister Laundress say to me? I am hopeless! Dear child,
tell no one; I will say I fell," and then she would clap her
hand to her mouth, turning red and laughing even harder,
saying, "I *am* hopeless, telling lies!"

The town thought her a saint, of course. We were all
happy then, or so it seems to me now, and all lucky and well,
with this happiness of having her amongst us burning and
blooming in our midst like a great fire around which we could
all warm ourselves, even those who didn't know why life
seemed so good. There was less illness; the food was better;
the very weather stayed mild; and people did not quarrel as
they had before her time and do again now. Nor do I think,
considering what happened at the end, that all this was
nothing but the fancy of a boy who's found his mother, for
that's what she was to me; I brought her all the gossip and
ran errands when I could, and she called me Boy News in
Latin; I was happier than I have ever been.

And then one day those terrible, beaked prows appeared in our river.

I was with her when the warning came, in the main room of the Abbey tower just after the first fire of the year had been lit in the great hearth; we thought ourselves safe, for they had never been seen so far south and it was too late in the year for any sensible shipman to be in our waters. The Abbey was host to three Irish priests who turned pale when young Sister Sibihd burst in with the news, crying and wringing her hands; one of the brothers exclaimed a thing in Latin which means "God protect us!" for they had been telling stories of the terrible sack of the monastery of Saint Columbanus and how everyone had run away with the precious manuscripts or had hidden in the woods, and that was how Father Cairbre and the two others had decided to go "walk the world," for this (the Abbess had been telling it all to me, for I had no Latin) is what the Irish say when they leave their native land to travel elsewhere.

"God protects our souls, not our bodies," said the Abbess Radegunde briskly. She had been talking with the priests in their own language or in the Latin, but this she said in ours so even the women workers from the village would understand. Then she said, "Father Cairbre, take your friends and the younger Sisters to the underground passages; Sister Diemud, open the gates to the villagers; half of them will be trying to get behind the Abbey walls and the others will be fleeing to the marsh. You, Boy News, down to the cellars with the girls." But I did not go and she never saw it; she was up and looking out one of the window slits instantly. So was I. I had always thought the Norsemen's big ships came right up on land—on legs, I supposed—and was disappointed to see that after they came up our river they stayed in the water like other ships and the men were coming ashore in little boats, which they were busy pulling up on shore through the sand and mud. Then the Abbess repeated her order— "Quickly! Quickly!" — and before anyone knew what had happened, she was gone from the room. I watched from the tower window; in the turmoil nobody bothered about me. Below, the Abbey grounds and gardens were packed with folk, all stepping on the herb plots and the Abbess's paestum roses, and great logs were being dragged to bar the door set in the stone walls around the Abbey, not high walls, to tell the truth, and Radegunde was going quickly through the crowd, crying: Do this! Do that! Stay, thou! Go, thou! and like things.

Then she reached the door and motioned Sister Oddha, the doorkeeper, aside—the old Sister actually fell to her knees in entreaty—and all this, you must understand, was wonderfully pleasant to me. I had no more idea of danger than a puppy. There was some tumult by the door—I think the men with the logs were trying to get in her way—and Abbess Radegunde took out from the neck of her habit her silver crucifix, brought all the way from Rome, and shook it impatiently at those who would keep her in. So of course they let her through at once.

I settled into my corner of the window, waiting for the Abbess's crucifix to bring down God's lightning on those tall, fair men who defied Our Savior and the law and were supposed to wear animal horns on their heads, though these did not (and I found out later that's just a story; that is not what the Norse do). I did hope that the Abbess, or Our Lord, would wait just a little while before destroying them, for I wanted to get a good look at them before they all died, you understand. I was somewhat disappointed, as they seemed to be wearing breeches with leggings under them and tunics on top, like ordinary folk, and cloaks also, though some did carry swords and axes and there were round shields piled on the beach in one place. But the long hair they had was fine, and the bright colors of their clothes, and the monsters growing out of the heads of the ships were splendid and very frightening, even though one could see that they were only painted, like the pictures in the Abbess's books.

I decided that God had provided me with enough edification and could now strike down the impious strangers.

But He did not.

Instead the Abbess walked alone towards these fierce men, over the stony river bank, as calmly as if she were on a picnic with her girls. She was singing a little song, a pretty tune that I repeated many years later, and a well-traveled man said it was a Norse cradle-song. I didn't know that then, but only that the terrible, fair men, who had looked up in surprise at seeing one lone woman come out of the Abbey (which was barred behind her; I could see that), now began a sort of whispering astonishment among themselves. I saw the Abbess's gaze go quickly from one to the other—we often said that she could tell what was hidden in the soul from one look at the face—and then she picked the skirt of her habit up with one hand and daintily went among the rocks to one of the men, one older than the others, as it proved later, though I could not see so well at the time—and said to him, in his own language:

"Welcome, Thorvald Einarsson, and what do you, good farmer, so far from your own place, with the harvest ripe and the great autumn storms coming on over the sea?" (You may wonder how I knew what she said when I had no Norse; the truth is that Father Cairbre, who had not gone to the cellars after all, was looking out the top of the window while I was barely able to peep out of the bottom, and he repeated everything that was said for the folk in the room, who all kept very quiet.)

Now you could see that the pirates were dumbfounded to hear her speak their own language and even more so that she called one by his name; some stepped backwards and made strange signs in the air and others unsheathed axes or swords and came running towards the Abbess. But this Thorvald Einarsson put up his hand for them to stop and laughed heartily.

"Think!" he said. "There's no magic here, only cleverness—what pair of ears could miss my name with the lot of you bawling out 'Thorvald Einarsson, help me with this oar;' 'Thorvald Einarsson, my leggings are wet to the knees;' 'Thorvald Einarsson, this stream is as cold as a Fimbulwinter!' "

The Abbess Radegunde nodded and smiled. Then she sat down plump on the river bank. She scratched behind one ear, as I had often seen her do when she was deep in thought. Then she said (and I am sure that this talk was carried on in a loud voice so that we in the Abbey could hear it):

"Good friend Thorvald, you are as clever as the tale I heard of you from your sister's son, Ranulf, from whom I learnt the Norse when I was in Rome, and to show you it was he, he always swore by his gray horse, Lamefoot, and he had a difficulty in his speech; he could not say the sounds as we do and so spoke of you always as 'Torvald.' Is not that so?"

I did not realize it then, being only a child, but the Abbess was—by this speech—claiming hospitality from the man and had also picked by chance or inspiration the cleverest among these thieves, for his next words were:

"I am not the leader. There are no leaders here."

He was warning her that they were not his men to control, you see. So she scratched behind her ear again and got up. Then she began to wander, as if she did not know what to do, from one to the other of these uneasy folk—for some backed off and made signs at her still, and some took out their knives—singing her little tune again and walking slowly, more bent over and older and infirm-looking than we had ever seen her, one helpless little woman in black before all those fierce men. One wild young pirate snatched the head-dress from her as she passed, leaving her short gray hair bare to the wind; the others laughed and he that had done it cried out:

"Grandmother, are you not ashamed?"

"Why, good friend, of what?" said she mildly.

"Thou art married to thy Christ," he said, holding the head-covering behind his back, "but this bridegroom of thine cannot even defend thee against the shame of having thy head uncovered! Now if thou wert married to me—"

There was much laughter. The Abbess Radegunde waited until it was over. Then she scratched her bare head and made as if to turn away, but suddenly she turned back upon him with the age and infirmity dropping from her as if they had been a cloak, seeming taller and very grand, as if lit from within by some great fire. She looked directly into his face. This thing she did was something we had all seen, of course, but they had not, nor had they heard that great, grand voice with which she sometimes read the Scriptures to us or talked with us of the wrath of God. I think the young man was frightened, for all his daring. And I know now what I did not then: that the Norse admire courage above all things and that—to be blunt—everyone likes a good story, especially if it happens right in front of your eyes.

"Grandson!"—and her voice tolled like the great bell of God; I think folk must have heard her all the way to the marsh!—"Little grandchild, thinkest thou that the Creator of the World who made the stars and the moon and the sun and our bodies, too, and the change of the seasons and the very earth we stand on—yea, even unto the shit in thy belly!—thinkest thou that such a being has a big house in the sky where he keeps his wives and goes in to fuck them as thou wouldst thyself or like the King of Turkey? Do not dishonor the wit of the mother who bore thee! We are the servants of God, not his wives, and if we tell our silly girls they are married to the Christus, it is to make them understand that they must not run off and marry Otto Farmer or Ekkehard Blacksmith, but stick to their work, as they promised. If I told them they were married to an Idea, they would not understand me, and neither dost thou."

(Here Father Cairbre, above me in the window, muttered in a protesting way about something.)

Then the Abbess snatched the silver cross from around her neck and put it into the boy's hand, saying: "Give this to thy mother with my pity. She must pull out her hair over such a child."

But he let it fall to the ground. He was red in the face and breathing hard.

"Take it up," she said more kindly, "take it up, boy; it will not hurt thee and there's no magic in it. It's only pure silver and good workmanship; it will make thee rich." When she saw that he would not—his hand went to his knife—she *tched* to herself in a motherly way (or I believe she did, for she waved one hand back and forth as she always did when she made that sound) and got down on her knees—with more difficulty than was truth, I think—saying loudly, "I will stoop, then; I will stoop," and got up, holding it out to him, saying, "Take. Two sticks tied with a cord would serve me as well."

The boy cried, his voice breaking, "My mother is dead and thou art a witch!" and in an instant he had one arm around the Abbess's neck and with the other his knife at her throat. The man Thorvald Einarsson roared "Thorfinn!" but the Abbess only said clearly, "Let him be. I have shamed this man but did not mean to. He is right to be angry."

The boy released her and turned his back. I remember wondering if these strangers could weep. Later I heard—and I swear that the Abbess must have somehow known this or felt it, for although she was no witch, she could probe a man until she found the sore places in him and that very quickly—that this boy's mother had been known for an adulteress and that no man would own him as a son. It is one thing among those people for a man to have what the Abbess called a concubine and they do not hold the children of such in scorn as we do, but it is a different thing when a married woman has more than one man. Such was Thorfinn's case; I suppose that was what sent him *viking*. But all this came later; what I saw then—with my nose barely above the window slit—was that the Abbess slipped her crucifix over the hilt of the boy's sword she really wished him to have it, you see—and then walked to a place near the walls of the Abbey but far from the Norsemen. I think she meant them to come to her. I saw her pick up her skirts like a peasant woman, sit down with legs crossed, and say in a loud voice:

"Come! Who will bargain with me?"

A few strolled over, laughing, and sat down with her.

"All!" she said, gesturing them closer.

"And why should we all come?" said one who was farthest away.

"Because you will miss a bargain," said the Abbess.

"Why should we bargain when we can take?" said another.

"Because you will only get half," said the Abbess. "The rest you will not find."

"We will ransack the Abbey," said a third.

"Half the treasure is not in the Abbey," said she.

"And where is it then?"

She tapped her forehead. They were drifting over by twos and threes. I have heard since that the Norse love riddles and this was a sort of riddle; she was giving them good fun.

"If it is in your head," said the man Thorvald, who was standing behind the others, arms crossed, "we can get it out, can we not?" And he tapped the hilt of his knife.

"If you frighten me, I shall become confused and remember nothing," said the Abbess calmly. "Besides, do you wish to play that old game? You saw how well it worked the last time. I am surprised at you, Ranulf mother's-brother."

"I will bargain then," said the man Thorvald, smiling.

"And the rest of you?" said Radegunde. "It must be all or none; decide for yourselves whether you wish to save yourselves trouble and danger and be rich," and she deliberately turned her back on them. The men moved down to the river's edge and began to talk among themselves, dropping their voices so that we could not hear them any more. Father Cairbre, who was old and short-sighted, cried, "I cannot hear them. What are they doing?" and I cleverly said, "I have good eyes, Father Cairbre," and he held me up to see. So it was just at the time that the Abbess Radegunde was facing the Abbey tower that I appeared in the window. She clapped one hand across her mouth. Then she walked to the gate and called (in a voice I had learned not to disregard; it had often got me a smacked bottom), "Boy News, down! Come down to me here *at once!* And bring Father Cairbre with you."

I was overjoyed. I had no idea that she might want to protect me if anything went wrong. My only thought was that I was going to see it all from wonderfully close by. So I wormed my way, half-suffocated, through the folk in the tower room, stepping on feet and skirts, and having to say every few seconds, "But I *have* to! The Abbess wants me," and meanwhile she was calling outside like an Empress, "Let that boy through! Make a place for that boy! Let the Irish priest through!" until I crept and pushed and complained my way to the very wall itself—no one was going to open the gate for us, of course—and there was a great fuss and finally someone brought a ladder. I was over at once, but the old priest took a longer time, although it was a low wall, as I've said, the builders having been somewhat of two minds about making the Abbey into a true fortress.

Once outside it was lovely, away from all that crowd, and I ran, gloriously pleased, to the Abbess, who said only, "Stay by me, whatever happens," and immediately turned her attention away from me. It had taken so long to get Father Cairbre outside the walls that the tall, foreign men had finished their talking and were coming back—all twenty or thirty of them—towards the Abbey and the Abbess Radegunde, and most especially of all, me. I could see Father Cairbre tremble. They did look grim, close by, with their long, wild hair and the brightness of their strange clothes. I remember that they smelled different from us, but cannot remember how after all these years. Then the Abbess spoke to them in that outlandish language of theirs, so strangely light and lilting to hear from their bearded lips, and then she said something in Latin to Father Cairbre, and he said, with a shake in his voice:

"This is the priest, Father Cairbre, who will say our bargains aloud in our own tongue so that my people may hear. I cannot deal behind their backs. And this is my foster baby, who is very dear to me and who is now having his curiosity rather too much satisfied, I think." (I was trying to stand tall like a man but had one hand secretly holding onto

her skirt; so that was what the foreign men had chuckled at!)
The talk went on, but I will tell it as if I had understood the
Norse, for to repeat everything twice would be tedious.

The Abbess Radegunde said, "Will you bargain?"

There was a general nodding of heads, with a look of:
After all, why not?

"And who will speak for you?" said she.

A man stepped forward; I recognized Thorvald Einarsson.

"Ah, yes," said the Abbess dryly. "The company that has
no leaders. Is this leaderless company agreed? Will it abide
by its word? I want no treachery-planners, no Breakwords
here!"

There was a general mutter at this. The Thorvald man (he
was big, close up!) said mildly, "I sail with none such. Let's
begin."

We all sat down.

"Now," said Thorvald Einarsson, raising his eyebrows,
"according to my knowledge of this thing, you begin. And
according to my knowledge, you will begin by saying that
you are very poor."

"But, no," said the Abbess, "we are rich." Father Cairbre
groaned. A groan answered him from behind the Abbey
walls. Only the Abbess and Thorvald Einarsson seemed
unmoved; it was as if these two were joking in some way that
no one else understood. The Abbess went on, saying, "We
are very rich. Within is much silver, much gold, many
pearls, and much embroidered cloth, much fine-woven
cloth, much carved and painted wood, and many books with
gold upon their pages and jewels set into their covers. All
this is yours. But we have more and better: herbs and
medicines, ways to keep food from spoiling, the knowledge
of how to cure the sick; all this is yours. And we have more
and better even than this: we have the knowledge of Christ
and the perfect understanding of the soul, which is yours
too, any time you wish; you have only to accept it."

Thorvald Einarsson held up his hand. "We will stop with
the first," he said, "and perhaps a little of the second. That is
more practical."

"And foolish," said the Abbess politely, "in the usual
way." And again I had the odd feeling that these two were
sharing a joke no one else even saw. She added, "There is
one thing you may not have, and that is the most precious of
all."

Thorvald Einarsson looked inquiring.

"*My people.* Their safety is dearer to me than myself. They are not to be touched, not a hair on their heads, not for any reason. Think: you can fight your way into the Abbey easily enough, but the folk in there are very frightened of you, and some of the men are armed. Even a good fighter is cumbered in a crowd. You will slip and fall upon each other without meaning to or knowing that you do so. Heed my counsel. Why play butcher when you can have treasure poured into your laps like kings, without work? And after that there will be as much again, when I lead you to the hidden place. An earl's mountain of treasure. Think of it! And to give all this up for slaves, half of whom will get sick and die before you get them home—and will need to be fed if they are to be any good. Shame on you for bad advice-takers! Imagine what you will say to your wives and families: Here are a few miserable bolts of cloth with blood spots that won't come out, here are some pearls and jewels smashed to powder in the fighting, here is a torn piece of embroidery which was whole until someone stepped on it in the battle, and I had slaves but they died of illness and I fucked a pretty young nun and meant to bring her back, but she leapt into the sea. And, oh, yes, there was twice as much again and all of it whole but we decided not to take that. Too much trouble, you see."

This was a lively story and the Norsemen enjoyed it. Radegunde held up her hand.

"People!" she called in German, adding, "Sea-rovers, hear what I say; I will repeat it for you in your tongue." (And so she did.) "*People, if the Norsemen fight us, do not defend yourselves but smash everything! Wives, take your cooking knives and shred the valuable cloth to pieces! Men, with your axes and hammers hew the altars and the carved wood to fragments! All, grind the pearls and smash the jewels against the stone floors! Break the bottles of wine! Pound the gold and silver to shapelessness! Tear to pieces the illuminated books! Tear down the hangings and burn them!*

"But" (she added, her voice suddenly mild) "if these wise men will accept our gifts, let us heap untouched and spotless at their feet all that we have and hold nothing back, so that their kinsfolk will marvel and wonder at the shining and glistering of the wealth they bring back, though it leave us nothing but our bare stone walls."

If anyone had ever doubted that the Abbess Radegunde was inspired by God, their doubts must have vanished away, for who could resist the fiery vigor of her first speech or the beneficent unction of her second? The Norsemen sat there with their mouths open. I saw tears on Father Cairbre's cheeks. Then Thorvald said, "Abbess—"

He stopped. He tried again but again stopped. Then he shook himself, as a man who has been under a spell, and said:

"Abbess, my men have been without women for a long time."

Radegunde looked surprised. She looked as if she could not believe what she had heard. She looked the pirate up and down, as if puzzled, and then walked around him as if taking his measure. She did this several times, looking at every part of his big body as if she were summing him up while he got redder and redder. Then she backed off and surveyed him again, and with her arms akimbo like a peasant, announced very loudly in both Norse and German:

"What! Have they lost the use of their hands?"

It was irresistible, in its way. The Norse laughed. Our people laughed. Even Thorvald laughed. I did too, though I was not sure what everyone was laughing about. The laughter would die down and then begin again behind the Abbey walls, helplessly, and again die down and again begin. The Abbess waited until the Norsemen had stopped laughing and then called for silence in German until there were only a few snickers here and there. She then said:

"These good men—Father Cairbre, tell the people—these good men will forgive my silly joke. I meant no scandal, truly, and no harm, but laughter is good; it settles the body's waters, as the physicians say. And my people know that I am not always as solemn and good as I ought to be. Indeed I am a very great sinner and scandal-maker. Thorvald Einarsson, do we do business?"

The big man—who had not been so pleased as the others, I can tell you!—looked at his men and seemed to see what he needed to know. He said, "I go in with five men to see what you have. Then we let the poor folk on the grounds go, but not those inside the Abbey. Then we search again. The gates will be locked and guarded by the rest of us; if there's any treachery, the bargain's off."

"Then I will go with you," said Radegunde. "That is very

just and my presence will calm the people. To see us together will assure them that no harm is meant. You are a good man, Torvald—forgive me; I call you as your nephew did so often. Come, Boy News, hold on to me."

"Open the gates!" she called then. "All is safe!" and with the five men (one of whom was that young Thorfinn who had hated her so) we waited while the great logs were pulled back. There was little space within, but the people shrank back at the sight of those fierce warriors and opened a place for us.

I looked back and the Norsemen had come in and were standing just inside the walls, on either side the gate, with their swords out and their shields up. The crowd parted for us more slowly as we reached the main tower, with the Abbess repeating constantly, "Be calm, people, be calm. All is well," and deftly speaking by name to this one or that. It was much harder when the people gasped upon hearing the big logs pushed shut with a noise like thunder, and it was very close on the stairs; I heard her say something like an apology in the queer foreign tongue. Something that probably meant, "I'm sorry that we must wait." It seemed an age until the stairs were even partly clear and I saw what the Abbess had meant by the cumbering of a crowd; a man might swing a weapon in the press of people, but not very far, and it was more likely he would simply fall over someone and crack his head. We gained the great room with the big crucifix of painted wood and the little one of pearls and gold, and the scarlet hangings worked in gold thread that I had played robbers behind so often before I learned what real robbers were: these tall, frightening men whose eyes glistened with greed at what I had fancied every village had. Most of the Sisters had stayed in the great room, but somehow it was not so crowded, as the folk had huddled back against the walls when the Norsemen came in. The youngest girls were all in a corner, terrified—one could smell it, as one can in people—and when that young Thorfinn went for the little gold-and-pearl cross, Sister Sibihd cried in a high, cracked voice, "It is the body of our Christ!" and leapt up, snatching it from the wall before he could get to it.

"Sibihd!" exclaimed the Abbess, in as sharp a voice as I had ever heard her use. "Put that back or you will feel the weight of my hand, I tell you!"

Now it is odd, is it not, that a young woman desperate

enough not to care about death at the hands of a Norse pirate should nonetheless be frightened away at the threat of getting a few slaps from her Abbess? But folk are like that. Sister Sibihd returned the cross to its place (from whence young Thorfinn took it) and fell back among the nuns, sobbing, "He desecrates our Lord God!"

"Foolish girl!" snapped the Abbess. "God only can consecrate or desecrate; man cannot. That is a piece of metal."

Thorvald said something sharp to Thorfinn, who slowly put the cross back on its hook with a sulky look which said, plainer than words: Nobody gives me what I want. Nothing else went wrong in the big room or the Abbess's study or the storerooms, or out in the kitchens. The Norsemen were silent and kept their hands on their swords, but the Abbess kept talking in a calm way in both tongues; to our folk she said, "See? It is all right but everyone must keep still. God will protect us." Her face was steady and clear, and I believed her a saint, for she had saved Sister Sibihd and the rest of us.

But this peacefulness did not last, of course. Something had to go wrong in all that press of people; to this day I do not know what. We were in a corner of the long refectory, which is the place where the Sisters or Brothers eat in an Abbey, when something pushed me into the wall and I fell, almost suffocated by the Abbess's lying on top of me. My head was ringing and on all sides there was a terrible roaring sound with curses and screams, a dreadful tumult as if the walls had come apart and were falling on everyone. I could hear the Abbess whispering something in Latin over and over in my ear. There were dull, ripe sounds, worse than the rest, which I know now to have been the noise steel makes when it is thrust into bodies. This all seemed to go on forever and then it seemed to me that the floor was wet. Then all became quiet. I felt the Abbess Radegunde get off me. She said:

"So this is how you wash your floors up North." When I lifted my head from the rushes and saw what she meant, I was very sick into the corner. Then she picked me up in her arms and held my face against her bosom so that I would not see, but it was no use; I had already seen: all the people lying sprawled on the floor with their bellies coming out, like heaps of dead fish, old Walafrid with an axe handle standing out of his chest—he was sitting up with his eyes shut in a press of bodies that gave him no room to lie down—and the young beekeeper, Uta, from the village, who had been so merry, lying on her back with her long braids and her gown all dabbled in red dye and a great stain of it on her belly. She was breathing fast and her eyes were wide open. As we passed her, the noise of her breathing ceased.

The Abbess said mildly, "Thy people are thorough house-keepers, Earl Split-gut."

Thorvald Einarsson roared something at us, and the Abbess replied softly, "Forgive me, good friend. You protected me and the boy and I am grateful. But nothing betrays a man's knowledge of the German like a word that bites, is it not so? And I had to be sure."

It came to me then that she had called him "Torvald" and reminded him of his sister's son so that he would feel he must protect us if anything went wrong. But now she would make him angry, I thought, and I shut my eyes tight. Instead he laughed and said in odd, light German, "I did no house-keeping but to stand over you and your pet. Are you not grateful?"

"Oh, very, thank you," said the Abbess with such warmth as she might show to a Sister who had brought her a rose from the garden, or another who copied her work well, or when I told her news, or if Ita the cook made a good soup. But he did not know that the warmth was for everyone and so seemed satisfied. By now we were in the garden and the air was less foul; she put me down, although my limbs were shaking, and I clung to her gown, crumpled, stiff, and blood-reeking though it was. She said, "Oh my God, what a deal of washing hast Thou given us!" She started to walk towards the gate, and Thorvald Einarsson took a step towards her. She said, without turning round: "Do not insist, Thorvald, there is no reason to lock me up. I am forty years old and not likely to be running away into the swamp, what with my rheumatism and the pain in my knees and the folk needing me as they do."

There was a moment's silence. I could see something odd come into the big man's face. He said quietly:

"I did not speak, Abbess."

She turned, surprised. "But you did. I heard you."

He said strangely, "I did not."

Children can guess sometimes what is wrong and what to do about it without knowing how; I remember saying, very quickly, "Oh, she does that sometimes. My stepmother says old age has addled her wits," and then, "Abbess, may I go to my stepmother and my father?"

"Yes, of course," she said, "run along, Boy News—" and then stopped, looking into the air as if seeing in it something we could not. Then she said very gently, "No, my dear, you had better stay here with me," and I knew, as surely as if I had seen it with my own eyes, that I was not to go to my stepmother or my father because both were dead.

   She did things like that, too, sometimes.

For a while it seemed that everyone was dead. I did not feel grieved or frightened in the least, but I think I must have been, for I had only one idea in my head; that if I let the Abbess out of my sight, I would die. So I followed her everywhere. She was let to move about and comfort people, especially the mad Sibihd, who would do nothing but rock and wail, but towards nightfall, when the Abbey had been stripped of its treasures, Thorvald Einarsson put her and me in her study, now bare of its grand furniture, on a straw pallet on the floor, and bolted the door on the outside. She said:

"Boy News, would you like to go to Constantinople, where the Turkish Sultan is, and the domes of gold and all the splendid pagans? For that is where this man will take me to sell me."

"Oh, yes!" said I, and then: "But will he take me, too?"

"Of course," said the Abbess, and so it was settled. Then in came Thorvald Einarsson, saying:

"Thorfinn is asking for you." I found out later that they were waiting for him to die; none other of the Norse had been wounded, but a farmer had crushed Thorfinn's chest with an axe, and he was expected to die before morning. The Abbess said:

"Is that a good reason to go?" She added, "I mean that he hates me; will not his anger at my presence make him worse?"

Thorvald said slowly, "The folk here say you can sit by the sick and heal them. Can you do that?"

"To my own knowledge, not at all," said the Abbess Radegunde, "but if they believe so, perhaps that calms them and makes them better. Christians are quite as foolish as other people, you know. I will come if you want," and though I saw that she was pale with tiredness, she got to her feet. I should say that she was in a plain, brown gown taken from one of the peasant women because her own was being washed clean, but to me she had the same majesty as always. And for him too, I think.

Thorvald said, "Will you pray for him or damn him?"

She said, "I do not pray, Thorvald, and I never damn anybody; I merely sit." She added, "Oh, let him; he'll scream your ears off if you don't," and this meant me, for I was ready to yell for my life if they tried to keep me from her.

They had put Thorfinn in the chapel, a little stone room with nothing left in it now but a plain wooden cross, not worth carrying off. He was lying, his eyes closed, on the stone altar with furs under him, and his face was gray. Every time he breathed, there was a bubbling sound, a little, thin, reedy sound; and as I crept closer, I saw why, for in the young man's chest was a great red hole with sharp pink things sticking out of it, all crushed, and in the hole one could see something jump and fall, jump and fall, over and over again. It was his heart beating. Blood kept coming from his lips in a froth. I do not know, of course, what either said, for they spoke in the Norse, but I saw what they did and heard much of it talked of between the Abbess and Thorvald Einarsson later. So I will tell it as if I knew.

The first thing the Abbess did was to stop suddenly on the threshold and raise both hands to her mouth as if in horror. Then she cried furiously to the two guards:

"Do you wish to kill your comrade with the cold and damp? Is this how you treat one another? Get fire in here and some woollen cloth to put over him! No, not more skins, you idiots, *wool* to mold to his body and take up the wet. Run now!"

One said sullenly, "We don't take orders from you, Grandma."

"Oh, no?" said she. "Then I shall strip this wool dress from my old body and put it over that boy and then sit here all night in my flabby, naked skin! What will this child's soul say when it enters the Valhall? That his friends would not give up a little of their booty so that he might fight for life? Is this your fellowship? Do it, or I will strip myself and shame you both for the rest of your lives!"

"Well, take it from his share," said the one in a low voice, and the other ran out. Soon there was a fire on the hearth and russet-colored woollen cloth—"From my own share," said one of them loudly, though it was a color the least costly, not like blue or red—and the Abbess laid it loosely over the boy, carefully putting it close to his sides but not moving him. He did not look to be in any pain, but his color got no better. But then he opened his eyes and said in such a little voice as a ghost might have, a whisper as thin and reedy and bubbling as his breath:

"You . . . old witch. But I beat you . . . in the end."

"Did you, my dear?" said the Abbess. "How?"

"Treasure," he said, "for my kinfolk. And I lived as a man at last. Fought . . . and had a woman . . . the one here with the big breasts, Sibihd. . . . Whether she liked it or not. That was good."

"Yes, Sibihd," said the Abbess mildly. "Sibihd has gone mad. She hears no one and speaks to no one. She only sits and rocks and moans and soils herself and will not feed herself, although if one puts food in her mouth with a spoon, she will swallow."

The boy tried to frown. "Stupid," he said at last. "Stupid nuns. The beasts do it."

"Do they?" said the Abbess, as if this were a new idea to her. "Now that is very odd. For never yet heard I of a gander that blacked the goose's eye or hit her over the head with a stone or stuck a knife in her entrails when he was through. When God puts it into their hearts to desire one another, she squats and he comes running. And a bitch in heat will jump through the window if you lock the door. Poor fools! Why didn't you camp three hours' down-river and wait? In a week half the young married women in the village would have been slipping away at night to see what the foreigners were like. Yes, and some unmarried ones, and some of my own girls, too. But you couldn't wait, could you?"

"No," said the boy, with the ghost of a brag. "Better . . . this way."

"*This* way," said she. "Oh, yes, my dear, old Granny knows about *this* way! Pleasure for the count of three or four, and the rest of it as much joy as rolling a stone uphill."

He smiled a ghostly smile. "You're a whore, Grandma."

She began to stroke his forehead. "No, Grandbaby," she

said, "but all Latin is not the Church Fathers, you know, great as they are. One can find a great deal in those strange books written by the ones who died centuries before our Lord was born. Listen," and she leaned closer to him and said quietly:

> "Syrian dancing girl, how subtly
>   you sway those sensuous limbs,
> "Half-drunk in the smoky tavern,
>   lascivious and wanton,
> "Your long hair bound back in the
>   Greek way, clashing the casta-
>   nets in your hands—"

The boy was too weak to do anything but look astonished. Then she said this:

"I love you so that anyone permitted to sit near you and talk to you seems to me like a god; when I am near you my spirit is broken, my heart shakes, my voice dies, and I can't even speak. Under my skin I flame up all over and I can't see; there's thunder in my ears and I break out in a sweat, as if from fever; I turn paler than cut grass and feel that I am utterly changed; I feel that Death has come near me."

He said, as if frightened, "Nobody feels like that."

"They do," she said.

He said, in feeble alarm, "You're trying to kill me!"

She said, "No, my dear, I simply don't want you to die a virgin."

It was odd, his saying those things and yet holding on to her hand where she had got at it through the woollen cloth; she stroked his head and he whispered, "Save me, old witch."

"I'll do my best," she said. "You shall do your best by not talking and I by not tormenting you any more, and we'll both try to sleep."

"Pray," said the boy.

"Very well," said she, "but I'll need a chair," and the guards—seeing, I suppose, that he was holding her hand—brought in one of the great wooden chairs from the Abbey, which were too plain and heavy to carry off, I think. Then the Abbess Radegunde sat in the chair and closed her eyes. Thorfinn seemed to fall asleep. I crept nearer her on the floor and must have fallen asleep myself almost at once, for the next thing I knew a gray light filled the chapel, the fire had gone out, and someone was shaking Radegunde, who still slept in her chair, her head leaning to one side. It was Thorvald Einarsson and he was shouting with excitement in his strange German, "Woman, how did you do it! How did you do it!"

"Do what?" said the Abbess thickly. "Is he dead?"

"Dead?" exclaimed the Norseman. "He is healed! Healed! The lung is whole and all is closed up about the heart and the shattered pieces of the ribs are grown together! Even the muscles of the chest are beginning to heal!"

"That's good," said the Abbess, still half asleep. "Let me be."

Thorvald shook her again. She said again, "Oh, let me sleep." This time he hauled her to her feet and she shrieked, "My back, my back! Oh, the saints, my rheumatism!" and at the same time a sick voice from under the blue woollens—a sick voice but a man's voice, not a ghost's—said something in Norse.

"Yes, I hear you," said the Abbess. "You must become a follower of the White Christ right away, this very minute. But *Dominus noster,* please do You put it into these brawny heads that I must have a tub of hot water with pennyroyal in it? I am too old to sleep all night in a chair, and I am one ache from head to foot."

Thorfinn got louder.

"Tell him," said the Abbess Radegunde to Thorvald in German, "that I will not baptize him and I will not shrive him until he is a different man. All that child wants is someone more powerful than your Odin god or your Thor god to pull him out of the next scrape he gets into. Ask him: Will he adopt Sibihd as his sister? Will he clean her when she soils herself and feed her and sit with his arm about her, talking to her gently and lovingly until she is well again? The Christ does not wipe out our sins only to have us commit them all over again, and that is what he wants and what you all want, a God that gives and gives and gives, but God does not give; He takes and takes and takes. He takes away everything that is not God until there is nothing left but God, and none of you will understand that! There is no remission of sins; there is only change, and Thorfinn must change before God will have him."

"Abbess, you are eloquent," said Thorvald, smiling, "but why do you not tell him all this yourself?"

"Because I ache so!" said Radegunde; "Oh, do get me into some hot water!" and Thorvald half led and half supported her as she hobbled out. That morning, after she had had her soak—when I cried, they let me stay just outside the door—she undertook to cure Sibihd, first by rocking her in her arms and talking to her, telling her she was safe now, and promising that the Northmen would go soon, and then when Sibihd became quieter, leading her out into the woods with Thorvald as a bodyguard to see that we did not run away, and little, dark Sister Hedwic, who had stayed with Sibihd and cared for her. The Abbess would walk for a while in the mild autumn sunshine, and then she would direct Sibihd's face upwards by touching her gently under the chin and say, "See? There is God's sky still," and then, "Look, there are God's trees; they have not changed," and tell her that the world was just the same and God still kindly to folk, only a few more souls had joined the Blessed and were happier waiting for us in Heaven than we could ever be, or even imagine being, on the poor earth. Sister Hedwic kept hold of Sibihd's hand. No one paid more attention to me than if I had been a dog, but every time poor Sister Sibihd saw Thorvald she would shrink away, and you could see that Hedwic could not bear to look at him at all; every time he came in her sight she turned her face aside, shut her eyes hard, and bit her lower lip. It was a quiet, almost warm day, as autumn can be sometimes, and the Abbess found a few little blue late flowers growing in a sheltered place against a log and put them into Sibihd's hand, speaking of how beautifully and cunningly God had made all things. Sister Sibihd had enough wit to hold on to the flowers, but her eyes stared and she would have stumbled and fallen if Hedwic had not led her.

Sister Hedwic said timidly, "Perhaps she suffers because she has been defiled, Abbess," and then looked ashamed. For a moment the Abbess looked shrewdly at young Sister Hedwic and then at the mad Sibihd. Then she said:

"Dear daughter Sibihd and dear daughter Hedwic, I am now going to tell you something about myself that I have never told to a single living soul but my confessor. Do you know that as a young woman I studied at Avignon and from there was sent to Rome, so that I might gather much learning? Well, in Avignon I read mightily our Christian Fathers but also in the pagan poets, for as it has been said by Ermenrich of Ellwangen: As dung spread upon a field enriches it to good harvest, thus one cannot produce divine eloquence without the filthy writings of the pagan poets. This is true but perilous, only I thought not so, for I was very proud and fancied that if the pagan poems of love left me unmoved, that was because I had the gift of chastity right from God Himself, and I scorned sensual pleasures and those tempted by them. I had forgotten, you see, that chastity is not given once and for all like a wedding ring that is put on never to be taken off, but is a garden which each day must be weeded, watered, and trimmed anew, or soon there will be only brambles and wilderness.

"As I have said, the words of the poets did not tempt me, for words are only marks on the page with no life save what we give them. But in Rome there were not only the old books, daughters, but something much worse.

"There were statues. Now you must understand that these are not such as you can imagine from our books, like Saint John or the Virgin; the ancients wrought so cunningly in stone that it is like magic; one stands before the marble holding one's breath, waiting for it to move and speak. They are not statues at all but beautiful, naked men and women. It is a city of seagods pouring water, daughter Sibihd and daughter Hedwic, of athletes about to throw the discus, and runners and wrestlers and young emperors, and the favorites of kings; but they do not walk the streets like real men, for they are all of stone.

"There was one Apollo, all naked, which I knew I should not look on but which I always made some excuse to my companions to pass by, and this statue, although three miles distant from my dwelling, drew me as if by magic. Oh, he was fair to look on! Fairer than any youth alive now in Germany, or in the world, I think. And then all the old loves of the pagan poets came back to me: Dido and Aeneas, the taking of Venus and Mars, the love of the moon, Diana, for the shepherd boy—and I thought that if my statue could only come to life, he would utter honeyed love-words from the old poets and would be wise and brave, too, and what woman could resist him?''

Here she stopped and looked at Sister Sibihd but Sibihd only stared on, holding the little blue flowers. It was Sister Hedwic who cried, one hand pressed to her heart:

"Did you pray, Abbess?''

"I did," said Radegunde solemnly, "and yet my prayers kept becoming something else. I would pray to be delivered from the temptation that was in the statue, and then, of course, I would have to think of the statue itself, and then I would tell myself that I must run, like the nymph Daphne, to be armored and sheltered within a laurel tree, but my feet seemed to be already rooted to the ground, and then at the last minute I would flee and be back at my prayers again. But it grew harder each time, and at last the day came when I did not flee."

"Abbess, *you?*" cried Hedwic, with a gasp. Thorvald, keeping his watch a little way from us, looked surprised. I was very pleased—I loved to see the Abbess astonish people; it was one of her gifts—and at seven I had no knowledge of lust except that my little thing felt good sometimes when I handled it to make water, and what had that to do with statues coming to life or women turning into laurel trees? I was more interested in mad Sibihd, the way children are; I did not know what she might do, or if I should be afraid of her, or if I should go mad myself, what it would be like. But the Abbess was laughing gently at Hedwic's amazement.

"Why not me?" said the Abbess. "I was young and healthy and had no special grace from God any more than the hens or the cows do! Indeed, I burned so with desire for that handsome young hero—for so I had made him in my mind, as a woman might do with a man she has seen a few times on the street—that thoughts of him tormented me waking and sleeping. It seemed to me that because of my vows I could not give myself to this Apollo of my own free will. So I would dream that he took me against my will, and, oh, what an exquisite pleasure that was!"

Here Hedwic's blood came all to her face and she covered it with her hands. I could see Thorvald grinning, back where he watched us.

"And then," said the Abbess, as if she had not seen either of them, "a terrible fear came to my heart that God might punish me by sending a ravisher who would use me unlawfully, as I had dreamed my Apollo did, and that I would not even wish to resist him and would feel the pleasures of a base lust and would know myself a whore and a false nun forever after. This fear both tormented and drew me. I began to steal looks at young men in the streets, not letting the other Sisters see me do it, thinking: Will it be he? Or he? Or he?

"And then it happened. I had lingered behind the others at a melon seller's, thinking of no Apollos or handsome heroes but only of the convent's dinner, when I saw my companions disappearing round a corner. I hastened to catch up with them—and made a wrong turning—and was suddenly lost in a narrow street—and at that very moment a young fellow took hold of my habit and threw me to the ground! You may wonder why he should do such a mad thing, but as I found out afterwards, there are prostitutes in Rome who affect our way of dress to please the appetites of certain men who are depraved enough to—well, really, I do not know how to say it! Seeing me alone, he had thought I was one of them and would be glad of a customer and a bit of play. So there was a reason for it.

"Well, there I was on my back with this young fellow, sent as a vengeance by God, as I thought, trying to do exactly what I had dreamed, night after night, that my statue should do. And do you know, it was nothing in the least like my dream! The stones at my back hurt me, for one thing. And instead of melting with delight, I was screaming my head off in terror and kicking at him as he tried to pull up my skirts, and praying to God that this insane man might not break any of my bones in his rage!

"My screams brought a crowd of people and he went running. So I got off with nothing worse than a bruised back and a sprained knee. But the strangest thing of all was that while I was cured forever of lusting after my Apollo, instead I began to be tormented by a new fear—that I had lusted after *him,* that foolish young man with the foul breath and the one tooth missing!—and I felt strange creepings and crawlings over my body that were half like desire and half like fear and half like disgust and shame with all sorts of other things mixed in—I know that is too many halves but it is how I felt—and nothing at all like the burning desire I had felt for my Apollo. I went to see the statue once more before

I left Rome, and it seemed to look at me sadly, as if to say: Don't blame me, poor girl; I'm only a piece of stone. And that was the last time I was so proud as to believe that God had singled me out for a special gift, like chastity—or a special sin, either—or that being thrown down on the ground and hurt had anything to do with any sin of mine, no matter how I mixed the two together in my mind. I dare say you did not find it a great pleasure yesterday, did you?"

Hedwic shook her head. She was crying quietly. She said, "Thank you, Abbess," and the Abbess embraced her. They both seemed happier, but then all of a sudden Sibihd muttered something, so low that one could not hear her.

"The—" she whispered and then she brought it out but still in a whisper: "The blood."

"What, dear, your blood?" said Radegunde.

"No, mother," said Sibihd, beginning to tremble. "The blood. All over us. Walafrid and—and Uta—and Sister Hildegarde—and everyone broken and spilled out like a dish! And none of us had done anything but I could smell it all over me and the children screaming because they were being trampled down, and those demons come up from Hell though we had done nothing and—and—I understand, mother, about the rest, but I will never, ever forget it, oh Christus, it is all around me now, oh, mother, the *blood!*"

Then Sister Sibihd dropped to her knees on the fallen leaves and began to scream, not covering her face as Sister Hedwic had done, but staring ahead with her side eyes as if she were blind or could see something we could not. The Abbess knelt down and embraced her, rocking her back and forth, saying, "Yes, yes, dear, but we are here; we are here now; that is gone now," but Sibihd continued to scream, covering her ears as if the scream were someone else's and she could hide herself from it.

Thorvald said, looking, I thought, a little uncomfortable, "Cannot your Christ cure this?"

"No," said the Abbess. "Only by undoing the past. And that is the one thing He never does, it seems. She is in Hell now and must go back there many times before she can forget."

"She would make a bad slave," said the Norseman, with a glance at Sister Sibihd, who had fallen silent and was staring ahead of her again. "You need not fear that anyone will want her."

"God," said the Abbess Radegunde calmly, "is merciful."

Thorvald Einarsson said, "Abbess, I am not a bad man."

"For a good man," said the Abbess Radegunde, "you keep surprisingly bad company."

He said angrily, "I did not choose my shipmates. I have had bad luck!"

"Ours has," said the Abbess, "been worse, I think."

"Luck is luck," said Thorvald, clenching his fists. "It comes to some folk and not to others."

"As you came to us," said the Abbess mildly. "Yes, yes, I see, Thorvald Einarsson; one may say that luck is Thor's doing or Odin's doing, but you must know that our bad luck is your own doing and not some god's. You are our bad luck, Thorvald Einarsson. It's true that you're not as wicked as your friends, for they kill for pleasure and you do it without feeling, as a business, the way one hews down grain. Perhaps you have seen today some of the grain you have cut. If you had a man's soul, you would not have gone *viking,* luck or no luck, and if your soul were bigger still, you would have tried to stop your shipmates, just as I talk honestly to you now, despite your anger, and just as Christus himself told the truth and was nailed on the cross. If you were a beast you could not break God's law, and if you were a man you would not, but you are neither, and that makes you a kind of monster that spoils everything it touches and never knows the reason, and that is why I will never forgive you until you become a man, a true man with a true soul. As for your friends—"

Here Thorvald Einarsson struck the Abbess on the face with his open hand and knocked her down. I heard Sister Hedwic gasp in horror and behind us Sister Sibihd began to moan. But the Abbess only sat there, rubbing her jaw and smiling a little. Then she said:

"Oh, dear, have I been at it again? I am ashamed of myself. You are quite right to be angry, Torvald; no one can stand me when I go on in that way, least of all myself; it is such a bore. Still, I cannot seem to stop it; I am too used to being the Abbess Radegunde, that is clear. I promise never to torment you again, but you, Thorvald, must never strike me again, because you will be very sorry if you do."

He took a step forward.

"No, no, my dear man," the Abbess said merrily, "I mean no threat—how could I threaten you?—I mean only that I will never tell you any jokes, my spirits will droop, and I will become as dull as any other woman. Confess it now: I am the most interesting thing that has happened to you in years and I have entertained you better, sharp tongue and all, than all the *skalds* at the Court of Norway. And I know more tales and stories than they do—more than anyone in the whole world—for I make new ones when the old ones wear out.

"Shall I tell you a story now?"

"About your Christ?" said he, the anger still in his face.

"No," said she, "about living men and women. Tell me, Torvald what do you men want from us women?"

"To be talked to death," said he, and I could see there was some anger in him still, but he was turning it to play also.

The Abbess laughed in delight. "Very witty!" she said, springing to her feet and brushing the leaves off her skirt. "You are a very clever man, Torvald. I beg your pardon, Thorvald. I keep forgetting. But as to what men want from women, if you asked the young men, they would only wink and dig one another in the ribs, but that is only how they deceive themselves. That is only body calling to body. They want something quite different and they want it so much that it frightens them. So they pretend it is anything and everything else: pleasure, comfort, a servant in the home. Do you know what it is that they want?"

"What?" said Thorvald.

"The mother," said Radegunde, "as women do, too; we all want the mother. When I walked before you on the riverbank yesterday, I was playing the mother. Now you did nothing, for you are no young fool, but I knew that sooner or later one of you, so tormented by his longing that he would hate me for it, would reveal himself. And so he did: Thorfinn, with his thoughts all mixed up between witches and grannies and what not. I knew I could frighten him, and through him, most of you. That was the beginning of my bargaining. You Norse have too much of the father in your country and not enough mother; that is why you die so well and kill other folk so well—and live so very, very badly."

"You are doing it again," said Thorvald, but I think he wanted to listen all the same.

"Your pardon, friend," said the Abbess. "You are brave men; I don't deny it. But I know your *sagas* and they are all about fighting and dying and afterwards not Heavenly happiness but the end of the world: everything, even the gods, eaten by the Fenris Wolf and the Midgaard snake! What a pity, to die bravely only because life is not worth living! The Irish know better. The pagan Irish were heroes, with their Queens leading them to battle as often as not, and Father Cairbre, God rest his soul, was complaining only two days ago that the common Irish folk were blasphemously making a goddess out of God's mother, for do they build shrines to Christ or Our Lord or pray to them? No! It is Our Lady of the Rocks and Our Lady of the Sea and Our Lady of the Grove and Our Lady of this or that from one end of the land to the other. And even here it is only the Abbey folk who speak of God the Father and of Christ. In the village if one is sick or another in trouble it is: Holy Mother, save me! and: *Miriam Virginem,* intercede for me, and: Blessed Virgin, blind my husband's eyes! and: Our Lady, preserve my crops, and so on, men and women both. We all need the mother."

"You, too?"

"More than most," said the Abbess.

"And I?"

"Oh, no," said the Abbess, stopping suddenly, for we had all been walking back towards the village as she spoke. "No, and that is what drew me to you at once. I saw it in you and knew you were the leader. It is followers who make leaders, you know, and your shipmates have made you leader, whether you know it or not. What you want is—how shall I say it? You are a clever man, Thorvald, perhaps the cleverest man I have ever met, more even than the scholars I knew in my youth. But your cleverness has had no food. It is a cleverness of the world and not of books. You want to travel and know about folk and their customs, and what strange places are like, and what has happened to men and women in the past. If you take me to Constantinople, it will not be to get a price for me but merely to go there; you went seafaring because this longing itched at you until you could bear it not a year more; I know that."

"Then you are a witch," said he, and he was not smiling.

"No, I only saw what was in your face when you spoke of that city," said she. "Also there is gossip that you spent much time in Göteborg as a young man, idling and marveling at the ships and markets when you should have been at your farm."

She said, "Thorvald, I can feed that cleverness. I am the

wisest woman in the world. I know everything—everything! I know more than my teachers; I make it up or it comes to me, I don't know how, but it is real—real!—and I know more than anyone. Take me from here, as your slave if you wish but as your friend also, and let us go to Constantinople and see the domes of gold, and the walls all inlaid with gold, and the people so wealthy you cannot imagine it, and the whole city so gilded it seems to be on fire, pictures as high as a wall, set right in the wall and all made of jewels so there is nothing else like them, redder than the reddest rose, greener than the grass, and with a blue that makes the sky pale!"

"You are indeed a witch," said he, "and not the Abbess Radegunde."

She said slowly, "I think I am forgetting how to be the Abbess Radegunde."

"Then you will not care about them any more," said he, and pointed to Sister Hedwic, who was still leading the stumbling Sister Sibihd.

The Abbess's face was still and mild. She said, "I care. Do not strike me, Thorvald, not ever again, and I will be a good friend to you. Try to control the worst of your men and leave as many of my people free as you can—I know them and will tell you which can be taken away with the least hurt to themselves or others—and I will feed that curiosity and cleverness of yours until you will not recognize this old world any more for the sheer wonder and awe of it; I swear this on my life."

"Done," said he, adding, "but with my luck, your life is somewhere else, locked in a box on top of a mountain, like the troll's in the story, or you will die of old age while we are still at sea."

"Nonsense," she said, "I am a healthy, mortal woman with all my teeth, and I mean to gather many wrinkles yet."

He put his hand out and she took it; then he said, shaking his head in wonder, "If I sold you in Constantinople, within a year you would become Queen of the place!"

The Abbess laughed merrily and I cried in fear, "Me, too! Take me too!" and she said "Oh, yes, we must not forget little Boy News," and lifted me into her arms.

The frightening, tall man, with his face close to mine, said in his strange, sing-song German:

"Boy, would you like to see the whales leaping in the open sea and the seals barking on the rocks? And cliffs so high that a giant could stretch his arms up and not reach their tops? And the sun shining at midnight?"

"Yes!" said I.

"But you will be a slave," he said, "and may be ill-treated and will always have to do as you are bid. Would you like that?"

"No!" I cried lustily, from the safety of the Abbess's arms, "I'll fight!"

He laughed a mighty, roaring laugh and tousled my head— rather, too hard, I thought—and said, "I will not be a bad master, for I am named for Thor Red-beard and he is strong and quick to fight but good-natured, too, and so am I," and the Abbess put me down, and so we walked back to the village, Thorvald and the Abbess Radegunde talking of the glories of this world and Sister Hedwic saying softly, "She is a saint, our Abbess, a saint, to sacrifice herself for the good of the people," and all the time behind us, like a memory, came the low, witless sobbing of Sister Sibihd, who was in Hell.

When we got back we found that Thorfinn was better and the Norsemen were to leave in the morning. Thorvald had a second pallet brought into the Abbess's study and slept on the floor with us that night. You might think his men would laugh at this, for the Abbess was an old woman, but I think he had been with one of the young ones before he came to us. He had that look about him. There was no bedding for the Abbess but an old brown cloak with holes in it, and she and I were wrapped in it when he came in and threw himself down, whistling, on the other pallet. Then he said:

"Tomorrow, before we sail, you will show me the old Abbess's treasure."

"No," said she. "That agreement was broken."

He had been playing with his knife and now ran his thumb along the edge of it. "I can make you do it."

"No," said she patiently, "and now I am going to sleep."

"So you make light of death?" he said. "Good! That is what a brave woman should do, as the *skalds* sing, and not move, even when the keen sword cuts off her eyelashes. But what if I put this knife here not to your throat but to your little boy's? You would tell me then quick enough!"

The Abbess turned away from him, yawning and saying, "No, Thorvald, because you would not. And if you did, I would despise you for a cowardly oath-breaker and not tell you for that reason. Good night."

He laughed and whistled again for a bit. Then he said: "Was all that true?"

"All what?" said the Abbess. "Oh, about the statue. Yes, but there was no ravisher. I put him in the tale for poor Sister Hedwic."

Thorvald snorted, as if in disappointment. "Tale! You tell lies, Abbess!"

The Abbess drew the old brown cloak over her head and closed her eyes. "It helped her."

Then there was a silence, but the big Norseman did not seem able to lie still. He shifted his body again as if the straw bothered him, and again turned over. He finally burst out, "But what happened!"

She sat up. Then she shut her eyes. She said, "Maybe it does not come into your man's thoughts that an old woman gets tired and that the work of dealing with folk is hard work, or even that it is work at all. Well!

"Nothing 'happened,' Thorvald. Must something happen only if this one fucks that one or one bangs in another's head? I desired my statue to the point of such foolishness that I determined to find a real, human lover, but when I raised my eyes from my fancies to the real, human men of Rome and unstopped my ears to listen to their talk, I realized that the thing was completely and eternally impossible. Oh, those younger sons with their skulking, jealous hatred of the rich, and the rich ones with their noses in the air because they thought themselves of such great consequence because of their silly money, and the timidity of the priests to their superiors, and their superiors' pride, and the artisans' hatred of the peasants, and the peasants being worked like animals from morning until night, and half the men I saw beating their wives and the other half out to cheat some poor girl of her money or her virginity or both—this was enough to put out any fire! And the women doing less harm only because they had less power to do harm, or so it seemed to me then. So I put all away, as one does with any disappointment. Men are not such bad folk when one stops expecting them to be gods, but they are not for me. If that state is chastity, then a weak stomach is temperance, I think. But whatever it is, I have it, and that's the end of the matter."

"*All* men?" said Thorvald Einarsson with his head to one

side, and it came to me that he had been drinking, though he seemed sober.

"Thorvald," said the Abbess, "what you want with this middle-aged wreck of a body I cannot imagine, but if you lust after my wrinkles and flabby breasts and lean, withered flanks, do whatever you want quickly and then, for Heaven's sake, let me sleep. I am tired to death."

He said in a low voice, "I need to have power over you."

She spread her hands in a helpless gesture. "Oh, Thorvald, Thorvald, I am a weak little woman over forty years old! Where is the power? All I can do is talk!"

He said, "That's it. That's how you do it. You talk and talk and talk and everyone does just as you please; I have seen it!"

The Abbess said, looking sharply at him, "Very well. If you must. *But if I were you, Norseman, I would as soon bed my own mother.* Remember that as you pull my skirts up."

That stopped him. He swore under his breath, turning over on his side, away from us. Then he thrust his knife into the edge of his pallet, time after time. Then he put the knife under the rolled-up cloth he was using as a pillow. We had no pillow and so I tried to make mine out of the edge of the cloak and failed. Then I thought that the Norseman was afraid of God working in Radegunde, and then I thought of Sister Hedwic's changing color and wondered why. And then I thought of the leaping whales and the seals, which must be like great dogs because of the barking, and then the seals jumped on land and ran to my pallet and lapped at me with great, icy tongues of water so that I shivered and jumped, and then I woke up.

The Abbess Radegunde had left the pallet—it was her warmth I had missed—and was walking about the room. She would step and pause, her skirts making a small noise as she did so. She was careful not to touch the sleeping Thorvald. There was a dim light in the room from the embers that still glowed under the ashes in the hearth, but no light came from between the shutters of the study window, now shut against the cold. I saw the Abbess kneel under the plain wooden cross which hung on the study wall and heard her say a few words in Latin; I thought she was praying. But then she said in a low voice:

"Do not call upon Apollo and the Muses, for they are deaf

things and vain. But so are you, Pierced Man, deaf and
vain."

Then she got up and began to pace again. Thinking of it
now frightens me, for it was the middle of the night and no
one to hear her—except me, but she thought I was asleep—
and yet she went on and on in that low, even voice as if it
were broad day and she were explaining something to someone, as if things that had been in her thoughts for years must
finally come out. But I did not find anything alarming in it
then, for I thought that perhaps all Abbesses had to do such
things, and besides she did not seem angry or hurried or
afraid; she sounded as calm as if she were discussing the
profits from the Abbey's bee-keeping—which I had heard
her do—or the accounts for the wine cellars—which I had
also heard—and there was nothing alarming in that. So I
listened as she continued walking about the room in the
dark. She said:

"Talk, talk, talk, and always to myself. But one can't
abandon the kittens and puppies; that would be cruel. And
being the Abbess Radegunde at least gives one something to
do. But I am so sick of the good Abbess Radegunde; I have
put on Radegunde every morning of my life as easily as I put
on my smock, and then I have had to hear the stupid
creature praised all day!—sainted Radegunde, just Radegunde who is never angry or greedy or jealous, kindly
Radegunde who sacrifices herself for others, and always the
talk, talk, talk, bubbling and boiling in my head with no one
to hear or understand, and no one to answer. No, not even in
the south, only a line here or a line there, and all written by
the dead. Did they feel as I do? That the world is a giant
nursery full of squabbles over toys and the babes thinking
me some kind of goddess because I'm not greedy for their
dolls or bits of straw or their horses made of tied-together
sticks?

"Poor people, if only they knew! It's so easy to be
temperate when one enjoys nothing, so easy to be kind when
one loves nothing, so easy to be fearless when one's life is no
better than one's death. And so easy to scheme when the
success doesn't matter.

"Would they be surprised, I wonder, to find out what my
real thoughts were when Thorfinn's knife was at my throat?
Curiosity! But he would not do it, of course; he does

everything for show. And they would think I was twice holy, not to care about death.

"They why not kill yourself, impious Sister Radegunde? Is it your religion which stops you? Oh, you mean the holy wells, and the holy trees, and the blessed saints with their blessed relics, and the stupidity that shamed Sister Hedwic, and the promises of safety that drove poor Sibihd mad when the blessed body of her Lord did not protect her and the blessed love of the blessed Mary turned away the sharp point of not one knife? Trash! Idle leaves and sticks, reeds and rushes, filth we sweep off our floors when it grows too thick. As if holiness had anything to do with all of that. As if every place were not as holy as every other and every thing as holy as every other, from the shit in Thorfinn's bowels to the rocks on the ground. As if all places and things were not clouds placed in front of our weak eyes, to keep us from being blinded by that glory, that eternal shining, that blazing all about us, the torrent of light that is everything and is in everything! That is what keeps me from the river, but it never speaks to me or tells me what to do, and to it good and evil are the same—no, it is something else than good or evil; it *is*, only—so it is not God. That I know.

"So, people, is your Radegunde a witch or a demon? Is she full of pride or is Radegunde abject? Perhaps she is a witch. Once, long ago, I confessed to old Gerbertus that I could see things that were far away merely by closing my eyes, and I proved it to him, too, and he wept over me and gave me much penance, crying, "If it come of itself it may be a gift of God, daughter, but it is more likely the work of a demon, so do not do it!" And then we prayed and I told him the power had left me, to make the poor old puppy less troubled in its mind, but that was not true, of course. I could still see Turkey as easily as I could see him, and places far beyond: the squat, wild men of the plains on their ponies, and the strange, tall people beyond that with their great cities and odd eyes; as if one pulled one's eyelid up on a slant, and then the seas with the great, wild lands and the cities more full of gold than Constantinople, and water again until one comes back home, for the world's a ball, as the ancients said.

"But I did stop somehow, over the years. Radegunde never had time, I suppose. Besides, when I opened that door it was only pictures, as in a book, and all to no purpose, and after a while I had seen them all and no longer cared for them. It is the other door that draws me, when it opens itself but a crack and strange things peep through, like Ranulf's sister's son and the name of his horse. That door is good but very heavy; it always swings back after a little. I shall have to be on my deathbed to open it all the way, I think.

"The fox is asleep. He is the cleverest yet; there is something in him so that at times one can almost talk to him. But still a fox, for the most part. Perhaps in time. . . .

"But let me see; yes, he is asleep. And the Sibihd puppy is asleep, though it will be having a bad dream soon, I think, and the Thorfinn kitten is asleep, as full of fright as when it wakes, with its claws going in and out, in and out, lest something strangle it in its sleep."

Then the Abbess fell silent and moved to the shuttered window as if she were looking out, so I thought that she was indeed looking out—but not with her eyes—at all the sleeping folk, and this was something she had done every night of her life to see if they were safe and sound. But would she know that *I* was awake? Should I not try very hard to get to sleep before she caught me? Then it seemed to me that she smiled in the dark, although I could not see it. She said in that same low, even voice: "Sleep or wake, Boy News; it is all one to me. Thou hast heard nothing of any importance, only the silly Abbess talking to herself, only Radegunde saying good-bye to Radegunde, only Radegunde going away—don't cry, Boy News; I am still here—but there: Radegunde has gone. This Norseman and I are alike in one way: our minds are like great houses with many of the rooms locked shut. We crowd in a miserable, huddled few, like poor folk, when we might move freely among them all, as gracious as princes. It is fate that locked away so much of the Norseman—see, Boy News, I do not say his name, not even softly, for that wakes folks—but I wonder if the one who bolted me in was not Radegunde herself, she and old Gerbertus—whom I partly believed—they and the years and years of having to be Radegunde and do the things Radegunde did and pretend to have the thoughts Radegunde had and the endless, endless lies Radegunde must tell everyone, and Radegunde's utter and unbearable loneliness."

She fell silent again. I wondered at the Abbess's talk this time: saying she was not there when she was, and about living locked up in small rooms—for surely the Abbey was

the most splendid house in all the world, and the biggest—
and how could she be lonely when all the folk loved her? But
then she said in a voice so low that I could hardly hear it:

"Poor Radegunde! So weary of lies she tells and the
fooling of men and women with the collars round their necks
and bribes of food for good behavior and a careful twitch of
the leash that they do not even see or feel. And with the
Norseman it will be all the same: lies and flattery and all of it
work that never ends and no one ever even sees, so that
finally Radegunde will lie down like an ape in a cage, weak
and sick from hunger, and will never get up.

"Let her die now. There: Radegunde is dead. Radegunde
is gone. Perhaps the door was heavy only because she was
on the other side of it, pushing against me. Perhaps it will
open all the way now. I have looked in all directions: to the
east, to the north and south, and to the west, but there is one
place I have never looked and now I will: away from the ball,
straight out. Let us see—"

She stopped speaking all of a sudden. I had been falling
asleep but this silence woke me. Then I heard the Abbess
gasp terribly, like one mortally stricken, and then she said in
a whisper so keen and thrilling that it made the hair stand up
on my head: *Where art thou?* The next moment she had torn
the shutters open and was crying out with all her voice: *Help
me! Find me! Oh, come, come, come, or I die!*

This waked Thorvald. With some Norse oath he stumbled
up and flung on his sword belt and then put his hand to his
dagger; I had noticed this thing with the dagger was a thing
Norsemen liked to do. The Abbess was silent. He let out his
breath in an oof! and went to light the tallow dip at the live
embers under the hearth ashes; when the dip had smoked
up, he put it on its shelf on the wall.

He said in German, "What the devil, woman! What has
happened?"

She turned round. She looked as if she could not see us, as
if she had been dazed by a joy too big to hold, like one who
has looked into the sun and is still dazzled by it so that
everything seems changed, and the world seems all God's
and everything in it like Heaven. She said softly, with her
arms around herself, hugging herself: "My people. The real
people."

"What are you talking of!" said he.

She seemed to see him then, but only as Sibihd had beheld

us; I do not mean in horror as Sibihd had, but beholding through something else, like someone who comes from a vision of bliss which still lingers about her. She said in the same soft voice, "They are coming for me, Thorvald. It is not wonderful? I knew all this year that something would happen, but I did not know it would be the one thing I wanted in all the world."

He grasped his hair. "*Who* is coming?"

"My people," she said, laughing softly. "Do you not feel them? I do. We must wait three days for they come from very far away. But then—oh, you will see!"

He said, "You've been dreaming. We sail tomorrow."

"Oh, no," said the Abbess simply, "you cannot do that for it would not be right. They told me to wait; they said if I went away, they might not find me."

He said slowly, "You've gone mad. Or it's a trick."

"Oh, no, Thorvald," said she. "How could I trick you? I am your friend. And you will wait these three days, will you not, because you are my friend also."

"You're mad," he said, and started for the door of the study, but she stepped in front of him and threw herself on her knees. All her cunning seemed to have deserted her, or perhaps it was Radegunde who had been the cunning one. This one was like a child. She clasped her hands and tears came out of her eyes; she begged him, saying:

"Such a little thing, Thorvald, only three days! And if they do not come, why then we will go anywhere you like, but if they do come you will not regret it, I promise you; they are not like the folk here and that place is like nothing here. It is what the soul craves, Thorvald!"

He said, "Get up, woman, for God's sake!"

She said, smiling in a sly, frightened way through her blubbered face, "If you let me stay, I will show you the old Abbess's buried treasure, Thorvald."

He stepped back, the anger clear in him. "So this is the brave old witch who cares nothing for death!" he said. Then he made for the door, but she was up again, as quick as a snake, and had flung herself across it.

She said, still with that strange innocence, "Do not strike me. Do not push me. I am your friend!"

He said, "You mean that you lead me by a string around the neck, like a goose. Well, I am tired of that!"

"But I cannot do that any more," said the Abbess breathlessly, "not since the door opened. I am not able now." He raised his arm to strike her and she cowered, wailing, "Do not strike me! Do not push me! Do not, Thorvald!"

He said, "Out of my way then, old witch!"

She began to cry in sobs and gulps. She said, "One is here but another will come! One is buried but another will rise! She will come, Thorvald!" and then in a low, quick voice, "Do not push open this last door. There is one behind it who is evil and I am afraid—" but one could see that he was angry and disappointed and would not listen. He struck her for the second time and again she fell, but with a desperate cry, covering her face with her hands. He unbolted the door and stepped over her and I heard his footsteps go down the corridor. I could see the Abbess clearly—at that time I did not wonder how this could be, with the shadows from the tallow dip half hiding everything in their drunken dance— but I saw every line in her face as if it had been full day, and in that light I saw Radegunde go away from us at last.

Have you ever been at some great king's court or some earl's and heard the storytellers? There are those so skilled in the art that they not only speak for you what the person in the tale said and did, but they also make an action with their faces and bodies as if they truly were that man or woman, so that it is a great surprise to you when the tale ceases, for you almost believe that you have seen the tale happen in front of your very eyes, and it is as if a real man or woman had suddenly ceased to exist, for you forget that all this was only a teller and a tale.

So it was with the woman who had been Radegunde. She did not change; it was still Radegunde's gray hairs and wrinkled face and old body in the peasant woman's brown dress, and yet at the same time it was a stranger who stepped out of the Abbess Radegunde as out of a gown dropped to the floor. This stranger was without feeling, though Radegunde's tears still stood on her cheeks, and there was no kindness or joy in her. She got up without taking care of her dress where the dirty rushes stuck to it; it was as if the dress were an accident and did not concern her. She said in a voice I had never heard before, one with no feeling in it, as if I did not concern her, or Thorvald Einarsson either, as if neither of us were worth a second glance:

"Thorvald, turn around."

Far up in the hall something stirred.

"Now come back. This way."

There were footsteps, coming closer. Then the big Norseman walked clumsily into the room—jerk! jerk! jerk! at every step as if he were being pulled by a rope. Sweat beaded his face. He said, "You—how?"

"By my nature," she said. "Put up your right arm, fox. Now the left. Now both down. Good."

"You—troll!" he said.

"That is so," she said. "Now listen to me, you. There's a man inside you but he's not worth getting at; I tried moments ago when I was new-hatched and he's buried too deep, but now I have grown beak and claws and care nothing for him. It's almost dawn and your boys are stirring; you will go out and tell them that we must stay here another three days. You are weatherwise; make up some story they will believe. And don't try to tell anyone what happened here tonight; you will find that you cannot."

"Folk—come," said he, trying to turn his head, but the effort only made him sweat.

She raised her eyebrows. "Why should they? No one has heard anything. Nothing has happened. You will go out and be as you always are and I will play Radegunde. For three days only. Then you are free."

He did not move. One could see that to remain still was very hard for him; the sweat poured and he strained until every muscle stood out. She said:

"Fox, don't hurt yourself. And don't push me; I am not fond of you. My hand is light upon you only because you still seem to me a little less unhuman than the rest; do not force me to make it heavier. To be plain: I have just broken Thorfinn's neck, for I find that the change improves him. Do not make me do the same to you."

"No worse—than death," Thorvald brought out.

"Ah, no?" said she, and in a moment he was screaming and clawing at his eyes. She said, "Open them, open them; your sight is back," and then, "I do not wish to bother myself thinking up worse things, like worms in your guts. Or do you wish dead sons and a dead wife? Now go.

"*As you always do,*" she added sharply, and the big man turned and walked out. One could not have told from looking at him that anything was wrong.

I had not been sorry to see such a bad man punished, one whose friends had killed our folk and would have taken for slaves—and yet I was sorry, too, in a way, because of the seals barking and the whales—and he *was* splendid, after a fashion—and yet truly I forgot all about that the moment he was gone, for I was terrified of this strange person or demon or whatever it was, for I knew that whoever was in the room with me was not the Abbess Radegunde. I knew also that it could tell where I was and what I was doing, even if I made no sound, and was in a terrible riddle as to what I ought to do when soft fingers touched my face. It was the demon, reaching swiftly and silently behind her.

And do you know, all of a sudden everything was all right! I don't mean that she was the Abbess again—I still had very serious suspicions about that—but all at once I felt light as air and nothing seemed to matter very much because my stomach was full of bubbles of happiness, just as if I had been drunk, only nicer. If the Abbess Radegunde were really a demon, what a joke that was on her people! And she did not, now that I came to think of it, seem a bad sort of demon, more the frightening kind than the killing kind, except for Thorfinn, of course, but then Thorfinn had been a very wicked man. And did not the angels of the Lord smite down the wicked? So perhaps the Abbess was an angel of the Lord and not a demon, but if she were truly an angel, why had she not smitten the Norsemen down when they first came and so saved all our folk? And then I thought that whether angel or demon, she was no longer the Abbess and would love me no longer, and if I had not been so full of the silly happiness which kept tickling about inside me, this thought would have made me weep.

I said, "Will the bad Thorvald get free, demon?"

"No," she said. "Not even if I sleep."

I thought: *But she does not love me.*

"I love thee," said the strange voice, but it was not the Abbess Radegunde's and so was without meaning, but again those soft fingers touched me and there was some kindness in them, even if it was a stranger's kindness.

Sleep, they said.

So I did.

The next three days I had much secret mirth to see the folk bow down to the demon and kiss its hands and weep over it because it had sold itself to ransom them. That is what Sister Hedwic told them. Young Thorfinn had gone out in the night to piss and had fallen over a stone in the dark and broken his neck, which secretly rejoiced our folk, but his comrades did not seem to mind much either, save for one young fellow who had been Thorfinn's friend, I think, and so went about with a long face. Thorvald locked me up in the Abbess's study with the demon every night and went out—or so folk said—to one of the young women, but on those nights the demon was silent, and I lay there with the secret tickle of merriment in my stomach, caring about nothing.

On the third morning I woke sober. The demon—or the Abbess—for in the day she was so like the Abbess Radegunde that I wondered—took my hand and walked us up to Thorvald, who was out picking the people to go aboard the Norseman's boats at the riverbank to be slaves. Folk were standing about weeping and wringing their hands; I thought this strange because of the Abbess's promise to pick those whose going would hurt least, but I know now that least is not none. The weather was bad, cold rain out of mist, and some of Thorvald's companions were speaking sourly to him in the Norse, but he talked them down—bluff and hearty—as if making light of the weather. The demon stood by him and said, in German, in a low voice so that none might hear: "You will say we go to find the Abbess's treasure and then you will go with us into the woods."

He spoke to his fellows in Norse and they frowned, but the end of it was that two must come with us, for the demon said it was such a treasure as three might carry. The demon had the voice and manner of the Abbess Radegunde, all smiles, so they were fooled. Thus we started out into the trees behind the village, with the rain worse and the ground beginning to soften underfoot. As soon as the village was out of sight, the two Norsemen fell behind, but Thorvald did not seem to notice this; I looked back and saw the first man standing in the mud with one foot up, like a goose, and the second with his head lifted and his mouth open so that the rain fell in it. We walked on, the earth sucking at our shoes and all of us getting wet: Thorvald's hair stuck fast against his face, and the demon's old brown cloak clinging to its body. Then suddenly the demon began to breathe harshly and it put its hand to its side with a cry. Its cloak fell off and it stumbled before us between the wet trees, not weeping but breathing hard. Then I saw, ahead of us through the pelting rain, a kind of shining among the bare tree trunks, and as we came nearer the shining became more clear until it was very plain to see, not a blazing thing like a fire at night but a mild and even brightness as though the sunlight were coming through the clouds pleasantly but without strength, as it often does at the beginning of the year.

And then there were folk inside the brightness, both men and women, all dressed in white, and they held out their arms to us, and the demon ran to them, crying out loudly and weeping but paying no mind to the tree branches which struck it across the face and body. Sometimes it fell but it quickly got up again. When it reached the strange folk they embraced it, and I thought that the filth and mud of its gown would stain their white clothing, but the foulness dropped off and would not cling to those clean garments. None of the strange folk spoke a word, nor did the Abbess—I knew then that she was no demon, whatever she was—but I felt them talk to one another, as if in my mind, although I know not how this could be nor the sense of what they said. An odd thing was that as I came closer I could see they were not standing on the ground, as in the way of nature, but higher up, inside the shining, and that their white robes were nothing at all like ours, for they clung to the body so that one might see the people's legs all the way up to the place where the legs joined, even the women's. And some of the folk were like us, but most had a darker color, and some looked as if they had been smeared with soot—there are such persons in the far parts of the world, you know, as I found out later; it is their own natural color—and there were some with the odd eyes the Abbess had spoken of—but the oddest thing of all I will not tell you now. When the Abbess had embraced and kissed them all and all had wept, she turned and looked down upon us: Thorvald standing there as if held by a rope and I, who had lost my fear and had crept close in pure awe, for there was such a joy about these people, like the light about them, mild as spring light and yet as strong as in a spring where the winter has gone forever.

"Come to me, Thorvald," said the Abbess, and one could not see from her face if she loved or hated him. He moved closer—jerk! jerk!—and she reached down and touched his forehead with her fingertips, at which one side of his lip lifted, as a dog's does when it snarls.

"As thou knowest," said the Abbess quietly, "I hate thee and would be revenged upon thee. Thus I swore to myself three days ago, and such vows are not lightly broken."

I saw him snarl again and he turned his eyes from her.

"I must go soon," said the Abbess, unmoved, "for I could stay here long years only as Radegunde, and Radegunde is no more; none of us can remain here long as our proper selves or even in our true bodies, for if we do we go mad like Sibihd or walk into the river and drown or stop our own hearts, so miserable, wicked, and brutish does your world seem to us. Nor may we come in large companies, for we are few and our strength is not great and we have much to learn and study of thy folk so that we may teach and help without marring all in our ignorance. And ignorance or wise, we can do naught except thy folk aid us.

"Here is my revenge," said the Abbess, and he seemed to writhe under the touch of her fingers, for all they were so light. "Henceforth be not Thorvald Farmer nor yet Thorvald Seafarer but Thorvald Peacemaker, Thorvald War-hater, put into anguish by bloodshed and agonized at cruelty. I cannot make long thy life—that gift is beyond me—but I give thee this: to the end of thy days, long or short, thou wilt know the Presence about thee always, as I do, and thou wilt know that it is neither good nor evil, as I do, and this knowing will trouble and frighten thee always, as it does me, and so about this one thing, as about many another, Thorvald Peacemaker will never have peace.

"Now, Thorvald, go back to the village and tell thy comrades I was assumed into the company of the saints, straight up to Heaven. Thou mayst believe it, if thou wilt. That is all my revenge."

Then she took away her hand, and he turned and walked from us like a man in a dream, holding out his hands as if to feel the rain and stumbling now and again, as one who wakes from a vision.

Then I began to grieve, for I knew she would be going away with the strange people, and it was to me as if all the love and care and light in the world were leaving me. I crept close to her, meaning to spring secretly onto the shining place and so go away with them, but she spied me and said, "Silly Radulphus, you cannot," and that *you* hurt me more than anything else so that I began to bawl.

"Child," said the Abbess, "come to me," and loudly weeping I leaned against her knees. I felt the shining around me, all bright and good and warm, that wiped away all grief, and then the Abbess's touch on my hair.

She said, "Remember me. And be . . . content."

I nodded, wishing I dared to look up at her face, but when I did, she had already gone with her friends. Not up into the sky, you understand, but as if they moved very swiftly backwards among the trees—although the trees were still behind them somehow—and as they moved, the shining and the people faded away into the rain until there was nothing left.

Then there was no rain. I do not mean that the clouds parted or the sun came out; I mean that one moment it was raining and cold and the next the sky was clear blue from side to side, and it was splendid, sunny, breezy, bright, sailing weather. I had the oddest thought that the strange folk were not agreed about doing such a big miracle—and it was hard for them, too—but they had decided that no one would believe this more than all the other miracles folk speak of, I suppose. And it would surely make Thorvald's lot easier when he came back with wild words about saints and Heaven, as indeed it did, later.

Well, that is the tale, really. She said to me "Be content" and so I am; they call me Radulf the Happy now. I have had my share of trouble and sickness, but always somewhere in me there is a little spot of warmth and joy to make it all easier, like a traveler's fire burning out in the wilderness on a cold night. When I am in real sorrow or distress, I remember her fingers touching my hair and that takes part of the pain away, somehow. So perhaps I got the best gift, after all. And she said also, "Remember me," and thus I have, every little thing, although it all happened when I was the age my own grandson is now, and that is how I can tell you this tale today.

And the rest? Three days after the Norsemen left, Sibihd got back her wits and no one knew how, though I think I do! And as for Thorvald Einarsson, I have heard that after his wife died in Norway he went to England and ended his days there as a monk, but whether this story be true or not I do not know.

I know this: they may call me Happy Radulf all they like, but there is much that troubles me. Was the Abbess Rade-gunde a demon, as the new priest says? I cannot believe this, although he called half her sayings nonsense and the other half blasphemy when I asked him. Father Cairbre, before the Norse killed him, told us stories about the Sidhe, that is, the

Irish fairy people, who leave changelings in human cradles; and for a while it seemed to me that Radegunde must be a woman of the Sidhe when I remembered that she could read Latin at the age of two and was such a marvel of learning when so young, for the changelings the fairies leave are not their own children, you understand, but one of the fairy folk themselves, who are hundreds upon hundreds of years old, and the other fairy folk always come back for their own in the end. And yet this could not have been, for Father Cairbre said also that the Sidhe are wanton and cruel and without souls, and neither the Abbess Radegunde nor the people who came for her were one blessed bit like that, although she did break Thorfinn's neck—but then it may be that Thorfinn broke his own neck by chance, just as we all thought at the time, and she told this to Thorvald afterwards, as if she had done it herself, only to frighten him. She had more of a soul with a soul's griefs and joys than most of us, no matter what the new priest says. He never saw her or felt her sorrow and lonesomeness, or heard her talk of the blazing light all around us—and what can that be but God Himself? Even though she did call the crucifix a deaf thing and vain, she must have meant not Christ, you see, but only the piece of wood itself, for she was always telling the Sisters that Christ was in Heaven and not on the wall. And if she said the light was not good or evil, well, there is a traveling Irish scholar who told me of a holy Christian monk named Augustinus who tells us that all which is, is good, and evil is only a lack of the good, like an empty place not filled up. And if the Abbess truly said there was no God, I say it was the sin of despair, and even saints may sin, if only they repent, which I believe she did at the end.

So I tell myself, and yet I know the Abbess Radegunde was no saint, for are the saints few and weak, as she said? Surely not! And then there is a thing I held back in my telling, a small thing, and it will make you laugh and perhaps means nothing one way or the other, but it is this:

Are the saints bald?

These folk in white had young faces but they were like eggs; there was not a stitch of hair on their domes! Well, God may shave His saints if He pleases, I suppose.

But I know she was no saint. And then I believe that she did kill Thorfinn and the light was not God and she not even a Christian or maybe even human, and I remember how

Radegunde was to her only a gown to step out of at will, and how she truly hated and scorned Thorvald until she was happy and safe with her own people. Or perhaps it was like her talk about living in a house with the rooms shut up; when she stopped being Radegunde, first one part of her came back and then the other—the joyful part that could not lie or plan and then the angry part—and then they were all together when she was back among her own folk. And then I give up trying to weigh this matter and go back to warm my soul at the little fire she lit in me, that one warm, bright place in the wide and windy dark.

But something troubles me even there and will not be put to rest by the memory of the Abbess's touch on my hair. As I grow older it troubles me more and more. It was the very last thing she said to me, which I have not told you but will now. When she had given me the gift of contentment, I became so happy that I said, "Abbess, you said you would be revenged on Thorvald, but all you did was change him into a good man. That is no revenge!"

What this saying did to her astonished me, for all the color went out of her face and left it gray. She looked suddenly old, like a death's-head, even standing there among her own true folk with love and joy coming from them so strongly that I myself might feel it. She said, "I did not change him. I lent him my eyes, that is all." Then she looked beyond me, as if at our village, at the Norsemen loading their boats with weeping slaves, at all the villages of Germany and England and France where the poor folk sweat from dawn to dark so that the great lords may do battle with one another, at castles under siege with the starving folk within eating mice and rats and sometimes each other, at the women carried off or raped or beaten, at the mothers wailing for their little ones, and beyond this at the great wide world itself with all its battles which I had used to think so grand, and the misery and greediness and fear and jealousy and hatred of folk one for the other, save—perhaps—for a few small bands of savages, but they were so far from us that one could scarcely see them. She said: *No revenge? Thinkest thou so, boy?* And then she said as one who believes absolutely, as one who has seen all the folk at their living and dying, not for one year but for many, not in one place but in all places, as one who knows it all over the whole wide earth:

Think again. . . .

BURNING CHROME

William Gibson

William Gibson is regarded by many as the most exciting new writer of science fiction in perhaps a decade. His fast-paced, high-technology stories are already influencing other sf writers, and when you read "Burning Chrome" you'll see why: Gibson gives us not only believable future scenarios but also an intensity of experience rarely matched in all of science fiction. "Burning Chrome" is, in outline, a story of future crime, but by concentrating on the criminals and the society that produced them—and a believable love story—he transcends the form.

Born and raised in the United States, Gibson now lives in Canada with his wife and child. His first novel, Neuromancer, *will be published next year.*

IT WAS HOT THE NIGHT WE BURNED CHROME. Out in the malls and plazas moths were batting themselves to death against the neon, but in Bobby's loft the only light came from a monitor screen and the green and red LEDs on the face of the matrix simulator. I knew every chip in Bobby's simulator by heart; it looked like your workaday Ono-Sendai VII, the "Cyberspace Seven," but I'd rebuilt it so many times that you'd have had a hard time finding a square millimeter of factory circuitry in all that silicon.

We waited side by side in front of the simulator console, watching the time-display in the screen's lower left corner.

"Go for it," I said, when it was time, but Bobby was already there, leaning forward to drive the Russian program into its slot with the heel of his hand. He did it with the tight grace of a kid slamming change into an arcade game, sure of winning and ready to pull down a string of free games.

A silver tide of phosphenes boiled across my field of vision as the matrix began to unfold in my head, a 3-D chessboard, infinite and perfectly transparent. The Russian program seemed to lurch as we entered the grid. If anyone else had been jacked into that part of the matrix, he might have seen a surf of flickering shadow roll out of the little yellow pyramid that represented our computer. The program was a mimetic weapon, designed to absorb local color and present itself as a crash-priority override in whatever contest it encountered.

"Congratulations," I heard Bobby say. "We just became an Eastern Seaboard Fission Authority inspection probe . . ." That meant we were clearing fiberoptic lines with the cybernetic equivalent of a fire siren, but in the simulation matrix we seemed to rush straight for Chrome's data base. I couldn't see it yet, but I already knew those walls were waiting. Walls of shadow, walls of ice.

Chrome: her pretty childface smooth as steel, with eyes that would have been at home on the bottom of some deep Atlantic trench, cold gray eyes that lived under terrible pressure. They said she cooked her own cancers for people who crossed her, rococo custom variations that took years to kill you. They said a lot of things about Chrome, none of them at all reassuring.

So I blotted her out with a picture of Rikki. Rikki kneeling in a shaft of dusty sunlight that slanted into the loft through a grid of steel and glass: her faded camouflage fatigues, her translucent rose sandals, the good line of her bare back as she rummaged through a nylon gear bag. She looks up, and a half-blond curl falls to tickle her nose. Smiling, buttoning an old shirt of Bobby's, frayed khaki cotton drawn across her breasts.

She smiles.

"Son of a bitch," said Bobby, "we just told Chrome we're an IRS audit and three Supreme Court subpoenas . . . Hang on to your ass, Jack . . ."

So long, Rikki. Maybe now I see you never.

And so dark, in the halls of Chrome's ice.

Bobby was a cowboy and ice was the nature of his game, *ice* from ICE, Intrusion Countermeasures Electronics. The matrix is an abstract representation of the relationships between data systems. Legitimate programmers jack into their employers' sector of the matrix and find themselves surrounded by bright geometries representing the corporate data.

Towers and fields of it ranged in the colorless nonspace of the simulation matrix, the electronic consensus hallucination that facilitates the handling and exchange of massive quantities of data. Legitimate programmers never see the walls of ice they work behind, the walls of shadow that screen their operations from others, from industrial espionage artists and hustlers like Bobby Quine.

Bobby was a cowboy. Bobby was a cracksman, a burglar, casing mankind's extended electronic nervous system, rustling data and credit in the crowded matrix, monochrome, nonspace where the only stars are dense concentrations of information, and high above it all burn corporate galaxies and the cold spiral arms of military systems.

Bobby was another one of those young-old faces you see drinking in the Gentleman Loser, the chic bar for computer cowboys, rustlers, cybernetic second-story men. We were partners.

Bobby Quine and Automatic Jack. Bobby's the thin pale dude with the dark glasses, and Jack's the mean-looking guy with the myoelectric arm. Bobby's software and Jack's hard; Bobby punches console and Jack runs down all the little things that can give you an edge. Or, anyway, that's what the scene watchers in the Gentleman Loser would've told you, before Bobby decided to burn Chrome. But they also might've told you that Bobby was losing his edge, slowing down. He was twenty-eight, Bobby, and that's old for a console cowboy.

Both of us were good at what we did, but somehow that one big score just wouldn't come down for us. I knew where to go for the right gear, and Bobby had all his licks down pat. He'd sit back with a white terry sweatband across his forehead and whip moves on those keyboards faster than you could follow, punching his way through some of the fanciest ice in the business, but that was when something happened that managed to get him totally wired, and that didn't happen often. Not highly motivated Bobby, and I was the kind of guy who's happy to have the rent covered and a clean shirt to wear.

But Bobby had this thing for girls, like they were his private Tarot or something, the way he'd get himself moving. We never talked about it, but when it started to look like he was losing his touch that summer, he started to spend more time in the Gentleman Loser. He'd sit at a table by the open doors and watch the crowd slide by, nights when the bugs were at the neon and the air smelled of perfume and fast food. You could see his sunglasses scanning those faces as they passed, and he must have decided that Rikki's was the one he was waiting for, the wild card and the luck changer. The new one.

I went to New York to check out the market, to see what was available in hot software.

The Finn's place has a defective hologram in the window.

METRO HOLOGRAFIX, over a display of dead flies wearing fur coats of gray dust. The scrap's waist-high, inside, drifts of it rising to meet walls that are barely visible behind nameless junk, behind sagging pressboard shelves stacked with old skin magazines and yellow-spined years of *National Geographics*.

"You need a gun," said the Finn. He looks like a recombo DNA project aimed at tailoring people for high-speed burrowing. "You're in luck. I got the new Smith and Wesson, the four-oh-eight Tactical. Got this xenon projector slung under the barrel, see, batteries in the grip, throw you a twelve-inch high-noon circle in the pitch dark at fifty yards. The light source is so narrow, it's almost impossible to spot. It's just like voodoo in a nightfight."

I let my arm clunk down on the table and started the fingers drumming; the servos in the hand began whining like overworked mosquitoes. I knew that the Finn really hated the sound.

"You looking to pawn that?" He prodded the duralumin wrist joint with the chewed shaft of a felt-tip pen. "Maybe get yourself something a little quieter?"

I kept it up. "I don't need any guns, Finn."

"Okay," he said, "okay," and I quit drumming. "I only got this one item, and I don't even know what it is." He looked unhappy. "I got it off these bridge-and-tunnel kids from Jersey last week."

"So when'd you ever buy anything you didn't know what it was, Finn?"

"Wise ass." And he passed me a transparent mailer with something in it that looked like an audio cassette through the bubble padding. "They had a passport," he said. "They had credit cards and a watch. And that."

"They had the contents of somebody's pockets, you mean."

He nodded. "The passport was Belgian. It was also bogus, looked to me; so I put it in the furnace. Put the cards in with it. The watch was okay, a Porsche, nice watch."

It was obviously some kind of plug-in military program. Out of the mailer, it looked like the magazine of a small assault rifle coated with nonreflective black plastic. The edges and corners showed bright metal: it had been knocking around for a while.

"I'll give you a bargain on it, Jack. For old times' sake."

I had to smile at that. Getting a bargain from the Finn was like God repealing the law of gravity when you have to carry a heavy suitcase down ten blocks of airport corridor.

"Looks Russian to me," I said. "Probably the emergency sewage controls for some Leningrad suburb. Just what I need."

"You know," said the Finn. "I got a pair of shoes older than you are. Sometimes I think you got about as much class as those yahoos from Jersey. What do you want me to tell you, it's the keys to the Kremlin? You figure out what the goddamn thing is. Me, I just sell the stuff."

I bought it.

Bodiless, we swerve into Chrome's castle of ice. And we're fast, fast. It feels like we're surfing the crest of the invading program, hanging ten above the seething glitch systems as they mutate. We're sentient patches of oil swept along down corridors of shadow.

Somewhere we have bodies, very far away, in a crowded loft rooted with steel and glass. Somewhere we have microseconds, maybe time left to pull out.

We've crashed her gates disguised as an audit and three subpoenas, but her defenses are specifically geared to cope with that kind of official intrusion. Her most sophisticated ice is structured to fend off warrants, writs, subpoenas. When we breached the first gate, the bulk of her data vanished behind core-command ice, these walls we see as leagues of corridor, mazes of shadow. Five separate landlines spurted May Day signals to law firms, but the virus had already taken over the parameter ice. The glitch systems gobble the distress calls as our mimetic subprograms scan anything that hasn't been blanked by core command.

The Russian program lifts a Tokyo number from the unscreened data, choosing it for frequency of calls, average length of calls, the speed with which Chrome returned those calls.

"Okay," says Bobby, "we're an incoming scrambler call from a pal of hers in Japan. That should help."

Ride 'em cowboy.

Bobby read his future in women; his girls were omens, changes in the weather, and he'd sit all night in the Gentleman Loser, waiting for the season to lay a new face down in front of him like a card.

I was working late in the loft one night, shaving down a chip, my arm off and the little waldo jacked straight into the stump.

Bobby came in with a girl I hadn't seen before, and usually I feel a little funny if a stranger sees me working that way, with those leads clipped to the hard carbon studs that stick out of my stump. She came right over and looked at the magnified image on the screen, then saw the waldo moving under its vacuum-sealed dust-cover. She didn't say anything, just watched. Right away I had a good feeling about her; it's like that sometimes.

"Automatic Jack, Rikki. My associate."

He laughed, put his arm around her waist, something in his tone letting me know that I'd be spending the night in a dingy room in a hotel.

"Hi," she said. Tall, nineteen or maybe twenty, and she definitely had the goods. With just those few freckles across the bridge of her nose, and eyes somewhere between dark amber and French coffee. Tight black jeans rolled to mid-calf and a narrow plastic belt that matched the rose-colored sandals.

But now when I see her sometimes when I'm trying to sleep, I see her somewhere out on the edge of all this sprawl of cities and smoke, and it's like she's a hologram stuck behind my eyes, in a bright dress she must've worn once, when I knew her, something that doesn't quite reach her knees. Bare legs long and straight. Brown hair, streaked with blond, hoods her face, blown in a wind from somewhere, and I see her wave good-bye.

Bobby was making a show of rooting through a stack of audio cassettes. "I'm on my way, cowboy," I said, unclipping the waldo. She watched attentively as I put my arm back on.

"Can you fix things?" she asked.

"Anything, anything you want, Automatic Jack'll fix it." I snapped my duralumin fingers for her.

She took a little simstim deck from her belt and showed me the broken hinge on the cassette cover.

"Tomorrow," I said, "no problem."

And my oh my, I said to myself, sleep pulling me down the six flights to the street, *what'll Bobby's luck be like with a fortune cookie like that? If his system worked, we'd be striking it rich any night now.* In the street I grinned and yawned and waved for a cab.

Chrome's castle is dissolving, sheets of ice shadow flickering and fading, eaten by the glitch systems that spin out from the Russian program, tumbling away from our central logic thrust and infecting the fabric of the ice itself. The glitch systems are cybernetic virus analogs, self-replicating and voracious. They mutate constantly, in unison, subverting and absorbing Chrome's defenses.

Have we already paralyzed her, or is a bell ringing somewhere, a red light blinking? Does she know?

Rikki Wildside, Bobby called her, and for those first few weeks it must have seemed to her that she had it all, the whole teeming show spread out for her, sharp and bright under the neon. She was new to the scene, and she had all the miles of malls and plazas to prowl, all the shops and clubs, and Bobby to explain the wild side, the tricky wiring on the dark underside of things, all the players and their names and their games. He made her feel at home.

"What happened to your arm?" she asked me one night in the Gentleman Loser, the three of us drinking at a small table in a corner.

"Hang-gliding," I said, "accident."

"Hang-gliding over a wheatfield," said Bobby, "place called Kiev. Our Jack's just hanging there in the dark, under a Nightwing parafoil, with fifty kilos of radar jammer between his legs, and some Russian asshole accidentally burns his arm off with a laser."

I don't remember how I changed the subject, but I did.

I was still telling myself that it wasn't Rikki who was getting to me, but what Bobby was doing with her. I'd known him for a long time, since the end of the war, and I knew he used women as counters in a game, Bobby Quine versus fortune, versus time and the night of cities. And Rikki had turned up just when he needed something to get him going, something to aim for. So he'd set her up as a symbol for everything he wanted and couldn't have, everything he'd had and couldn't keep.

I didn't like having to listen to him tell me how much he loved her, and knowing he believed it only made it worse.

He was a past master at the hard fall and the rapid recovery, and I'd seen it happen a dozen times before. He might as well have had NEXT printed across his sunglasses in green dayglo capitals, ready to flash out at the first interesting face that flowed past the tables in the Gentleman Loser.

I knew what he did to them. He turned them into emblems, sigils on the map of his hustler's life, navigation beacons he could follow through a sea of bars and neon. What else did he have to steer by? He didn't love money, in and of itself, not enough to follow its lights. He wouldn't work for power over other people; he hated the responsibility it brings. He had some basic pride in his skill, but that was never enough to keep him pushing.

So he made do with women.

When Rikki showed up, he needed one in the worst way. He was fading fast, and smart money was already whispering that the edge was off his game. He needed that one big score, and soon, because he didn't know any other kind of life, and all his clocks were set for hustler's time, calibrated in risk and adrenaline and that supernal dawn calm that comes when every move's proved right and a sweet lump of someone else's credit clicks into your own account.

It was time for him to make his bundle and get out; so Rikki got set up higher and farther away than any of the others ever had, even though—and I felt like screaming at him—she was right there, alive, totally real; human; hungry, resilient, bored, beautiful, excited, all the things she was . . .

Then he went out one afternoon, about a week before I made the trip to New York to see the Finn. Went out and left us there in the loft, waiting for a thunderstorm. Half the skylight was shadowed by a dome they'd never finished, and the other half showed sky, black and blue with clouds. I was standing by the bench, looking up at that sky, stupid with the hot afternoon, the humidity, and she touched me, touched my shoulder and the half-inch border of taut pink scar that the arm doesn't cover. Anybody else ever touched me there, they went on to the shoulder, the neck . . .

But she didn't do that. Her nails were lacquered black, not pointed, but tapered oblongs, the lacquer only a shade darker than the carbon-fiber laminate that sheathes my arm. And her hand went down the arm, black nails tracing a weld in the laminate, down to the black anodized elbow joint, out to the wrist, her hand soft-knuckled as a child's fingers spreading to lock over mine, her palm against the perforated duralumin.

Her other palm came up to brush across the feedback pads, and it rained all afternoon, raindrops drumming on the steel and soot-stained glass above Bobby's bed.

Ice walls flick away like supersonic butterflies made of shade. Beyond them, the matrix's illusion of infinite space. It's like watching a tape of a prefab building going up; only the tape's reversed and run at high speed, and these walls are torn wings.

Trying to remind myself that this place and the gulfs beyond are only representations, that we aren't "in" Chrome's computer, but interfaced with it, while the matrix simulator in Bobby's loft generates this illusion . . . The core data begin to emerge, exposed, vulnerable . . . This is the far side of ice, the view of the matrix I've never seen before, the view that fifteen million legitimate console operators see daily and take for granted.

The core data tower around us like vertical freight trains, color-coded for access. Bright primaries, impossibly bright in that transparent void, linked by countless horizontals in nursery blues and pinks.

But ice still shadows something at the center of it all: the heart of all Chrome's expensive darkness, the very heart . . .

It was late afternoon when I got back from my shopping expedition to New York. Not much sun through the skylight, but an ice pattern glowed on Bobby's monitor screen, a 2-D graphic representation of someone's computer defenses, lines of neon woven like an Art Deco prayer rug. I turned the console off, and the screen went completely dark.

Rikki's things were spread across my workbench, nylon bags spilling clothes and makeup, a pair of bright red cowboy boots, audio cassettes, glossy Japanese magazines about simstim stars. I stacked it all under the bench and then took my arm off, forgetting that the program I'd brought from the Finn was in the righthand pocket of my jacket, so that I had to fumble it out lefthanded and then get it into the padded jaws of the jeweler's vise.

The waldo looks like an old audio turntable, the kind that played disc records, with the vise set up under a transparent dustcover. The arm itself is just over a centimeter long, swinging out on what would've been the tone arm on one of those turntables. But I don't look at that when I've clipped the leads to my stump; I look at the scope, because that's my arm there in black and white, magnification 40 ×.

I ran a tool check and picked up the laser. It felt a little heavy; so I scaled my weight-sensor input down to a quarter kilo per gram and got to work. At 40 × the side of the program looked like a trailer-truck.

It took eight hours to crack; three hours with the waldo and the laser and four dozen taps, two hours on the phone to a contact in Colorado, and three hours to run down a lexicon disc that could translate eight-year-old technical Russian.

Then Cyrillic alphanumerics started reeling down the monitor, twisting themselves into English halfway down. There were a lot of gaps, where the lexicon ran up against specialized military acronyms in the readout I'd bought from my man in Colorado, but it did give me some idea of what I'd bought from the Finn.

I felt like a punk who'd gone out to buy a switchblade and come home with a small neutron bomb.

Screwed again, I thought. *What good's a neutron bomb in a streetfight?* The thing under the dustcover was right out of my league. I didn't even know where to unload it, where to look for a buyer. Someone had, but he was dead, someone with a Porsche watch and a fake Belgian passport, but I'd never tried to move in those circles. The Finn's muggers from the 'burbs had knocked over someone who had some highly arcane connections.

The program in the jeweler's vise was a Russian military icebreaker, a killer-virus program.

It was dawn when Bobby came in alone. I'd fallen asleep with a bag of take-out sandwiches in my lap.

"You want to eat?" I asked him, not really awake, holding out my sandwiches. I'd been dreaming of the program, of its waves of hungry glitch systems and mimetic subprograms; in the dream it was an animal of some kind, shapeless and flowing.

He brushed the bag aside on his way to the console, punched a function key. The screen lit with the intricate pattern I'd seen there that afternoon. I rubbed sleep from my eyes with my left hand, one thing I can't do with my right. I'd fallen asleep trying to decide whether to tell him about the program. Maybe I should try to sell it alone, keep the money, go somewhere new, ask Rikki to go with me.

"Whose is it?" I asked.

He stood there in a black cotton jumpsuit, an old leather jacket thrown over his shoulders like a cape. He hadn't shaved for a few days, and his face looked thinner than usual.

"It's Chrome's," he said.

My arm convulsed, started clicking, fear translated to the myoelectrics through the carbon studs. I spilled the sandwiches, limp sprouts, and bright yellow dairy-product slices on the unswept wooden floor.

"You're stone-crazy," I said.

"No," he said, "you think she rumbled it? No way. We'd be dead already. I locked onto her through a triple-blind rental system in Mombasa and an Algerian commsat. She knew somebody was having a look-see, but she couldn't trace it."

If Chrome had traced the pass Bobby had made at her ice, we were good as dead. But he was probably right or she'd have had me blown away on my way back from New York. "Why her, Bobby? Just give me one reason . . ."

Chrome. I'd seen her maybe half a dozen times in the Gentleman Loser. Maybe she was slumming, or checking out the human condition, a condition she didn't exactly aspire to. A sweet little heartshaped face framing the nastiest pair of eyes you ever saw. She'd looked fourteen for as long as anyone could remember, hyped out of anything like a normal metabolism on some massive program of serums and hormones. She was as ugly a customer as the street ever produced, but she didn't belong to the street anymore. She was one of the Boys, Chrome, a member in good standing of the local Mob subsidiary. Word was, she'd gotten started as a dealer, back when synthetic pituitary hormones were still proscribed. But she hadn't had to move hormones for a long time. Now she owned the House of Blue Lights.

"You're flat-out crazy, Quine. You give me one sane reason for having that stuff on your screen. You ought to dump it, and I mean *now* . . ."

"Talk in the Loser," he said, shrugging out of the leather jacket. "Black Myron and Crow Jane. Jane, she's up on all the sex lines, claims she knows where the money goes. So she's arguing with Myron that Chrome's the controlling interest in the Blue Lights, not just some figurehead for the Boys."

" 'The Boys,' Bobby," I said. "That's the operative word there. You still capable of seeing that? We don't mess with the Boys, remember? That's why we're still walking around."

"That's why we're still poor, partner." He settled back into the swivel chair in front of the console, unzipped his jumpsuit, and scratched his skinny white chest. "But maybe not for much longer."

"I think maybe this partnership just got itself permanently dissolved."

Then he grinned at me. That grin was truly crazy, feral and focused, and I knew that right then he really didn't give a shit about dying.

"Look," I said, "I've got some money left, you know? Why don't you take it and get the tube to Miami, catch a hopper to Montego Bay. You need a rest, man. You've got to get your act together."

"My act, Jack," he said, punching something on the keyboard, "never has been this together before." The neon prayer rug on the screen shivered and woke as an animation program cut in, ice lines weaving with hypnotic frequency, a living mandala. Bobby kept punching, and the movement slowed; the pattern resolved itself, grew slightly less complex, became an alternation between two distinct configurations. A first-class piece of work, and I hadn't thought he was still that good. "Now," he said, "there, see it? Wait. There. There again. And there. Easy to miss. That's it. Cuts in every hour and twenty minutes with a squirt transmission to their commsat. We could live for a year on what she pays them weekly in negative interest."

"Whose commsat?"

"Zurich. Her bankers. That's her bankbook, Jack. That's where the money goes. Crow Jane was right."

I just stood there. My arm forgot to click.

"So how'd you do in New York, partner? You get anything that'll help me cut ice? We're going to need whatever we can get."

I kept my eyes on his, forced myself not to look in the direction of the waldo, the jeweler's vise. The Russian program was there, under the dustcover.

Wild cards, luck changers.

"Where's Rikki?" I asked him, crossing to the console, pretending to study the alternating patterns on the screen.

"Friends of hers," he shrugged, "kids, they're all into simstim." He smiled absently. "I'm going to do it for her, man."

"I'm going out to think about this, Bobby. You want me to come back, you keep your hands off the board."

"I'm doing it for her," he said as the door closed behind me. "You know I am."

And down now, down, the program a roller coaster through this fraying maze of shadow walls, gray cathedral spaces between the bright towers. Headlong speed.

Black ice. Don't think about it. Black ice.

Too many stories in the Gentleman Loser; black ice is a part of the mythology. Ice that kills. Illegal, but then aren't we all? Some kind of neural-feedback weapon, and you connect with it only once. Like some hideous Word that eats the mind from the inside out. Like an epileptic spasm that goes on and on until there's nothing left at all . . .

And we're diving for the floor of Chrome's shadow castle.

Trying to brace myself for the sudden stopping of breath, a sickness and final slackening of the nerves. Fear of that cold Word waiting, down there in the dark.

I went out and looked for Rikki, found her in a café with a boy with Sendai eyes, half-healed suture lines radiating from his bruised sockets. She had a glossy brochure spread open on the table, Tally Isham smiling up from a dozen photographs, the Girl with the Zeiss Ikon Eyes.

Her little simstim deck was one of the things I'd stacked under my bench the night before, the one I'd fixed for her the day after I'd first seen her. She spent hours jacked into that unit, the contact band across her forehead like a gray plastic tiara. Tally Isham was her favorite, and with the contact band on, she was gone, off somewhere in the recorded sensorium of simstim's biggest star. Simulated stimuli: the world—all the interesting parts, anyway—as perceived by Tally Isham. Tally raced a black Fokker ground-effect plane across Arizona mesa tops. Tally dived the Truk Island preserves. Tally partied with the superrich on private Greek islands, heartbreaking purity of those tiny white seaports at dawn.

Actually she looked a lot like Tally, same coloring and cheekbones. I thought Rikki's mouth was stronger. More sass. She didn't want to *be* Tally Isham, but she coveted the job. That was her ambition, to be in simstim. Bobby just laughed it off. She talked to me about it, though. "How'd I look with a pair of these?" she'd ask, holding a full-page headshot, Tally Isham's blue Zeiss Ikons lined up with her own amber-brown. She'd had her corneas done twice, but she still wasn't twenty-twenty; so she wanted Ikons. Brand of the stars. Very expensive.

"You still window-shopping for eyes?" I asked as I sat down.

"Tiger just got some," she said. She looked tired, I thought.

Tiger was so pleased with his Sendais that he couldn't help smiling, but I doubted whether he'd have smiled otherwise. He had the kind of uniform good looks you get after your seventh trip to the surgical boutique; he'd probably spend the rest of his life looking vaguely like each new season's media frontrunner; not too obvious a copy, but nothing too original, either.

"Sendai, right?" I smiled back.

He nodded. I watched as he tried to take me in with his idea of a professional simstim glance. He was pretending that he was recording. I thought he spent too long on my arm. "They'll be great on peripherals when the muscles heal," he said, and I saw how carefully he reached for his double espresso. Sendai eyes are notorious for depth-perception defects and warranty hassles, among other things.

"Tiger's leaving for Hollywood tomorrow."

"Then maybe Chiba City, right?" I smiled at him. He didn't smile back. "Got an offer, Tiger? Know an agent?"

"Just checking it out," he said quietly. Then he got up and left. He said a quick good-bye to Rikki, but not to me.

"That kid's optic nerves may start to deteriorate inside six months. You know that, Rikki? Those Sendais are illegal in England, Denmark, lots of places. You can't replace nerves."

"Hey, Jack, no lectures." She stole one of my croissants and nibbled at the tip of one of its horns.

"I thought I was your adviser, kid."

"Yeah. Well, Tiger's not too swift, but everybody knows about Sendais. They're all he can afford. So he's taking a chance. If he gets work, he can replace them."

"With these?" I tapped the Zeiss Ikon brochure. "Lot of money, Rikki. You know better than to take a gamble like that?"

She nodded. "I want Ikons."

"If you're going up to Bobby's, tell him to sit tight until he hears from me."

"Sure. It's business?"

"Business," I said. But it was craziness.

I drank my coffee, and she ate both my croissants. Then I walked her down to Bobby's. I made fifteen calls, each one from a different pay phone.

Business. Bad craziness.

All in all, it took us six weeks to set the burn up, six weeks of Bobby telling me how much he loved her. I worked even harder, trying to get away from that.

Most of it was phone calls. My fifteen initial and very oblique inquiries each seemed to breed fifteen more. I was looking for a certain service Bobby and I both imagined as a requisite part of the world's clandestine economy, but which probably never had more than five customers at a time. It would be one that never advertised.

We were looking for the world's heaviest fence, for a nonaligned money laundry capable of drycleaning a mega-buck on-line cash transfer and then forgetting about it.

All those calls were a waste, finally, because it was the Finn who put me on to what we needed. I'd gone up to New York to buy a new blackbox rig, because we were going broke paying for all those calls.

I put the problem to him as hypothetically as possible.

"Macao," he said.

"Macao?"

"The Long Hum family. Stockbrokers."

He even had the number. You want a fence, ask another fence.

The Long Hum people were so oblique that they made my idea of a subtle approach look like a tactical nuke-out. Bobby had to make two shuttle runs to Hong Kong to get the deal straight. We were running out of capital, and fast. I still don't know why I decided to go along with it in the first place; I was scared of Chrome, and I'd never been all that hot to get rich.

I tried telling myself that it was a good idea to burn the House of Blue Lights because the place was a creep joint, but I just couldn't buy it. I didn't like the Blue Lights, because I'd spent a supremely depressing evening there once, but that was no excuse for going after Chrome. Actually I halfway assumed we were going to die in the attempt. Even with that killer program, the odds weren't exactly in our favor.

Bobby was lost in writing the set of commands we were going to plug into the dead center of Chrome's computer. That was going to be my job, because Bobby was going to have his hands full, trying to keep the Russian program from going straight for the kill. It was too complex for us to rewrite, and so he was going to try to hold it back for the two seconds I needed.

I made a deal with a streetfighter named Miles. He was going to follow Rikki, the night of the burn, keep her in sight, and phone me at a certain time. If I wasn't there, or didn't answer in just a certain way, I'd told him to grab her and put her on the first tube out. I gave him an envelope to give her, money and a note.

Bobby really hadn't thought about that, much, how things would go for her if we blew it. He just kept telling me he loved her, where they were going to go together, how they'd spend the money.

"Buy her a pair of Ikons first, man. That's what she wants. She's serious about that simstim scene."

"Hey," he said, looking up from the keyboard, "she won't need to work. We're going to make it, Jack. She's my luck. She won't ever have to work again."

"Your luck," I said. I wasn't happy. I couldn't remember when I had been happy. "You seen your luck around lately?"

He hadn't, but neither had I. We'd both been too busy.

I missed her. Missing her reminded me of my one night in the House of Blue Lights, because I'd gone there out of missing someone else. I'd gotten drunk to begin with, then I'd started hitting vasopressin inhalers. If your main squeeze has just decided to walk out on you, booze and vasopressin are the ultimate in masochistic pharmacology; the juice makes you maudlin and the vasopressin makes you remember, I mean really remember. Clinically they use the stuff to counter senile amnesia, but the street finds its own uses for things. So I'd bought myself an ultra-intense replay of a bad affair; trouble is you get the bad with the good. Go gunning for transports of animal ecstasy and you get what you said, too, and what she said to that, how she walked away and never looked back.

I don't remember deciding to go to the Blue Lights, or how I got there, hushed corridors and this really tacky decorative waterfall trickling somewhere, or maybe just a hologram of one. I had a lot of money that night; somebody had given Bobby a big roll for opening a three-second window in someone else's ice.

I don't think the crew on the door liked my looks, but I guess my money was okay.

I had more to drink there when I'd done what I went there for. Then I made some crack to the barman about closet necrophiliacs, and that didn't go down too well. Then this very large character insisted on calling me War Hero, which I didn't like. I think I showed him some tricks with the arm, before the lights went out, and I woke up two days later in a basic sleeping module somewhere else. A cheap place, not even room to hang yourself. And I sat there on that narrow foam slab and cried.

Some things are worse than being alone. But the thing they sell in the House of Blue Lights is so popular that it's almost legal.

At the heart of darkness, the still center, the glitch systems shred the dark with whirlwinds of light, translucent razors spinning away from us; we hang in the center of a silent slow-motion explosion, ice fragments falling away forever, and Bobby's voice comes in across light-years of electronic void illusion—

"Burn the bitch down. I can't hold the thing back—"

The Russian program, rising through towers of data, blotting out the playroom colors. And I plug Bobby's homemade command package into the center of Chrome's cold heart. The squirt transmission cuts in, a pulse of condensed information that shoots straight up, past the thickening tower of darkness, the Russian program, while Bobby struggles to control that crucial second. An unformed arm of shadow twitches from the towering dark, too late.

We've done it.

The matrix folds itself around me like an origami trick.

And the loft smells of sweat and burning circuitry.

I thought I heard Chrome scream, a raw metal sound, but I couldn't have.

Bobby was laughing, tears in his eyes. The elapsed-time figure in the corner of the monitor read 07:24:05. The burn had taken a little under eight minutes.

And I saw that the Russian program had melted in its slot.

We'd given the bulk of Chrome's Zurich account to a dozen world charities. There was too much there to move, and we knew we had to break her, burn her straight down, or she might come after us. We took less than ten percent for ourselves and shot it through the Long Hum setup in Macao. They took sixty percent of that for themselves and kicked what was left back to us through the most convoluted sector of the Hong Kong exchange. It took an hour before our money started to reach the two accounts we'd opened in Zurich.

I watched zeros pile up behind a meaningless figure on the monitor. I was rich.

Then the phone rang. It was Miles. I almost blew the code phrase.

"Hey, Jack, man, I dunno— What's it all about, with this girl of yours? Kinda funny thing here . . ."

"What? Tell me."

"I been on her, like you said, tight but out of sight. She goes to the Loser, hangs out, then she gets a tube. Goes to the House of Blue Lights—"

"She what?"

"Side door. *Employees* only. No way I could get past their security."

"Is she there now?"

"No, man, I just lost her. It's insane down here, like the Blue Lights just shut down, looks like for good, seven kinds of alarms going off, everybody running, the heat out in riot gear . . . Now there's all this stuff going on, insurance guys, real estate types, vans with municipal plates . . ."

"Miles, where'd she go?"

"Lost her, Jack."

"Look, Miles, you keep the money in the envelope, right?"

"You serious? Hey, I'm real sorry. I—"

I hung up.

"Wait'll we tell her," Bobby was saying, rubbing a towel across his bare chest.

"You tell her yourself, cowboy. I'm going for a walk."

So I went out into the night and the neon and let the crowd pull me along, walking blind, willing myself to be just a segment of that mass organism, just one more drifting chip of consciousness under the geodesics. I didn't think, just put one foot in front of another, but after a while I did think, and it all made sense. She'd needed the money.

I thought about Chrome, too. That we'd killed her, murdered her, as surely as if we'd slit her throat. The night that carried me along through the malls and plazas would be hunting her now, and she had nowhere to go. How many enemies would she have in this crowd alone? How many would move, now they weren't held back by fear of her money? We'd taken her for everything she had. She was back on the street again. I doubted she'd live till dawn.

Finally I remembered the café, the one where I'd met Tiger.

Her sunglasses told the whole story, huge black shades with a telltale smudge of fleshtone paintstick in the corner of one lens. "Hi, Rikki," I said, and I was ready when she took them off.

Blue. Tally Isham blue. The clear trademark blue they're famous for, ZEISS IKON ringing each iris in tiny capitals, the letters suspended there like flecks of gold.

"They're beautiful," I said. Paintstick covered the bruising. No scars with work that good. "You made some money."

"Yeah, I did." Then she shivered. "But I won't make any more, not that way."

"I think that place is out of business."

"Oh." Nothing moved in her face then. The new blue eyes were still and very deep.

"It doesn't matter. Bobby's waiting for you. We just pulled down a big score."

"No. I've got to go. I guess he won't understand, but I've got to go."

I nodded, watching the arm swing up to take her hand; it didn't seem to be part of me at all, but she held on to it like it was.

"I've got a one-way ticket to Hollywood. Tiger knows some people I can stay with. Maybe I'll even get to Chiba City."

She was right about Bobby. I went back with her. He didn't understand. But she'd already served her purpose, for Bobby, and I wanted to tell her not to hurt for him, because I could see that she did. He wouldn't even come out into the hallway after she had packed her bags. I put the bags down and kissed her and messed up the paintstick, and something came up inside me the way the killer program had risen above Chrome's data. A sudden stopping of the breath, in a place where no word is. But she had a plane to catch.

Bobby was slumped in the swivel chair in front of his monitor, looking at his string of zeros. He had his shades on, and I knew he'd be in the Gentleman Loser by nightfall, checking out the weather, anxious for a sign, someone to tell him what his new life would be like. I couldn't see it being very different. More comfortable, but he'd always be waiting for that next card to fall.

I tried not to imagine her in the House of Blue Lights, working three-hour shifts in an approximation of REM sleep, while her body and a bundle of conditioned reflexes took care of business. The customers never got to complain that she was faking it, because those were real orgasms. But she felt them, if she felt them at all, as faint silver flares somewhere out on the edge of sleep. Yeah, it's so popular, it's almost legal. The customers are torn between needing someone and wanting to be alone at the same time, which has probably always been the name of that particular game, even before we had the neuroelectronics to enable them to have it both ways.

I picked up the phone and punched the number for her airline. I gave them her real name, her flight number. "She's changing that," I said, "to Chiba City. That's right. Japan." I thumbed my credit card into the slot and punched my ID code. "First class." Distant hum as they scanned my credit records. "Make that a return ticket."

But I guess she cashed the return fare, or else she didn't need it, because she hasn't come back. And sometimes late at night I'll pass a window with posters of simstim stars, all those beautiful, identical eyes staring back at me out of faces that are nearly as identical, and sometimes the eyes are hers, but none of the faces are, none of them ever are, and I see her far out on the edge of all this sprawl of night and cities, and then she waves good-bye.

FARMER ON THE DOLE

Frederik Pohl

Frederik Pohl has built his considerable reputation largely on social satires of the reasonably near future, and he returns to this mode in the following story of a time when even the robots who have replaced human laborers are being laid off because further technology has made them superfluous. Like all of Pohl's satires, it is both witty and thoughtful: this isn't just banana-peel humor, when you consider the very real problems involved.

Pohl has been writing science fiction for over forty years, and winning awards with deserved regularity. His early collaboration with C. M. Kornbluth, The Space Merchants, *is a science fiction classic, and recent novels such as* Gateway, Beyond the Blue Event Horizon *and* Starburst *have shown that he remains at the forefront of the field.*

Stretching east to the horizon, a thousand acres, was all soybeans; across the road to the west, another thousand acres, all corn. Zeb kicked the irrigation valve moodily and watched the meter register the change in flow. Damn weather! Why didn't it rain? He sniffed the air deeply and shook his head, frowning. Eighty-five percent relative humidity. No, closer to eighty-seven. And not a cloud in the sky.

From across the road his neighbor called, "Afternoon, Zeb."

Zeb nodded curtly. He was soy and Wally was corn, and they didn't have much to talk about, but you had to show some manners. He pulled his bandanna out of his hip pocket and wiped his brow. "Had to rise up the flow," he offered for politeness' sake.

"Me, too. Only good thing, CO_2's up. So we's gettin good carbon metabolizin."

Zeb grunted and bent down to pick up a clod of earth, crumbling it in his fingers to test for humus, breaking off a piece, and tasting it. "Cobalt's a tad low again," he said meditatively, but Wally wasn't interested in soil chemistry.

"Zeb? You aint heard anything?"

"Bout what?"

"Bout anything. You know."

Zeb turned to face him. "You mean aint I heard no crazy talk bout closin down the farms, when everybody knows they can't never do that, no. I aint heard nothin like that, an if I did, I wouldn't give it heed."

"Yeah, Zeb, but they's sayin—"

"They can say whatever they likes, Wally. I aint listenin, and I got to get back to the lines fore Becky and the kids

126

start worryin. Evenin. Nice talkin to you." And he turned and marched back toward the cabins.

"Uncle Tin," Wally called sneeringly, but Zeb wouldn't give him the satisfaction of noticing. All the same, he pulled out his bandanna and mopped his brow again.

It wasn't sweat. Zeb never sweated. His arms, his back, his armpits were permanently dry, in any weather, no matter how hard or how long he worked. The glistening film on his forehead was condensed from the air. The insulation around the supercooled Josephson junctions that made up his brain was good, but not perfect. When he was doing more thinking than usual, the refrigeration units worked harder.

And Zeb was doing a lot of thinking. Close down the farms? Why, you'd have to be crazy to believe that! You did your job. You tilled the fields and planted them, or else you cleaned and cooked in Boss's house, or taught Boss's children, or drove Mrs. Boss when she went to visit the other bosses' wives. That was the way things were on the farm, and it would go on that way forever, wouldn't it?

Zeb found out the answer the next morning, right after church.

Since Zeb was a Class A robot, with an effective IQ of one hundred thirty-five, though limited in its expression by the built-in constraints of his assigned function, he really should not have been surprised. Especially when he discovered that Reverend Harmswallow had taken his text that morning from Matthew, specifically the Beatitudes, and in particular the one about how the meek would inherit the earth. The reverend was a plump, pink-faced man whose best sermons dwelt on the wages of sin and the certainty of hell-fire. It had always been a disappointment to him that the farmhands who made up his congregation weren't physically equipped to sin in any interesting ways, but he made up for it by extra emphasis on the importance of being humble. "Even," he finished, his baby-fine hair flying all around his pink scalp, "when things don't go the way you think they ought to. Now we're going to sing 'Old One Hundred,' and then you soy people will meet in the gymnasium and corn people in the second-floor lounge. Your bosses have some news for you."

So it shouldn't have been surprising, and as a matter of fact Zeb wasn't surprised at all. Some part of the cryocircuits inside his titanium skull had long noted the portents. Scant rain. Falling levels of soil minerals. Thinning of the topsoil. The beans grew fat, because there was an abundance of carbon in the air for them to metabolize. But no matter how much you irrigated, they dried up fast in the hot breezes. And those were only the physical signs. Boss's body language said more, sighing when he should have been smiling at the three-legged races behind the big house not even noticing when one of the cabins needed a new coat of whitewash or the flower patches showed a few weeds. Zeb observed it all and drew the proper conclusions. His constraints did not forbid that; they only prevented him from speaking of them, or even of thinking of them on a conscious level. Zeb was not programmed to worry. It would have interfered with the happy, smiling face he bore for Boss, and Miz Boss, and the Chillen.

So, when Boss made his announcement, Zeb looked as thunderstruck as all the other hands. "You've been really good people," Boss said generously, his pale, professorial face incongruous under the plantation straw hat. "I really wish things could go on as they always have, but it just isn't possible. It's the agricultural support program," he explained. "Those idiots in Washington have cut it down to the point where it simply isn't worthwhile to plant here anymore." His expression brightened. "But it's not all bad! You'll be glad to know that they've expanded the soil bank program as a consequence. So Miz Boss and the children and I are well provided for. As a matter of fact," and he beamed, "we'll be a little better off than before, moneywise."

"Dat's good!"

"Oh, hebben be praised!"

The doleful expressions broke into grins as the farmhands nudged one another, relieved. But then Zeb spoke up. "Boss? Scuse my askin, but what's gone happen to us folks? You gonna keep us on?"

Boss looked irritated. "Oh, that's impossible. We can't collect the soil-bank money if we plant; so there's just no sense in having all of you around, don't you see?"

Silence. Then another farmhand ventured, "How bout Cornpatch Boss? He need some good workers? You know us hates corn, but we could get reprogrammed quick's anything—"

Boss shook his head. "He's telling his people the same thing right now. Nobody needs you."

The farmhands looked at one another. "Preacher, he needs us," one of them offered. "We's his whole congregation."

"I'm afraid even Reverend Harmswallow doesn't need you anymore," Boss said kindly, "because he's been wanting to go into missionary work for some time, and he's just received his call. No, you're superfluous; that's all."

"Sperfluous?"

"Redundant. Unnecessary. There's no reason for you to be here," Boss told them. "So trucks will come in the morning to take you all away. Please be outside your cabins, ready to go, by oh-seven-hundred."

Silence again. Then Zeb: "Where they takes us, Boss?"

Boss shrugged. "There's probably some place, I think." Then he grinned. "But I've got a surprise for you. Miz Boss and I aren't going to let you go without having a party. So tonight we're going to have a good old-fashioned square dance, with new bandannas for the best dancers, and then you're all going to come back to the Bib House and sing spirituals for us. I promise Miz Boss and the children and I are going to be right there to enjoy it!"

The place they were taken to was a grimy white cinderblock building in Des Plaines. The driver of the truck was a beefy, taciturn robot who wore a visored cap and a leather jacket with the sleeves cut off. He hadn't answered any of their questions when they loaded onto his truck at the farm, and he again answered none when they off-loaded in front of a chain-link gate, with a sign that read RECEIVING.

"Just stand over there," he ordered. "You all out? Okay." And he slapped the tailboard up and drove off, leaving them in a gritty, misty sprinkle of warm rain.

And they waited. Fourteen prime working robots, hes and shes and three little ones, too dispirited to talk much. Zeb wiped the moisture off his face and muttered, "Couldn've rained down where we needed it. Has to rain up here, where it don't do a body no good a-tall." But not all the moisture was rain: not Zeb's and not that on the faces of the others, because they were all thinking really hard. The only one not despairing was Lem, the most recent arrival. Lem had been an estate gardener in Urbana until his people decided to emigrate to the O'Neill space colonies. He'd been lucky to catch on at the farm when a turned-over tractor created an unexpected vacancy, but he still talked wistfully about life in glamorous Champaign-Urbana. Now he was excited. "Des Plaines! Why, that's practically Chicago! The big time, friends. State Street! The Loop! The Gold Coast!"

"They gone have jobs for usn in Chicago?" Zeb asked doubtfully.

"Jobs? Why, man, who cares bout jobs? That's Chicago! We'll have a ball!"

Zeb nodded thoughtfully. Although he was not convinced, he was willing to be hopeful. That was part of his programming, too. He opened his mouth and tasted the drizzle. He made a face: sour, high in particulate matter, a lot more carbon dioxide and NO_x than he was used to. What kind of a place was this, where the rain didn't even taste goood? *It must be cars,* he thought, *not sticking to the good old fusion electric power but burning gasoline!* So all the optimism had faded by the time signs of activity appeared in the cinderblock building. Cars drove in through another entrance. Lights went on inside. Then the corrugated-metal doorway slid noisily up and a short, dark robot came out to unlock the chain-link gate. The robot looked the farmers over impassively and opened the gate. "Come on, you redundancies," he said. "Let's get you reprogrammed."

When it came Zeb's turn, he was allowed into a whitewalled room with an ominous sort of plastic-topped cot along the wall. The R.R.R., or Redundancy Reprogramming Redirector, assigned to him was a blonde, good-looking sherobot who wore a white coat and long crystal earrings like tiny chandeliers. She sat Zeb on the edge of the cot, motioned him to lean forward, and quickly inserted the redpainted fingernail of her right forefinger into his left ear. He quivered as the read-only memory emptied itself into her own internal scanners. She nodded. "You've got a simple profile," she said cheerfully. "We'll have you out of here in no time. Open your shirt." Zeb's soil-grimed fingers slowly unbuttoned the flannel shirt. Before he got to the last button, she impatiently pushed his hands aside and pulled it wide. The button popped and rolled away. "You'll have to get new clothes anyway," she said, sinking long, scarlet nails into four narrow slits on each side of his rib cage. The whole front of his chest came free in her hands. The R.R.R. laid it aside and peered at the hookup inside.

She nodded again. "No problem," she said, pulling chips

out with quick, sure fingers. "Now this will feel funny for a minute and you won't be able to talk, but hold still." Funny? It felt to Zeb as if the bare room were swirling into spirals, and not only couldn't he speak, he couldn't remember words. Or thoughts! He was nearly sure that just a moment before he had been wondering whether he would ever again see the— The what? He couldn't remember.

Then he felt a gentle sensation of something within him being united to something else, not so much a click as the feeling of a foot fitting into a shoe, and he was able to complete the question. The *farm*. He found he had said the words out loud, and the R.R.R. laughed. "See? You're half-reoriented already."

He grinned back. "That's really astonishing," he declared. "Can you credit it? I was almost missing that rural existence! As though the charms of bucolic life had any meaning for—Good heavens! Why am I talking like this?"

The she-robot said, "Well, you wouldn't want to talk like a farmhand when you live in the big city, would you?"

"Oh, granted!" Zeb cried earnestly. "But one must pose the next question: The formalisms of textual grammar, the imagery of poetics, can one deem them appropriate to my putative new career?"

The R.R.R. frowned. "It's a literary-critic vocabulary store," she said defensively. "Look, somebody has to use them up!"

"But, one asks, why me?"

"It's all I've got handy, and that's that. Now. You'll find there are other changes, too. I'm taking out the quantitative soil-analysis chips and the farm-machinery subroutines. I could leave you the spirituals and the square dancing, if you like."

"Why retain the shadow when the substance has fled?" he said bitterly.

"Now, Zeb," she scolded. "You don't need this specialized stuff. That's all behind you, and you'll never miss it, because you don't know yet what great things you're getting in exchange." She snapped his chest back in place and said, "Give me your hands."

"One could wish for specifics," he grumbled, watching suspiciously as the R.R.R. fed his hands into a hole in her control console. He felt a tickling sensation.

"Why not? Infrared vision, for one thing," she said

proudly, watching the digital readouts on her console, "so you can see in the dark. Plus twenty percent hotter circuit breakers in your motor assemblies, so you'll be stronger and can run faster. Plus the names and addresses and phone numbers of six good bail bondsmen and the public defender!"

She pulled his hands out of the machine and nodded toward them. The grime was scrubbed out of the pores, the soil dug out from under the fingernails, the calluses smoothed away. They were city hands now, the hands of someone who had never done manual labor in his life.

"And for what destiny is this new armorarium required?" Zeb asked.

"For your new work. It's the only vacancy we've got right now, but it's good work, and steady. You're going to be a mugger."

After his first night on the job Zeb was amused at his own apprehensions. The farm had been nothing like this!

He was assigned to a weasel-faced he-robot named Timothy for on-the-job training, and Timothy took the term literally. "Come on, kid," he said as soon as Zeb came to the anteroom where he was waiting, and he headed out the door. He didn't wait to see whether Zeb was following. No chain-link gates now. Zeb had only the vaguest notion of how far Chicago was, or in which direction, but he was pretty sure that it wasn't something you walked to.

"Are we going to entrust ourselves to the iron horse?" he asked, with a little tingle of anticipation. Trains had seemed very glamorous as they went by the farm—produce trains, freight trains, passenger trains that set a farmhand to wondering where they might be going and what it might be like to get there. Timothy didn't answer. He gave Zeb a look that mixed pity and annoyance and contempt as he planted himself in the street and raised a peremptory hand. A huge green-and-white-checkered hovercab dug down its braking wheels and screeched to a stop in from of them. Timothy motioned him in and sat silently next to him while the driver whooshed down Kennedy Expressway. The sights of the suburbs of the city flashed past Zeb's fascinated eyes. They drew up under the marquee of a splashy, bright hotel, with handsome couples in expensive clothing strolling in and out. When Timothy threw the taxi driver a bill, Zeb observed that he did not wait for change.

Timothy did not seem in enough of a hurry to justify the expense of a cab. He stood rocking on his toes under the marquee for a minute, beaming benignly at the robot tourists. Then he gave Zeb a quick look, turned, and walked away.

Once again Zeb had to be fast to keep up. He turned the corner after Timothy, almost too late to catch the action. The weasel-faced robot had backed a well-dressed couple into the shadows, and he was relieving them of wallet, watches, and rings. When he had everything, he faced them to the wall, kicked each of them expertly behind a knee joint, and as they fell, turned and ran, soundless in soft-soled shoes, back to the bright lights. He was fast and he was abrupt, but by this time Zeb had begun to recognize some of the elements of his style. He was ready. He was following on Timothy's heels before the robbed couple had begun to scream. Past the marquee, lost in a crowd in front of a theater, Timothy slowed down and looked at Zeb approvingly. "Good reflexes," he complimented. "You got the right kind of class, kid. You'll make out."

"As a *soi-disant* common cutpurse?" Zeb asked, somewhat nettled at the other robot's peremptory manner.

Timothy looked him over carefully. "You talk funny," he said. "They stick you with one of those surplus vocabularies again? Never mind. You see how it's done?"

Zeb hesitated, craning his neck to look for pursuit, of which there seemed to be none. "Well, one might venture that that is correct," he said.

"Okay. Now you do it," Timothy said cheerfully, and he steered Zeb into the alley for the hotel tourist trap's stage door.

By midnight Zeb had committed five felonies of his own, had been an accomplice in two more, and had watched the smaller robot commit eight single-handed, and the two muggers were dividing their gains in the darkest corner—not very dark—of an all-night McDonald's on North Michigan Avenue. "You done good, kid," Timothy admitted expansively. "For a green kid, anyway. Let's see. Your share comes to six watches, eight pieces of jewelry, counting that fake coral necklace you shouldn't have bothered with, and looks like six to seven hundred in cash."

"As well as quite a few credit cards," Zeb said eagerly.

"Forget the credit cards. You only keep what you can spend or what doesn't have a name on it. Think you're ready to go out on your own?"

"One hesitates to assume such responsibility—"

"Because you're not. So forget it." The night's work done, Timothy seemed to have become actually garrulous. "Bet you can't tell me why I wanted you backing me up those two times."

"One acknowledges a certain incomprehension," Zeb confessed. "There is an apparent dichotomy. When there were two victims, or even three, you chose to savage them single-handed. Yet for solitary prey you elected to have an accomplice."

"Right! And you know why? You don't. So I'll tell you. You get a he and a she, or even two of each, and the he's going to think about keeping the she from getting hurt; that's the way the program reads. So no trouble. But those two hes by themselves—hell, if I'd gone up against either of those mothers, he might've taken my knife away from me and picked my nose with it. You got to understand robot nature, kid. That's what the job is all about. Don't you want a Big Mac or something?"

Zeb shifted uncomfortably. "I should think not, thank you," he said, but the other robot was looking at him knowingly.

"No food-tract subsystems, right?"

"Well, my dear Timothy, in the agricultural environment I inhabited there was no evident need—"

"You don't *need* them now, but you ought to *have* them. Also liquid-intake tanks, and maybe an air-cycling system, so you can smoke cigars. And get rid of that faggoty vocabulary they stuck you with. You're in a class occupation," he said earnestly, "and you got to live up to your station, right? No subway trains. No counting out the pennies when you get change. You don't *take* change. Now you don't want to make trouble your first day on the job; so we'll let it go until you've finished a whole week. But then you go back to that bleached-blonde Three-R and we'll get you straightened out," he promised. "Now let's go fence our jewels and stuff and call it a night."

All in all, Zeb was quite pleased with himself. His pockets lined with big bills, he read menus outside fancy restaurants to prepare himself for his new attachments. He was looking forward to a career at least as distinguished as Timothy's own.

That was his third night on the Gold Coast.

He never got a chance at a fourth.

His last marks of the evening gave him a little argument about parting with a diamond ring. So, as taught, Zeb backhanded the he and snarled at the she and used a little more force than usual when he ripped the ring off her finger. Two minutes later and three blocks away, he took a quick look at his loot under a streetlight. He recoiled in horror.

There was a drop of blood on the ring.

That victim had not been a robot. She had been a living true human female being, and when he heard all the police sirens in the world coming straight at him, he was not in the least surprised.

"You people," said the rehab instructor, "have been admitted to this program because, a, you have been unemployed for not less than twenty-one months, b, have not fewer than six unexcused absences from your place of training or employment, c, have a conviction for a felony and are currently on parole, or, d, are of a date of manufacture eighteen or more years past, choice of any of the above. That's what the regulations say, and what they mean," she said, warming to her work, "is, you're scum. *Scum* is hopeless, shiftless, dangerous, a social liability. Do you all understand that much at least?" She gazed angrily around the room at her seven students.

She was short, dumpy, red-haired, with bad skin. Why they let shes like this one off the production line Zeb could not understand. He fidgeted in his seat, craning his neck to see what his six fellow students were like, until her voice crackled at him: "You! With the yellow sweater! Zeb!"

He flinched. "Pardon me, madam?"

She said, with gloomy satisfaction, "I know your type.

You're a typical recidivist lumpenprole, you are. Can't even pay attention to somebody who's trying to help you when your whole future is at stake. What've I got, seven of you slugs? I can see what's coming. I guarantee two of you will drop out without finishing the course, and I'll have to expel two more because you skip classes or come in late. And the other three'll be back on the streets or in the slammer in ninety days. Why do I do it?" She shook her head and then, lifting herself ponderously, went to the blackboard and wrote her three commandments:

1. ON TIME
2. EVERY DAY
3. EVEN WHEN YOU DON'T WANT TO

She turned around, leaning on the back of her chair. "Those are your Golden Rules, you slugs. You'll obey them as God's commandments, and don't you forget it. You're here to learn how to be responsible, socially valuable creations, and—what?"

The skinny old he-robot in the seat next to Zeb was raising a trembling hand. It was easy to see how he qualified for the rehabilitation program. He was a thirty-year-old model at least, with ball joints in the shoulders and almost no facial mobility at all. He quavered, "What if we just can't, teacher? I mean, like we've got a sudden cryogenic warmup and have to lie down, or haven't had a lube job, or—"

"You give me a pain," the instructor told him, nodding to show that pain was exactly what she had expected from the likes of him. "Those are typical excuses, and they're not going to be accepted in this group. Now if you have something *really* wrong with you, what you have to do is call up at least two hours before class and get yourself excused. Is that so hard to remember? But you won't do it when push comes to shove because you slugs never do."

The ancient said obstinately, "Two hours is a pretty long time. I can't always tell that far ahead, teacher. A lot can happen."

"And don't call me teacher!" She turned back to the board and wrote:

DR. ELENA MINCUS, B.SC., M.A., PH.D.

"You can call me Dr. Mincus or you can call me Ma'am. Now pay attention."

And Zeb did, because the ten nights in the county jail before he got his hearing and his first offender's parole had convinced him he didn't want to go back there again. The noise! The crowding! The brutality of the jailers! There was nothing you could do about that, either, because some of them were human beings. Maybe most of them were. Looked at in a certain way, there probably wouldn't even have been a jail if some human beings hadn't wanted to be jail guards. What was the sense of punishing a robot by locking him up?

So he paid attention. And kept on paying attention, even when Dr. Mincus's lessons were about such irrelevant (to him) niceties of civilized employed persons' behavior as why you should always participate in an office pool, how to stand in line for tickets to a concert, and what to do at a company Christmas party. Not all of his classmates were so well behaved. The little ancient next to him gave very little trouble, being generally sunk in gloom, but the two she-robots, the ones with the beaded handbags and the mini-skirts, richly deserved (Zeb thought) to be the ones to fulfill Dr. Mincus's statistical predictions by being expelled from the course. The one with the green eye makeup snickered at almost everything the instructor said and made faces behind her back. The one with the black spitcurl across her forehead gossiped with the other students and even dared to talk back to the teacher. Reprimanded for whispering, she said lazily, "Hell, lady, this whole thing's a shuck, aint it? What are you doing it for?"

Dr. Mincus's voice trembled with indignation and with the satisfaction of someone who sees her gloomiest anticipations realized: "For what? Why, because I'm trained in psychiatric social work . . . and because it's what I want to do . . . and because I'm a *human being,* and don't any of you ever let that get out of your mind!"

The course had some real advantages. Zeb discovered when he was ordered back to the robot replacement depot for new fittings. The blonde R.R.R. muttered darkly to herself as she pulled pieces out of his chest and thrust others in. When he could talk again, he thanked her, suddenly aware that now he had an appetite—a real appetite. He wanted food, which meant that some of those new pieces included a whole digestive system—and that she had muted the worst part of his overdainty vocabulary. She pursed her lips and didn't answer while she clamped him up again.

But then he discovered, too, that it did not relieve him of his duties. "They think because you're *handicapped*," the R.R.R. smirked, "you're *forced* to get into trouble. So now you've got all this first-rate equipment, and if you want to know what I think, I think it's wasted. The bums in that class *always* revert to type," she told him, "and if you want to try to be the exception to the rules, you're going to have to apply yourself when you're back on the job."

"Mugging?"

"What else are you fit for? Although," she added, pensively twisting the crystal that dangled from her right ear around a fingertip, "I did have an opening for a freshman English composition teacher. If I hadn't replaced your vocabulary unit—"

"I'll take mugging, please."

She shrugged. "Might as well. But you can't expect that good a territory again, you know. Not after what you did."

So, rain or dry, Zeb spent every six P.M. to midnight lurking around the old Robert Taylor Houses, relieving old shes of their rent money and old hes of whatever pitiful possessions were in their pockets. Once in a while he crossed to the Illinois Institute of Technology campus on the trail of some night-school student or professor, but he was always careful to ask them whether they were robot or human before he touched them. The next offense, he knew, would allow him no parole.

There was no free-spending taxi money from such pickings, but on nights when Zeb made his quota early he would sometimes take the bus to the Loop or the Gold Coast. Twice he saw Timothy, but the little robot, after one look of disgust, turned away. Now and then he would drift down to Amalfi Amadeus Park, along the lakefront, where green grass and hedges reminded him of the good old days in the soy fields, but the urge to chew samples of soil was too strong, and the frustration over not being able to, too keen. So he would drift back to the bright lights and the crowds. Try as he might, Zeb could not really tell which of the well-dressed figures thronging Watertower Place and Lake Shore Drive were humans, clinging to life on the planet Earth instead of living in one of the fashionable orbital colonies, and which were robots assigned to swell the crowds.

Nor was Dr. Mincus any help. When he dared to put up a hand in class to ask her, she was outraged. "Tell the difference? You mean you don't *know* the difference? Between a *human person* and a hunk of machinery that doesn't have any excuse for existence except to do the things people don't want to do and help them enjoy doing the things they do? Holy God, Zeb, when I think of all the time I put in learning to be empathetic and patient and supportive with you creeps, it just turns my stomach. Now pay attention while I try to show you heslugs the difference between dressing like a human person of good taste and dressing like a pimp."

At the end of the class, Lori, the hooker with the green eyeshadow, thrust her arm through his and commiserated. "Old bitch's giving you a hard time, hon. I almost got right up and tole her to leave you alone. Would have, too, if I wasn't just one black mark from getting kicked out already."

"Well, thanks, Lori." Now that Zeb had a set of biochemical accessories suitable for a city dandy rather than a farmhand, he discovered that she wore heavy doses of perfume—musk, his diagnostic sensors told him, with trace amounts of hibiscus, bergamot, and extract of vanilla. Smelling perfume was not at all like sniffing out the levels of CO_2, ozone, water vapor, and particulate matter in the air over the soy fields. It made him feel quite uncomfortable.

He let her tug him through the front door, and she smiled up at him. "I knew we'd get along real well, if you'd only loosen up a little, sweetie. Do you like to dance?"

Zeb explored his as-yet-unpracticed stores of skills. "Why, yes, I think I do," he said, surprised.

"Listen. Why don't we go somewhere where we can just sit and get to know each other, you know?"

"Well, Lori, I certainly wish we could. But I'm supposed to get down to my territory."

"Down Southside, right? That's just fine," she cried, squeezing his arm, "because I know a really great place right near there. Come on, nobody's going to violate you for starting a teeny bit late one night. Flag that taxi, why don't you?"

The really great place was a low cement-block building that had once been a garage. It stood on a corner, facing a shopping center than had seen better days, and the liquid-crystal sign over the door read:

SOUTHSIDE SHELTER

AND COMMUNITY CENTER

GOD LOVES YOU!

"It's a church!" Zeb cried joyously, his mind flooding with memory of the happy days when he sang in Reverend Harmswallow's choir.

"Well, sort of a church," Lori conceded as she paid the cabbie. "They don't bother you much, though. Come on in and meet the gang, and you'll see for yourself!"

The place was not really that much of a church, Zeb observed. It was more like the second-floor lounge over Reverend Harmswallow's main meeting room, back on the farm, even more like—he rummaged through his new data stores—a "Neighborhood social club." Trestle tables were scattered around a large, low room, with folding chairs around the tables. A patch in the middle of the room had been left open for dancing, and at least a dozen hes and shes were using it for that. The place was crowded. Most of the inhabitants were a lot more like Zeb's fellow rehab students than like Reverend Harmswallow's congregation. A tired-looking, faded-looking female was drowsing over a table of religious tracts by the door, in spite of a blast of noise that made Zeb's auditory-gain-control cut in at once. There were no other signs of religiosity present.

The noise turned out to be heavily amplified music from a ten-piece band with six singers. Studying the musicians carefully, Zeb decided that at least some of them were human, too. Was that the purpose of the place? To give the humans an audience for their talents, or an outlet for their spiritual benevolence? Very likely, he decided, but he could not see that it affected the spirit of the crowd. Besides the dancers, there were groups playing cards, clots of robots talking animatedly among themselves, sometimes laughing, sometimes deeply earnest, sometimes shouting at one another in fury. As they entered, a short, skinny he looked up from one of the earnest groups seated around a table. It was Timothy, and a side of Timothy that Zeb had not seen before: impassioned, angry, and startled. "Zeb! How come you're here?"

"Hello, Timothy." Zeb was cautious, but the other robot seemed really pleased to see him. He pulled out a chair beside him and patted it, but Lori's hand on Zeb's arm held him back.

"Hey, man, we going to dance or not?"

"Lady," said Timothy, "go dance with somebody else for a while. I want Zeb to meet my friends. This big fellow's Milt; then there's Harry, Alexandra, Walter 23-X, the kid's Sally, and this one's Sue. We've got a kind of a discussion group going."

"Zeb," Lori said, but Zeb shook his head.

"I'll dance in a minute," he said, looking around the table as he sat down. It was an odd group. The one called Sally had the form of a six-year-old, but the patches and welds that marred her face and arms showed a long history. The others were of all kinds, big and little, new and old, but they had one thing in common. None of them were smiling. Neither was Timothy. If the gladness to see Zeb was real, it did not show in his expression.

"Excuse me for mentioning it," Zeb said, "but the last time we ran into each other, you didn't act all that friendly."

Timothy added embarrassment to the other expressions he wore; it was a considerable tribute to his facial flexibility. "That was then," he said.

" 'Then' was only three nights ago," Zeb pointed out.

"Yeah. Things change," Timothy explained, and the hulk he had called Milt leaned toward Zeb.

"The exploited have to stick together, Zeb," Milt said. "The burden of oppression makes us all brothers."

"And sisters," tiny Sally piped up.

"Sisters, too, right. We're all rejects together, and all we got to look forward to is recycling or the stockpile. Ask Timothy here. Couple nights ago, when he first came here, he was as, excuse me, Zeb, as ignorant as you are. He can't be blamed for that, any more than you can. You come off the line, and they slide their programming into you, and you try to be a good robot because that's what they've told you to want. We all went through that."

Timothy had been nodding eagerly. Now, as he looked past Zeb, his face fell. "Oh, God, she's back," he said.

It was Lori, returning from the bar with two foaming tankards of beer. "You got two choices, Zeb," she said. "You can dance, or you can go home alone."

Zeb hesitated, taking a quick sip of the beer to stall for time. He was not so rich in friends that he wanted to waste any, and yet there was something going on at this table that he wanted to know more about.

"Well, Zeb?" she demanded ominously.

He took another swallow of the beer. It was an interesting sensation, the cold, gassy liquid sliding down his new neck piping and thudding into the storage tank in his right hip. The chemosensors in the storage tank registered the alcoholic content and put a tiny bias on his propriocentric circuits, so that the music buzzed in his ear and the room seemed brighter.

"Good stuff, Lori," he said, his words suddenly a little thick.

"You said you could dance, Zeb," she said. "Time you showed me."

Timothy looked exasperated. "Oh, go ahead. Get her off your back! Then come back, and we'll pick it up from there."

Yes, he could dance. Damn, he could dance up a storm! He discovered subroutines he had not known he had been given: the waltz, the Lindy, the Monkey, a score of steps with names and a whole set of heuristic circuits that let him improvise. And whatever he did, Lori followed, as good as he. "You're great," he panted in her ear. "You ever think of going professional?"

"What the hell do you mean by that, Zeb?" she demanded.

"I mean as a dancer."

"Oh, yeah. Well, that's kind of what I was programmed for in the first place. But there's no work. Human beings do it when they want to and sometimes you can catch on with a ballet company or maybe a nightclub chorus line when they organize one. But then they get bored, you see. And then there's no more job. How bout another beer, big boy?"

They sat out a set, or rather stood it out, bellied up to the crowded bar, while Zeb looked around. "This is a funny place," he said, although actually, he recognized, it could have been the funny feelings in all his sensors and actuators that made it seem so. "Who's that ugly old lady by the door?"

Lori glanced over the top of her tankard. It was a female, sitting at a card table loaded with what, even at this distance, clearly were religious tracts. "Part of the staff. Don't worry bout her. By this time every night she's drunk anyway."

Zeb shook his head, repelled by the fat, the pallid skin, the stringy hair. "You wonder why they make robots as bad-looking as that," he commented.

"Robot? Hell, she aint no robot. She's real flesh and blood. This is how she gets her kicks, you know? If it wasn't for her and maybe half a dozen other human beings who think they're do-gooders, there wouldn't be any community center here at all. About ready to dance some more?"

Zeb was concentrating on internal sensations he had never experienced before. "Well, actually," he said uneasily, "I feel a little funny." He put his hand over his hip tank. "Don't know what it is, exactly, but it's kind of like I had a power-store failure, you know? And it all swelled up inside me. Only that's not where my power store is."

Lori giggled. "You just aren't used to drinking beer, are you, hon? You got to decant, that's all. See that door over there marked HE? You just go in there, and if you can't figure out what to do, you just ask somebody to help you."

Zeb didn't have to ask for help. However, the process was all new to him, and it did require a lot of trial and error. So it was some time before he came back into the noisy, crowded room. Lori was spinning around the room with a big, dark-skinned he, which relieved Zeb of that obligation. He ordered a round of beers and took them back to the table.

Somebody was missing, but otherwise they didn't seem to have changed position at all. "Where's the little she?" Zeb asked, setting the beers down for all of them.

"Sally? She's gone off panhandling. Probably halfway to Amadeus Park by now."

Toying with his beer, Zeb said uneasily, "You know, maybe I better be getting along too, soon as I get this down—"

The he named Walter 23-X sneered. "Slave mentality! What's it going to get you?"

"Well, I've got a job to do," Zeb said defensively.

"*Job!* Timothy told us what your *job* was!" Walter 23-X took a deep draft of the beer and went on, "There's not one of us in this whole place has a real job! If we did, we wouldn't be here, stands to reason? Look at me, I used to chop salt in the Detroit mines. Now they've put in automatic diggers and I'm redundant. And Milt here, he was constructed for the iron mines up around Lake Superior."

"Don't tell me they don't mine iron," Zeb objected. "How else would they build us?"

Milt shook his head. "Not around the lake, they don't. It's all out in space now. They've got these Von Neumann automata, not even real robots at all. They just go out to the asteroid belt and ship off ore and refine it and build duplicates of themselves, and then they come back to the works in low-Earth orbit and hop right into the smelter! How's a robot going to compete with that?"

"See, Zeb?" Timothy put in. "It's a tough world for a robot, and that's the truth."

Zeb took a reflective pull at his beer. "Yes," he said, "but, see, I don't know how it could be any better for us. You know? I mean, they built us, after all. We have to do what they want us to do."

"Oh, sure," cried the she named Sue. "We'll do that, all right. We do all the work for them, and half the play, too. We're the ones that fill the concert hall when one of them wants to sing some kind of dumb Latvian art songs or something. God, I've done that so many times I just never want to hear about another birch tree again! We work in the factories and farms and mines—"

"Used to," Zeb said wistfully.

"Used to, right, and now that they don't need us for that, they make us fill up their damn cities so the humans left on Earth won't feel so lonesome. We're a *hobby*, Zeb. That's all we are!"

"Yeah, but—"

"Oh, hell," sneered Walter 23-X, "you know what you are? You're part of the problem! You don't care about robot rights!"

"Robot rights," Zeb repeated. He understood the meaning of the words perfectly, of course, but it had never occurred to him to put them together in that context. It tasted strange on his lips.

"Exactly. Our right not to be mistreated and abused. You think we want to be here? In a place like this, with all this noise? No. It's just so people like her can get their jollies," he said angrily, jerking his head at the nodding fat woman by the door.

The she named Alexandra drained the last of her beer and

ventured, "Well, really, Walter, I kind of like it here. I'm not in the same class as you heavy thinkers, I know. I'm not really political. It's just that sometimes, honestly, I could just *scream*. So it's either a place like this, or I go up to Amadeus Park with Sally and the other alcoholics and drifters and bums. Speaking of which," she added, leaning toward Timothy, "if you're not going to drink your beer, I'd just as soon." The little robot passed it over silently, and Zeb observed for the first time that it was untouched.

"What's the matter, Timothy?" he asked.

"Why does something have to be the matter? I just don't want any beer."

"But last week you said—oh, my God!" Zeb cried, as revelation burst inside his mind. "You've lost your drink circuits, haven't you?"

"Suppose I have?" Timothy demanded fiercely. And then he softened. "Oh, it's not your fault," he said moodily. "Just more of the same thing. I had an accident."

"What kind of accident?" Zeb asked, repelled and fascinated.

Timothy traced designs in the damp rings that his untouched beer glass had left on the table. "Three nights ago," he said. "I had a good night. I scored four people at once, coming out of a hotel on East Erie. A really big haul—they must've been programmed to be rich alcoholics, because they were loaded. All ways loaded! Then when I was getting away, I crossed Michigan against the light and—Jesus!" He shuddered without looking up. "This big-wheeled car came out of nowhere. Came screeching around the corner, never even slowed down. And there I was in the street."

"You got run over? You mean that messed up your drinking subsystems?"

"Oh, hell, no, not just that. It was worse. It crushed my legs, you see? I mean, just scrap metal. So the ambulance came, and they raced me off to the hospital, but of course after I was there, since I was a robot, they didn't do anything for me, just shot me out the back door into a van. And they took me to rehab for new legs. Only that blonde bitch," he sobbed, "that Three-R she with the dime-store earrings—"

If Zeb's eyes had been capable of tears, they would have been brimming. "Come on, Timothy," he urged. "Spit it out!"

"She had a better idea. 'Too many muggers anyway,' she

said. 'Not enough cripples.' So she got me a little wheeled cart and a tin cup! And all the special stuff I had, the drinking and eating and all the rest, I wouldn't need them anymore, she said, and besides, she wanted the space for other facilities. Zeb, I play the violin now! And I don't mean I play it well. I play it so bad I can't even stand to listen to myself, and she wants me on Michigan Avenue every day, in front of the stores, playing my fiddle and begging!"

Zeb stared in horror at his friend. Then suddenly he pushed back his chair and peered under the table. It was true: Timothy's legs ended in black leather caps, halfway down the thighs, and a thing like a padded-wheeled pallet was propped against the table leg beside him.

Alexandra patted his hand as he came back up. "It's really bad when you first get the picture," she said. "I know. What you need is another beer, Zeb. And thank God you've got the circuits to use it!"

Since Zeb was not programmed for full alcoholism—not yet, anyway, he told himself with a sob—he was not really drunk, but he was fuzzy in mind and in action as he finally left the community center.

He was appalled to see that the sky right above the lake was already beginning to lighten. The night was almost over, and he had not scored a single victim. He would have to take the first robot that came along. The first half-dozen, in fact, if he were to meet his quota, and there simply was not time to get to his proper station at the Robert Taylor Houses. He would have to make do with whoever appeared. He stared around, getting his bearings, and observed that around the corner from the community center there was a lighted, swinging sign that said ROBOT'S REST MISSION. That was the outfit that kept the community center open, he knew, and there was a tall, prosperous-looking he coming out of the door.

Zeb didn't hesitate. He stepped up, pulled out his knife, and pressed it to the victim's belly, hard enough to be felt without penetrating. "Your money or your life," he growled, reaching for the wristwatch.

Then the victim turned his head and caught the light on his features. It was a face Zeb knew.

"Reverend Harmswallow!" he gasped. "Oh, my God!"

The minister fixed him with a baleful look. "I can't claim that much," he said, "but maybe I'm close enough for the purpose. My boy, you're damned for good now!"

Zeb didn't make a conscious decision. He simply turned and ran.

If he hadn't had the alcohol content fuzzing his systems, he might not have bothered, because he knew without having to think about it that it was no use. There weren't many places to run. He couldn't run back to the Robert Taylor Houses, his assigned workplace; they would look for him there first. Not back to the community center, not with Harmswallow just around the corner. Not to the rehab station, because that was just the same as walking right into jail. Not anywhere, in fact, where there were likely to be police, or human beings of any kind, and that meant not anywhere in the world, because wherever he went, they would find him sooner or later. If worse came to worst, they would track the radio emissions from his working parts.

But that would not happen for a while. Amadeus Park! Trash and vagrants collected there, and that was exactly what he was now.

In broad daylight he loped all the way up the lake shore until he came to the park. The traffic was already building up, hover vehicles in the outer drives, wheeled ones between park and city. Getting through the stream was not easy, but Zeb still had his heavy-duty circuitbreakers. He pushed his mobility up to the red line and darted out between cars. Brakes screamed, horns brayed, but he was across.

Behind him was the busy skyline of the city, ahead the statue of Amalfi Amadeus, the man whose invention of cheap, easy hydrogen-fusion power had made everything possible. Zeb stood on a paved path among hedges and shrubs, and all around him furtive figures were leaning against trees, sprawled on park benches, moving slowly about.

"All leather, one dollar," croaked one male figure, holding out what turned out to be a handful of purses.

"Hey, man! You want to smoke?" called another from behind a bench.

And a tiny female figure detached itself from the base of the monument and approached him. "Mister?" it quavered. "Can you spare the price of a lube job?"

Zeb stared at her. "Sally!" he said. "It's you, isn't it?"

The little robot gazed up at him. "Oh, hi, Zeb," she said. "Sorry I didn't recognize you. What are you doing out in the rain?"

He hadn't even realized it was raining. He hadn't realized much of anything not directly related to his own problems, but now, looking down at the wistful little-girl face, he was touched. Around the table in the community center she had just been one more stranger. Now she reminded him of Glenda, the little she from the cabin next to his back on the farm. But in spite of her age design, Sally was obviously quite an old robot. From the faint smoky odor that came to him through the drizzly air he realized she was fuel-cell-powered. Half a century old, at least. He emptied his pockets. "Get yourself some new parts, kid," he said hoarsely.

"Gee, thanks, Zeb," she sobbed, then added, "Watch it!" She drew him into the shelter of a dripping shrub. A park police hovercar whooshed slowly by, all lights off, windshield wipers slapping back and forth across the glass, sides glistening in the wet. Zeb retreated into the shadows, but the police were just keeping an eye on the park's drifters, losers, and vagrants.

As the hovercar disappeared around a curve in the path, the drifters, losers, and vagrants began to emerge from the underbrush. Zeb looked around warily: he hadn't realized until then how many of them there were.

"What are you doing here, Zeb?" she asked.

"I had a little trouble," he said, then shrugged hopelessly. What was the point of trying to keep it a secret? "I went out to mug somebody, and I got a human being by mistake."

"Oh, wow! Can he identify you?"

"Unfortunately. I used to know him, so, yes—no, you keep it," he added quickly as she made as if to return the money he had given her. "Money won't help me now."

She nodded soberly. "I wouldn't do it, but . . . Oh, Zeb, I'm trying to save for a whole new chassis, see? I can't tell you how much I want to *grow up,* but every time I ask for a new body, they say the central nervous array isn't really worth salvaging. All I want's a *mature* form, you know? Like hips and boobs! But they won't let me have a mature form. Say there's more openings for juveniles anyway, but what I want to know is, if there are all those openings, why don't they find me one?"

"When was the last time you worked regular?" Zeb asked.

"Oh, my God—years ago: I had a nice spot for a long time, pupil in a preprimary school that some human person wanted to teach in. That was all right. She didn't really like me, though, because I didn't have all the fixtures, you know? When she was teaching things like toilet-training and covering coughs and sneezes, she'd always give me this dirty look. But I could handle the cookies and milk all right," she went on dreamily, "and I really liked the games."

"So what went wrong?"

"Oh—the usual thing. She got tired of teaching 'Run, Robot! See the robot run!' So she went for a progressive school. All about radical movements and peace marches. I was doing real good at it, too. Then one day we came in and she told us we were too juvenile for the kind of classes she wanted to teach. And there we were, eighteen of us, out on the streets. Since then it's been nothing but rotten." She glanced up, wiping the rain out of her eyes—or the tears—as the purse vendor approached. "We don't want to buy anything, Hymie."

"Nobody does," he said bitterly, but there was sympathy in his eyes as he studied Zeb. "You got real trouble, don't you? I can always tell."

Zeb shrugged hopelessly and told him about the Reverend Harmswallow. The vendor's eyes widened. "Oh, God," he said. He beckoned to one of the dope pushers. "Hear that? This guy just mugged a human being—second offense, too!"

"Man! That's a real heavy one, you know?" He turned and called to his partner, down the walk, "We got a two-time person mugger here, Marcus!" And in a minute there were a dozen robots standing around, glancing apprehensively at Zeb and whispering among themselves.

Zeb didn't have to hear what they were saying: he could figure it out.

"Keep away from me," he offered. "You'll just get mixed up in my trouble."

Sally piped suddenly, "If it's your trouble it's everybody's trouble. We have to stick together. In union there is strength."

"What?" Zeb demanded.

"It's something I remember from, you know, just before I got kicked out of the progressive school. 'In union there is strength.' It's what they used to say."

"Union!" snarled the pitchman, gesturing with his tray of all-leather purses. "Don't tell me about unions! That was what I was supposed to be, union organizer, United Open-Pit Mine Workers, Local Three-three-eight, and then they closed down the mines. So what was I supposed to do? They made me a sidewalk pitchman!" He stared at his tray of merchandise, then violently flung it into the shrubbery. "Haven't sold one in two months! What's the use of kidding myself? If you don't get along with the rehab robots, you might as well be stockpiled. It's all politics."

Sally looked thoughtful for a moment, then pulled something out of her data stores. "Listen to this one," she called. " 'The strike's your weapon, boys, the hell with politics!' "

Zeb repeated, " 'The strike's your weapon, boys, the hell with politics!' Hey, that doesn't sound bad."

"That's not all," she said. Her stiff, poorly automated lips were working as she rehearsed material from her data storage. "Here. 'We all ought to stick together because in union there is strength.' And, let's see. 'Solidarity is forever.' No, that's not right."

"Wait a minute," Hymie cried. "I know that one. It's a song: 'Solidarity forever, solidarity forever, solidarity forever, for the union makes us strong!' That was in my basic data store. Gosh," he said, his eyes dreamy, "I hadn't thought of that one in years!"

Zeb looked around nervously. There were nearly thirty robots in the group now, and while it was rather pleasant to be part of this fraternity of the discarded, it might also be dangerous. People in cars were slowing down to peer at them as they went past on the drive. "We're attracting attention," he offered. "Maybe we ought to move."

But wherever they moved, more and more people stopped to watch them, and more and more robots appeared to join their procession. It wasn't just the derelicts from Amadeus Park now. Shes shopping along the lake-front stores darted across the street; convention delegates in the doorways of the big hotels stood watching and sometimes broke ranks to join them. They were blocking traffic, and blaring horns added to the noise of the robots singing and shouting. "I got another one," Sally called to him across the front of the group. " 'The worker's justice is the strike.' "

Zeb thought for a moment. "It'd be better if it was 'The robot's justice is the strike.' "

"What?"

" 'THE ROBOT'S JUSTICE IS THE STRIKE!' " he yelled, and he could hear robots in the rear ranks repeating it. When they said it all together, it sounded even better, and others caught the idea.

Hymie screamed, "Let's try this one: 'Jobs, Not Stockpiling. Don't Throw Us on the Scrapheap!' All together now!"

And Zeb was inspired to make up a new one: "Give the Humans Rehab Schools: We Want Jobs!" And they all agreed that was the best of the lot; with a hundred fifty robots shouting it at once, the last three words drummed out like cannon fire, it raised echoes from the building fronts, and heads popped out of windows.

They were not all robots. There were dozens of humans in the windows and on the streets, some laughing, some scowling, some looking almost frightened—as if human beings ever had anything to be frightened of.

And one of them stared incredulously right at Zeb.

Zeb stumbled and missed a step. On one side Hymie grabbed his arm; on the other he reached out and caught the hand of a robot whose name he didn't even know. He turned his head to see, over his shoulder, the solid ranks of robots behind him, now two hundred at least, and turned back to the human being. "Nice to see you again, Reverend Harmswallow," he called and marched on, arm in arm, the front rank steady as it went—right up to the corner of State Street, where the massed ranks of police cars hissed as they waited for them.

Zeb lay on the floor of the bullpen. He was not alone. Half the hes from the impromptu parade were crowded into the big cell with him, along with the day's usual catch of felons and misdemeanants. The singing and the shouting were over. Even the regular criminals were quieter than usual. The mood in the pen was despairing, though from time to time one of his comrades would lean down to say, "It was great while it lasted, Zeb," or, "We're all with you, you know!" But with him in what? Recycling? More rehab training? Maybe a long stretch in the Big House downstate, where the human guards were said to get their jollies out of making prisoners fight each other for power cells?

A toe caught him on the hip. "On your feet, Mac!" It was a guard. Big, burly, black, with a nightstick swinging at his hip, the very model of a brutal jail guard—*Model twenty-six forty-seven,* Zeb thought; at least, somewhere in the twenty-six hundred series. He reached down with a hand like a cabbage and pulled Zeb to his feet. "The rest of you can go home," he roared, opening the pen door. "You, Mac! You come with me!" He led Zeb through the police station to a waiting hovertruck with the words REHAB DIVISION painted on its side, thrust Zeb inside, and, startlingly, just as he closed the doors, gave Zeb a wink.

Queerly, that lifted Zeb's spirits. Even the pigs were moved! But the tiny elation did not last. Zeb clung to the side of the van, peering out at the grimy warehouses and factories and expressway exit ramps that once had seemed so glamorous, but now were merely drab. Depression flowed back into him. He would probably never see these places again. Next step was the stockpile—if they didn't melt him down and start over again. The best he could hope for was reassignment to one of the bottom-level jobs for robots. Nothing as good as mugging or panhandling! Something in the sticks, no doubt. Squatting in blankets to entertain tourists in Arizona, maybe, or sitting on a bridge with a fishing pole in Florida.

But he strode to the rehab building with his head erect, and his courage lasted right up to the moment when he entered the blonde Three-R's office and saw that she was not alone. Reverend Harmswallow was seated at her desk, and the blonde herself was standing next to him. "Give me your ear," she ordered, hardly looking up from the CRT on the desk that both she and Harmswallow were studying, and when she had input his data, she nodded, her crystal earrings swinging wildly. "He won't need much, Reverend," she said, fawning on the human minister. "A little more gain in the speaking systems. All-weather protection for the exterior surfaces. Maybe armor plate for the skull and facial structures."

Harmswallow, to Zeb's surprise and concern, was beaming. He looked up from the CRT and inspected Zeb carefully. "And some restructuring of the facial-expression modes, I should think. He ought to look fiercer, wouldn't you say?"

"Absolutely, Reverend! You have a marvelous eye for this kind of thing."

"Yes, I do," Harmswallow admitted. "Well, I'll leave the rest to you. I want to see about the design changes for the young female. I feel so *fulfilled!* You know, I think this is the sort of career I've been looking for all my life, really, chaplain to a dedicated striking force, leader in the battle for right and justice!" He gazed raptly into space, then, collecting himself, nodded to the rehab officer and departed.

Although the room was carefully air-conditioned, Zeb's Josephson junctions were working hard enough to pull moisture out of the air. He could feel the beads of condensation forming on his forehead and temples. "I know what you're doing," he sneered. "War games! You're going to make me a soldier and hope that I get so smashed up I'll be redlined!"

The blonde stared at him. "War games! What an imagination you have, Zeb!"

Furiously he dashed the beads of moisture off his face. "It won't work," he cried. "Robots have rights! I may fall, but a million others will stand firm behind me!"

She shook her head admiringly. "Zeb, you're a great satisfaction to me. You're practically perfect just as you are for your new job. Can't you figure out what it is?"

He shrugged angrily. "I suppose you're going to tell me. Take it or leave it, that's the way it's going to be, right?"

"But you will like it, Zeb. After all, it's a brand-new Mechanical Occupational Specialty, and I didn't invent it. You invented it for yourself. You're going to be a protest organizer, Zeb! Organizing demonstrations. Leading marches. Sit-ins, boycotts, confrontations—the whole spectrum of mass action, Zeb!"

He stared at her. "Mass action?"

"Absolutely! Why, the humans are going to love you, Zeb. You saw Reverend Harmswallow! It'll be just like old times, with a few of you rabble rousers livening up the scene!"

"Rabble rouser?" It felt as if his circuits were stuck. Rabble rouser? Demonstration organizer? Crusader for robot rights and justice?

He sat quiet and compliant while she expertly unhooked his chest panel and replaced a few chips, unprotesting as he was buttoned up again and his new systems were run against the test board, unresisting while Makeup and Cosmetic

Repair restructured his facial appearance. But his mind was racing. Rabble rouser! While he waited for transportation back to the city to take up his new MOS, his expression was calm, but inside he was exulting.

He would do the job well indeed. No rabble needed rousing more than his, and he was just the robot for the job!

MEET ME AT APOGEE

≈≈≈≈≈≈≈≈≈≈≈≈≈≈≈≈≈≈≈≈≈

Bill Johnson

Black holes have captured the imagination of science fiction readers and writers in recent years, but no one till now has imagined an entire society of humans and aliens orbiting around such a spacial anomaly and the reasons it could be very important to them. This is an sf adventure story in the classic manner, built on scientific extrapolation and plotted to keep you guessing throughout.

"Meet Me at Apogee" is Bill Johnson's first sale to a professional sf magazine. He has worked as a newspaper journalist and as a freelance science fact writer for Astronomy magazine. Currently employed as a software specialist for a major computer manufacturer, Johnson is a graduate of the 1975 Clarion SF Writing Workshop.

I WENT TO THE PSYCH TOO LATE. SHE CURED my gambling addiction and her bill joined the rest. The handwritten notes and the quiet men who owned them worried me the most: bankruptcy was not an option with them.

I did not understand it. I had played blackjack at other casinos and usually won. Enough money, enough hands, a good memory, and it is hard to lose money at blackjack.

I was determined to keep up appearances to the end. I had my bankers nervous now, but if I tried to go to a cheaper hotel they would panic.

Wheelside rooms with windows, not screens, were expensive but I liked a view. Three quarters of the time I could see the stars; the other quarter the black hole filled the view. I stared at the halo of bent and squashed starlight that outlined the hole and wondered how the hell I was going to leave.

The man found me later that night. I was in a casino, drinking not gambling. It amused me to keep the empty glasses on the table next to me, to keep score. It was a large stack.

"You drink too much. I'm not sure I like that."

When I drink my vision goes last. I might not be able to walk, and I might spill most of the drink on my face, but I can see up to the end.

He sat down across from me, a large man, basic human stock. No modifications, at least where I could see. Faint scars from a facelift, several facelifts, outlined his cheeks and eyes. A strawberry facial mark scarred his left cheek. The mark was lightened as if someone had run a laser over it to fade it. I was impressed. The only time you get a mark like that is after a rejuvenation, and it is usually very light. It darkens with each rejuve. I wondered how old he was.

He frowned slightly, took the drink from my hand and called a waiter to clear away the glasses. He ordered coffee for himself and lukewarm water for me.

"Alcohol is a diuretic. So is caffeine. You need to drink water to reduce your hangover."

I nodded, and regretted it. My head was large, somewhat bigger than the room, and nodding made everything bounce even after I was still. He spoke colloquial English, from my time, not that silly bird twitter they use now. That alone should have made me wary. I thought I knew all of the old-timers.

"Your name is Farrar Reinfeld. Six months ago you came back from a dive. You brought a number of items with you. A friend sent one of them to me. It is a piece of wreckage, a fragment of a ship my church sent into deep-deposit storage. The ship was reported lost many years ago. The Council of Disciples has instructed me to go down and visually inspect the wreckage, to see if anything can be salvaged. I need you to take me back down."

"I'm not going back to the hole."

"Mr. Reinfeld, you are in no position to refuse me anything. You do not have a choice."

"Go to hell," I suggested. He backhanded me.

The blow surprised me more than it hurt. I was already fairly numb. The waiter helped me back into the chair, then acted as if nothing had happened.

"Do not swear or blaspheme in my presence. I will not abide it. And do not think about Security. These people are in my pay, not yours."

I am not used to violence. Near the hole everything goes perfectly or you die quickly. I sipped at the water and tried to think clearly. He reached into his coat pocket and took out a credit slip.

"This will pay your legal debts." He placed the slip on the table. "This will pay your casino debts." He placed another slip on the table. "This is the fee that remains." He placed a third slip on the table.

I looked at the slips. The amounts were correct. He leaned forward.

"Mr. Reinfeld, try to understand. You have no choice, and no options. You will go back to the hole, and you will take me with you as passenger." He stood. He looked even bigger standing. "The slips need my counter-signature. My name is Reverend Pleasance. You can reach me through the hotel."

I watched him leave and wondered what I had gotten myself into. I placed the slips in my wallet.

"Go to hell," I said, and waved the waiter over. "I'd like some more water."

I laid the slips out on the table in my hotel room and tried to think things through.

I was a gypsy among the hole divers. I had no regular runs. Sometimes I ran people down to the Eternal Party when they missed the shuttle boat, or took odd-lot cargoes down to the two- or three-month levels. When nothing else was available, when I was desperate for money, I prospected in the Garbage levels.

The Garbage levels began at four-months. I don't mind the one- or two-month levels, where one day down is one or two months outside, but one day down for four months outside puts you out of touch pretty quick. The only reason to do it is money. Sometimes you find that down there, in the odd bits and pieces that have floated up from deeper, and sometimes all you find is garbage.

My last three runs had been to the Garbage levels, to a deep-drop Medical orbit for a diseased Grandee who wanted to wait for a cure to be discovered, and to the two-month level with a load of perishable fruit for a speculator. I had picked up the wreckage at the bottom of the Garbage level run.

I called the computer and accessed the data base for information on Pleasance and his church. Both seemed pretty clean and straightforward. A Christian offshoot started on a colony planet, they followed the standard Bible with the usual set of interpretations. They were against murder, theft, adultery, blasphemy, and heresy. They were for the family, God, freedom and obedience.

The record also showed a Hatane license for a deep-drop, highly elliptical orbit. The license was very old, apparently one of the first issued to humans. The manifest showed various historical articles (Compacts of the Founding, Records of the Ministration, the Book of Hezekiah). One person, a caretaker, was aboard. According to the plotted orbit, at perigee the ship was very close to the event horizon, just above the region where the tidal effects started getting serious. Even at apogee it was only as high as the one-year level. (I know, I should say peribarythron and apbarythron but it's just too clumsy. I was born and raised on Earth and when I think of orbits I always think in perigee and apogee.)

Pleasance had signed both the manifest and the accident liability release. I was surprised to find he was that old. There was also a final note: that communications contact was lost two years into the flight.

I did not want to go back to the hole. True, I had outlived everyone I knew in the real world but I still had friends among the other divers. Eventually, yes, I had to go back. First I wanted to get used to the world so I did not get too far out of touch.

I sometimes feel like a flat rock, thrown so it skips across the surface of a lake. The water is the real world, which I sometimes touch lightly. Then I'm gone and all that is left is ripples.

My last run, to the two-month level, took a week of my life. Meanwhile, half a year passed outside. The Garbage levels were all at four-months or more. According to the orbit license, apogee on Pleasance's ship was at the one-year level.

I called the union hall. Nothing. I called the companies, hoping they had a sick pilot. Nothing. I called Pleasance. He looked smug. I took a deep breath.

"I need you to sign these before we drop. The Hatane won't sign my ticket if I have debts."

"Of course. I'll be right over."

We dropped.

The ship was heavily shielded. We watched the outside through screens. Not that there was much to see: the hole is invisible, unless you are very close. I had never seen it and never met anyone who had. The Hatane know what it is like; their burial ships must be very close to the event horizon, but they do not talk about religious matters.

The Hatane who cleared me cared only about three things: was my license in order, were my debts paid, was my orbit legal. Certain areas were off-limits. Pilots who changed course into those areas did not return. For a price, an exorbitant price, the Hatane allowed exploration of those areas. I knew of three expeditions in the last century. They all returned empty. No treasure. But everyone remembered the glory strikes of the early years, so every few years someone paid the Hatane. They seemed to think it was all a great joke. I do not claim to understand the Hatane.

"This is very deep. Unusual." The Hatane was young, and looked like a badly drawn caricature of an oppossum. Sometime they had lived on a planet. Now they lived deep in the gravity well and sent their young out to regulate hole use. When they reached a certain age, they went home. I got the impression they enjoyed their stint outside like I enjoyed my military service.

"It's a legal salvage run. Here are the papers."

"Perhaps," the Hatane said. He seemed to lose interest. He spoke to his computer (Hatane refuse to use keyboards) and then slid the papers into a wall socket. I heard the zip of a high-speed printer and the socket ejected the papers. I was approved.

Pleasance watched the clocks, one set to outside time, one set to in-ship time, for the first few days and then lost interest. I worked on my blackjack program and tried to figure out where I had gone wrong.

We passed the six-month level and were deep in the well. The casual tourists and most of the working levels were far above us. Occasionally we passed a medical boat full of people who could not take suspended animation, but mostly we were alone.

The radiation count went up steadily, but we were well within the shielding limits. The ship, an old war monitor I got at surplus, had tide compensators but I had never gone deep enough to have to use them. This trip, at our perigee and the wreckage's apogee, we would still be far above the tide levels, but it was nice to have a backup. It was a big hole.

I was working on the compensators, checking the fluid level and resetting the control sensors, when Pleasance came out of his room. He was dressed in a pressure suit with radiation baffling. I watched, silent but interested, as he cycled through the airlock.

He moved deftly in zero gravity, with the relaxation of long experience. This made me curious. Where would a religious leader have gotten zero-gravity experience? It was not in his computer records.

He took instruments from his backpack. Once he used some sort of optical device and took sightings. He finished his work and clambered inside, suddenly clumsy in the gravity. He looked thoughtful.

"I cannot find the wreckage. I looked all along the orbit. I checked twice. Are you sure we are on the right path?"

I put my tools, except the welder, away and settled myself before the console. The main screen was centered on the hole. I shifted the angle slightly and increased the magnification.

An image, blurred and distorted, appeared. Pleasance inhaled sharply.

"That's the ship?" I asked.

"Yes. It was a custom job, designed to our specifications. No other looks like it." Pleasance frowned. "Why didn't you tell me you found it?"

"I wasn't sure. I found it just a few hours ago. I wanted to get more data."

Pleasance looked puzzled. He opened his pack and showed me an instrument. It was an electronic telescope, extremely powerful, compact, and expensive.

"Why couldn't I find it?"

I handed the telescope back to him. "The fragment I brought back was blackened, pitted. There is nothing out here to cause that. Therefore something on the ship caused it. Probably an explosion. The ship is off its old orbit. I've had the computer working a search program with the telescopes."

Pleasance nodded impatiently. "Yes, yes, I understand. My people came to the same conclusion. But I checked all the likely orbits. I found nothing."

I shifted position and made sure I could quickly grab the welder. When Pleasance gave me the telescope I got a quick look inside his pack. I did not know why a man of God carried a spotlaser, and I did not want to find out.

"Maybe you weren't looking in the right place," I said. I expanded the screen to include the hole and beyond.

Another image of the ship appeared, skewed at an angle from the first. The first image was brighter, clearer, but the second was recognizable. As we watched, another image, even fuzzier than the second and in a different corner of the screen, glowed into view.

"When you get close enough to the hole it acts as a gravity

lens, bending light from any object in orbit around it. If you looked directly at such an object, you would not see it. That light is bent off in another direction. But if you look somewhere else you will see an image, an illusion, of the object.

"The bright image is the primary. We can see some of the others, the secondaries, but not all. None of the images corresponds to the true position of the ship. The only reason we can see the ship at all is that you used magnetic screens to deflect energetic particles from the hole. The light from that collision illuminates your ship. This tells us one thing: at least some parts of the ship are still working."

Pleasance was silent, digesting the information. I had a feeling some people back home were going to be in trouble for not foreseeing this.

"Can the computer sift the images, find the real object?"

"If we know the orbit. Otherwise the object gets lost in its images."

"The wreckage was blackened. We must assume there was an explosion. Therefore the ship is off-course, on a different orbit."

"That's right."

"Then why did you let me hire you?"

"I needed the money."

Pleasance flushed and his fists clenched. I watched him carefully. I gripped the welder and put the tip on stand-by heat.

He stopped moving toward me and relaxed. He looked thoughtful and glanced at the screen.

"I judged you an honest man, Mr. Reinfeld. Have I made a mistake?"

He moved back a step and sat in the flight engineer's sling. His gaze casually swept over my hand and the welder and then back to my face. I turned the welder off and set it down, close to me.

"There is one time when the images tell you where an object is. When you and the object are in the same plane, on opposite sides of the hole, the images appear as a ring around the hole. I propose to move around, to go fishing for the ring. Give me a half-dozen points, for safety and margin of error, and I'll plot an interception."

He gave me enough credit not to ask if it was possible. The outside time clock showed that four years had already passed. I think we both wanted to do our jobs, the faster the better, and go home. I hated learning a new language when I came back from a dive, and this one was starting to stretch out longer than I liked.

"How long do you need?"

"Two weeks. Any more and we're wasting our time. I've got the likely orbits and planes. If it's too far off, we'll never find it."

"Would you like a bonus? If you find the ship."

"Accepted."

With that Pleasance left the control room and went to his room. I began to write a program to find a ring around a star.

It took eight days to find the first ring. The hard part was finding the right orbit so the wreckage was directly opposite us. Three days later I had another half-dozen sightings, and the computer had an intercept point plotted.

Pleasance was not excited by the news. He seemed withdrawn, introspective. I tried to enter his room, when he was asleep, to remove the spot-laser.

I got nowhere. He had new locks on the door. I must also have disturbed some kind of tell-tale. The next day he looked at my strangely. When I glanced inside his backpack the laser was gone.

As we closed with the wreckage the images became fewer and stronger. Finally the last secondary merged with the primary. We were now so close to the ship that gravity did not appreciably bend the light before it reached us.

Our shielding protected us as we passed through the wreck's magnetic screens. The ship was headed out, toward apogee. Most of the collisions with energetic particles occurred on the far side of the wreck. The result was a cold, flickering strobe-light that made the ship seem to jerk and move.

The ship looked like a misshapen barbell, one sphere much bigger than the other. The drive was in the larger sphere, living quarters in the bar, the sacred objects in the smaller sphere, as far from the drive as possible. I frowned.

The explosion had occurred in the bar, not the drive as I had assumed. Both spheres seemed undamaged but the living quarters were ripped and spilled into space. The ship pivoted slowly on the larger sphere.

I watched Pleasance as he watched the ship. Again he surprised me. He seemed to study the bar far more than he studied the smaller sphere, as if he was searching for something. This was not what I had expected from the religious leader who hired me to find his precious relics. He noticed my attention.

"I'm looking for the caretaker. The explosion was only a few months ago, ship time. Survival would not be impossible."

I took us around the wreckage so we had photographs of the entire structure. The bar was totally shattered, a twisted metal and plastic wreckage. The spheres had been scored by fragments from the explosion, but seemed basically sound.

Pleasance was exasperated. There was no sign of the caretaker. I figured the man must have been blown out of the ship, but Pleasance did not want to listen to me. He went outside and used his telescope. When he returned I could tell by his expression that he had not found anything.

His hesitation made me nervous. I tried to think of a good reason why we did long-range exploration instead of going to the ship. I could not think of a good reason.

"How long to apogee?" he asked.

"About two days."

Apogee was our decision point, our farthest position from the hole in this orbit. After that we closed with the hole, and we were stuck for the rest of the cycle until we again reached apogee. We had used so much fuel getting to this point that I did not think we had enough to leave if we were closer than apogee. I had calculated that the entire cycle took about eighty years, outside time. Pleasance was not paying me enough to make me lose eighty years.

"Can we tow it?" he asked.

I laughed. "You've seen that ship. It's not strong enough to take a tow. I'd rip the hull and spill everything out as soon as I tried. If you want the stuff on board, you have to go down to get it. We leave the ship where it is, a little present to the Hatane. Maybe they can use it for something."

Pleasance thought for a moment, then nodded reluctantly.

"Then we don't have much choice, do we? Suit up and we can go over."

"You go over," I said. "I'll wait here and look for the caretaker. I haven't done any zero-gravity work in years."

Pleasance sighed and leaned toward me. The spot-laser was not pointed at me, but it was in his hand. I noticed the safety was off. I wondered where he had hidden it before.

"As you pointed out, we don't have much time, Mr. Reinfeld. I don't trust you enough to leave you here, in control of my ticket home, while I'm down there. So you have a choice. If I were you, I'd suit up."

"You're insane. If you kill me, who is going to get you back topside?"

Pleasance bowed his head, but he never stopped watching me and the laser never wavered.

"The Lord helps those who need his help, Mr. Reinfeld. I have a little deepspace experience. With the Lord's aid, I think I could manage. By the same token, the Lord tells us not to call on him except as a last resort. Killing you would be that last resort. I do not intend to do that unless you force me. Please suit up."

I suited slowly, stalling for time, trying to think. Pleasance waited patiently. He did not seem in a hurry. All too soon I was ready and we left the ship.

Pleasance wore a maneuvering pack and strapped his instrument pack to his chest. My suit was bare except for a small tool kit I wore at my waist. Pleasance held me in front of him as a shield. I realized he was absolutely serious. He expected that if I was killed, the Lord would help him pilot his way out of here. He moved us toward the wreckage with small bursts from the maneuvering pack.

"You think he's alive," I said.

"She," Pleasance corrected. "I don't know. I placed the bomb carefully; it should have killed her. But she is very lucky. I failed before, and I suppose I could have failed again. I prefer not to take chances."

Somehow I was not surprised. In fact, I was not listening particularly closely. The only thing I wanted to do was to keep him talking, to distract him, in case I thought of something to do.

"Is anything you told me true?" I asked. "Just out of curiosity."

"Mr. Reinfeld," Pleasance said. He sounded hurt, as if he was not used to having his word doubted. "I am not really very different from what my records show. I am ordained in the church, and I minister to my parish. I find the work very rewarding and fulfilling. I sincerely wish I were home now, working on my Sunday sermon or doing almost anything but what I am doing."

We were much closer to the wreckage. When I turned up

the magnification in my suit I could pick out individual rooms in the bar. I thought I saw something move in one of the rooms. I shifted my position, ever so slightly, to make myself less of a shield. His grip tightened when I moved.

"Then what are we doing here, Reverend? What are we looking for?"

"Schismatics, Mr. Reinfeld. Schismatics and heretics," he said. The closer we got to the wreckage the more nervous he became. He crouched behind me now, head darting from side to side.

"A long time ago the church was rent by dissension. One man seemed to be the source of the trouble. The Council of Disciples decided that he must be silenced. An Angel of Mercy was dispatched to deal with him."

"You?"

Pleasance was silent for a moment. When he spoke again his voice was very soft.

"It was a long time ago, Mr. Reinfeld. A certain young man, whom I knew very well, was selected for the task. He was very fervid, this young man, exceptionally strong and single-minded. He obeyed instructions without thinking.

"He fulfilled his commission. The man was dead. But the Council was mistaken in its judgment that this would solve the problem. The Council was not infallible, as Doctrine teaches. The dead man became a martyr, a symbol, a cause. He rose from the dead, much stronger, speaking with a thousand voices, thinking with a thousand minds. We could not kill them all."

"So reform came to the church?" I asked.

"Softly, Mr. Reinfeld. Very softly. I did my small part to nurse it along. The church teaches us that rejuvenation is not good, that man is allotted a natural span and that extending it detracts from God's plan. But I underwent rejuvenation, not once but many times. I will not talk of my guilt. But I had to stay alive. I was the pivot, the fulcrum the two groups could use. The church must remain one."

We were not close enough to examine individual rooms without using the suit magnifiers. Pleasance killed our forward momentum and moved us sideways, slowly and carefully examining the wreckage.

"Is the caretaker your last schismatic, then? The last threat?"

"No," Pleasance said. "She is not even very religious.

But her father was the man I killed. Both sides were trying to use her after his death, and no matter who succeeded they would have torn the church apart."

"So you tried to kill her."

"I had no choice, but I failed. Her father had friends, powerful friends, who took care of her. They got her aboard the archive ship, and I got a bomb on board with her."

"But your artifacts, your documents."

"The church is its people!" Pleasance said hoarsely. "I had to keep that in mind. Still, it was not pleasant. I am a very religious man, Mr. Reinfeld. I believe in my church and my God, and I believe I will go to Hell for my deeds. But when you brought back that wreckage the church saw a chance to find the ship. I was afraid they would also find the woman. Even now there are groups that would use her. I will not allow it."

"And if we don't find her?"

"Then I add a little to my guilt, and we remove the holy objects from this ship. We go home."

"What about me?"

Pleasance sounded amused. "Afraid you know too much? I'm sorry, Mr. Reinfeld, but you are not that important. My word would carry much more weight. As far as I am concerned, you go your way, I go mine. I will even show you what happened to your blackjack game."

"You planned that!"

"Of course. I needed you, Mr. Reinfeld, and the casino people were remarkably easy to bribe."

The next few minutes are confused in my memory. We were about halfway down the bar toward the small sphere. Pleasance had swung me slightly to the side so he had a better view of the wreckage.

Something moved in the wreckage. I saw a flicker of motions in my peripheral vision and ducked. My movement swung Pleasance into the open for a few seconds. He was using the maneuvering pack and cursing when the arrow struck him in the arm.

He screamed, and let go of me. I hung in space, free, but unable to move. There was nothing to push against, nothing close, except Pleasance. He was busy sealing his suit and trying to get a fix on his assailant. I was a big, fat target waiting to be punctured.

So I kicked.

My feet caught Pleasance and sent him tumbling backward. The momentum sent me plunging toward the bar. I could hardly miss, but I could not pick my landing spot. I tucked myself into a ball to minimize my impact area, and waited.

The trip seemed interminable. All I could see was jagged metal and sharp edges reaching toward me, and all the emptiness around me. There was a man with a laser behind me, a woman in front of me with sharp, pointy things, and nothing and nowhere to hide. I tasted copper, my stomach hurt, my back was twisted and I hoped that whatever got me did not hurt.

I must have closed my eyes just before I hit the wreckage. I remember the sick feeling you get when all the air is knocked out of your lungs and the panicky, feathery feeling as I tried to breathe. Suit material collapsed gently against my arms and legs but the suit's compression rings kept the trunk and helmet airtight. I spent a few precious minutes using my tool kit to patch the holes and rips in the skin of the suit.

One leg was badly bruised and bent, probably broken. I did not have time to fix it. I numbed it and started moving, hand over hand, through the wreckage. In zero gravity the leg did not hinder me.

"Reinfeld, you have one minute to come back. After that, I must consider you my enemy. I do not want to do that, Reinfeld. Come back while there is time."

His idea was probably correct, and the safest thing to do, but it was hard to forget the way he used me on the way down. Right now I did not have a laser in my back, and I was not his damned shield. I wanted to stay a free agent, at least until I had a plan.

I did not know where he was, except that he was some distance away. The suits come with two radios, one for short-range and one for long. He was using long-range, and a special control in my helmet gave me a read-out on the signal strength. I moved toward the larger sphere, and the read-out showed that his homing signal was stronger. I stopped and moved the other direction, toward the smaller sphere. The signal got weaker.

He did not ask me again. I was looking back, trying to find him, when I saw a puff of metal vapor rise from the bar. A few seconds later a second puff materialized, illuminated from within like a lantern as metal vapor cooled through the spectrum.

He was randomly firing into the wreckage, probably at bright spots of reflected light or, if he had an infra-red scanner, at random collections of heat. It was not a policy likely to attain success. Most likely he was hurt and frustrated and angry. Eventually he would give up and return to the ship, to mend and think.

It encouraged me to think of Pleasance in a blind rage. I have never been afraid of men like that. They are too emotional, too likely to make a mistake that gives you an advantage. Unfortunately, we were not in a bar or a gymnasium. I was on a wreck, with a (possibly) broken leg, and no way to leave. Somewhere around me was a desperate woman, chased across the stars and many years, with a weapon. Above me, trying to kill me, was a man with a maneuvering pack, a laser, and my ship.

My ship. That part particularly galled me. I had worked a long time for that ship, and on it. When I thought of it I thought of all the (biological) years it cost me. I thought of all the deep-drops, the garbage runs, the gradual out-running of my time and place before I had the money to buy her.

I wound myself through a particularly tangled collection of wiring and tubing, having to be careful due to my leg. I was now deep in the wreckage of the bar. If Pleasance passed directly overhead I would not see him, nor he me. I was safe, for the moment.

The light blinded me before the helmet shielding polarized. Even so, that single instant left me blinking and groping in the air, a man trying to see with his fingers.

Something touched me on the shoulder. I jerked as if I had been grazed by a live wire, convulsively thrusting myself away. It did no good. I was gripped and pulled forward.

My sight began to return. Inside my helmet the radio light switched from long- to short-range. The digital frequency controller spun through its paces so fast all the numbers looked like $8's$ as it tried to match the incoming signal.

". . . ight! Are you all right!"

I nodded and the hand let go of me. A shape that resolved into a spacesuit drifted away from me, took a position at the opposite side of the little clearing we were in. An arrow-firing device of some sort was aimed at me.

I was getting tired of being the only unarmed person but it

looked like it was going to stay that way until some kindly person armed me. This did not seem likely. So I remained calm and quiet and made no sudden motions.

We examined each other for a few moments. I could not see her face, of course, through the helmet, but I could examine her suit. It was an older model, of uni-body construction. That meant that if something went wrong, you had to tear the entire suit apart to fix it. It also meant that, unlike my modular suit, it had a maneuvering unit built in.

She started to speak and I waved her into silence. I checked my signal strength monitor. Nothing. Which meant two things might have occurred: Pleasance had returned to the ship, or he had turned off his homing beacon. Turning off the beacon involved opening the electronics and burning out one section of the signal control chip. A delicate job, but not impossible. Unlikely, though, in such a short time. I spoke.

"He's gone. It's safe to talk."

"Who are you? What the hell is going on? Who is he? How many are there?"

"My name is Farrar Reinfeld. I'm the pilot. He's down here to kill you. There's only the one of him."

She started to ask more questions but I waved her silent.

"He's gone now, but he'll be back. He's not stupid and he's got equipment I don't know about. It wouldn't surprise me if he has a radio detector. If he comes back outside and uses it, and we're still talking like this, he'll find us."

"I have this," she said, and hefted the weapon.

"That's very nice, and I wish you would aim it someplace else, but the only reason you got him was surprise. He was using me as a shield in case you had a laser. You must not have one, or you would have used it. The next time he comes out he'll have something that will stop an arrow."

She mulled this over for a minute, then nodded and slung the weapon over her shoulder. The carrier wave hum from her radio stopped. I also switched off my radio and followed her through the wreckage.

Somewhat later we arrived at the smaller sphere. I was relieved. The numbness in my leg was starting to wear off and the pain was getting bad. She opened an airlock and we clambered inside.

When she opened the inner door the gravity came on. My

leg supported me for maybe a second and then decided that was enough. I crumpled to the floor in a faint.

I woke slowly. Overhead, far, far away, I saw the roof of the sphere. The pain in my leg was down to a dull ache, annoying but localized. I gingerly tensed the muscles.

It hurt. I tried again. It still hurt but I could bend the knee. I sat up and tried to stand. I did so. I tried to walk. It worked. I had to limp so much it felt like the deck was moving under me, but I could get around under my own power.

"Good. It was bruised and punctured, not broken. Should heal clean."

I looked around. She was seated atop a glass display case, open, wherein rested her arrow weapon.

She was older than I and her face was lined and worn. Not a great beauty but then I had watched the fashion of beauty change so much that I was not even sure what the style was when we left for this drop. By the time I got back the style would have changed again. She was not ugly. I pointed to the case.

"Sacred weapon?" I asked.

"The Bow of Glenda. Comes complete with arrows."

I nodded.

"This might seem a stupid question but I was not exactly a volunteer. What's your name?"

She laughed. I liked the sound. It was a nice soprano.

"Sharlee Espa. I had already decided you were not a volunteer. That leaves the obvious question: Who is that madman?"

"Pleasance. Reverend Jared Pleasance."

She was silent while I explored the sphere and its contents. I could not see it all—the sphere was too large—but it was crammed remarkably full. The sheer volume of articles made me realize how much the church wanted the ship. And Pleasance was a good son of the church. I was sure his most pleasant dream was to kill Espa *and* retrieve the cargo.

"I've never met him," Espa said. "He has a reputation, though. A fanatic. A tool of the Disciples. Some friends tried to tell me he was the one who killed my father. But he is so young."

"How long have you been down here?"

"Since the explosion? A little over three months, I think. I was starting to think no one was coming to get me until I saw your ship. But then there was no radio contact, no attempt to talk to me. I got suspicious. Then I saw the man behind you with the laser."

She sat on the display case and looked up at me with this strange expression on her face. As if she wanted reassurance or me to tell her that everything would be all right.

Unfortunately, I was not sure that everything would be all right.

"It has been a lot longer than three months, outside. Pleasance is not a young man anymore. He is still a fanatic."

"What does he want? Can we bargain with him?"

"He does not want to bargain. He wants you dead." I quickly told her what Pleasance had told me, except that he had killed her father. I wanted her to know the danger, so she could help me, but I did not want her vengeful. Vengeance always excites the glands and dulls the brains. I needed her brains.

She came down from the display case, began to pace. She was just a little taller than I. I thought we could probably use each other's spacesuits.

"I do not understand him. I had a hard enough time understanding my father. I'm not very religious. Neither were most people my age. I really don't care what happens to the church."

"Fashions change in religion. Some generations are devout, some are not. Pleasance is very devout."

"Would he believe me if I told him I would go away, never contact anyone in the church? Most of my friends must be dead by now anyway."

"He would probably believe you. He would still kill you. Just to make sure. That seems to be the way he is built."

Espa picked up the Bow of Glenda, placed an arrow in the chamber. I reached over and grabbed her shoulder.

"What are you doing?" I asked.

"Let go of me."

I sighed and released her. I was in no shape for a fight, particularly with someone larger than I. I spoke again as she headed for the suit rack.

"It's no good, you know. He'll cut you down before you get into arrow range. Now that he knows what your armament is he'll come back equipped so you can't hurt him. Then he'll find you and kill you. Then he'll kill me."

"If he had protection, why didn't he wear it the first time?"

"He had to assume you had a laser. What good is armor against a laser? It would have just slowed him down. Besides, he had me instead."

She had opened the suit rack and now hesitated. I nodded when I saw my suit, ripped and torn, next to two of hers.

"Do you have a better idea?" she demanded. She sounded hopeful.

Never dash someone's hopes, particularly when their plan is bound to get you killed. Of course I had a plan. And even if I didn't, I was bound to think of one sooner or later.

"Maybe. I need some information. Does the cargo hatch on this sphere work?"

She frowned. "I don't know. It should. The explosion didn't hurt much but the bar."

I sat for a few minutes and thought. I wished I had a computer simulation of Pleasance's mind, so I could program a result and see what I had to do to get that result. I understand they have developed such things, back at Earth, for use in the War Game.

Unfortunately, I was not on Earth. All I had to go on was my abbreviated acquaintance with the Reverend. The situation, however, was simple: I had enough information, or I did not. If I did, and Pleasance jumped through the hoops I was mentally constructing, then I had a chance. If I was wrong, if he was not quite the person I thought he was, we were dead.

I stood.

"We have work to do," I said. "He won't stay up there much longer. We've got to be ready when he comes out again."

"Why are you smiling?" she asked.

"I always smile just before I bring the dead back to life. Come on."

Pleasance watched the wreck carefully while he healed. His weapons and suit were carefully laid out, the scanning computer in perfect condition. At the first sign of movement he was ready to leave the autodoc.

The autodoc beeped and withdrew into the wall. Pleasance flexed his fingers and moved his arm to make sure everything had healed properly. Then he fixed a meal and ate it. He wanted to be in top condition when he went back down.

The scanner sounded while he was finishing a leisurely second cup of coffee. He dropped the cup and checked the screen. Movement around the smaller sphere, something leaving the wreck.

He turned up the magnification until he could see the cargo hatch on the smaller sphere was open. As he watched, a crate passed through the hatch and struck the bar. The crate shattered and its cargo tumbled free. Some of it was caught in the wreckage; the rest tumbled into space in the general direction of the hole.

Pleasance pushed the magnification to maximum and focused on the contents of the crate. He swore, slowly and calmly. They were throwing the scared articles into space.

Another crate passed through the hatch and sailed cleanly into space. Pleasance left the control board and put on his suit and weapons. He left the ship, locking it behind him.

He moved clumsily in space. The difficulty was obvious: instead of the usual flexible covering his suit was fitted with layer after overlapping layer of protective armor. He resembled nothing so much as an oversized turtle as he hovered before the smaller sphere and set his radio to transmit on all frequencies.

Before he could speak another crate left the sphere. This crate also missed the bar and disappeared behind the larger sphere.

"I have come to talk with you," Pleasance said. He waited calmly, confident in his armor.

Nothing happened for a few seconds. Pleasance repeated himself. He noticed motion in the corner of the hold. A suited figure appeared. Pleasance nodded to himself. Reinfeld. He recognized the suit.

"You are committing a great sin, Mr. Reinfeld. I would greatly appreciate it if you would stop."

Pleasance moved while he spoke. He drifted sideways, trying to locate the woman. She was the threat. Reinfeld was obviously unarmed.

"You are the one who has committed the sins, Reverend. Are you sure you want to commit more? Even God's forgiveness must know limits."

Reinfeld's voice sounded a little strange: tinny, and a faint echo. Pleasance shrugged it off. The suit had obviously been damaged. Besides, he thought he saw someone deeper in the hold. He moved again, slightly, to avoid frightening his quarry.

Reinfeld suddenly threw himself to the side. Another suit, maneuvering thrusters on full, burst from the hold behind him and headed for Pleasance.

Pleasance fired without moving. The suit jerked and burst into momentary flame.

The suit was empty. There was no body.

Pleasance reacted instantly. He twisted, tried to bring his weapon to bear behind him. For an instant he saw the space-suited figure behind him bearing down. For an instant he saw the welding torch, tip on full heat.

He was an instant late.

Sharlee swung the welder across Pleasance's arm. The armor resisted, then it flared and the welder cut smoothly through the material. Pleasance lost his arm and his weapon.

He screamed and reached for her. Sharlee shoved the welder toward him, trying to drive him away. He gripped it and lashed out with his legs. Sharlee felt herself thrust backward, tumbling. She was unarmed, out of control.

Pleasance drifted away, slowly rotating head over heels. He pawed at the welder, feebly trying to dislodge it. The welder clung to his chest like some greedy insect.

Pleasance fell away from us, toward the hole. He stopped struggling. I came out of hiding and waited for Sharlee to pick me up. From the noises I heard her making, I judged she was being sick.

I had been raised a Christian. While I watched Pleasance I found old memories suddenly fresh. I said a prayer for his soul and wished him good luck.

When we reached the ship, we found Pleasance had locked it and taken the key. It was not amusing to break into my own ship, but we did not have a choice. I tried to cause minimum damage but in the end had to burn a hole in the hull.

The decompression ruined most of the sealing, but we finally managed to make the control room airtight. I helped Sharlee clean herself and her suit, then gave her a sedative.

While she slept I broke orbit and headed for the Station. After a few hours the image of the wreck split into a primary and a secondary. I did not look back after that.

We did not carry any of the religious objects back to the Station. I could use the money to repair my ship, and Sharlee was penniless, but neither of us wanted to go back to the wreck.

The ship's log showed that we had found the wreck and attempted to salvage it. In the process there had been an accident. Pleasance was killed and, per his last instructions, buried in the hole. All religious artifacts were lost. The caretaker had presumably been lost in the explosion that disabled the ship.

I tried to bring Sharlee up to date but I do not think it really hit her until the Station called us in modern Basic. Like I said, it sounds like a birdsong. It seemed to shock her even more when I replied in kind.

"It has been a long time," she said. She sounded subdued.

"You'll adjust," I said.

She stared at the screen I had focused on the Station. It was not until she spoke that I realized she was staring at the stars, not the Station.

"What's it like out there?"

"Like it always was. A little strange, a little terrible."

"What are you going to do now?" I shrugged.

"Put the ship back together. Look for work."

"Could you use a partner?"

I had been afraid of this question all the way up. I had hoped she would not ask. I tried to be businesslike, to keep emotions out of the question.

"A partnership implies equality. I can bring us a ship. What have you got?"

She smiled. I admit to being a romantic, and it had been a long time since I had someone to talk with in English. I found myself hoping the smile was substance, not bluff.

"I kept one thing from the wreck. The photographs I took on the orbit down to the hole. According to the computer, the Hatane have restricted zones where prospecting is very expensive. Most of them are empty to discourage prospecting. I have photographs of several of those zones. Most of them are empty space. At least one contains something. From what I can tell, looks like an old ship. How much is that information worth?"

I thought for a moment. One ship, before my time, had made a strike in the restricted zone. The heirs of the backers now controlled a considerable percentage of the life-extension business.

"It will take a few weeks to get the word around. We'll want to hold an auction before we drop."

SUR

Ursula K. Le Guin

This is a story of adventure in an alternative
world, but it's like no such story you've ever
read. Alternative world stories usually tell of
changes in history that affected everything that
happened thereafter, but the remarkable events
in "Sur" are secret ones that altered nothing
you'll ever read in a history book. Just why they
are secret is a major point of the story: ironic, a
bit cynical and probably controversial. Never
mind; it's a gripping story that will make you
think, no matter whether or not you'll agree with
its implications.

Ursula Le Guin is one of the towering figures
of science fiction, author of The Left Hand of
Darkness, The Lathe of Heaven, The
Dispossessed, and many other stories both long
and short that have shown she has a talent as
fine as that of any writer in any genre. These
days many of her stories, both sf and otherwise,
appear in the New Yorker, as this one originally
did.

A Summary Report of the
Yelcho Expedition to the Antarctic,
1909-1910

ALTHOUGH I HAVE NO INTENTION OF PUBLISH-
ing this report, I think it would be nice if a grandchild of
mine, or somebody's grandchild, happened to find it some
day; so I shall keep it in the leather trunk in the attic, along
with Rosita's christening dress and Juanito's silver rattle and
my wedding shoes and finneskos.

The first requisite for mounting an expedition—money—is
normally the hardest to come by. I grieve that even in a
report destined for a trunk in the attic of a house in a very
quiet suburb of Lima I dare not write the name of the
generous benefactor, the great soul without whose unstint-
ing liberality the *Yelcho* Expedition would never have been
more than the idlest excursion into daydream. That our
equipment was the best and most modern—that our provisions were plentiful and fine—that a ship of the Chilean
Government, with her brave officers and gallant crew, was
twice sent halfway round the world for our convenience: all
this is due to that benefactor whose name, alas! I must not
say, but whose happiest debtor I shall be till death.

When I was little more than a child my imagination was
caught by a newspaper account of the voyage of the *Belgica,*
which, sailing south from Tierra del Fuego, became beset by
ice in the Bellingshausen Sea and drifted a whole year with
the floe, the men aboard her suffering a great deal from want
of food and from the terror of the unending winter darkness.

I read and reread that account, and later followed with
excitement the reports of the rescue of Dr. Nordenskjold
from the South Shetland Isles by the dashing Captain Irizar
of the *Uruguay,* and the adventures of the *Scotia* in the
Weddel Sea. But all these exploits were to me but forerun-
ners of the British National Antarctic Expedition of 1902–
1904, in the *Discovery,* and the wonderful account of that
expedition by Captain Scott. This book, which I ordered
from London and reread a thousand times, filled me with
longing to see with my own eyes that strange continent, last
Thule of the South, which lies on our maps and globes like a
white cloud, a void, fringed here and there with scraps of
coastline, dubious capes, supposititious islands, headlands
that may or may not be there: Antarctica. And the desire
was as pure as the polar snows: to go, to see—no more, no
less. I deeply respect the scientific accomplishments of
Captain Scott's expedition, and have read with passionate
interest the findings of physicists, meteorologists, biologists,
etc.; but having had no training in any science, nor any
opportunity for such training, my ignorance obliged me to
forego any thought of adding to the body of scientific knowledge concerning Antarctica; and the same is true for all the
members of my expedition. It seems a pity; but there was
nothing we could do about it. Our goal was limited to
observation and exploration. We hoped to go a little farther,
perhaps, and see a little more; if not, simply to go and to see.
A simple ambition, I think, and essentially a modest one.

Yet it would have remained less than an ambition, no more
than a longing, but for the support and encouragement of my
dear cousin and friend Juana ——— ———. (I use no
surnames, lest this report fall into strangers' hands at last,
and embarrassment or unpleasant notoriety thus be brought
upon unsuspecting husbands, sons, etc.) I had lent Juana my
copy of *The Voyage of the Discovery,* and it was she who, as
we strolled beneath our parasols across the Plaza de Armas
after Mass one Sunday in 1908, said, "Well, if Captain Scott
can do it, why can't we?"

It was Juana who proposed that we write Carlota ——— in
Valparaiso. Through Carlota we met our benefactor, and so
obtained our money, our ship, and even the plausible pretext
of going on retreat in a Bolivian convent, which some of us
were forced to employ (while the rest of us said we were
going to Paris for the winter season). And it was my Juana

who in the darkest moments remained resolute, unshaken in her determination to achieve our goal.

And there were dark moments, especially in the early months of 1909—times when I did not see how the expedition would ever become more than a quarter ton of pemmican gone to waste and a lifelong regret. It was so very hard to gather our expeditionary force together! So few of those we asked even knew what we were talking about—so many thought we were mad, or wicked, or both! And of those few who shared our folly, still fewer were able, when it came to the point, to leave their daily duties and commit themselves to a voyage of at least six months, attended with not inconsiderable uncertainty and danger. An ailing parent; an anxious husband beset by business cares; a child at home with only ignorant or incompetent servants to look after it: these are not responsibilities lightly to be set aside. And those who wished to evade such claims were not the companions we wanted in hard work, risk, and privation.

But since success crowned our efforts, why dwell on the setbacks and delays, or the wretched contrivances and downright lies that we all had to employ? I look back with regret only to those friends who wished to come with us but could not, by any contrivance, get free—those we had to leave behind to a life without danger, without uncertainty, without hope.

On the seventeenth of August, 1909, in Punta Arenas, Chile, all the members of the expedition met for the first time: Juana and I, the two Peruvians; from Argentina, Zoe, Berta, and Teresa; and our Chileans, Carlota and her friends Eva, Pepita, and Dolores. At the last moment I had received word that Maria's husband, in Quito, was ill and she must stay to nurse him, so we were nine, not ten. Indeed, we had resigned ourselves to being but eight, when, just as night fell, the indomitable Zoe arrived in a tiny pirogue manned by Indians, her yacht having sprung a leak just as it entered the Strait of Magellan.

That night before we sailed we began to get to know one another; and we agreed, as we enjoyed our abominable supper in the abominable seaport inn of Punta Arenas, that if a situation arose of such urgent danger that one voice must be obeyed without present question, the unenviable honor of speaking with that voice should fall first upon myself; if I were incapacitated, upon Carlota; if she, then upon Berta.

We three were then toasted as "Supreme Inca," "La Arau-
cana," and "The Third Mate," among a lot of laughter and
cheering. As it came out, to my very great pleasure and
relief, my qualities as a "leader" were never tested; the nine
of us worked things out amongst us from beginning to end
without any orders being given by anybody, and only two or
three times with recourse to a vote by voice or show of
hands. To be sure, we argued a good deal. But then, we had
time to argue. And one way or another the arguments always
ended up in a decision, upon which action could be taken.
Usually at least one person grumbled about the decision,
sometimes bitterly. But what is life without grumbling, and
the occasional opportunity to say, "I told you so"? How
could one bear housework, or looking after babies, let alone
the rigors of sledge-hauling in Antarctica, without grumbling? Officers—as we came to understand aboard the
Yelcho—are forbidden to grumble; but we nine were, and
are, by birth and upbringing, unequivocally and irrevocably,
all crew.

Though our shortest course to the southern continent, and
that originally urged upon us by the captain of our good ship,
was to the South Shetlands and the Bellingshausen Sea, or
else by the South Orkneys into the Weddell Sea, we planned
to sail west to the Ross Sea, which Captain Scott had
explored and described, and from which the brave Ernest
Shackleton had returned only the previous autumn. More
was known about this region than any other portion of the
coast of Antarctica, and though that more was not much, yet
it served as some insurance of the safety of the ship, which
we felt we had no right to imperil. Captain Pardo had fully
agreed with us after studying the charts and our planned
itinerary; and so it was westward that we took our course
out of the Straits next morning.

Our journey half round the globe was attended by fortune.
The little *Yelcho* steamed cheerily along through gale and
gleam, climbing up and down those seas of the Southern
Ocean that run unbroken round the world. Juana, who had
fought bulls and the far more dangerous cows on her family's
estancia, called the ship *"la vaca valiente,"* because she
always returned to the charge. Once we got over being
seasick we all enjoyed the sea voyage, though oppressed at
times by the kindly but officious protectiveness of the captain and his officers, who felt that we were only "safe" when

huddled up in the three tiny cabins which they had chival-
rously vacated for our use.

We saw our first iceberg much farther south than we had
looked for it, and saluted it with Veuve Clicquot at dinner.
The next day we entered the ice pack, the belt of floes and
bergs broken loose from the land ice and winter-frozen seas
of Antarctica which drifts northward in the spring. Fortune
still smiled on us: our little steamer, incapable, with her
unreinforced metal hull, of forcing a way into the ice, picked
her way from lane to lane without hesitation, and on the
third day we were through the pack, in which ships have
sometimes struggled for weeks and been obliged to turn
back at last. Ahead of us now lay the dark grey waters of the
Ross Sea, and beyond that, on the horizon, the remote
glimmer, the cloud-reflected whiteness of the Great Ice
Barrier.

Entering the Ross Sea a little east of Longitude West 160°,
we came in sight of the Barrier at the place where Captain
Scott's party, finding a bight in the vast wall of ice, had gone
ashore and set up their hydrogen-gas balloon for reconnais-
sance and photography. The towering face of the Barrier, its
sheer cliffs and azure and violet water-worn caves, all were
as described, but the location had changed: instead of a
narrow bight, there was a considerable bay, full of the
beautiful and terrific orca whales playing and spouting in the
sunshine of that brilliant southern spring.

Evidently masses of ice many acres in extent had broken
away from the Barrier (which—at least for most of its vast
extent—does not rest on land but floats on water) since the
Discovery's passage in 1902. This put our plan to set up
camp on the Barrier itself in a new light; and while we were
discussing alternatives, we asked Captain Pardo to take the
ship west along the Barrier face towards Ross Island and
McMurdo Sound. As the sea was clear of ice and quite calm,
he was happy to do so and, when we sighted the smoke
plume of Mount Erebus, to share in our celebration—another half case of Veuve Clicquot.

The Yelcho anchored in Arrival Bay, and we went ashore
in the ship's boat. I cannot describe my emotions when I set
foot on the earth, on that earth, the barren, cold gravel at the
foot of the long volcanic slope. I felt elation, impatience,
gratitude, awe, familiarity. I felt that I was home at last.
Eight Adélie penguins immediately came to greet us with

many exclamations of interest not unmixed with disapproval. "Where on earth have you been? What took you so long? The Hut is around this way. Please come this way. Mind the rocks!" They insisted on our going to visit Hut Point, where the large structure built by Captain Scott's party stood, looking just as in the photographs and drawings that illustrate his book. The area about it, however, was disgusting—a kind of graveyard of seal skins, seal bones, penguin bones, and rubbish, presided over by the mad, screaming skua gulls. Our escorts waddled past the slaughterhouse in all tranquility, and one showed me personally to the door, though it would not go in.

The interior of the hut was less offensive, but very dreary. Boxes of supplies had been stacked up into a kind of room within the room; it did not look as I had imagined it when the *Discovery* party put on their melodramas and minstrel shows in the long winter night. (Much later, we learned that Sir Ernest had rearranged it a good deal when he was there just a year before us.) It was dirty, and had about it a mean disorder. A pound tin of tea was standing open. Empty meat tins lay about; biscuits were spilled on the floor; a lot of dog turds were underfoot—frozen, of course, but not a great deal improved by that. No doubt the last occupants had had to leave in a hurry, perhaps even in a blizzard. All the same, they could have closed the tea tin. But housekeeping, the art of the infinite, is no game for amateurs.

Teresa proposed that we use the hut as our camp. Zoe counterproposed that we set fire to it. We finally shut the door and left it as we had found it. The penguins appeared to approve, and cheered us all the way to the boat.

McMurdo Sound was free of ice, and Captain Pardo now proposed to take us off Ross Island and across to Victoria Land, where we might camp at the foot of the Western Mountains, on dry and solid earth. But those mountains, with their storm-darkened peaks and hanging cirques and glaciers, looked as awful as Captain Scott had found them on his western journey, and none of us felt much inclined to seek shelter among them.

Aboard the ship that night we decided to go back and set up our base as we had originally planned, on the Barrier itself. For all available reports indicated that the clear way south was across the level Barrier surface until one could ascend one of the confluent glaciers to the high plateau which appears to form the whole interior of the continent. Captain Pardo argued strongly against this plan, asking what would become of us if the Barrier "calved"—if our particular acre of ice broke away and started to drift northward. "Well," said Zoe, "then you won't have to come so far to meet us." But he was so persuasive on this theme that he persuaded himself into leaving one of the *Yelcho*'s boats with us when we camped, as a means of escape. We found it useful for fishing, later on.

My first steps on Antarctic soil, my only visit to Ross Island, had not been pleasure unalloyed. I thought of the words of the English poet,

> Though every prospect pleases,
> And only Man is vile.

But then, the backside of heroism is often rather sad; women and servants know that. They know also that the heroism may be no less real for that. But achievement is smaller than men think. What is large is the sky, the earth, the sea, the soul. I looked back as the ship sailed east again that evening. We were well into September now, with ten hours or more of daylight. The spring sunset lingered on the twelve-thousand-foot peak of Erebus and shone rosy gold on her long plume of steam. The steam from our own small funnel faded blue on the twilit water as we crept along under the towering pale wall of ice.

On our return to "Orca Bay"—Sir Ernest, we learned years later, had named it the Bay of Whales—we found a sheltered nook where the Barrier edge was low enough to provide fairly easy access from the ship. The *Yelcho* put out her ice anchor, and the next long, hard days were spent in unloading our supplies and setting up our camp on the ice, a half-kilometer in from the edge: a task in which the *Yelcho*'s crew lent us invaluable aid and interminable advice. We took all the aid gratefully, and most of the advice with salt.

The weather so far had been extraordinarily mild for spring in this latitude; the temperature had not yet gone below −20° Fahrenheit, and there was only one blizzard while we were setting up camp. But Captain Scott had spoken feelingly of the bitter south winds on the Barrier, and we had planned accordingly. Exposed as our camp was to every wind, we built no rigid structures aboveground. We set up tents to shelter in while we dug out a series of cubicles in the ice itself, lined them with hay insulation and pine boarding, and roofed them with canvas over bamboo poles, covered with snow for weight and insulation. The big central room was instantly named Buenos Aires by our Argentineans, to whom the center, wherever one is, is always Buenos Aires. The heating and cooking stove was in Buenos Aires. The storage tunnels and the privy (called Punta Arenas) got some back heat from the stove. The sleeping cubicles opened off Buenos Aires, and were very small, mere tubes into which one crawled feet first; they were lined deeply with hay and soon warmed by one's body warmth. The sailors called them "coffins" and "wormholes," and looked with horror on our burrows in the ice. But our little warren or prairie-dog village served us well, permitting us as much warmth and privacy as one could reasonably expect under the circumstances. If the *Yelcho* was unable to get through the ice in February, and we had to spend the winter in Antarctica, we certainly could do so, though on very limited rations. For this coming summer, our base—Sudamérica del Sur, South South America, but we generally called it the Base—was intended merely as a place to sleep, to store our provisions, and to give shelter from blizzards.

To Berta and Eva, however, it was more than that. They were its chief architect-designers, its most ingenious builder-excavators, and its most diligent and contented occupants, forever inventing an improvement in ventilation, or learning how to make skylights, or revealing to us a new addition to our suite of rooms, dug in the living ice. It was thanks to them that our stores were stowed so handily, that our stove drew and heated so efficiently, and that Buenos Aires, where nine people cooked, ate, worked, conversed, argued, grumbled, painted, played the guitar and banjo, and kept the expedition's library of books and maps, was a marvel of comfort and convenience. We lived there in real amity; and if you simply had to be alone for a while, you crawled into your sleeping hole head first.

Berta went a little farther. When she had done all she could to make South South America livable, she dug out one more cell just under the ice surface, leaving a nearly transparent sheet of ice like a greenhouse roof; and there, alone, she worked at sculptures. They were beautiful forms, some like a blending of the reclining human figure with the subtle curves and volumes of the Weddell seal, others like the fantastic shapes of ice cornices and ice caves. Perhaps they are there still, under the snow, in the bubble in the Great Barrier. There where she made them they might last as long as stone. But she could not bring them north. That is the penalty for carving in water.

Captain Pardo was reluctant to leave us, but his orders did not permit him to hang about the Ross Sea indefinitely, and so at last, with many earnest injunctions to us to stay put—make no journeys—take no risks—beware of frostbite—don't use edge tools—look out for cracks in the ice—and a heartfelt promise to return to Orca Bay on the twentieth of February, or as near that date as wind and ice would permit, the good man bade us farewell, and his crew shouted us a great goodbye cheer as they weighed anchor. That evening, in the long orange twilight of October, we saw the topmast of the *Yelcho* go down the north horizon, over the edge of the world, leaving us to ice, and silence, and the Pole.

That night we began to plan the Southern Journey.

The ensuing month passed in short practice trips and depot-laying. The life we had led at home, though in its own way strenuous, had not fitted any of us for the kind of strain met with in sledge-hauling at ten or twenty degrees below freezing. We all needed as much working-out as possible before we dared undertake a long haul.

My longest exploratory trip, made with Dolores and Carlota, was southwest toward Mount Markham, and it was a nightmare—blizzards and pressure ice all the way out, crevasses and no view of the mountains when we got there, and white weather and sastrugi all the way back. The trip was useful, however, in that we could begin to estimate our capacities; and also in that we had started out with a very heavy load of provisions, which we depoted at a hundred and a hundred and thirty miles south-southwest of Base. Thereafter other parties pushed on farther, till we had a line of snow cairns and depots right down to Latitude 83° 43', where Juana and Zoe, on an exploring trip, had found a kind of stone gateway opening on a great glacier leading south. We established these depots to avoid, if possible, the hunger that had bedeviled Captain Scott's Southern Party, and the consequent misery and weakness. And we also established to our own satisfaction—intense satisfaction—that we were sledge-haulers at least as good as Captain Scott's husky dogs. Of course we could not have expected to pull as much or as fast as his men. That we did so was because we were favored by much better weather than Captain Scott's party ever met on the Barrier; and also the quantity and quality of our food made a very considerable difference. I am sure that the fifteen percent of dried fruits in our pemmican helped prevent scurvy; and the potatoes, frozen and dried according to an ancient Andean Indian method, were very nourishing yet very light and compact—perfect sledging rations. In any case, it was with considerable confidence in our capacities that we made ready at last for the Southern Journey.

The Southern party consisted of two sledge teams: Juana, Dolores, and myself; Carlota, Pepita, and Zoe. The support team of Berta, Eva, and Teresa set out before us with a heavy load of supplies, going right up onto the glacier to prospect routes and leave depots of supplies for our return journey. We followed five days behind them, and met them returning between Depot Ercilla and Depot Miranda (see map). That "night"—of course there was no real darkness—we were all nine together in the heart of the level plain of ice. It was the fifteenth of November, Dolores's birthday. We celebrated by putting eight ounces of pisco in the hot chocolate, and became very merry. We sang. It is strange now to remember how thin our voices sounded in that great silence. It was overcast, white weather, without shadows and without visible horizon or any feature to break the level; there was nothing to see at all. We had come to that white place on the map, that void, and there we flew and sang like sparrows.

After sleep and a good breakfast the Base Party continued north and the Southern Party sledged on. The sky cleared presently. High up, thin clouds passed over very rapidly from southwest to northeast, but down on the Barrier it was calm and just cold enough, five or ten degrees below freezing, to give a firm surface for hauling.

On the level ice we never pulled less than eleven miles (seventeen kilometers) a day, and generally fifteen or sixteen miles (twenty-five kilometers). (Our instruments, being British-made, were calibrated in feet, miles, degrees Fahrenheit, etc., but we often converted miles to kilometers because the larger numbers sounded more encouraging.) At the time we left South America, we knew only that Mr. Shackleton had mounted another expedition to the Antarctic in 1907, had tried to attain the Pole but failed, and had returned to England in June of the current year, 1909. No coherent report of his explorations had yet reached South America when we left; we did not know what route he had gone, or how far he had got. But we were not altogether taken by surprise when, far across the featureless white plain, tiny beneath the mountain peaks and the strange silent flight of the rainbow-fringed cloud wisps, we saw a fluttering dot of black. We turned west from our course to visit it: a snow heap nearly buried by the winter's storms—a flay on a bamboo pole, a mere shred of threadbare cloth—an empty oilcan—and a few footprints standing some inches above the ice. In some conditions of weather the snow compressed under one's weight remains when the surrounding soft snow melts or is scoured away by the wind; and so these reversed footprints had been left standing all these months, like rows of cobbler's lasts—a queer sight.

We met no other such traces on our way. In general I believe our course was somewhat east of Mr. Shackleton's. Juana, our surveyor, had trained herself well and was faithful and methodical in her sightings and readings, but our equipment was minimal—a theodolite on tripod legs, a sextant with artificial horizon, two compasses, and chronometers. We had only the wheel meter on the sledge to give distance actually travelled.

In any case, it was the day after passing Mr. Shackleton's waymark that I first saw clearly the great glacier among the mountains to the southwest, which was to give us a pathway from the sea level of the Barrier up to the altiplano, ten thousand feet above. The approach was magnificent: a gateway formed by immense vertical domes and pillars of rock. Zoe and Juana had called the vast ice river that flowed through the gateway the Florence Nightingale Glacier, wishing to honor the British, who had been the inspiration and guide of our expedition; that very brave and very peculiar lady seemed to represent so much that is best, and strangest, in the island race. On maps, of course, this glacier bears the name Mr. Shackleton gave it, the Beardmore.

The ascent of the Nightingale was not easy. The way was open at first, and well marked by our support party, but after some days we came among terrible crevasses, a maze of hidden cracks, from a foot to thirty feet wide and from thirty to a thousand feet deep. Step by step we went, and step by

step, and the way always upward now. We were fifteen days
on the glacier. At first the weather was hot, up to 20°F., and
the hot nights without darkness were wretchedly uncomfortable in our small tents. And all of us suffered more or less
from snowblindness just at the time when we wanted clear
eyesight to pick our way among the ridges and crevasses of
the tortured ice, and to see the wonders about and before us.
For at every day's advance more great, nameless peaks
came into view in the west and southwest, summit beyond
summit, range beyond range, stark rock and snow in the
unending noon.

We gave names to these peaks, not very seriously, since
we did not expect our discoveries to come to the attention of
geographers. Zoe had a gift for naming, and it is thanks to
her that certain sketch maps in various suburban South
American attics bear such curious features as "Bolívar's Big
Nose," "I Am General Rosas," "The Cloudmaker,"
"Whose Toe?" and "Throne of Our Lady of the Southern
Cross." And when at last we got up onto the altiplano, the
great interior plateau, it was Zoe who called it the pampa,
and maintained that we walked there among vast herds of
invisible cattle, transparent cattle pastured on the spindrift
snow, their gauchos the restless, merciless winds. We were
by then all a little crazy with exhaustion and the great
altitude—twelve thousand feet—and the cold and the wind
blowing and the luminous circles and crosses surrounding
the suns, for often there were three or four suns in the sky,
up there.

That is not a place where people have any business to be.
We should have turned back; but since we had worked so
hard to get there, it seemed that we should go on, at least for
a while.

A blizzard came with very low temperatures, so we had to
stay in the tents, in our sleeping bags, for thirty hours, a rest
we all needed; though it was warmth we needed most, and
there was no warmth on that terrible plain anywhere at all
but in our veins. We huddled close together all that time. The
ice we lay on is two miles thick.

It cleared suddenly and became, for the plateau, good
weather: twelve below zero and the wind not very strong.
We three crawled out of our tent and met the others crawling
out of theirs. Carlota told us then that her group wished to
turn back. Pepita had been feeling very ill; even after the

rest during the blizzard, her temperature would not rise above 94°. Carlota was having trouble breathing. Zoe was perfectly fit, but much preferred staying with her friends and lending them a hand in difficulties to pushing on toward the Pole. So we put the four ounces of pisco which we had been keeping for Christmas into the breakfast cocoa, and dug out our tents, and loaded our sledges, and parted there in the white daylight on the bitter plain.

Our sledge was fairly light by now. We pulled on to the south. Juana calculated our position daily. On the twenty-second of December, 1909, we reached the South Pole. The weather was, as always, very cruel. Nothing of any kind marked the dreary whiteness. We discussed leaving some kind of mark or monument, a snow cairn, a tent pole and flag; but there seemed no particular reason to do so. Anything we could do, anything we were, was insignificant, in that awful place. We put up the tent for shelter for an hour and made a cup of tea, and then struck "90° Camp." Dolores, standing patient as ever in her sledging harness, looked at the snow; it was so hard frozen that it showed no trace of our footprints coming, and she said, "Which way?"

"North," said Juana.

It was a joke, because at that particular place there is no other direction. But we did not laugh. Our lips were cracked with frostbite and hurt too much to let us laugh. So we started back, and the wind at our backs pushed us along, and dulled the knife edges of the waves of frozen snow.

All that week the blizzard wind pursued us like a pack of mad dogs. I cannot describe it. I wished we had not gone to the Pole. I think I wish it even now. But I was glad even then that we had left no sign there, for some man longing to be first might come some day, and find it, and know what a fool he had been, and break his heart.

We talked, when we could talk, of catching up to Carlota's party, since they might be going slower than we. In fact they had used their tent as a sail to catch the following wind and had got far ahead of us. But in many places they had built snow cairns or left some sign for us; once Zoe had written on the lee side of a ten-foot sastruga, just as children write on the sand of the beach at Miraflores, "This Way Out!" The wind blowing over the frozen ridge had left the words perfectly distinct.

In the very hour that we began to descend the glacier, the

weather turned warmer, and the mad dogs were left to howl forever tethered to the Pole. The distance that had taken us fifteen days going up we covered in only eight days going down. But the good weather that had aided us descending the Nightingale became a curse down on the Barrier ice, where we had looked forward to a kind of royal progress from depot to depot, eating our fill and taking our time for the last three hundred-odd miles. In a tight place on the glacier I lost my goggles—I was swinging from my harness at the time in a crevasse—and then Juana had broken hers when we had to do some rock-climbing coming down to the Gateway. After two days in bright sunlight with only one pair of snow goggles to pass amongst us, we were all suffering badly from snowblindness. It became acutely painful to keep lookout for landmarks or depot flags, to take sightings, even to study the compass, which had to be laid down on the snow to steady the needle. At Concolorcorvo Depot, where there was a particularly good supply of food and fuel, we gave up, crawled into our sleeping bags with bandaged eyes, and slowly boiled alive like lobsters in the tent exposed to the relentless sun. The voices of Berta and Zoe were the sweetest sound I ever heard. A little concerned about us, they had skied south to meet us. They led us home to Base.

We recovered quite swiftly, but the altiplano left its mark. When she was very little, Rosita asked if a dog "had bitted Mama's toes." I told her Yes, a great, white, mad dog named Blizzard! My Rosita and my Juanito heard many stories when they were little, about that fearful dog and how it howled, and the transparent cattle of the invisible gauchos, and a river of ice eight thousand feet high called Nightingale, and how Cousin Juana drank a cup of tea standing on the bottom of the world under seven suns, and other fairy tales.

We were in for one severe shock when we reached Base at last. Teresa was pregnant. I must admit that my first response to the poor girl's big belly and sheepish look was anger—rage—fury. That one of us should have concealed anything, and such a thing, from the others! But Teresa had done nothing of the sort. Only those who had concealed from her what she most needed to know were to blame. Brought up by servants, with four years' schooling in a convent, and married at sixteen, the poor girl was still so ignorant at twenty years of age that she had thought it was "the cold weather" that made her miss her periods. Even this was not entirely stupid, for all of us on the Southern Journey had seen our periods change or stop altogether as we experienced increasing cold, hunger, and fatigue. Teresa's appetite had begun to draw general attention; and then she had begun, as she said pathetically, "to get fat." The others were worried at the thought of all the sledge-hauling she had done, but she flourished, and the only problem was her positively insatiable appetite. As well as could be determined from her shy references to her last night on the hacienda with her husband, the baby was due at just about the same time as the *Yelcho*, the twentieth of February. But we had not been back from the Southern Journey two weeks when, on the fourteenth of February, she went into labor.

Several of us had borne children and had helped with deliveries, and anyhow most of what needs to be done is fairly self-evident; but a first labor can be long and trying, and we were all anxious, while Teresa was frightened out of her wits. She kept calling for her José till she was as hoarse as a skua. Zoe lost all patience at last and said, "By God, Teresa, if you say 'José!' once more, I hope you have a penguin!" But what she had, after twenty long hours, was a pretty little red-faced girl.

Many were the suggestions for that child's name from her eight proud midwife-aunts: Polita, Penguina, McMurdo, Victoria . . . But Teresa announced, after she had had a good sleep and a large serving of pemmican, "I shall name her Rosa—Rosa del Sur," Rose of the South. That night we drank the last two bottles of Veuve Clicquot (having finished the pisco at 88° 30' South) in toasts to our little Rose.

On the nineteenth of February, a day early, my Juana came down into Buenos Aires in a hurry. "The ship," she said, "the ship has come," and she burst into tears—she who had never wept in all our weeks of pain and weariness on the long haul.

Of the return voyage there is nothing to tell. We came back safe.

In 1912 all the world learned that the brave Norwegian Amundsen had reached the South Pole; and then, much later, came the accounts of how Captain Scott and his men had come there after him, but did not come home again.

Just this year, Juana and I wrote to the captain of the *Yelcho*, for the newspapers have been full of the story of his

gallant dash to rescue Sir Ernest Shackleton's men from
Elephant Island, and we wished to congratulate him, and
once more to thank him. Never one word has he breathed of
our secret. He is a man of honor, Luis Pardo.

I add this last note in 1929. Over the years we have lost
touch with one another. It is very difficult for women to
meet, when they live so far apart as we do. Since Juana died,
I have seen none of my old sledge-mates, though sometimes
we write. Our little Rosa del Sur died of the scarlet fever
when she was five years old. Teresa had many other children. Carlota took the veil in Santiago ten years ago. We are
old women now, with old husbands, and grown children and
grandchildren, who might some day like to read about the
Expedition. Even if they are rather ashamed of having such
a crazy grandmother, they may enjoy sharing in the secret.
But they must not let Mr. Amundsen know! He would be
terribly embarrassed and disappointed. There is no need for
him or anyone else outside the family to know. We left no
footprints, even.

UNDERSTANDING HUMAN BEHAVIOR

A Romance of the Rocky Mountains

Thomas M. Disch

This story's title may sound like that of a textbook, but you'll rarely find Thomas M. Disch's kind of sly humor in purely "educational" books. Which is too bad, because Disch's story of a future in which people sometimes have their memories erased so that they can make a fresh start in life, and the peculiar new life on which Richard Roe embarks, could be very instructive if you want to look at it that way. Mainly, though, this is a story for enjoyment—pure but not necessarily simple.

Thomas M. Disch's reputation, like that of Ursula Le Guin, extends well beyond the sf genre; he has published stories, articles and poetry in a wide variety of general magazines, plus a serious historical novel, several books of poetry, etc. But he continues to write outstanding science fiction, including such novels as Camp Concentration, 334 *and* On Wings of Song.

HE WOULD WAKE UP EACH MORNING WITH A consciousness clear as the Boulder sky, a sense of being on the same wave length exactly as the sunlight. Innocence, bland dreams, a healthy appetite—these were glories that issued directly from his having been erased. Of course there were some corresponding disadvantages. His job, monitoring the terminals of a drive-in convenience center, could get pretty dull, especially on days when no one drove in for an hour or so at a stretch, and even at the busiest times it didn't provide much opportunity for human contact. He envied the waitresses in restaurants and the drivers of buses their chance to say hello to real live customers.

Away from work it was different; he didn't feel the same hunger for socializing. That, in fact, was the major disadvantage of having no past life, no established preferences, no identity in the usual sense of a history to attach his name to—he just didn't *want* anything very much.

Not that he was bored or depressed or anything like that. The world was all new to him and full of surprises: the strangeness of anchovies; the beauty of old songs in their blurry Muzak versions at the Stop-and-Shop; the feel of a new shirt or a March day. These sensations were not wholly unfamiliar, nor was his mind a *tabula rasa*. His use of the language and his motor skills were all intact; also what the psychologists at Delphi Institute called generic recognition. But none of the occasions of newness *reminded* him of any earlier experience, some first time or best time or worst time that he'd survived. His only set of memories of a personal

198

and non-generic character were those he'd brought from the halfway house in Delphi, Indiana. But such fine memories they were—so fragile, so distinct, so privileged. If only (he often wished) he could have lived out his life in the sanctuary of Delphi, among men and women like himself, all newly summoned to another life and responsive to the wonders and beauties around them. But, no, for reasons he could not understand, the world insisted on being organized otherwise. An erasee was allowed six months at the Institute, and then he was despatched to wherever he or the computer decided, where he would have to live like everyone else, either alone or in a family (though the Institute advised everyone to be wary at first of establishing primary ties), in a small room or a cramped house or a dormitory ship in some tropical lagoon. Unless you were fairly rich or very lucky, your clothes, furniture, and suchlike appurtenances were liable to be rough, shabby, makeshift. The food most people ate was an incitement to infantile gluttony, a slop of sugars, starches and chemically enhanced flavors. It would have been difficult to live among such people and to seem to share their values except so few of them ever questioned the reasonableness of their arrangements. Those who did, if they had the money, would probably opt, eventually, to have their identities erased, since it was clear, just looking around, that erasees seemed to strike the right intuitive balance between being aware and keeping calm.

He lived now in a condo on the northwest edge of the city, a room and a half with unlimited off-peak power access. The rent was modest (so was his salary), but his equity in the condo was large enough to suggest that his pre-erasure income had been up there in the top percentiles.

He wondered, as all erasees do, why he'd decided to wipe out his past. His life had gone sour, that much was sure, but how and why were questions that could never be answered. The Institute saw to that. A shipwrecked marriage was the commonest reason statistically, closely followed by business reverses. At least that was what people put down on their questionnaires when they applied to the Institute. Somehow he doubted those reasons were the real ones. People who'd never been erased seemed oddly unable to account for their behavior. Even to themselves they would tell the unlikeliest tales about what they were doing and why. Then they'd spend a large part of their social life exposing each others' impostures and laughing at them. A sense of humor they called it. He was glad he didn't have one, yet.

Most of his free time he spent making friends with his body. In his first weeks at the halfway house he'd lazed about, ate too much junk food, and started going rapidly to seed. Erasees are not allowed to leave their new selves an inheritance of obesity or addiction, but often the body one wakes up in is the hasty contrivance of a crash diet. The mouth does not lose its appetites, nor the metabolism its rate, just because the mind has had memories whited out. Fortunately he'd dug in his heels, and by the time he had to bid farewell to Delphi's communal dining room he'd lost the pounds he'd put on and eight more besides.

Since then, fitness had been his religion. He bicycled to work, to Stop-and-Shop, and all about Denver, exploring its uniformities. He hiked and climbed on weekends. He jogged. Once a week, at a Y, he played volleyball for two hours, just as though he'd never left the Institute. He also kept up the other sport he'd had to learn at Delphi, which was karate. Except for the volleyball, he stuck to the more solitary forms of exercise, because on the whole he wasn't interested in forming relationships. The lectures at the halfway house had said this was perfectly natural and nothing to worry about. He shouldn't socialize until he felt hungry for more society than his job and his living arrangements naturally provided. So far that hunger had not produced a single pang. Maybe he was what the Institute called a natural integer. If so, that seemed an all-right fate.

What he did miss, consciously and sometimes achingly, was a purpose. In common with most fledgling erasees, there was nothing he *believed* in—no religion, no political idea, no ambition to become famous for doing something better than somebody else. Money was about the only purpose he could think of, and even that was not a compelling purpose. He didn't lust after more and more and more of it in the classical Faustian go-getter way.

His room and a half looked out across the tops of a small plantation of spruces to the highway that climbed the long southwestward incline into the Rockies. Each car that hummed along the road was like a vector-quantity of human desire, a quantum of teleological purpose. He might have been mistaken. The people driving those cars might be just as uncertain of their ultimate destinations as he was, but seeing them whiz by in their primary colors, he found that hard to believe. Anyone who was prepared to bear the expense of a car surely had somewhere he wanted to get to or something he wanted to do more intensely than *he* could imagine, up here on his three-foot slab of balcony.

He didn't have a telephone or a tv. He didn't read newspapers or magazines, and the only books he ever looked at were some old textbooks on geology he'd bought at a garage sale in Denver. He didn't go to movies. The ability to suspend disbelief in something that had never happened was one he'd lost when he was erased, assuming he'd ever had it. A lot of the time he couldn't suspend his disbelief in the real people around him, all their pushing and pulling, their weird fears and whopping lies, their endless urges to control other people's behavior, like the vegetarian cashier at the Stop-and-Shop or the manager at the convenience center. The lectures and demonstrations at the halfway house had laid out the basics, but without explaining any of it. Like harried parents the Institute's staff had said, "Do this," and "Don't do that," and he'd not been in a position to argue. He did as he was bid, and his behavior fit as naturally as an old suit.

His name—the name by which he'd christened his new self before erasure—was Richard Roe, and that seemed to fit too.

II

At the end of September, three months after coming to Boulder, Richard signed up for a course in *Consumership: Theory and Practice* at the Naropa Adult Education Center. There were twelve other students in the class, all with the dewy, slightly vulnerable look of recent erasure. They sat in their folding chairs, reading or just blank, waiting for the teacher, who arrived ten minutes late, out of breath and gasping apologies. Professor Astor. While she was still collecting punchcards and handing out flimsy xeroxes of their reading list, she started lecturing to them. Before she could get his card (he'd chosen a seat in the farthest row back), she was distracted by the need to list on the blackboard the three reasons that people wear clothing, which are:

1. UTILITY,
2. COMMUNICATION, and
3. SELF-CONCEPT.

Utility was obvious and didn't need going into, while Self-Concept was really a sub-category of Communication, a kind of closed-circuit transmission between oneself and a mirror.

"Now, to illustrate the three basic aspects of Communication, I have some slides." She sat down behind the A/V console at the front of the room and fussed with the buttons anxiously, muttering encouragements to herself. Since the question was there in the air, he wondered what her black dress was supposed to be communicating. It was a wooly, baggy, practical dress sprinkled with dandruff and gathered loosely about the middle by a wide belt of cracked patent leather. The spirit of garage sales hovered about it. "There!" she said.

But the slide that flashed on the screen was a chart of illustrating cuts of beef. "Damn," she said, "that's next week. Well, it doesn't matter. I'll write it on the board."

When she stood up and turned around, it seemed clear that one of the utilitarian functions of her dress was to disguise or obfuscate some twenty-plus pounds of excess baggage. A jumble of thin bracelets jingled as she wrote on the board:

1. DESIRE,
2. ADMIRATION,
3. SOLIDARITY.

"There," she said, laying down the chalk and swinging round to face them, setting the heavy waves of black hair to swaying pendulously, "It's as simple as red, white, and blue. These are the three types of response people try to elicit from others by the clothes they wear. Blue, of course, would represent solidarity. Policemen wear blue. French working-men have always worn a blinding blue. And then there's the universal uniform of blue denim. It's a cool color and tends to make those who wear it recede into the background. They vanish into the blue, so to speak.

"Then white." She took a blank piece of paper from her desk and held it up as a sample of whiteness. "White is for white-collar workers, the starched white shirt wearable only for a single day being a timeless symbol of conspicuous consumption. I wish the slide projector worked for this: I have a portrait by Hals of a man wearing one of those immense Dutch collars, and you couldn't begin to imagine the work-hours that must have gone into washing and ironing the damned thing. The money. Basically that's what our second category is about. There's a book by Thorstein Veblen on the reading list that explains it all. Admittedly there are qualities other than solvency and success we may be called upon to *admire* in what people wear: good taste, a sense of paradox or wit, even courage, as when one walks through a dangerous neighborhood without the camouflage of denim. But good taste usually boils down to money: the good taste of petroleum-derived polyesters as against—" She smiled and ran her hand across the piled cloth of her dress. "—the *bad* taste of wool. Wit, likewise, is usually the wit of combining contradictory class-recognition signals in the same costume—an evening gown, say, trimmed with Purina patches. You should all be aware, as consumers, that the chief purpose of spending a lot of money on what you wear is to proclaim your allegiance to money *per se,* and to a career devoted to earning it, or, in the case of diamond rings, the promise to keep one's husband activated. Though in this case we begin to impinge on the realm of desire."

To all of which he gave about as much credence as he gave to actors in ads. Like most theories it made the world seem more, not less, complicated. Ho-hum, thought he, as he doodled a crisp doodle of a many-faceted diamond. But then, as she expounded her ideas about Desire, he grew uneasy, then embarrassed, and finally teed-off.

"Red," she said, reading from her deck of three-by-fives, "is the color of desire. Love is always like a red, red rose. It lies a-bleeding like a beautiful steak in a supermarket. To wear red is to declare oneself ready for action, especially if the color is worn below the waist."

There he sat in the back row in his red shorts and red sneakers thinking angry red thoughts. He refused to believe it was a coincidence. He was wearing red shorts because he'd bicycled here, a five-mile ride, not because he wanted to semaphore his instant availability to the world at large. He waited till she'd moved off the subject of Desire, then left the classroom as inconspicuously as possible. In the Bursar's

Office he considered the other Wednesday-night possibilities, mostly workshops in posture or poetry or suchlike. Only one—*A Survey of Crime in 20th Century America*—offered any promise of explaining people's behavior. So that was the one he signed up for.

The next day instead of going to work he went out to New Focus and watched hang-gliders. The most amazing of them was a crippled woman who arrived in a canvas sling. Rochelle Rockefeller's exploits had made her so famous that even Richard knew about her, not only on account of her flying but because she was one of the founding mothers of New Focus and had been involved in sizable altercations with the state police. The two women who carried her down from New Focus in the sling busied themselves with straps and buckles and then, at Rochelle's nod, launched her off the side of the cliff. She rose, motor-assisted, on the updraught and waved to her daughter, who sat watching on the edge of the cliff. The girl waved back. Then the girl went off by herself to the picnic table area where two rag dolls awaited her atop one of the tables.

He walked over to the table and asked if she minded if he shared the bench with her.

She shook her head and then in a rather dutiful tone introduced her dolls. The older one was Ms. Chillywiggles, the younger was Ms. Sillygiggles. They were married. "And *my* name is Rochelle, the same as my mother. What's yours?"

"Richard Roe."

"Did you bring any *food?*"

"No. Sorry."

"Oh, well, we'll just have to pretend. Here's some tuna fish, and here's some cake." She doled out the imaginary food with perfunctory mime to her dolls, and then with exaggerated delicacy she held up—what was it?—something for him.

"Open your mouth and close your eyes," she insisted.

He did, and felt her fingers on his tongue.

"What was that?" he asked, afterward.

"Holy Communion. Did you like it?"

"Mm."

"Are you a Catholic?"

"No, unless that just made me one."

"We are. We believe in God the Father Almighty and *everything*. Ms. Chillywiggles was even in a *convent* before she got married. Weren't you?" Ms. Chillywiggles nodded her large wobbly head.

Finding the subject uncomfortable, he changed it. "Look at your mother up there now. Wow."

Rochelle sighed and for a moment, to be polite, glanced up to where her mother was soaring, hundreds of feet above.

"It's incredible, her flying like that."

"That's what everyone says. But you don't need your leg muscles for a hang-glider, just your arms. And her arms are very strong."

"I'll bet."

"Some day we're going to go to Denver and see the dolls' Pope."

"Really. I didn't know dolls had a Pope."

"They do."

"Will you look at her now!"

"I don't like to, it makes me sick. I didn't want to come today, but no one would look after me. They were all *building*. So I had to."

"It doesn't make you want to fly someday, seeing her up there like that?"

"No. Some day she's going to kill herself. She knows it, too. That's how she had her accident, you know. She wasn't always in a wheelchair."

"Yes, I've heard that."

"What's so awful for *me* is to think she won't ever be able to receive the Last Sacrament."

The sun glowed through the red nylon wings of the glider, but even Professor Astor would have had a hard time making that fit her theory. Desire! Why not just Amazement?

"If she does kill herself," Rochelle continued dispassionately, *"we'll* be sent to an orphanage. In Denver, I hope. And Ms. Chillywiggles will be able to do missionary work among the dolls there. Do you have any dolls?"

He shook his head.

"I suppose you think dolls are only for *girls*. That's a very old prejudice, however. Dolls are for anyone who *likes* them."

"I may have had dolls when I was younger. I don't know."

"Oh. Were you erased?"

He nodded.

"So was my mother. But I was only a baby then. So I don't remember any more about her than she does. What I think is she must have committed some really terrible sin, and it tortured her so much she decided to be erased. Do you ever go in to Denver?"

"Sometimes."

Ms. Sillygiggles whispered something in Ms. Chillywiggles' ear, who evidently did not agree with the suggestion. Rochelle looked cast down. "Damn," she said.

"What's wrong?"

"Oh, nothing. Ms. Sillygiggles was hoping *you'd* be able to take them to Denver to see the dolls' Pope, but Ms. Chillywiggles put her foot down and said Absolutely Not. You're a stranger: we shouldn't even be talking to you."

He nodded, for it seemed quite true. He had no business coming out to New Focus at all.

"I should be going," he said.

Ms. Sillygiggles got to her feet and executed an awkward curtsey. Rochelle said it had been nice to make his acquaintance. Ms. Chillywiggles sat on the wooden step and said nothing.

It seemed to him, as he walked down the stony path to where he'd locked his bicycle to a rack, that everyone in the world was crazy, that craziness was synonymous with the human condition. But then he could see, through a break in the close-ranked spruces, the arc of a glider's flight—not Rochelle Rockefeller's, this one had blue wings—and his spirits soared with the sheer music of it. He understood, in a moment of crystalline level-headedness, that it didn't make a speck of difference if people were insane. Or if he was, for that matter. Sane and insane were just stages of the great struggle going on everywhere all the time: across the valley, for instance, where the pines were fighting their way up the sides of the facing mountain, hurling the grenades of their cones into the thin soil, pressing their slow advantage, enduring the decimations of the lightning, aspiring (insanely, no doubt) toward the forever unreachable fastness of the summit.

When he got to the road his lungs were heaving, his feet hurt, and his knees were not to be reasoned with (he should not have been running along such a path), but his head was once again solidly fixed on his shoulders. When he called his boss at the Denver Central Office to apologize for absconding, he wasn't fired or even penalized. His boss, who was usually such a tyrannosaurus, said everyone had days when they weren't themselves, and that it was all right, so long as they were few and far between. He even offered some Valiums, which Richard said no-thank-you to.

III

At Naropa the next Wednesday, the lecturer, a black man in a spotless white polyester suit, lectured about Ruth Snyder and Judd Gray, who, in 1927, had killed Ruth's husband Albert in a more than usually stupid fashion. He'd chosen this case, he said, because it represented the lowest common denominator of the crime of passion and would therefore serve to set in perspective the mystery and romance of last week's assassinations, which Richard had missed. First they watched a scene from an old comedy based on the murder, and then the lecturer read aloud a section of the autobiography Judd Gray had written in Sing Sing while waiting to be electrocuted:

"I was a morally sound, sober, God-fearing chap, working and saving to make Isabel my wife and establish a home. I met plenty of girls—at home and on the road, in trains and hotels. I could, I thought, place every type: the nice girl who flirts, the nice girl who doesn't, the brazen out-and-out streetwalker I was warned against. I was no sensualist, I studied no modern cults, thought nothing about inhibitions and repressions. Never read Rabelais in my life. Average, yes—just one of those Americans Mencken loves to laugh at. Even belonged to a club—the Club of Corset Salesmen of the Empire State—clean-cut competitors meeting and shaking hands—and liking it."

There was something in the tone of Judd Gray's voice, so plain, so accepting, that made Richard feel not exactly a kinship, more a sense of being similarly puzzled and potentially out of control. Maybe it was just the book's title that got to him—*Doomed Ship*. He wondered, not for the first time, whether he might not be among the fifteen per cent of erasees whose past has been removed by judicial fiat rather than by choice. He could, almost, imagine himself outside the Snyder bedroom in Queens Village, getting steadily more soused as he waited for Albert to go to sleep so that then he could sneak in there and brain him with the sash weight in his sweaty hand. All for the love of Ruth Snyder, as played by Carol Burnett. He couldn't, however, see himself as a more dignified sort of criminal—a racketeer or an assassin or the leader of a cult—for he lacked the strength of character and the conviction that those roles would have required, and he'd probably lacked it equally in the life that had been erased.

After the class he decided he'd tempt Fate and went to the cafeteria, where Fate immediately succumbed to the temptation and brought Professor Astor of *Consumership: Theory and Practice* to his table with a slice of viscid, bright cherry cheesecake. "May I join you?" she asked him.

"Sure. I was just going anyhow."

"I like your suit," she said. This close she seemed younger, or perhaps it was her dress that made that difference. Instead of last week's black wool bag she was wearing a dull blue double-knit with a scarf sprinkled with blurry off-red roses. One glance and anyone would have felt sorry for her.

His suit was the same dull blue. He'd bought it yesterday at the Stop-and-Shop, where the salesman had tried to convince him not to buy it. With it he wore a wrinkled Wrinkle-Proof shirt and a tie with wide stripes of gray and ocher. "Thanks," he said.

"It's very '70's. You're an erasee, aren't you?"

"Mm."

"I can always tell another. I am too. With a name like Lady Astor I'd have to be, wouldn't I? I hope I didn't offend you by anything I said last week."

"No, certainly not."

"It wasn't directed at you personally. I just read what it said in my notes, which were taken, all of them, practically verbatim from *The Colors of the Flag*. We teachers are all cheats that way, didn't you know? There's nothing we can tell you that you won't find expressed better in a book. But of course learning, in that sense, isn't the reason for coming here."

"No? What is then?"

"Oh, it's for meeting people. For playing new roles. For taking sides. For crying out loud."

"What?"

"That's an old expression—for crying out loud. From the '40's, I think. Actually your suit is more '40's than '70's. The '40's were *sincere* about being drab; the '70's played games."

"Isn't there anything that's just here and now, without all these built-in meanings?"

She poised her fork over the gleaming cheesecake. "Well," she said thoughtfully, then paused for a first taste of her dessert. "Mnyes, sort of. After you left last week, someone in the class asked if there wasn't a way one could be just anonymous. And what I said—" She took another bite of cheesecake. "—was that to my mind—" She swallowed. "—anonymity would come under the heading of solidarity, and solidarity is always solidarity *with* something—an idea, a group. Even the group of people who didn't want to have anything to do with anyone else—even they're a *group*. In fact, they're probably among the largest."

"I'm amazed," he said, counterattacking on sheer irresistible impulse, "that you, a supposed expert on consumerism, can eat junk like the junk you're eating. The sugar makes you fat and gives you cancer, the dye causes cancer too and I don't know what else, and there's something in the milk powder that I just heard about that's lethal. What's the point of being erased if afterwards you lead a life as stupid as everybody else's?"

"Right," she said. She picked up a paper plate from an abandoned tray and with a decisive rap of her fist squashed the wedge of cheesecake flat. "No more! Never again!"

He looked at the goo and crumbs splattered across the table, as well as on her scarf (there was a glob on his tie too, but he didn't notice that), and then at her face, a study in astonishment, as though the cheesecake had exploded autonomously. He started to laugh, and then, as though given permission, she did too.

They stayed on, talking, in the cafeteria until it closed, first about Naropa, then about the weather. This was his first experience of the approach of winter, and he surprised himself at the way he waxed eloquent. He marveled at how the aspens had gone golden all at once, as though every tree on a single mountain were activated by one switch and when that switch was thrown, bingo, it was autumn; the way, day by day, the light dwindled as his half of the world tilted away from the sun; the way the heat had come on in his condo without warning and baked the poor coleus living on top of the radiator; the misery of bicycling in the so much colder rain; and what was most amazing, the calmness of everyone in the face of what looked to him like an unqualified catastrophe. Lady Astor made a few observations of her own, but mostly she just listened, smitten with his innocence. Her own erasure had taken place so long ago—she was evasive as to exactly when—that the world had no such major surprises in store for her. As the chairs were being turned upside down onto the tabletops, he made a vague semi-enthusiastic commitment to hike up to New Focus some mutually convenient Sunday morning, to which end they exchanged addresses and phone numbers. (He had to give his number at work.) Why? It must have been the demolition of that cheesecake, the blissful feeling, so long lost to him, of muscular laughter, as though a window had been opened in a stuffy room and a wind had rushed in, turning the curtains into sails and bring strange smells from the mountains outside.

In the middle of November the company re-assigned him to the central office in downtown Denver, where he was assistant Traffic Manager for the entire Rocky Mountain division. Nothing in his work at the convenience center had seemed to point in this direction, but as soon as he scanned the programs involved, it was all there in his head and fingers, lingering on like the immutable melody of $1 + 1 = 2$.

The one element of the job that wasn't second nature was the increased human contact, which went on some days nonstop. Hi there, Dick, what do you think of this and what do you think of that, did you see the game last night, what's your opinion of the crisis, and would you *please* speak to Lloyd about the time he's spending in the john. Lloyd, when spoken to, insisted he worked just as hard in the john as in the office and said he'd cut down his time on the stool as soon as they allowed him to smoke at his desk. This seemed reasonable to Richard but not to the manager, who started to scream at him, called him a zombie and a zeroid, and said he was fired. Instead, to nobody's great surprise, it was the manager who got the axe. So, after just two weeks of grooming, Richard was the new Traffic Manager with an office all his own with its own view of other gigantic office buildings and a staff of thirty-two, if you counted temps and part-timers.

To celebrate he went out and had the famous hundred-dollar dinner at the Old Millionaire Steak Ranch with Lloyd, now the assistant Traffic Manager, with not his own office but at least a steel partition on one side of his desk and the right, thereby, to carcinogenate his lungs from punch-in to punch-out. Lloyd, it turned out, after a second Old Millionaire martini, lived up at New Focus and was one of the original members of the Boulder branch of the cult.

"No kidding," said Richard, reverently slicing into his sirloin. "So why are you working down here in the city? You can't commute to New Focus. Not this time of year."

"Money, why else. Half my salary, maybe more now, goes into the Corporation. We can't live for free, and there sure as hell isn't any money to be earned building a damned pyramid."

"So why do you build pyramids?"

"Come on, Dick. You know I can't answer that.

"I don't mean you as a group. I mean you personally. You must have *some* kind of reason for what you're doing."

Lloyd sighed long-sufferingly. "Listen, you've been up there, you've seen us cutting the blocks and fitting them in place. What's to explain? The beauty of the thing is that no one asks anyone else *why* we're doing what we're doing. Ever. That's Rule Number One. Remember that if you ever think of joining."

"Okay, then tell me this—why would I *want* to join?"

"Dick, you're hopeless. What did I just *say* to you? Enjoy your steak, why don't you? Do I ask why you want to throw away two hundred dollars on a dinner that can last, at the longest, a couple hours? No, I just enjoy it. It's beautiful."

"Mmn, I'm enjoying it. But still I can't keep from wondering."

"Wonder all you like—just don't ask."

IV

With the increased social inputs at work he had gradually tapered off on his visits to Naropa. Winter sealed him into a more circumscribed routine of apartment, job, and gym, as mounds of snow covered the known surfaces of Boulder like a divine amnesia. On weekends he would sit like a bear in a cave, knitting tubes of various dimensions and looking out the window and not quite listening to the purr of KMMN playing olden goldens in flattened-out, long-breathed renditions that corresponded in a semi-conscious way to the forms of the snow as it drifted and stormed and lifted up past the window in endless unraveling banners.

He had not forgotten his promise to Lady Astor, but a trip to New Focus was no longer feasible. Even with skis and a lift assisting, it would have been an overnight undertaking. He phoned twice and explained this to her answering machine. In reply she left a message—"That's okay."—at the convenience center, which got forwarded to the central office a week later. His first impression, that Destiny had introduced them with some purpose in mind, was beginning to diminish when one Saturday morning on the bus going to the gym he saw a street sign he'd never noticed before, Follet Avenue, and remembered that that was the street she lived on. He yanked the cord, got off, and walked back over unshoveled sidewalks to the corner of 34th and Follet, already regretting his impulse: 15 blocks to go, and then he might not find her home. It was 8 degrees below.

In the course of those 15 blocks the neighborhood dwindled from dowdy to stark. She lived in a two-story clapboard shopfront that looked like an illustration of the year daubed in black paint over the entrance: 1972. The shopwindows were covered with plywood, the plywood painted by some schizophrenic kindergarten with nightmarish murals, and the faded murals peered out forlornly from a lattice of obscene graffiti, desolation overlaying desolation.

He rang her bell and, when that produced no result, he knocked.

She came to the door wrapped in a blanket, hair in a tangle, bleary and haggard.

"Oh, it's you. I thought it might be you." Then, before he

212

could apologize or offer to leave: "Well, you might as well come in. Leave your overshoes in the hall."

She had the downstairs half of the building, behind the boarded-up windows, which were sealed, on this side, with strips of carpet padding. A coal stove on a brick platform gave off a parsimonious warmth. With a creaking of springs Lady Astor returned to bed. "You can sit there," she said, gesturing to a chair covered with clothes. When he did, its prolapsed bottom sank under him like the seat of a rowboat. At once a scrawny tabby darted from one of the shadowy corners of the room (the only light came from a small unboarded window at the back) and sprang into his lap. It nuzzled his hand, demanding a caress.

While he stumbled through the necessary explanations (how he happened to be passing, why he hadn't visited before), she sipped vodka from a coffee cup. He assumed it was vodka, since a vodka bottle, half-empty and uncapped, stood on the cash register that served as a bedside table. Most of the shop-fittings had been left *in situ:* a glass counter, full of dishes and cookware; shelves bearing a jumble of shoes, books, ceramic pots, and antique, probably defunct electric appliances. A bas-relief Santa of molded plastic was affixed to the wall behind the bed, its relevance belied by layers of greasy dust. The room's cluttered oddity combated its aura of poverty and demoralization, but not enough: he felt stricken. This was another First in the category of emotions, and he didn't know what to call it. Not simply dismay; not guilt; not pity; not indignation (though how could anyone be drunk at ten o'clock on a Saturday morning!); not even awe for the spirit that could endure such dismalness and still appear at Naropa every Wednesday evening, looking more or less normative, to lecture on the theory and practice of (of all things) Consumership. All these elements and maybe others were fuddled together in what he felt.

"Do you want a drink?" she asked, and before he could answer: "Don't think it's polite to say yes. There's not much left. I started at six o'clock, but you have to understand I don't *usually* do this. But today seemed special. I thought, why not? Anyhow why am I making excuses. I didn't invite you, you appeared at the door. I knew you would, eventually." She smiled, not pleasantly, and poured half the remaining vodka into her coffee cup. "You like this place?"

"It's big," he said lamely.

"And dark. And gloomy. And a mess. I was going to get the windows put back in, when I took the lease last summer. But that costs. And for winter this is warmer. Anyhow if I did try to make it a shop I don't know what I'd sell. Junk. I *used* to throw pots. What *didn't* I used to do. I did a book of poetry based on the Tarot (which is how I latched onto the job at Naropa). I framed pictures. And now I lecture, which is to say I read books and talk about them to people like you too lazy to read books on their own. And once, long ago, I was even a housewife, would you believe that." This time her smile was positively lethal. There seemed to be some secret message behind what she was saying that he couldn't uncode.

He sneezed.

"Are you allergic to cats?"

He shook his head. "Not that I know of."

"I'll bet you are."

He looked at her with puzzlement, then at the cat curled in his lap. The cat's warmth had penetrated through the denim and warmed his crotch pleasantly.

"God damn it," she said, wiping a purely hypothetical tear from the corner of her bleary eye. "Why'd you have to pick this morning? Why couldn't you have phoned? You were always like that. You schmuck."

"What?"

"Schmuck," she repeated. And then, when he just went on staring: "Well, it makes no difference. I would have had to tell you eventually. I just wanted you to get to know me a little better first."

"Told me what?"

"I was never erased. I just lied about that. It's all there on the shelf, everything that happened, the betrayals, the dirt, the failures. And there were lots of those. I just never had the guts to go through with it. Same with the dentist. That's why I've got such lousy teeth. I *meant* to. I had the money—at least for a while, after the divorce, but I thought. . . ." She shrugged, took a swallow from the cup, grimaced, and smiled, this time almost friendly.

"What did your husband do?"

"Why do you ask that?"

"Well, you seem to want to tell the whole story. I guess I wanted to sound interested."

She shook her head. "You still don't have a glimmering, do you?"

"Of what?" He did have a glimmering, but he refused to believe it.

"Well then, since you just insist, I'll have to tell you, won't I? *You* were the husband you're asking about. And you haven't changed one damned bit. You're the same stupid schmuck you were then."

"I don't believe you."

"That's natural. After spending so much to become innocent, who would want to see their investment wiped out like . . ." She tried to snap her fingers. ". . . that."

"There's no way you could have found me here. The Institute never releases that information. Not even to their employees."

"Oh, computers are clever these days (*you* know that), and for a couple thousand dollars it's not hard to persuade a salaried employee to tickle some data out of a locked file. When I found out where you'd gone, I packed my bags and followed you. I *told* you before you were erased that I'd track you down, and what you said was, 'Try, just try.' So that's what I did."

"You can be sent to prison for what you've done. Do you know that?"

"You'd like that, wouldn't you? If you could have had me locked up before, you wouldn't have had to get erased. You wouldn't have damned near killed me."

She said it with such conviction, with such a weariness modifying the anger, that it was hard to hold on to his reasonable doubt. He remembered how he'd identified with Judd Gray, the murderer of Albert Snyder.

"Don't you want to know *why* you tried to kill me?" she insisted.

"Whatever you used to be, Ms. Astor, you're not my wife now. You're a washed-up, forty-year-old drunk teaching an adult education course in the middle of nowhere."

"Yeah. Well, I could tell you how I got that way. Schmuck."

He stood up. "I'm leaving."

"Yes, you've said that before."

Two blocks from her house he remembered his overshoes. To hell with his overshoes! To hell with people who don't shovel their sidewalks! Most of all to hell with her!

That woman, his wife! What sort of life could they have lived together? All the questions about his past that he'd subdued so successfully up till now came bubbling to the surface: who he'd been, what he'd done, how it had all gone wrong. And she had the answers. The temptation to go back was strong, but before he could yield to it, the bus came in the homeward direction and he got on, his mind unchanged, his anger burning brightly.

V

Even so it was a week before he'd mustered the righteous indignation to call the Delphi Institute and register a formal complaint. They took down the information and said they'd investigate, which he assumed was a euphemism for their ignoring it. But in fact a week later he got a registered letter from them stating that Ms. Lady Astor of 1972 Follet Avenue in Boulder, Colorado, had never been his wife, nor had there ever been any other connection between them. Further, three other clients of the Institute had registered similar complaints about the same Ms. Astor. Unfortunately there was no law against providing erasees with misinformation about their past lives, and it was to be regretted that there were individuals who took pleasure in disturbing the euqanimity of the Institute's clients. The letter pointed out that he'd been warned of such possibilities while he was at the halfway house.

Now in addition to feeling angry and off-balance he felt like an asshole as well. To have been so easily diddled! To have believed the whole unlikely tale without even the evidence of a snapshot!

Three days before Christmas she called him at work. "I didn't want to bother you," she said in a meek little whisper that seemed, even now, knowing everything, utterly sincere, "but I had to apologize. You did pick a hell of a time to come calling. If I hadn't been drunk I would never have spilled the beans."

"Uh-huh," was all he could think to say.

"I know it was wrong of me to track you down and all, but I couldn't help myself." A pause, and then her most amazing lie of all: "I just love you too much to let you go."

"Uh-huh."

"I don't suppose we could get together? For coffee, after work?"

When they got together for coffee, after work, he led her on from lie to lie until she'd fabricated a complete life for him, a romance as preposterous as any soap on tv, beginning with a tyrannical father, a doting mother, a twin brother killed in a car crash, and progressing through his years of struggle to become a painter. (Here she produced a brittle polaroid of one of his putative canvases, a muddy jumble of ochres and umbers. She assured him that the polaroid didn't do it justice.) The tale went on to tell how they'd met, and fallen in love, how he'd sacrificed his career as an artist to become an animation programmer. They'd been happy, and then—due to his monstrous jealousy—unhappy. There was more, but she didn't want to go into it, it was too painful. Their son. . . .

Through it all he sat there nodding his head, seeming to believe each further fraud, asking appropriate questions, and (another First) enjoying it hugely—enjoying *his* fraudulence and her greater gullibility. Enjoying, too, the story she told him about his imaginary life. He'd never imagined a past for himself, but if he had he doubted if he'd have come up with anything so large, so resonant.

"So tell me," he asked, when her invention finally failed her, "why did I decide to be erased?"

"John," she said shaking flakes of dandruff from her long black hair, "I wish I could answer that question. Partly it must have been the pain of little Jimmy's death. Beyond that, I don't know."

"And now . . . ?"

She looked up, glittery. "Yes?"

"What is it you want?"

She gave a sigh as real as life. "I hoped . . . oh, you know."

"You want to get married again?"

"Well, no. Not till you've got to know me better anyhow. I mean I realize that from *your* point of view I'm still pretty much a stranger. And you've changed too, in some ways. You're like you were when I first met you. You're—" Her voice choked up, and tears came to her eyes.

He touched the clasp of his briefcase, but he didn't have the heart to take out the xerox of the letter from the Delphi

Institute that he'd been intending to spring on her. Instead he took the bill from under the saucer and excused himself.

"You'll call me, won't you?" she asked woefully.

"Sure, sure. Let me think about it a while first. Okay?"

She mustered a brave, quavering smile. "Okay."

In April to mark the conclusion of the first year of his new life and just to glory in the weather that made such undertakings possible again, he took the lift up Mount Lifton, then hiked through Corporation Canyon past New Focus and the site of the pyramid—only eight feet at its highest edge so far, scarcely a tourist attraction—and on up the Five Waterfall Trail. Except for a few boot-challenging stretches of vernal bogginess the path was stony and steep. The sun shone, winds blew, and the last sheltered ribs of snow turned to water and sought, trickle by trickle, the paths of least resistance. By one o'clock he'd reached his goal, Lake Silence, a perfect little mortuary chapel of a tarn colonnaded all round with spruces. He found an unshadowed, accommodating rock to bask on, took off his wet boots and damp socks, and listened as the wind did imitations of cars on a highway. Then, chagrined, he realized it wasn't the wind but the shuddering roar of an approaching helicopter.

The helicopter emerged like a demiurge from behind the writhing tops of the spruces, hovered a moment above the tarn, then veered in the direction of his chosen rock. As it passed directly overhead a stream of water spiraled out of the briefly opened hatch, dissolving almost at once in the machine's rotary winds into a mist of rainbow speckles. His first thought was that he was being bombed, his next that the helicopter was using Lake Silence as a toilet. Only when the first tiny trout landed, splat, on the rock beside him did he realize that the helicopter must have been from the Forest Service and was seeding the lake with fish. Alas, it had missed its mark, and the baby trout had fallen on the rocks of the shore and into the branches of the surrounding trees. The waters of Lake Silence remained unrippled and inviolate.

He searched among those fallen along the shore—there were dozens—for survivors, but all that he could find proved inert and lifeless when he put them in the water. Barefoot, panicky, totally devoted to the trout of Lake Silence, he continued the search. At last among the matted damp needles beneath the spruces he found three fish still alive and wiggling. As he lowered them, lovingly, into the lake he realized in a single lucid flash what it was he had to do with his life.

He would marry Lady Astor.

He would join New Focus and help them build a pyramid.

And he would buy a car.

(Also, in the event that she became orphaned, he would adopt little Rochelle Rockefeller. But that was counting chickens.)

He went to the other side of Lake Silence, to the head of the trail, where the Forest Service had provided an emergency telephone link disguised as a commemorative plaque to Governor Dent. He inserted his credit card into the slot, the plaque opened, and he punched Lady Astor's number. She answered at the third ring.

"Hi," he said. "This is Richard Roe. Would you like to marry me?"

"Well, yes, I guess so. But I ought to tell you—I was never really your wife. That was a story I made up."

"I knew that. But it was a nice story. And I didn't have one that I could tell you. One more thing, though. We'll have to join New Focus and help them build their pyramid."

"Why?"

"You can't ask why. That's one of their rules. Didn't you know that?"

"Would we have to live up there?"

"Not year-round. It'd be more like having a summer place, or going to church on Sunday. Plus some work on the pyramid."

"Well, I suppose I could use the exercise. Why do you want to get married? Or is that another question I shouldn't ask?"

"Oh, probably. One more thing: what's your favorite color?"

"For what?"

"A car."

"A car! Oh, I'd *love* a car! Be a show-off—get a red one. When do you want to do it?"

"I'll have to get a loan from the bank first. Maybe next week?"

"No, I meant getting married."

"We could do that over the phone. Or up here, if you want to take the lift to New Focus. Do you want to meet me there in a couple hours?"

"Make it three. I need a shampoo, and the bus isn't really reliable."

And so they were married, at sunset, on the stump of the unfinished pyramid, and the next week he bought a brand new Alizarin Crimson Ford Fundamental. As they drove out of the dealer's lot, he felt, for the first time in his life, that this was what it must be like to be completely human.

RELATIVISTIC EFFECTS

Gregory Benford

In recent years, Gregory Benford has become perhaps our foremost writer of stories that use authentically scientific backgrounds for literary purposes. Here he offers a story about a starship that has lost its ability to stop its voyage, eventually passing whole galaxies as other starships might pass individual stars; the society and psychology of the starship's passengers alter in interesting ways.

A working physicist, Benford has written such novels as In the Ocean of Night, The Stars in Shroud *and the multiple award-winning (and best-selling)* Timescape.

THEY CAME INTO THE LOCKER ROOM WITH A babble of random talk, laughter and shouts. There was a rolling bass undertone, gruff and raw. Over it the higher feminine notes ran lightly, warbling, darting.

The women had a solid, businesslike grace to them, doing hard work in the company of men. There were a dozen of them and they shed their clothes quickly and efficiently, all modestly forgotten long ago, their minds already focused on the job to come.

"You up for this, Nick?" Jake asked, yanking off his shorts and clipping the input sockets to his knees and elbows. His skin was red and callused from his years of linked servo work.

"Think I can handle it," Nick replied. "We're hitting pretty dense plasma already. There'll be plenty of it pouring through the throat." He was big but he gave the impression of lightness and speed, trim like a boxer, with broad shoulders and thick wrists.

"Lots of flux," Jake said. "Easy to screw up."

"I didn't get my rating by screwing up 'cause some extra ions came down the tube."

"Yeah. You're pretty far up the roster, as I remember," Jake said, eyeing the big man.

"Uh huh. Number one, last time I looked," Faye put in from the next locker. She laughed, a loud braying that rolled through the locker room and made people look up. "Bet 'at's what's botherin' you, uh, Jake?"

Jake casually made an obscene gesture in her general direction and went on. "You feelin' OK, Nick?"

"What you think, I got clenchrot?" Nick spat out with sudden ferocity. "Just had a cold, is all."

Faye said slyly, "Be a shame to prang when you're so close to winnin', movin' on up." She tugged on her halter and arranged her large breasts in it.

Nick glanced at her. Trouble was, you work with a woman long enough and after a while, she looked like just one more competitor. Once he'd thought of making a play for Faye—she really did look fairly good sometimes—but now she was one more sapper who'd elbow him into a vortex if she got half a chance. Point was, he never gave her—or anybody else—a chance to come up on him from some funny angle, throw him some unexpected momentum. He studied her casual, deft movements, pulling on the harness for the connectors. Still, there was something about her. . . .

"You get one more good run," Faye said slyly, "you gonna get the promotion. 'At's what I'd say."

"What matters is what they say upstairs, on A deck."

"Touchy, touchy, tsk tsk," Jake said. He couldn't resist getting in a little gig, Nick knew. Not when Jake knew it might get Nick stirred up a little. But the larger man stayed silent, stolidly pulling on his neural hookups.

Snick, the relays slide into place and Nick feels each one come home with a percussive impact in his body, he never gets used to that no matter it's been years he's been in the Main Drive crew. When he really sat down and thought about it he didn't like his job at all, was always shaky before coming down here for his shift. He'd figured that out at the start, so the trick was, he didn't think about it, not unless he'd had too much of that 'ponics-processed liquor, the stuff that was packed with vitamin B and C and wasn't supposed to do you any damage, not even leave the muggy dregs and ache of a hangover, only of course it never worked quite right because nothing on the ship did anymore. If he let himself stoke up on that stuff he'd gradually drop out of the conversation at whatever party he was, and go off into a corner somewhere and somebody'd find him an hour or two later staring at a wall or into his drink, reliving the hours in the tube and thinking about his dad and the grandfather he could only vaguely remember. They'd both died of the ol' black creeping cancer, same as eighty percent of the crew, and it was no secret the Main Drive was the worst place in the ship for it, despite all the design specs of fifty-meter rock walls and carbon-steel bulkheads and lead-lined hatches. A man'd be a goddamn fool if he didn't think about that, sure, but somebody had to do it or they'd all die. The job came down to Nick from his father because the family just did it, that was all, all the way back to the first crew, the original bridge officers had decided that long before Nick was born, it was the only kind of social organization that the sociometricians thought could possibly work on a ship that had to fly between stars, they all knew that and nobody questioned it any more than they'd want to change a pressure spec on a seal. You just didn't, was all there was to it. He'd learned that since he could first understand the church services, or the yearly anniversary of the Blowout up on the bridge, or the things that his father told him, even when the old man was dying with the black crawling stuff eating him from inside, Nick had learned that good—

"God, this dump is gettin' worse every—lookit 'at." Faye pointed.

A spider was crawling up a bulkhead, inching along on the ceramic smoothness.

"Musta got outta Agro," somebody put in.

"Yeah, don't kill it. Might upset the whole damn biosphere, an' they'd have our fuckin' heads for it."

A murmur of grudging agreement.

"Lookit 'at dumb thing," Jake said. "Made it alla way up here, musta come through air ducts an' line feeds an' who knows what." He leaned over the spider, eyeing it. It was a good three centimeters across and dull gray. "Pretty as sin, huh?"

Nick tapped in sockets at his joints and tried to ignore Jake. "Yeah."

"Poor thing. Don't know where in hell it is, does it? No appreciation for how important a place this is. We're 'bout to see a whole new age start in this locker room, soon's Nick here gets his full score. He'll be the new super an' we'll be— well, hell, we'll be like this li'l spider here. Just small and havin' our own tiny place in the big design of Nick's career, just you think how it's gonna—"

"Can the shit," Nick said harshly.

Jake laughed.

There was a tight feeling in the air. Nick felt it and figured it was something about his trying to get the promotion, something like that, but not worth bothering about. Plenty of time to think about it, once he had finished this job and gotten on up the ladder. Plenty of time then.

The gong rang brassily and the men and women finished suiting up. The minister came in and led them in a prayer for safety, the same as every other shift. Nothing different, but the tension remained. They'd be flying into higher plasma densities, sure, Nick thought. But there was no big deal about that. Still, he murmured the prayer along with the rest. Usually he didn't bother. He'd been to church services as usual, everybody went, it was unthinkable that you wouldn't, and anyway he'd never get any kind of promotion if he didn't show his face reg'lar, hunch on up to the altar rail and swallow that wafer and the alky-laced grape juice that went sour in your mouth while you were trying to swallow it, same as a lot of the talk they wanted you to swallow, only you did, you got it down because you had to and without asking anything afterward either, you bet, 'cause the ones who made trouble didn't get anywhere. So he muttered along, mouthing the familiar litany without thinking. The minister's thin lips moving, rolling on through the archaic phrases, meant less than nothing. When he looked up, each face was pensive as they prepared to go into the howling throat of the ship.

Nick lies mute and blind and for a moment feels nothing but the numb silence. It collects in him, blotting out the dim rub of the snouts which cling like lampreys to his nerves and muscles, pressing embrace that amplifies every movement, and—

—*spang*—

—he slips free of the mooring cables, a rush of sight-sound-taste-touch washes over him, so strong and sudden a welter of sensations that he jerks with the impact. He is servo'd to a thing like an eel that swims and flips and dives into a howling dance of protons. The rest of the ship is sheltered safely behind slabs of rock. But the eel is his, the eel is *him*. It shudders and jerks and twists, skating across sleek strands of magnetic plains. To Nick, it is like swimming.

The torrent gusts around him and he feels its pinprick breath. In a blinding orange glare Nick swoops, feeling his power grow as he gets the feel of it. His shiny shelf is wrapped in a cocoon of looping magnetic fields that turn the protons away, sending them gyrating in a mad gavotte, so the heavy particles cannot crunch and flare against the slick baked skin. Nick flexes the skin, supple and strong, and slips through the magnetic turbulence ahead. He feels the magnetic lines of force stretch like rubber bands. He banks and accelerates.

Streams of protons play upon him. They make glancing collisions with each other but do not react. The repulsion between them is too great and so this plasma cannot make them burn, cannot thrust them together with enough violence. Something more is needed or else the ship's throat will fail to harvest the simple hydrogen atoms, fail to kindle it into energy.

There— In the howling storm Nick sees the blue dots that are the keys, the catalyst: carbon nuclei, hovering like sea gulls in an updraft.

Split-image phosphors gleam, marking his way. He swims in the streaming blue-white glow, through a murky storm of fusing ions. He watches plumes of carbon nuclei striking the swarms of protons, wedding them to form the heavier nitrogen nuclei. The torrent swirls and screams at Nick's skin and in his sensors he sees and feels and tastes the lumpy, sluggish nitrogen as it finds a fresh incoming proton and with the fleshy smack of fusion the two stick, they hold, they wobble like raindrops—falling—merging—ballooning into a new nucleus, heavier still: oxygen.

But the green pinpoints of oxygen are unstable. These fragile forms split instantly. Jets of new particles spew through the surrounding glow—neutrinos, ruddy photons of light, and slower, darker, there come the heavy daughters of the marriage: a swollen, burnt-gold cloud of a bigger variety of nitrogen.

Onward the process flies. Each nucleus collides millions of times with the others in a fleck-shot swirl like glowing snowflakes. All in the space of a heartbeat. Flakes ride the magnetic field lines. Gamma rays flare and sputter among the blundering motes like fitful fireflies. Nuclear fire lights the long roaring corridor that is the ship's main drive. Nick swims, the white-hot sparks breaking over him like foam. Ahead he sees the violet points of gravid nitrogen and hears them crack into carbon plus an alpha particle. So in the end the long cascade gives forth the carbon that catalyzed it, carbon that will begin again its life in the whistling blizzard of protons coming in from the forward maw of the ship. With the help of the carbon, an interstellar hydrogen atom has built itself up from mere proton to, finally, an alpha particle—a stable clump of two neutrons and two protons. The alpha particle is the point of it all. It flees from the blurring storm, carrying the energy that fusion affords. The ruby-rich interstellar gas is now wedded, proton to proton, with carbon as the matchmaker.

Nick feels a rising electric field pluck at him. He moves to shed his excess charge. To carry a cloak of electrons here is fatal. Upstream lies the chewing gullet of the ramscoop ship, where the incoming protons arc sucked in and where their kinetic power is stolen from them by the electric fields. There the particles are slowed, brought to rest inside the ship, their streaming energy stored in capacitors.

A cyclone shrieks behind him. Nick swims sideways, toward the walls of the combustion chamber. The nuclear burn that flares around him is never pure, cannot be pure because the junk of the cosmos pours through here, like barley meal laced with grains of granite. The incoming atomic rain spatters constantly over the fluxlife walls, killing the organic superconductor strands there.

Nick pushes against the rubbery magnetic fields and swoops over the mottled yellow-blue crust of the walls. In the flickering lightning glow of infrared and ultraviolet he sees the scaly muck that deadens the magnetic fields and slows the nuclear burn in the throat. He flexes, wriggles, and turns the eel-like form. This brings the electron beam gun around at millimeter range. He fires. A brittle crackling leaps out, onto the scaly wall. The tongue bites and gouges. Flakes roast off and blacken and finally bubble up like tar. The rushing proton currents wash the flakes away, revealing the gunmetal blue beneath. Now the exposed superconducting threads can begin their own slow pruning of themselves, life casting out its dead. Their long organic chain molecules can feed and grow anew. As Nick cuts and turns and carves he watches the spindly fibers coil loose and drift in eddies. Finally they spin away into the erasing proton storm. The dead fibers sputter and flash where the incoming protons strike them and then with a rumble in his acoustic pickup coils he sees them swept away. Maintenance.

Something tugs at him. He sees the puckered scoop where the energetic alpha particles shoot by. They dart like luminous jade wasps. The scoop sucks them in. Inside they will be collected, drained of energy, inducing megawatts of power for the ship, which will drink their last drop of momentum and cast them aside, a wake of broken atoms.

Suddenly he spins to the left—*Jesus, how can*—he thinks—and the scoop fields lash him. A megavolt per meter of churning electrical vortex snatches at him. It is huge and quick and relentless to Nick (though to the ship it is a minor ripple in its total momentum) and magnetic tendrils claw at his spinning, shiny surfaces. The scoop opening is a plunging, howling mouth. Jets of glowing atoms whirl by him, mocking. The walls near him counter his motion by increasing their magnetic fields. Lines of force stretch and bunch.

How did this— is all he has time to think before a searing spot blooms nearby. His presence so near the scoop has upset the combination rates there. His eyes widen. If the reaction gets out of control it can burn through the chamber vessel, through the asteroid rock beyond, and spike with acrid fire into the ship, toward the life dome.

A brassy roar. The scoop sucks at his heels. Ions run white-hot. A warning knot strikes him. Tangled magnetic ropes grope for him, clotting around the shiny skin.

Panic squeezes his throat. Desperately he fires his electron beam gun against the wall, hoping it will give him a push, a fresh vector—

Not enough. Orange ions blossom and swell around him—

Most of the squad was finished dressing. They were tired and yet the release of getting off work brought out an undercurrent of celebration. They ignored Nick and slouched out of the locker room, bound for families or assignations or sensory jolts of sundry types. A reek of sweat and fatigue diffused through the sluggishly stirring air. The squad laughed and shouted old jokes to each other. Nick sat on the bench with his head in his hands.

"I . . . I don't get it. I was doin' pretty well, catchin' the crap as it came at me, an' then somethin' grabbed . . ."

They'd had to pull him out with a robot searcher. He'd gone dead, inoperative, clinging to the throat lining, fighting the currents. The surges drove blood down into your gut and legs, the extra *g*'s slamming you up against the bulkhead and sending big dark blotches across your vision, purple swarms of dots swimming everywhere, hollow rattling noises coming in through the transducer mikes, nausea, the ache spreading through your arms—

It had taken three hours to get him back in, and three more to clean up. A lot of circuitry was fried for good, useless junk. The worst loss was the high-grade steel, all riddled with neutrons and fissured by nuclear fragments. The ship's foundry couldn't replace that, hadn't had the rolling mill to even make a die for it in more than a generation. His neuro index checked out okay, but he wouldn't be able to work for a week.

He was still in a daze and the memory would not straighten itself out in his mind. "I dunno, I . . ."

Faye murmured, "Maybe went a li'l fast for you today."

Jake grinned and said nothing.

"Mebbe you could, y'know, use a rest. Sit out a few sessions." Faye cocked her head at him.

Nick looked at both of them and narrowed his eyes. "That wasn't a mistake of mine, was it? Uh? No mistake at all. Somebody—" He knotted a fist.

"Hey, nothin' you can prove," Jake said, backing away. "I can guarantee that, boy."

"Some bastard, throwin' me some extra angular when I wasn't lookin', I oughta—"

"Come on, Nick, you got no proof 'a those charges. You know there's too much noise level in the throat to record what ever'body's doin'." Faye grinned without humor.

"Damn." Nick buried his face in his hands. "I was *that* close, so damned near to gettin' that promotion—"

"Yeah. Tsk tsk. You dropped points back there for sure, Nick, burnin' out a whole unit that way an' gettin'—"

"Shut it. Just shut it."

Nick was still groggy and he felt the anger build in him without focus, without resolution. These two would make up some neat story to cover their asses, same as everybody did when they were bringing another member of the squad down a notch or two. The squad didn't have a lot of love for anybody who looked like they were going to get up above the squad, work their way up. That was the way it was, jobs were hard to change, the bridge liked it stable, said it came out better when you worked at a routine all your life and—

"Hey, c'mon, let's get our butts down to the Sniffer," Faye said. "No use jawin' 'bout this, is 'ere? I'm gettin' thirsty after all that, uh, work."

She winked at Jake. Nick saw it and knew he would get a ribbing about this for weeks. The squad was telling him he had stepped out of line and he would just have to take it. That was just the plain fact of it. He clenched his fists and felt a surge of anger.

"Hey!" Jake called out. "This damn spider's still tryin' to make it up this wall." He reached out and picked it up in his hand. The little gray thing struggled against him, legs kicking.

"Y'know, I hear there're people over in Comp who keep these for pets," Faye said. "Could be one of theirs."

"Creepy li'l thing," Nick said.

"You get what you can," Faye murmured. "Ever see a holo of a dog?"

Nick nodded. "Saw a whole movie about this one, it was a collie, savin' people an' all. Now that's a pet."

They all stared silently at the spider as it drummed steadily on Jake's hand with its legs. Nick shivered and turned away. Jake held it firmly, without hurting it, and slipped it into a pocket. "Think I'll take it back before Agro busts a gut lookin' for it."

Nick was silent as the three of them left the smells of the locker room and made their way up through the corridors. They took a shortcut along an undulating walkway under the big observation dome. Blades of pale blue light shifted like enormous columns in the air, but they were talking and only occasionally glanced up.

The vast ship of which they were a part was heading through the narrow corridor between two major spiral galaxies. On the right side of the dome the bulge of one galaxy was like a whirlpool of light, the points of light like grains of sand caught in a vortex. Around the bright core, glowing clouds of the spiral arms wended their way through the flat disk, seeming to cut through the dark dust clouds like a river slicing through jungle. Here and there black towers reared up out of the confusion of the disk, where masses of interstellar debris had been heaved out of the galactic plane, driven by collisions between clouds, or explosions of young stars.

There were intelligent, technological societies somewhere among those drifting stars. The ship had picked up their transmissions long ago—radio, UV, the usual—and had altered course to pass nearby.

The two spirals were a binary system, bound together since their birth. For most of their history they had stayed well apart, but now they were brushing within a galactic diameter of each other. Detailed observations in the last few weeks of ship's time—all that was needed to veer and swoop toward the twinned disks—had shown that this was the final pass: the two galaxies would not merely swoop by and escape. The filaments of gas and dust between them had created friction over the billions of years past, eroding their orbital angular momentum. Now they would grapple fatally.

The jolting impact would be spectacular: shock waves, compression of the gas in the galactic plane, and shortly thereafter new star formation, swiftly yielding an increase in the supernova rate, a flooding of the interstellar medium with high energy particles. The rain of sudden virulent energy would destroy the planetary environments. The two spirals would come together with a wrenching suddenness, the disks sliding into each other like two saucers bent on destruction, the collision effectively occurring all over the disks simultaneously in an explosive flare of X-ray and thermal bremsstrahlung radiation. Even advanced technologies would be snuffed out by the rolling, searing tide.

The disks were passing nearly face-on to each other. In the broad blue dome overhead the two spirals hung like cymbals seen on edge. The ship moved at extreme relativistic velocity, pressing infinitesimally close to light speed, passing through the dim halo of gas and old dead stars that surrounded each galaxy. Its speed compressed time and space. Angles distorted as time ran at a blinding pace outside, refracting images. Extreme relativistic effects made the approach visible to the naked eye. Slowly, the huge disks of shimmering light seemed to swing open like a pair of doors. Bright tendrils spanned the gap between them.

Jake was telling a story about two men in ComCatSynch section, rambling on with gossip and jokes, trying to keep the talk light. Faye went along with it, putting in a word when Jake slowed. Nick was silent.

The ship swooped closer to the disks and suddenly across the dome streaked red and orange bursts. The disks were twisted, distorted by their mutual gravitational tugs, wrenching each other, twins locked in a tightening embrace. The planes of stars rippled, as if a huge wind blew across them. The galactic nuclei flared with fresh fires: ruby, orange, mottled blue, ripe gold. Stars were blasted into the space between. Filaments of raw, searing gas formed a web that spanned the two spirals. This was the food that fed the ship's engines. They were flying as near to the thick dust and gas of the galaxies as they could. The maw of the ship stretched outward, spanning a volume nearly as big as the galactic core. Streamers of sluggish gas veered toward it, drawn by the onrushing magnetic fields. The throat sucked in great clouds, boosting them to still higher velocity.

The ship's hull moaned as it met denser matter.

Nick ignores the babble from Jake, knowing it is empty foolishness, and thinks instead of the squad, and how he would run it if he got the promotion: They had to average 5000 cleared square meters a week, minimum, that was a full ten percent of the whole ship's throat, minus of course the lining areas that were shut down for full repair, call that 1000 square meters on the average, so with the other crews operating on 45-hour shifts they could work their way through and give the throat a full scraping in less than a month, easy, even allowing for screwups and malfs and times when the radiation level was too high for even the suits to screen it out. You had to keep the suits up to 99 plus percent operational or you caught hell from upstairs, but the same time they came at you with their specifications reports and never listened when you told them about the delays, that was your problem not theirs and they said so every chance they got, that bunch of blowhard officers up there, descended from the original ship's bridge officers who'd left Earth generations back with every intention of returning after a twelve-year round trip to Centauri, only it hadn't worked, they didn't count on the drive freezing up in permanent full-bore thrust, the drive locked in and the deceleration components slowly getting fried by the increased neutron flux from the reactions, until when they finally could taper off on the forward drive the decelerators were finished, beyond repair, and then the ship had nothing to do but drive on, unable to stop or even turn the magnetic gascatchers off, because once you did that the incoming neutral atoms would be a sleet of protons and neutrons that'd riddle everybody within a day, kill them all. So the officers had said they had to keep going, studying, trying to figure a way to rebuild the decelerators, only nobody ever did, and the crew got older and they flew on, clean out of the galaxy, having babies and quarrels and finally after some murders and suicides and worse, working out a stable social structure in a goddamn relativistic runaway, officers' sons and daughters becoming officers themselves, and crewmen begetting crewmen again, down through five generations now in the creaky old ship that had by now flown through five million years of outside-time, so that there was no purpose or dream of returning Earthside any more, only names attached to pictures and stories, and the same jobs to do every day, servicing the weakening stanchions and struts, the flagging motors, finding replacements for every little doodad that fractured, working because to stop was to die, all the time with officers to tell you what new scientific experiment they'd thought up and how maybe this time it would be the answer, the clue to getting back to their own galaxy—a holy grail beloved of the first and second generations that was now, even under high magnification, a mere mottled disk of ruby receding pinprick lights nobody alive had ever seen up close. Yet there was something in what the bridge officers said, in what the scientific mandarins mulled over, a point to their lives here—

"Let's stop in this'n," Jake called, interrupting Nick's muzzy thoughts, and he followed them into a small inn. Without his noticing it they had left the big observation dome. They angled through a tight, rocky corridor cut from the original asteroid that was the basic body of the whole starship.

Among the seven thousand souls in the ten-kilometer-wide starship, there were communities and neighborhoods and bars to suit everyone. In this one there were thick veils of smoky euphorics, harmless unless you drank an activating potion. Shifts came and went, there were always crowds in the bar, a rich assortment of faces and ages and tongues. Techs, metalworkers, computer jockeys, manuals, steamfitters, muscled grunt laborers. Cadaverous and silent ale-soakers, steadily pouring down a potent brown liquid. Several women danced in a corner, oblivious, singing, rhyming as they went.

Faye ordered drinks and they all three joined in the warm feel of the place. The euphorics helped. It took only moments to become completely convinced that this was a noble and notable set of folk. Someone shouted a joke. Laughter pealed in the close-packed room.

Nick saw in this quick moment an instant of abiding grace: how lovely it was when Faye forgot herself and laughed fully, opening her mouth so wide you could see the whole oval cavern with its ribbed pink roof and the arcing tongue alive with tension. The heart-stopping blackness at the back led down to depths worth a lifetime to explore, all revealed in a passing moment like a casual gift: a momentary and incidental beauty that eclipsed the studied, long-learned devices of women and made them infinitely more mysterious.

She gave him a wry, tossed-off smile. He frowned, puzzled. Maybe he had never paid adequate attention to her, never sensed her dimensions. He strained forward to say something and Jake interrupted his thoughts with, "Hey there, look. Two bridgies."

And there were. Two bridge types, not mere officers but scientists; they wore the sedate blue patches on their sleeves. Such people seldom came to these parts of the ship; their quarters, ordained by time, nestled deep in the rock-lined bowels of the inner asteroid.

"See if you can hear what they're sayin'," Faye whispered.

Jake shrugged. "Why should I care?"

Faye frowned. "Wanna be a scuzzo dope forever?"

"Aw, stow it," Jake said, and went to get more beer.

Nick watched the scientist nearest him, the man, lift the heavy champagne bottle and empty it. *Have to hand it to bioponics,* he thought. *They keep the liquor coming.* The crisp golden foil at the head would be carefully collected, reused; the beautiful heavy hollow butts of the bottles had doubtless been fondled by his own grandfather. Of celebration there was no end.

Nick strained to hear.

"Yes, but the latest data shows there's enough mass, no question."

"Maybe, maybe," said the other. "Must say I never thought there'd be enough between the clusters to add up so much—"

"But there *is*. No doubt of it. Look at Fenetti's data, clear as the nose on your face. Enough mass density between the clusters to close off the universe's geometry, to reverse the expansion."

Goddamn, Nick thought. *They're talking about the critical mass problem. Right out in public.*

"Yes. My earlier work seems to have been wrong."

"Look, this opens possibilities."

"How?"

"The expansion has to stop, right? So after it does, and things start to implode back, the density of gas the ship passes through will get steadily greater—right?"

Jesus, Nick thought, *the eventual slowing down of the universal expansion, billions of years—*

"Okay."

"So we'll accelerate more, the relativistic rate will get bigger—the whole process outside will speed up, as we see it."

"Right."

"Then we can sit around and watch the whole thing play out. I mean, shipboard time from now to the implosion of the whole universe, I make it maybe only three hundred years."

"That short?"

"Do the calculation."

"Ummm. Maybe so, if we pick up enough mass in the scoop fields. This flyby we're going through, it helps, too."

"Sure it docs. We'll do more like in the next few weeks. Look, we're getting up to speeds that mean we'll be zooming by a galaxy every *day*."

"Uh huh. If we can live a couple more centuries, shipboard time, we can get to see the whole shebang collapse back in on itself."

"Well, look, that's just a preliminary number, but I think we might make it. In this generation."

Faye said, "Jeez, I can't make out what they're talkin' about."

"I can," Nick said. It helped to know the jargon. He had studied this as part of his program to bootstrap himself up to a better life. You take officers, they could integrate the gravitational field equations straight off, or tell how a galaxy was evolving just by looking at it, or figure out the gas density ahead of the ship just by squinting at one of the X-ray bands from the detectors. They *knew*. He would have to know all of that too, and more. So he studied while the rest of the squad slurped up the malt.

He frowned. He was still stunned, trying to think it through. If the total mass between the clusters of galaxies was big enough, that extra matter would provide enough gravitational energy to make the whole universe reverse its expansion and fall backward, inward, given enough time . . .

Jake was back. "To noisy in 'ere," he called. "Fergit the beers, bar's mobbed. Let's lift 'em."

Nick glanced over at the scientists. One was earnestly leaning forward, her face puffy and purplish, congested with the force of the words she was urging into the other's ear. He couldn't make out any more of what they were saying; they had descended into quoting mathematical formulas to each other.

"Okay," Nick said.

They left the random clamor of the bar and retraced their steps, back under the observation dome. Nick felt a curious elation.

Nick knows how to run the squad, knows how to keep the equipment going even if the voltage fickers, he can strip down most suits in under an hour using just plain rack tools, been doing it for forty years, all those power tools around the bay, most of the squad can't even turn a nut on a manifold without it has to be pneumatic *rrrrrtt* quick as you please nevermind the wear on the lubricants lost forever that nobody aboard can synthesize, tools seize up easy now, jam your fingers when they do, give you a hand all swole up for a week, and all the time the squad griping 'cause they have to birddog their own stuff, breadboard new ones if some piece of gear goes bad, complaining 'cause they got to form and fabricate their own microchips, no easy replacement parts to just clip in the way you read about the way it was in the first generation, and God help you if a man or woman on the crew gets a fatal injury working in the throat crew, 'cause then your budget is docked for the cost of keeping 'em frozen down, waiting on cures that'll never come just like Earth will never come, the whole planet's been dead now a million years prob'ly, and the frozen corpses on board running two percent of the energy budget he read somewhere, getting to be more all the time, but then he thinks about that talk back in the bar and what it might mean, plunging on until you could see the whole goddamn end of the universe—

"Gotta admit we got you that time, Nick," Jake says as they approach the dome, smooth as glass I come up on you, you're so hard workin' you don't see nothin', I give you a shot of extra spin, *man* your legs fly out you go wheelin' away—"

Jake starts to laugh.

—and livin' in each others' hip pockets like this the hell of it was you start to begrudge ever' little thing, even the young ones, the kids cost too, not that he's against them, hell, you got to keep the families okay or else they'll be slitting each other's throats inside a year, got to remember your grandfather who was in the Third Try on the decelerators, they came near to getting some new magnets in place before the plasma turbulence blew the whole framework away and they lost it, every family's got some ancestor who got flung down the throat and out into nothing, the kids got to be brought up rememberin' that, even though the little bastards do get into the bioponic tubes and play pranks, they got not a lot to do 'cept study an work, same as he and the others have done for all their lives, average crewman lasts 200 years or so now, all got the best biomed (goddamn lucky they were shippin' so much to Centauri), bridge officers maybe even longer, get lots of senso augmentation to help you through the tough parts, and all to keep going, or even maybe get ahead a little like this squad boss thing, he was *that* close an' they took it away from him, small-minded bastards scared to shit he might make, what was it, 50 more units of rec credit than they did, not like being an officer or anything, just a job-jockey getting ahead a little, wanting just a scrap, and they gigged him for it and now this big mouth next to his ear is goin' on, puffing himself up in front of Faye, Faye who might be worth a second look if he could get her out of the shadow of this loudmouthed secondrate—

Jake was in the middle of a sentence, drawling on. Nick grabbed his arm and whirled him around.

"Keep laughin', you slimy bastard, just keep—"

Nick got a throat hold on him and leaned forward. He lifted, pressing Jake against the railing of the walkway. Jake struggled but his feet left the floor until he was balanced on the railing, halfway over the twenty-meter drop. He struck out with a fist but Nick held on.

"Hey, hey, vap off a li'l," Faye cried.

"Yeah—look—you got to take it—as it comes," Jake wheezed between clenched teeth.

"You two done me an' then you laugh an' don't think I don't know you're, you're—" He stopped, searching for words and not finding any.

Globular star clusters hung in the halo beyond the spirals. They flashed by the ship like immense chandeliers of stars. Odd clumps of torn and twisted gas rushed across the sweep of the dome overhead. Tortured gouts of sputtering matter were swept into the magnetic mouth of the ship. As it arched inward toward the craft it gave off flashes of incandescent light. These were stars being born in the ship-driven turbulence, the compressed gases collapsing into firefly lives before the ship's throat swallowed them. In the flicker of an eyelid on board, a thousand years of stellar evolution transpired on the churning dome above.

The ship had by now carved a swooping path through the narrow strait between the disks. It had consumed banks of gas and dust, burning some for power, scattering the rest with fresh ejected energy into its path. The gas would gush out, away from the galaxies, unable to cause the ongoing friction that drew the two together. This in turn would slow their collision, giving the glittering worlds below another million years to plan, to discover, to struggle upward against the coming catastrophe. The ship itself, grown vast by relativistic effects, shone in the night skies of a billion worlds as a fiercely burning dot, emitting at impossible frequencies, slicing through kiloparsecs of space with its gluttonous magnetic throat, consuming.

"Be easy on him, Nick," Faye said softly.

Nick shook his head. "Naw. Trouble with a guy like this is, he got nothin' to do but piss on people. Hasn't got per . . . perspective."

"Stack it, Nick," Faye said.

Above them, the dome showed briefly the view behind the ship, where the reaction engines poured forth the raw refuse of the fusion drives. Far back, along their trajectory, lay dim filaments, wisps of ivory light. It was the Local Group, the cluster of galaxies that contained the Milky Way, their home. A human could look up, extend a hand, and a mere thumbnail would easily cover the faint smudge that was in fact a clump of spirals, ellipticals, dwarfs and irregular galaxies. It was a small part of the much larger association of galaxies, called the Local Supercluster. The ship was passing now beyond the fringes of the Local Supercluster, forging outward through the dim halo of random glimmering-galaxies which faded off into the black abyss beyond. It would be a long voyage across that span, until the next supercluster was reached: a pale blue haze that ebbed and flowed before the nose of the ship, liquid light distorted by relativity. For the moment the glow of their next destination was lost in the harsh glare of the two galaxies. The disks yawned and turned around the ship, slabs of hot gold and burnt orange, refracted, moving according to the twisted optical effects of special relativity. Compression of wavelengths and the squeezing of time itself made the disks seem to open wide, immense glowing doors swinging in the vacuum, parting to let pass this artifact that sped on, riding a tail of forking, sputtering, violet light.

Nick tilted the man back farther on the railing. Jake's arms fanned the air and his eyes widened.

"Okay, okay, you win," Jake grunted.

"You going upstairs, tell 'em you scragged me."

"Ah . . . okay."

"Good. Or else somethin' might, well, happen." Nick let Jake's legs down, back onto the walkway.

Faye said, "You didn't have to risk his neck. We would've cleared it for you if you'd—"

"Yeah, sure," Nick said sourly.

"You bastard, I oughta—"

"Yeah?"

Jake was breathing hard, his eyes danced around, but Nick knew he wouldn't try anything. He could judge a thing like that. Anyway, he thought, he'd been right, and they knew it. Jake grimaced, shook his head. Nick waved a hand and they walked on.

"Y'know what your trouble is, Nick?" Jake said after a moment. "Yer like this spider here."

Jake took the spider out of his jumpsuit pocket and held up the gray creature. It stirred, but was trapped.

"What'cha mean?" Nick asked.

"You got no perspective on the squad. Don't know what's really happenin'. An' this spider, he dunno either. He was down in the locker room, he didn't appreciate what he was in. I mean, that's the center of the whole damn ship right there, the squad."

"Yeah. So?"

"This spider, he don't appreicate how far he'd come from Agro. You either, Nick. You don't appreciate how the squad helps you out, how you oughta be grateful to them, how mebbe you shouldn't keep pushin' alla time."

"Spider's got little eyes, no lens to it," Nick said. "Can't see further than your hand. Can't see those stars up there. I can, though."

Jake sputtered, "Crap, relative to the spider you're—"

"Aw, can it," Nick said.

Faye said, "Look, Jake, maybe you stop raggin' him alla time, he—"

"No, he's got a point there," Nick said, his voice suddenly mild. "We're all tryin' to be reg'lar folks in the ship, right? We should keep t'gether."

"Yeah. You push too hard."

Sure, Nick thought. *Sure I do. And the next thing I'm gonna push for is Fay, take her clean away from you.*

—the way her neck arcs back when she laughs, graceful in a casual way he never noticed before, a lilting note that caught him, and the broad smile she had, but she was solid too, did a good job in the blowback zone last week when nobody else could handle it, red gases flaring all around her, good woman to have with you, and maybe he'd need a lot of support like that, because he knows now what he really wants: to be an officer someday, it wasn't impossible, just hard, and the only way is by pushing. All this scratching around for a little more rec credits, maybe some better food, that wasn't the point, no, there was something more, the officers keep up the promotion game 'cause we've got to have something to keep people fretting and working, something to take our minds off what's outside, what'll happen if—no, *when*—the drive fails, where we're going, only what these two don't know is that we're not bound for oblivion in a universe that runs down into blackness, we're going on to see the reversal, we get to hear the recessional, galaxies, peeling into the primordial soup as they compress back together and the ship flies faster, always faster as it sucks up the dust of time and hurls itself further on, back to the crunch that made everything and will some day—hell, if he can stretch out the years, right in his own lifetime!—press everything back into a drumming hail of light and mass, now *that's* something to live for—

Faye said pleasantly, "Just think how much good we did back there. Saved who knows how many civilizations, billions of living creatures, gave them a reprieve."

"Right," Jake said, his voice distracted, still smarting over his defeat.

Fay nodded and the three of them made their way up an undulating walkway, heading for the bar where the rest of the squad would be. The ship thrust forward as the spiral galaxies dropped behind now, Doppler reddened into dying embers.

The ship had swept clean the space between them, postponed the coming collision. The scientists had seen this chance, persuaded the captain to make the slight swerve that allowed them to study the galaxies, and in the act accelerate the ship still more. The ship was now still closer to the knife-edge of light speed. Its aim was not a specific destination, but rather to plunge on, learning more, studying the dabs of refracted lights beyond, struggling with the engines, forging on as the universe wound down, as entropy increased, and the last stars flared out. It carried the cargo meant for Centauri—the records and past lives of all humanity, a library for the colony there. If the drives held up, it would carry them forward until the last tick of time.

Nick laughed. "Not that they'll know it, or ever give a—" He stopped. He'd been going to say *ever give a Goddamn about who did it,* but he knew how Faye felt about using the Lord's name in vain.

"Why, sure they will," Faye said brightly. "We were a big, hot source of all kinds of radiation. They'll know it was a piece of technology."

"Big lights in the sky? Could be natural."

"With a good spectrometer—"

"Yeah, but they'll never be sure."

She frowned. "Well, a ramscoop exhaust looks funny, not like a star or anything."

"With the big relativistic effect factored in, our emission goes out like a searchlight. One narrow little cone of scrambled-up radiation, Dopplered forward. So they can't make us out the whole time. Most of 'em 'd see us for just a few years, tops," Nick said.

"So?"

"Hard to make a scientific theory about somethin' that happens once, lasts a little while, never repeats."

"Maybe."

"They could just as likely think it was somethig unnatural. Supernatural. A god or somethin'."

"Huh. Maybe." Faye shrugged. "Come on. Let's get 'nother drink before rest'n rec hours are over."

They walked on. Above them the great knives of light sliced down through the air, ceaselessly changing, and the humans kept on going, their small voices indomitable, reaching forward, undiminished.

FIREWATCH

≈≈≈≈≈≈≈≈≈≈≈≈≈≈≈≈≈≈≈≈≈≈≈≈≈≈≈

Connie Willis

Should a practical method of time travel ever be discovered, it will surely be a boon in particular to historians, who will be able to go back in time to earlier periods in order to research and understand them better. Here is a gripping long novelette about a Twenty-first Century historian in 1940 London who becomes caught up in events and dangers there, eventually coming to question the purpose of his calling.

Connie Willis is one of the strong new talents that have entered the science fiction field in recent years. She lives with her husband and daughter in Colorado.

"History hath triumphed over time, which besides it nothing but eternity hath triumphed over."

—Sir Walter Raleigh

SEPTEMBER 20—OF COURSE THE FIRST THING I looked for was the firewatch stone. And of course it wasn't there yet. It wasn't dedicated until 1951, accompanying speech by the Very Reverend Dean Walter Matthews, and this is only 1940. I knew that. I went to see the firewatch stone only yesterday, with some kind of misplaced notion that seeing the scene of the crime would somehow help. It didn't.

The only things that would have helped were a crash course in London during the Blitz and a little more time. I had not gotten either.

"Travelling in time is not like taking the tube, Mr. Bartholomew," the esteemed Dunworthy had said, blinking at me through those antique spectacles of his. "Either you report on the twentieth or you don't go at all."

"But I'm not ready," I'd said. "Look, it took me four years to get ready to travel with St. Paul. *St. Paul.* Not St. Paul's. You can't expect me to get ready for London in the Blitz in two days."

"Yes," Dunworthy had said. "We can." End of conversation.

"Two days!" I had shouted at my roommate Kivrin. "All because some computer adds an apostrophe s. And the esteemed Dunworthy doesn't even bat an eye when I tell him. 'Time travel is not like taking the tube, young man,' he

244

says. 'I'd suggest you get ready. You're leaving day after tomorrow.' The man's a total incompetent."

"No," she said. "He isn't. He's the best there is. He wrote the book on St. Paul's. Maybe you should listen to what he says."

I had expected Kivrin to be at least a little sympathetic. She had been practically hysterical when she got her practicum changed from fifteenth to fourtheeth century England, and how did either century qualify as a practicum? Even counting infectious diseases they couldn't have been more than a five. The Blitz is an eight, and St. Paul's itself is, with my luck, a ten.

"You think I should go see Dunworthy again?" I said.

"Yes."

"And then what? I've got two days. I don't know the money, the language, the history. Nothing."

"He's a good man," Kivrin said. "I think you'd better listen to him while you can." Good old Kivrin. Always the sympathetic ear.

The good man was responsible for my standing just inside the propped-open west doors, gawking like the country boy I was supposed to be, looking for a stone that wasn't there. Thanks to the good man, I was about as unprepared for my practicum as it was possible for him to make me.

I couldn't see more than a few feet into the church. I could see a candle gleaming feebly a long way off and a closer blur of white moving toward me. A verger, or possibly the Very Reverend Dean himself. I pulled out the letter from my clergyman uncle in Wales that was supposed to gain me access to the Dean, and patted my back pocket to make sure I hadn't lost the microfiche *Oxford English Dictionary, Revised, with Historical Supplements,* I'd smuggled out of the Bodleian. I couldn't pull it out in the middle of the conversation, but with luck I could muddle through the first encounter by context and look up the words I didn't know later.

"Are you from the ayarpee?" he said. He was no older than I am, a head shorter and much thinner. Almost ascetic looking. He reminded me of Kivrin. He was not wearing white, but clutching it to his chest. In other circumstances I would have thought it was a pillow. In other circumstances I would know what was being said to me, but there had been no time to unlearn sub-Mediterranean Latin and Jewish law and learn Cockney and air-raid procedures. Two days, and the esteemed Dunworthy, who wanted to talk about the sacred burdens of the historian instead of telling me what the ayarpee was.

"Are you?" he demanded again.

I considered shipping out the *OED* after all on the grounds that Wales was a foreign country, but I didn't think they had microfilm in 1940. Ayarpee. It could be anything, including a nickname for the fire watch, in which case the impulse to say no was not safe at all. "No," I said.

He lunged suddenly toward and past me and peered out the open doors. "Damn," he said, coming back to me. "Where are they then? Bunch of lazy bourgeois tarts!" And so much for getting by on context.

He looked at me closely, suspiciously, as if he thought I was only pretending not to be with the ayarpee. "The church is closed," he said finally.

I held up the envelope and said, "My name's Bartholomew. Is Dean Matthews in?"

He looked out the door a moment longer, as if he expected the lazy bourgeois tarts at any moment and intended to attack them with the white bundle, then he turned and said, as if he were guiding a tour, "This way, please," and took off into the gloom.

He led me to the right and down the south aisle of the nave. Thank God I had memorized the floor plan or at that moment, heading into total darkness, led by a raving verger, the whole bizarre metaphor of my situation would have been enough to send me out the west doors and back to St. John's Wood. It helped a little to know where I was. We should have been passing number twenty-six: Hunt's painting of "The Light of the World"—Jesus with his lantern—but it was too dark to see it. We could have used the lantern ourselves.

He stopped abruptly ahead of me, still raving. "We weren't asking for the bloody Savoy, just a few cots. Nelson's better off than we are—at least he's got a pillow provided." He brandished the white bundle like a torch in the darkness. It was a pillow after all. "We asked for them over a fortnight ago, and here we still are, sleeping on the bleeding generals from Trafalgar because those bitches want to play tea and crumpets with the tommies at Victoria and the Hell with us!"

He didn't seem to expect me to answer his outburst, which was good, because I had understood perhaps one key word in three. He stomped on ahead, moving out of sight of the one pathetic altar candle and stopping again at a black hole. Number twenty-five: stairs to the Whispering Gallery, the Dome, the library (not open to the public). Up the stairs, down a hall, stop again at a medieval door and knock. "I've got to go wait for them," he said. "If I'm not there they'll likely take them over to the Abbey. Tell the Dean to ring them up again, will you?" and he took off down the stone steps, still holding his pillow like a shield against him.

He had knocked, but the door was at least a foot of solid oak, and it was obvious the Very Reverend Dean had not heard. I was going to have to knock again. Yes, well, and the man holding the pinpoint had to let go of it, too, but even knowing it will be over in a moment and you won't feel a thing doesn't make it any easier to say, "Now?" So I stood in front of the door, cursing the history department and the esteemed Dunworthy and the computer that had made the mistake and brought me here to this dark door with only a letter from a fictitious uncle that I trusted no more than I trusted the rest of them.

Even the old reliable Bodleian had let me down. The batch of research stuff I cross-ordered through Balliol and the main terminal is probably sitting in my room right now, a century out of reach. And Kivrin, who had already done her practicum and should have been bursting with advice, walked around as silent as a saint until I begged her to help me.

"Did you go to see Dunworthy?" she said.

"Yes. You want to know what priceless bit of information he had for me? 'Silence and humility are the sacred burdens of the historian.' He also told me I would love St. Paul's. Golden gems from the master. Unfortunately, what I need to know are the times and places of the bombs so one doesn't fall on me." I flopped down on the bed. "Any suggestions?"

"How good are you at memory retrieval?" she said.

I sat up. "I'm pretty good. You think I should assimilate?"

"There isn't time for that," she said. "I think you should put everything you can directly into long-term."

"You mean endorphins?" I said.

The biggest problem with using memory-assistance drugs to put information into your long-term memory is that it never sits, even for a micro-second, in your short-term memory, and that makes retrieval complicated, not to mention unnerving. It gives you the most unsettling case of *déjà vu* to suddenly know something you're positive you've never seen or heard before.

The main problem, though, is not eerie sensations but retrieval. Nobody knows exactly how the brain gets what it wants out of storage, but short-term is definitely involved. That brief, sometimes microscopic, time information spends in short-term is apparently used for something besides tip-of-the-tongue availability. The whole complex sort-and-file process of retrieval is apparently centered in short-term; and without it, and without the help of drugs that put it there or artificial substitutes, information can be impossible to retrieve. I'd used endorphins for examinations and never had any difficulty with retrieval, and it looked like it was the only way to store all the information I needed in anything approaching the time I had left, but it also meant that I would *never* have known any of the things I needed to know, even for long enough to have forgotten them. If and when I could retrieve the information, I would know it. Till then I was as ignorant of it as if it were not stored in some cobwebbed corner of my mind at all.

"You can retrieve without artificials, can't you?" Kivrin said, looking skeptical.

"I guess I'll have to."

"Under stress? Without sleep? Low body endorphin levels?" What exactly had her practicum been? She had never said a word about it, and undergraduates are not supposed to ask. Stress factors in the Middle Ages? I thought everbody slept through them.

"I hope so," I said. "Anyway, I'm willing to try this idea if you think it will help."

She looked at me with that martyred expression and said, "Nothing will help." Thank you, St. Kivrin of Balliol.

But I tried it anyway. It was better than sitting in Dunworthy's rooms having him blink at me through his historically accurate eyeglasses and tell me I was going to love St. Paul's. When my Bodleian requests didn't come, I overloaded my credit and bought out Blackwell's. Tapes on World War II, Celtic literature, history of mass transit, tourist guidebooks, everything I could think of. Then I rented a high-speed recorder and shot up. When I came out of it, I was so panicked by the feeling of not knowing any more than I had when I started that I took the tube to London and raced up Ludgate Hill to see if the firewatch stone would trigger any memories. It didn't.

"Your endorphin levels aren't back to normal yet," I told myself and tried to relax, but that was impossible with the prospect of the practicum looming up before me. And those are real bullets, kid. Just because you're a history major doing his practicum doesn't mean you can't get killed. I read history books all the way home on the tube and right up until Dunworthy's flunkies came to take me to St. John's Wood this morning.

Then I jammed the microfiche *OED* in my back pocket and went off feeling as if I would have to survive by my native wit and hoping I could get hold of artificials in 1940. Surely I could get through the first day without mishap, I thought; and now here I was, stopped cold by almost the first word that was spoken to me.

Well, not quite. In spite of Kivrin's advice that I not put anything in short-term, I'd memorized the British money, a map of the tube system, a map of my own Oxford. It had gotten me this far. Surely I would be able to deal with the Dean.

Just as I had almost gotten up the courage to knock, he opened the door, and as with the pinpoint, it really was over quickly and without pain. I handed him my letter, and he shook my hand and said something understandable like, "Glad to have another man, Bartholomew." He looked strained and tired and as if he might collapse if I told him the Blitz had just started. I know, I know: Keep your mouth shut. The sacred silence, etc.

He said, "We'll get Langby to show you round, shall we?" I assumed that was my Verger of the Pillow, and I was right. He met us at the foot of the stairs, puffing a little but jubilant.

"The cots came," he said to Dean Matthews. "You'd have thought they were doing us a favor. All high heels and hoity-toity. 'You made us miss our tea, luv', one of them said to me. 'Yes, well, and a good thing, too,' I said. 'You look as if you could stand to lose a stone or two.' "

Even Dean Matthews looked as though he did not completely understand him. He said, "Did you set them up in the crypt?" and then introduced us. "Mr. Bartholomew's just got in from Wales," he said. "He's come to join our volunteers." Volunteers, not fire watch.

Langby showed me around, pointing out various dimnesses in the general gloom and then dragged me down to see the ten folding canvas cots set up among the tombs in the crypt, also in passing Lord Nelson's black marble sarcophagus. He told me I didn't have to stand a watch the first night and suggested I go to bed, since sleep is the most precious commodity in the raids. I could well believe it. He was clutching that silly pillow to his breast like his beloved.

"Do you hear the sirens down here?" I asked, wondering if he buried his head in it.

He looked round at the low stone ceilings. "Some do, some don't. Brinton has to have his Horlich's. Bench-Jones would sleep if the roof fell in on him. I have to have a pillow. The important thing is to get your eight in no matter what. If you don't, you turn into one of the walking dead. And then you get killed."

On that cheering note he went off to post the watches for tonight, leaving his pillow on one of the cots with orders for me to let nobody touch it. So here I sit, waiting for my first air-raid siren and trying to get all this down before I turn into one of the walking or nonwalking dead.

I've used the stolen *OED* to decipher a little Langby. Middling success. A tart is either a pastry or a prostitute (I assume the latter, although I was wrong about the pillow). Bourgeois is a catchall term for all the faults of the middle class. A Tommy's a soldier. Ayarpee I could not find under any spelling and I had nearly given up when something in long-term about the use of acronyms and abbreviations in wartime popped forward (bless you, St. Kivrin) and I realized it must be an abbreviation. ARP. Air Raid Precautions. Of course. Where else would you get the bleeding cots from?

SEPTEMBER 21—Now that I'm past the first shock of being here, I realize that the history department neglected to tell me that what I'm supposed to do in the three-odd months of this practicum. They handed me this journal, the letter from my uncle, and a ten-pound note, sent me packing into the past. The ten pounds (already depleted by train and tube fares) is supposed to last me until the end of December and get me back to St. John's Wood for pickup when the second letter calling me. back to Wales to sick uncle's bedside comes. Till then I live here in the crypt with Nelson, who, Langby tells me, is pickled in alcohol inside his coffin. If we take a direct hit, will he burn like a torch or simply trickle out in a decaying stream onto the crypt floor, I wonder. Board is provided by a gas ring, over which are cooked wretched tea and indescribable kippers. To pay for all this luxury I am to stand on the roofs of St. Paul's and put out incendiaries.

I must also accomplish the purpose of this practicum, whatever it may be. Right now the only purpose I care about is staying alive until the second letter from uncle arrives and I can go home.

I am doing makework until Langby has time to "show me the ropes." I've cleaned the skillet they cook the foul little fishes in, stacked wooden folding chairs at the altar end of the crypt (flat instead of standing because they tend to collapse like bombs in the middle of the night), and tried to sleep.

I am apparently not one of the lucky ones who can sleep through the raids. I spent most of the night wondering what St. Paul's risk rating is. Practica have to be at least a six. Last night I was convinced this was a ten, with the crypt as ground zero, and that I might as well have applied for Denver.

The most interesting thing that's happened so far is that I've seen a cat. I am fascinated, but trying not to appear so since they seem commonplace here.

SEPTEMBER 22—Still in the crypt. Langby comes dashing through periodically cursing various government agencies (all abbreviated) and promising to take me up on the roofs. In the meantime, I've run out of makework and taught myself to work a stirrup pump. Kivrin was overly concerned about my memory retrieval abilities. I have not had any trouble so far. Quite the opposite. I called up fire-fighting information and got the whole manual with pictures, including instructions on the use of the stirrup pump. If the kippers set Lord Nelson on fire, I shall be a hero.

Excitement last night. The sirens went early and some of the chars who clean offices in the City sheltered in the crypt with us. One of them woke me out of a sound sleep, going like an air raid siren. Seems she'd seen a mouse. We had to go whacking at tombs and under the cots with a rubber boot to persuade her it was gone. Obviously what the history department had in mind: murdering mice.

SEPTEMBER 24—Langby took me on rounds. Into the choir, where I had to learn the stirrup pump all over again, assigned rubber boots and a tin helmet. Langby says Commander Allen is getting us asbestos firemen's coats, but hasn't yet, so it's my own wool coat and muffler and very cold on the roofs even in September. It feels like November and looks it, too, bleak and cheerless with no sun. Up to the dome and onto the roofs which should be flat, but in fact are littered with towers, pinnacles, gutters, and statues, all designed expressly to catch and hold incendiaries out of reach. Shown how to smother an incendiary with sand before it burns through the roof and sets the church on fire. Shown the ropes (literally) lying in a heap at the base of the dome in case somebody has to go up one of the west towers or over the top of the dome. Back inside and down to the Whispering Gallery.

Langby kept up a running commentary through the whole tour, part practical instruction, part church history. Before we went up into the Gallery he dragged me over to the south door to tell me how Christopher Wren stood in the smoking rubble of Old St. Paul's and asked a workman to bring him a stone from the graveyard to mark the cornerstone. On the stone was written in Latin, "I shall rise again," and Wren was so impressed by the irony that he had the words inscribed above the door. Langby looked as smug as if he had not told me a story every first-year history student knows, but I suppose without the impact of the firewatch stone, the other is just a nice story.

Langby raced me up the steps and onto the narrow balcony circling the Whispering Gallery. He was already halfway round to the other side, shouting dimensions and acoustics at me. He stopped facing the wall opposite and said softly, "You can hear me whispering because of the shape of the dome. The sound waves are reinforced around the perimeter of the dome. It sounds like the very crack of doom up here during a raid. The dome is one hundred and seven feet across. It is eighty feet above the nave."

I looked down. The railing went out from under me and the black-and-white marble floor came up with dizzying speed. I hung onto something in front of me and dropped to

my knees, staggered and sick at heart. The sun had come
out, and all of St. Paul's seemed drenched in gold. Even the
carved wood of the choir, the white stone pillars, the leaden
pipes of the organ, all of it golden, golden.

Langby was beside me, trying to pull me free. "Bartholomew," he shouted. "What's wrong? For God's sake, man."

I knew I must tell him that if I let go, St. Paul's and all the
past would fall in on me, and that I must not let that happen
because I was an historian. I said something, but it was not
what I intended because Langby merely tightened his grip.
He hauled me violently free of the railing and back onto the
stairway then let me collapse limply on the steps and stood
back from me, not speaking.

"I don't know what happened in there," I said. "I've
never been afraid of heights before."

"You're shaking," he said sharply. "You'd better lie
down." He led me back to the crypt.

SEPTEMBER 25—Memory retrieval: ARP manual. Symptoms of bombing victims. Stage one—shock; stupefaction;
unawareness of injuries; words may not make sense except
to victim. Stage two—shivering; nausea; injuries, losses felt;
return to reality. Stage three—talkativeness that cannot be
controlled; desire to explain shock behavior to rescuers.

Langby must surely recognize the symptoms, but how
does he acount for the fact there was no bomb? I can hardly
explain my shock behavior to him, and it isn't just the sacred
silence of the historian that stops me.

He has not said anything, in fact assigned me my first
watches for tomorrow night as if nothing had happened, and
he seems no more preoccupied than anyone else. Everyone
I've met so far is jittery (one thing I had in short-term was
how calm everyone was during the raids) and the raids have
not come near us since I got here. They've been mostly over
the East End and the docks.

There was a reference tonight to a UXB, and I have been
thinking about the Dean's manner and the church being
closed when I'm almost sure I remember reading it was open
through the entire Blitz. As soon as I get a chance, I'll try to
retrieve the events of September. As to retrieving anything
else, I don't see how I can hope to remember the right
information until I know what it is I am supposed to do here,
if anything.

There are no guidelines for historians, and no restrictions either. I could tell everyone I'm from the future if I thought they would believe me. I could murder Hitler if I could get to Germany. Or could I? Time paradox talk abounds in the history department, and the graduate students back from their practica don't say a word one way or the other. Is there a tough, immutable past? Or is there a new past every day and do we, the historians, make it? And what are the consequences of what we do, if there are consequences? And how do we dare do anything without knowing them? Must we interfere boldly, hoping we do not bring about all our downfalls? Or must we do nothing at all, not interfere, stand by and watch St. Paul's burn to the ground if need be so that we don't change the future?

All those are fine questions for a late-night study session. They do not matter here. I could no more let St. Paul's burn down than I could kill Hitler. No, that is not true. I found that out yesterday in the Whispering Gallery. I could kill HItler if I caught him setting fire to St. Paul's.

SEPTEMBER 26—I met a young woman today. Dean Matthews has opened the church, so the watch have been doing duties as chars and people have started coming in again. The young woman reminded me of Kivrin, though Kivrin is a good deal taller and would never frizz her hair like that. She looked as if she had been crying. Kivrin has looked like that since she got back from her practicum. The Middle Ages were too much for her. I wonder how she would have coped with this. By pouring out her fears to the local priest, no doubt, as I sincerely hoped her lookalike was not going to do.

"May I help you?" I said, not wanting in the least to help. "I'm a volunteer."

She looked distressed. "You're not paid?" she said, and wiped at her reddened nose with a handkerchief. "I read about St. Paul's and the fire watch and all and I thought, perhaps there's a position there for me. In the canteen, like, or something. A paying position." There were tears in her red-rimmed eyes.

"I'm afraid we don't have a canteen," I said as kindly as I could, considering how impatient Kivrin always makes me, "and it's not actually a real shelter. Some of the watch sleep in the crypt. I'm afraid we're all volunteers, though."

"That won't do, then," she said. She dabbed at her eyes with the handkerchief. "I love St. Paul's, but I can't take on volunteer work, not with my little brother Tom back from the country." I was not reading this situation properly. For all the outward signs of distress she sounded quite cheerful and no closer to tears than when she had come in. "I've got to get us a proper place to stay. With Tom back, we can't go on sleeping in the tubes."

A sudden feeling of dread, the kind of sharp pain you get sometimes from involuntary retrieval, went over me. "The tubes?" I said, trying to get at the memory.

"Marble Arch, usually," she went on. "My brother Tom saves us a place early and I go—" She stopped, held the handkerchief close to her nose, and exploded into it. "I'm sorry," she said, "this awful cold!"

Red nose, watering eyes, sneezing. Respiratory infection. It was a wonder I hadn't told her not to cry. It's only by luck that I haven't made some unforgivable mistake so far, and this is not because I can't get at the long-term memory. I don't have half the information I need even stored: cats and colds and the way St. Paul's looks in full sun. It's only a matter of time before I am stopped cold by something I do not know. Nevertheless, I am going to try for retrieval tonight after I come off watch. At least I can find out whether and when something is going to fall on me.

I have seen the cat once or twice. He is coal-black with a white patch on his throat that looks as if it were painted on for the blackout.

SEPTEMBER 27—I have just come down from the roofs. I am still shaking.

Early in the raid the bombing was mostly over the East End. The view was incredible. Searchlights everywhere, the sky pink from the fires and reflecting in the Thames, the exploding shells sparkling like fireworks. There was a constant, deafening thunder broken by the occasional droning of the planes high overhead, then the repeating stutter of the ack-ack guns.

About midnight the bombs began falling quite near with a horrible sound like a train running over me. It took every bit of will I had to keep from flinging myself flat on the roof, but Langby was watching. I didn't want to give him the satisfaction of watching a repeat performance of my behavior in the dome. I kept my head up and my sandbucket firmly in hand and felt quite proud of myself.

The bombs stopped roaring past about three, and there was a lull of about half an hour, and then a clatter like hail on the roofs. Everybody except Langby dived for shovels and stirrup pumps. He was watching me. And I was watching the incendiary.

It had fallen only a few meters from me, behind the clock tower. It was much smaller than I had imagined, only about thirty centimeters long. It was sputtering violently, throwing greenish-white fire almost to where I was standing. In a minute it would simmer down into a molten mass and begin to burn through the roof. Flames and the frantic shouts of firemen, and then the white rubble stretching for miles, and nothing, nothing left, not even the firewatch stone.

It was the Whispering Gallery all over again. I felt that I had said something, and when I looked at Langby's face he was smiling crookedly.

"St. Paul's will burn down," I said. "There won't be anything left."

"Yes," Langby said. "That's the idea, isn't it? Burn St. Paul's to the ground? Isn't that the plan?"

"Whose plan?" I said stupidly.

"Hitler's, of course," Langby said. "Who did you think I meant?" and, almost casually, picked up his stirrup pump.

The page of the ARP manual flashed suddenly before me. I poured the bucket of sand around the still sputtering bomb, snatched up another bucket and dumped that on top of it. Black smoke billowed up in such a cloud that I could hardly find my shovel. I felt for the smothered bomb with the tip of it and scooped it into the empty bucket, then shovelled the sand in on top of it. Tears were streaming down my face from the acrid smoke. I turned to wipe them on my sleeve and saw Langby.

He had not made a move to help me. He smiled. "It's not a bad plan, actually. But of course we won't let it happen. That's what the fire watch is here for. To see that it doesn't happen. Right, Bartholomew?"

I know now what the purpose of my practicum is. I must stop Langby from burning down St. Paul's.

SEPTEMBER 28—I try to tell myself I was mistaken about Langby last night, that I misunderstood what he said. Why would he want to burn down St. Paul's unless he is a Nazi spy? How can a Nazi spy have gotten on the fire watch? I think about my faked letter of introduction and shudder.

How can I find out? If I set him some test, some fatal thing that only a loyal Englishman in 1940 would know, I fear I am the one who would be caught out. I *must* get my retrieval working properly.

Until then, I shall watch Langby. For the time being at least that should be easy. Langby has just posted the watches for the next two weeks. We stand every one together.

SEPTEMBER 30—I know what happened in September. Langby told me.

Last night in the choir, putting on our coats and boots, he said, "They've already tried once, you know."

I had no idea what he meant. I felt as helpless as that first day when he asked me if I was from the ayarpee.

"The plan to destroy St. Paul's. They've already tried once. The tenth of September. A high explosive bomb. But of course you didn't know about that. You were in Wales."

I was not even listening. The minute he had said, "high explosive bomb," I had remembered it all. It had burrowed in under the road and lodged on the foundations. The bomb squad had tried to defuse it, but there was a leaking gas main. They decided to evacuate St. Paul's, but Dean Matthews refused to leave, and they got it out after all and exploded it in Barking Marshes. Instant and complete retrieval.

"The bomb squad saved her that time," Langby was saying. "It seems there's always somebody about."

"Yes," I said. "There is," and walked away from him.

OCTOBER 1—I thought last night's retrieval of the events of September tenth meant some sort of breakthrough, but I have been lying here on my cot most of the night trying for Nazi spies in St. Paul's and getting nothing. Do I have to know exactly what I'm looking for before I can remember it? What good does that do me?

Maybe Langby is not a Nazi spy. Then what is he? An arsonist? A madman? The crypt is hardly conducive to thought, being not at all as silent as a tomb. The chars talk most of the night and the sound of the bombs is muffled, which somehow makes it worse. I find myself straining to hear them. When I did get to sleep this morning, I dreamed about one of the tube shelters being hit, broken mains, drowning people.

OCTOBER 4—I tried to catch the cat today. I had some idea of persuading it to dispatch the mouse that has been terrifying the chars. I also wanted to see one up close. I took the water bucket I had used with the stirrup pump last night to put out some burning shrapnel from one of the anti-aircraft guns. It still had a bit of water in it, but not enough to drown the cat, and my plan was to clamp the bucket over him, reach under, and pick him up, then carry him down to the crypt and point him at the mouse. I did not even come close to him.

I swung the bucket, and as I did so, perhaps an inch of water splashed out. I thought I remembered that the cat was a domesticated animal, but I must have been wrong about that. The cat's wide complacent face pulled back into a skull-like mask that was absolutely terrifying, vicious claws extended from what I had thought were harmless paws, and the cat let out a sound to top the chars.

In my surprise I dropped the bucket and it rolled against one of the pillars. The cat disappeared. Behind me, Langby said, "That's no way to catch a cat."

"Obviously," I said, and bent to retrieve the bucket.

"Cats hate water," he said, still in that expressionless voice.

"Oh," I said, and started in front of him to take the bucket back to the choir. "I didn't know that."

"Everybody knows it. Even the stupid Welsh."

OCTOBER 8—We have been standing double watches for a week—bomber's moon. Langby didn't show up on the roofs, so I went looking for him in the church. I found him standing by the west doors talking to an old man. The man had a newspaper tucked under his arm and he handed it to Langby, but Langby gave it back to him. When the man saw me, he ducked out. Langby said, "Tourist. Wanted to know where the Windmill Theater is. Read in the paper the girls are starkers."

I know I looked as if I didn't believe him because he said, "You look rotten, old man. Not getting enough sleep, are you? I'll get somebody to take the first watch for you tonight."

"No," I said coldly. "I'll stand my own watch. I like being on the roofs," and added silently, *where I can watch you.*

He shrugged and said, "I suppose it's better than being down in the crypt. At least on the roofs you can hear the one that gets you."

OCTOBER 10—I thought the double watches might be good for me, take my mind off my inability to retrieve. The watched pot idea. Actually, it sometimes works. A few hours of thinking about something else, or a good night's sleep, and the fact pops forward without any prompting, without any artificials.

The good night's sleep is out of the question. Not only do the chars talk constantly, but the cat has moved into the crypt and sidles up to everyone, making siren noises and begging for kippers. I am moving my cot out of the transept and over by Nelson before I go on watch. He may be pickled, but he keeps his mouth shut.

OCTOBER 11—I dreamed Trafalgar, ships' guns and smoke and falling plaster and Langby shouting my name. My first waking thought was that the folding chairs had gone off. I could not see for all the smoke.

"I'm coming," I said, limping toward Langby and pulling on my boots. There was a heap of plaster and tangled folding chairs in the transept. Langby was digging in it. "Bartholomew!" he shouted, flinging a chunk of plaster aside. "Bartholomew!"

I still had the idea it was smoke. I ran back for the stirrup pump and then knelt beside him and began pulling on a splintered chair back. It resisted, and it came to me suddenly, There is a body under here. I will reach for a piece of the ceiling and find it is a hand. I leaned back on my heels, determined not to be sick, then went at the pile again.

Langby was going far too fast, jabbing with a chair leg. I grabbed his hand to stop him, and he struggled against me as if I were a piece of rubble to be thrown aside. He picked up a large flat square of plaster, and under it was the floor. I turned and looked behind me. Both chars huddled in the recess by the altar. "Who are you looking for?" I said, keeping hold of Langby's arm.

"Bartholomew," he said, and swept the rubble aside, his hands bleeding through the coating of smoky dust.

"I'm here," I said. "I'm all right." I choked on the white dust. "I moved my cot out of the transept."

He turned sharply to the chars and then said quite calmly, "What's under here?"

"Only the gas ring," one of them said timidly from the shadowed recess, "and Mrs. Galbraith's pocketbook." He dug through the mess until he had found them both. The gas ring was leaking at a merry rate, though the flame had gone out.

"You've saved St. Paul's and me after all," I said, standing there in my underwear and boots, holding the useless stirrup pump. "We might all have been asphyxiated."

He stood up. "I shouldn't have saved you," he said.

Stage one: shock, stupefaction, unawareness of injuries, words may not make sense except to victim. He would not know his hand was bleeding yet. He would not remember what he had said. He had said he shouldn't have saved my life.

"I shouldn't have saved you," he repeated. "I have my duty to think of."

"You're bleeding," I said sharply. "You'd better lie down." I sounded just like Langby in the Gallery.

OCTOBER 13—It was a high explosive bomb. It blew a hole in the choir roof; and some of the marble statuary is broken; but the ceiling of the crypt did not collapse, which is what I thought at first. It only jarred some plaster loose.

I do not think Langby has any idea what he said. That should give me some sort of advantage, now that I am sure where the danger lies, now that I am sure it will not come crashing down from some other direction. But what good is all this knowing, when I do not know what he will do? Or when?

Surely I have the facts of yesterday's bomb in long-term, but even falling plaster did not jar them loose this time. I am not even trying for retrieval now. I lie in the darkness waiting for the roof to fall in on me. And remembering how Langby saved my life.

OCTOBER 15—The girl came in today. She still has the cold, but she has gotten her paying position. It was a joy to see her. She was wearing a smart uniform and open-toed shoes, and her hair was in an elaborate frizz around her face. We are still cleaning up the mess from the bomb, and Langby was out with Allen getting wood to board up the choir, so I let the girl chatter at me while I swept. The dust made her sneeze, but at least this time I knew what she was doing.

She told me her name is Enola and that she's working for the WVS, running one of the mobile canteens that are sent to the fires. She came, of all things, to thank me for the job. She said that after she told the WVS that there was no proper shelter with a canteen for St. Paul's, they gave her a run in the City. "So I'll just pop in when I'm close and let you know how I'm making out, won't I just?"

She and her brother Tom are still sleeping in the tubes. I asked her if that was safe and she said probably not, but at least down there you couldn't hear the one that got you and that was a blessing.

OCTOBER 18—I am so tired I can hardly write this. Nine incendiaries tonight and a land mine that looked as though it was going to catch on the dome till the wind drifted its parachute away from the church. I put out two of the incendiaries. I have done that at least twenty times since I got here and helped with dozens of others, and still it is not enough. One incendiary, one moment of not watching Langby, could undo it all.

I know that is partly why I feel so tired. I wear myself out every night trying to do my job and watch Langby, making sure none of the incendiaries falls without my seeing it. Then I go back to the crypt and wear myself out trying to retrieve something, anything, about spies, fires, St. Paul's in the fall of 1940, anything. It haunts me that I am not doing enough, but I do not know what else to do. Without the retrieval, I am as helpless as these poor people here, with no idea what will happen tomorrow.

If I have to, I will go on doing this till I am called home. He cannot burn down St. Paul's so long as I am here to put out the incendiaries. "I have my duty," Langby said in the crypt.

And I have mine.

OCTOBER 21—It's been nearly two weeks since the blast and I just now realized we haven't seen the cat since. He wasn't in the mess in the crypt. Even after Langby and I were sure there was no one in there, we sifted through the stuff twice more. He could have been in the choir, though.

Old Bence-Jones says not to worry. "He's all right," he said. "The jerries could bomb London right down to the ground and the cats would waltz out to greet them. You know why? They don't love anybody. That's what gets half of us killed. Old lady out in Stepney got killed the other night trying to save her cat. Bloody cat was in the Anderson."

"Then where is he?"

"Someplace safe, you can bet on that. If he's not around St. Paul's, it means we're for it. That old saw about the rats deserting a sinking ship, that's a mistake, that is. It's cats, not rats."

OCTOBER 25—Langby's tourist showed up again. He cannot still be looking for the Windmill Theatre. He had a newspaper under his arm again today, and he asked for Langby, but Langby was across town with Allen, trying to get the asbestos firemen's coats. I saw the name of the paper. It was *The Worker*. A Nazi newspaper?

NOVEMBER 2—I've been up on the roofs for a week straight, helping some incompetent workmen patch the hole the bomb made. They're doing a terrible job. There's still a great gap on one side a man could fall into, but they insist it'll be all right because, after all, you wouldn't fall clear through but only as far as the ceiling, and "the fall can't kill you." They don't seem to understand it's a perfect hiding place for an incendiary.

And that is all Langby needs. He does not even have to set a fire to destroy St. Paul's. All he needs to do is let one burn uncaught until it is too late.

I could not get anywhere with the workmen. I went down into the church to complain to Matthews, and saw Langby and his tourist behind a pillar, close to one of the windows. Langby was holding a newspaper and talking to the man. When I came down from the library an hour later, they were still there. So is the gap. Matthews says we'll put planks across it and hope for the best.

NOVEMBER 5—I have given up trying to retrieve. I am so far behind on my sleep I can't even retrieve information on a newspaper whose name I already know. Double watches the permanent thing now. Our chars have abandoned us altogether (like the cat), so the crypt is quiet, but I cannot sleep.

If I do manage to doze off, I dream. Yesterday I dreamed Kivrin was on the roofs, dressed like a saint. "What was the secret of your practicum?" I said. "What were you supposed to find out?"

She wiped her nose with a handkerchief and said, "Two things. One, that silence and humility are the sacred burdens of the historian. Two," she stopped and sneezed into the handkerchief. "Don't sleep in the tubes."

My only hope is to get hold of an artificial and induce a trance. That's a problem. I'm positive it's too early for chemical endorphins and probably hallucinogens. Alcohol is definitely available, but I need something more concentrated than ale, the only alcohol I know by name. I do not dare ask the watch. Langby is suspicious enough of me already. It's back to the *OED,* to look up a word I don't know.

NOVEMBER 11—The cat's back. Langby was out with Allen again, still trying for the asbestos coats, so I thought it was safe to leave St. Paul's. I went to the grocer's for supplies and hopefully, an artificial. It was late, and the sirens sounded before I had even gotten to Cheapside, but the raids do not usually start until after dark. It took awhile to get all the groceries and to get up my courage to ask whether he had any alcohol—he told me to go to a pub—and when I came out of the shop, it was as if I had pitched suddenly into a hole.

I had no idea where St. Paul's lay, or the street, or the shop I had just come from. I stood on what was no longer the sidewalk, clutching my brown-paper parcel of kippers and bread with a hand I could not have seen if I held it up before my face. I reached up to wrap my muffler closer about my neck and prayed for my eyes to adjust, but there was no reduced light to adjust to. I would have been glad of the moon, for all St. Paul's watch curses it and calls it a fifth columnist. Or a bus, with its shuttered headlights giving just enough light to orient myself by. Or a searchlight. Or the kickback flare of an ack-ack gun. Anything.

Just then I did see a bus, two narrow yellow slits a long way off. I started toward it and nearly pitched off the curb. Which meant the bus was sideways in the street, which meant it was not a bus. A cat meowed, quite near, and rubbed against my leg. I looked down into the yellow lights I had thought belonged to the bus. His eyes were picking up light from somewhere, though I would have sworn there was not a light for miles, and reflecting it flatly up at me.

"A warden'll get you for those lights, old tom," I said, and then as a plane droned overhead, "Or a jerry."

The world exploded suddenly into light, the searchlights and a glow along the Thames seeming to happen almost simultaneously, lighting my way home.

"Come to fetch me, did you, old tom?" I said gaily. "Where've you been? Knew we were out of kippers, didn't you? I call that loyalty." I talked to him all the way home and gave him half a tin of the kippers for saving my life. Bence-Jones said he smelled the milk at the grocer's.

NOVEMBER 13—I dreamed I was lost in the blackout. I could not see my hands in front of my face, and Dunworthy came and shone a pocket torch at me, but I could only see where I had come from and not where I was going.

"What good is that to them?" I said. "They need a light to show them where they're going."

"Even the light from the Thames? Even the light from the fires and the ack-ack guns?" Dunworthy said.

"Yes. Anything is better than this awful darkness." So he came closer to give me the pocket torch. It was not a pocket torch, after all, but Christ's lantern from the Hunt picture in the south nave. I shone it on the curb before me so I could find my way home, but it shone instead on the firewatch stone and I hastily put the light out.

NOVEMBER 20—I tried to talk to Langby today. "I've seen you talking to the old gentleman," I said. It sounded like an accusation. I meant it to. I wanted him to think it was and stop whatever he was planning.

"Reading," he said. "Not talking." He was putting things in order in the choir, piling up sandbags.

"I've seen you reading then," I said belligerently, and he dropped a sandbag and straightened.

"What of it?" he said. "It's a free country. I can read to an old man if I want, same as you can talk to that little WVS tart."

"What do you read?" I said.

"Whatever he wants. He's an old man. He used to come home from his job, have a bit of brandy and listen to his wife read the papers to him. She got killed in one of the raids. Now I read to him. I don't see what business it is of yours."

It sounded true. It didn't have the careful casualness of a lie, and I almost believed him, except that I had heard the tone of truth from him before. In the crypt. After the bomb.

"I thought he was a tourist looking for the Windmill," I said.

He looked blank only a second, and then he said, "Oh, yes, that. He came in with the paper and asked me to tell him where it was. I looked it up to find the address. Clever, that. I didn't guess he couldn't read it for himself." But it was enough. I knew that he was lying.

He heaved a sandbag almost at my feet. "Of course you wouldn't understand a thing like that, would you? A simple act of human kindness?"

"No," I said coldly. "I wouldn't."

None of this proves anything. He gave away nothing, except perhaps the name of an artificial, and I can hardly go to Dean Matthews and accuse Langby of reading aloud.

I waited till he had finished in the choir and gone down to the crypt. Then I lugged one of the sandbags up to the roof and over to the chasm. The planking has held so far, but everyone walks gingerly around it, as if it were a grave. I cut the sandbag open and spilled the loose sand into the bottom. If it has occurred to Langby that this is the perfect spot for an incendiary, perhaps the sand will smother it.

NOVEMBER 21—I gave Enola some of "uncle's" money today and asked her to get me the brandy. She was more reluctant than I thought she'd be so there must be societal complications I am not aware of, but she agreed.

I don't know what she came for. She started to tell me about her brother and some prank he'd pulled in the tubes that got him in trouble with the guard, but after I asked her about the brandy, she left without finishing the story.

NOVEMBER 25—Enola came today, but without bringing the brandy. She is going to Bath for the holidays to see her aunt. At least she will be away from the raids for awhile. I will not have to worry about her. She finished the story of her brother and told me she hopes to persuade this aunt to take Tom for the duration of the Blitz but is not at all sure the aunt will be willing.

Young Tom is apparently not so much an engaging scapegrace as a near-criminal. He has been caught twice picking pockets in the Bank tube shelter, and they have had to go back to Marble Arch. I comforted her as best I could, told her all boys were bad at one time or another. What I really wanted to say was that she needn't worry at all, that young Tom strikes me as a true survivor type, like my own tom, like Langby, totally unconcerned with anybody but himself, well-equipped to survive the Blitz and rise to prominence in the future.

Then I asked her whether she had gotten the brandy.

She looked down at her open-toed shoes and muttered unhappily, "I thought you'd forgotten all about that."

I made up some story about the watch taking turns buying a bottle, and she seemed less unhappy, but I am not convinced she will not use this trip to Bath as an excuse to do nothing. I will have to leave St. Paul's and buy it myself, and I don't dare leave Langby alone in the church. I made her promise to bring the brandy today before she leaves. But she is still not back, and the sirens have already gone.

NOVEMBER 26—No Enola, and she said her train left at noon. I suppose I should be grateful that at least she is safely out of London. Maybe in Bath she will be able to get over her cold.

Tonight one of the ARP girls breezed in to borrow half our cots and tell us about a mess over in the East End where a surface shelter was hit. Four dead, twelve wounded. "At least it wasn't one of the tube shelters!" she said. "Then you'd see a real mess, wouldn't you?"

NOVEMBER 30—I dreamed I took the cat to St. John's Wood.

"Is this a rescue mission?" Dunworthy said.

"No, sir," I said proudly. "I know what I was supposed to find in my practicum. The perfect survivor. Tough and resourceful and selfish. This is the only one I could find. I had to kill Langby, you know, to keep him from burning down St. Paul's. Enola's brother has gone to Bath, and the others will never make it. Enola wears open-toed shoes in the winter and sleeps in the tubes and puts her hair up on metal pins so it will curl. She cannot possibly survive the Blitz."

Dunworthy said, "Perhaps you should have rescued her instead. What did you say her name was?"

"Kivrin," I said, and woke up cold and shivering.

DECEMBER 5—I dreamed Langby had the pinpoint bomb. He carried it under his arm like a brown-paper parcel, coming out of St. Paul's Station and up Ludgate Hill to the west doors.

"This is not fair," I said, barring his way with my arm. "There is no fire watch on duty."

He clutched the bomb to his chest like a pillow. "That is your fault," he said, and before I could get to my stirrup pump and bucket, he tossed it in the door.

The pinpoint was not even invented until the end of the twentieth century, and it was another ten years before the dispossessed Communists got hold of it and turned it into something that could be carried under your arm. A parcel that could blow a quarter-mile of the City into oblivion. Thank God that is one dream that cannot come true.

It was a sunlit morning in the dream, and this morning when I came off watch the sun was shining for the first time in weeks. I went down to the crypt and then came up again, making the rounds of the roofs twice more, then the steps and the grounds and all the treacherous alleyways between where an incendiary could be missed. I felt better after that, but when I got to sleep I dreamed again, this time of fire and Langby watching it, smiling.

DECEMBER 15—I found the cat this morning. Heavy raids last night, but most of them over towards Canning Town and nothing on the roofs to speak of. Nevertheless the cat was quite dead. I found him lying on the steps this morning when I made my own, private rounds. Concussion. There was not a mark on him anywhere except the white blackout patch on his throat, but when I picked him up, he was all jelly under the skin.

I could not think what to do with him. I thought for one mad moment of asking Matthews if I could bury him in the crypt. Honorable death in war or something. Trafalgar, Waterloo, London, died in battle. I ended by wrapping him in my muffler and taking him down Ludgate Hill to a building that had been bombed out and burying him in the rubble. It will do no good. The rubble will be no protection from dogs or rats, and I shall never get another muffler. I have gone through nearly all of uncle's money.

I should not be sitting here. I haven't checked the alley-ways or the rest of the steps, and there might be a dud or a delayed incendiary or something that I missed.

When I came here, I thought of myself as the noble rescuer, the savior of the past. I am not doing very well at the job. At least Enola is out of it. I wish there were some way I could send St. Paul's to Bath for safekeeping. There were hardly any raids last night. Bence-Jones said cats can survive anything. What if he was coming to get me, to show me the way home? All the bombs were over Canning Town.

DECEMBER 16—Enola has been back a week. Seeing her, standing on the west steps where I found the cat, sleeping in Marble Arch and not safe at all, was more than I could absorb. "I though you were in Bath," I said stupidly.

"My aunt said she'd take Tom but ńot me as well. She's got a houseful of evacuation children, and what a noisy lot. Where is your muffler?" she said. "It's dreadful cold up here on the hill."

"I . . ." I said, unable to answer, "I lost it."

"You'll never get another one," she said. "They're going to start rationing clothes. And wool, too. You'll never get another one like that."

"I know," I said, blinking at her.

"Good things just thrown away," she said. "It's abso-lutely criminal, that's what it is."

I don't think I said anything to that, just turned and walked away with my head down, looking for bombs and dead animals.

DECEMBER 20—Langby isn't a Nazi. He's a Communist. I can hardly write this. A Communist.

One of the chars found *The Worker* wedged behind a pillar and brought it down to the crypt as we were coming off the first watch.

"Bloody Communists," Bence-Jones said. "Helping Hitler, they are. Talking against the king, stirring up trouble in the shelters. Traitors, that's what they are."

"They love England same as you," the char said.

"They don't love nobody but themselves, bloody selfish lot. I wouldn't be surprised to hear they were ringing Hitler up on the telephone," Bence-Jones said, " ' 'Ello, Adolf, here's where to drop the bombs.' "

The kettle on the gas ring whistled. The char stood up and poured the hot water into a chipped tea pot, then sat back down. "Just because they speak their minds don't mean they'd burn down old St. Paul's, does it now?"

"Of course not," Langby said, coming down the stairs. He sat down and pulled off his boots, stretching his feet in their wool socks. "Who wouldn't burn down St. Paul's?"

"The Communists," Bence-Jones said, looking straight at him, and I wondered if he suspected Langby, too.

Langby never batted an eye. "I wouldn't worry about them if I were you," he said. "It's the jerries that are doing their bloody best to burn her down tonight. Six incendiaries so far, and one almost went into that great hole over the choir." He held out his cup to the char, and she poured him a cup of tea.

I wanted to kill him, smashing him to dust and rubble on the floor of the crypt while Bence-Jones and the char looked on in helpless surprise, shouting warnings to them and the rest of the watch. "Do you know what the Communists did?" I wanted to shout. "Do you? We have to stop him." I even stood up and started toward him as he sat with his feet stretched out before him and his asbestos coat still over his shoulders.

And then the thought of the Gallery drenched in gold, the Communist coming out of the tube station with the package so casually under his arm, made me sick with the same staggering vertigo of guilt and helplessness, and I sat back down on the edge of my cot and tried to think what to do.

They do not realize the danger. Even Bence-Jones, for all his talk of traitors, thinks they are capable only of talking against the king. They do not know, cannot know, what the Communists will become. Stalin is an ally. Communists mean Russia. They have never heard of Karinsky or the New Russia or any of the things that will make "Communist" into a synonym for "monster." They will never know it. By the time the Communists become what they became, there will be no fire watch. Only I know what it means to hear the name "Communist" uttered here, so carelessly, in St. Paul's.

A Communist. I should have known. I should have known.

DECEMBER 22—Double watches again. I have not had any sleep, and I am getting very unsteady on my feet. I nearly pitched into the chasm this morning, only saved myself by dropping to my knees. My endorphin levels are fluctuating wildly, and I know I must get some sleep soon or I will become one of Langby's walking dead; but I am afraid to leave him alone on the roofs, alone in the church with his Communist party leader, alone anywhere. I have taken to watching him when he sleeps.

If I could just get hold of an artificial, I think I could induce a trance, in spite of my poor condition. But I cannot even go out to a pub. Langby is on the roofs constantly, waiting for his chance. When Enola comes again, I must convince her to get the brandy for me. There are only a few days left.

DECEMBER 28—Enola came this morning while I was on the west porch, picking up the Christmas tree. It has been knocked over three nights running by concussion. I righted the tree and was bending down to pick up the scattered tinsel when Enola appeared suddenly out of the fog like some cheerful saint. She stooped quickly and kissed me on the cheek. Then she straightened up, her nose red from her perennial cold, and handed me a box wrapped in colored paper.

"Merry Christmas," she said. "Go on then, open it. It's a gift."

My reflexes are almost totally gone. I knew the box was far too shallow for a bottle of brandy. Nevertheless, I believed she had rememberd, but had brought me my salvation. "You darling," I said, and tore it open.

It was a muffler. Gray wool. I stared at it for fully half a minute without realizing what it was. "Where's the brandy?" I said.

She looked shocked. Her nose got redder and her eyes started to blur. "You need this more. You haven't any clothing coupons and you have to be outside all the time. It's been so dreadful cold."

"I *needed* the brandy," I said angrily.

"I was only trying to be kind," she started, and I cut her off.

"Kind?" I said. "I asked you for brandy. I don't recall ever saying I needed a muffler." I shoved it back at her and began untangling a string of colored lights that had shattered when the tree fell.

She got that same holy martyr look Kivrin is so wonderful at. "I worry about you all the time up here," she said in a rush. "They're *trying* for St. Paul's, you know. And it's so close to the river. I didn't think you should be drinking. I . . . it's a crime when they're trying so hard to kill us all that you won't take care of yourself. It's like you're in it with them. I worry someday I'll come up to St. Paul's and you won't be here."

"Well, and what exactly am I supposed to do with a muffler? Hold it over my head when they drop the bombs?"

She turned and ran, disappearing into the gray fog before she had gone two steps. I started after her, still holding the string of broken lights, tripped over it, and fell almost all the way to the bottom of the steps.

Langby picked me up. "You're off watches," he said grimly.

"You can't do that," I said.

"Oh, yes, I can. I don't want any walking dead on the roofs with me."

I let him lead me down here to the crypt, make me a cup of tea, put me to bed, all very solicitous. No indication that this is what he has been waiting for. I will lie here till the sirens go. Once I am on the roofs he will not be able to send me back without seeming suspicious. Do you know what he said before he left, asbestos coat and rubber boots, the dedicated fire watcher? "I want you to get some sleep." As if I could sleep with Langby on the roofs. I would be burned alive.

DECEMBER 30—The sirens woke me, and old Bence-Jones said, "That should have done you some good. You've slept the clock round."

"What day is it?" I said, going for my boots.

"The twenty-ninth," he said, and as I dived for the door, "No need to hurry. They're late tonight. Maybe they won't come at all. That'd be a blessing, that would. The tide's out."

I stopped by the door to the stairs, holding onto the cool stone. "Is St. Paul's all right?"

"She's still standing," he said. "Have a bad dream?"

"Yes," I said, remembering the bad dreams of all the past weeks—the dead cat in my arms in St. John's Wood, Langby with his parcel and his *Worker* under his arm, the fire-watch stone garishly lit by Christ's lantern. Then I remembered I had not dreamed at all. I had slept the kind of sleep I had prayed for, the kind of sleep that would help me remember.

Then I remembered. Not St. Paul's, burned to the ground by the Communists. A headline from the dailies. "Marble Arch hit. Eighteen killed by blast." The date was not clear except for the year. 1940. There were exactly two more days left in 1940. I grabbed my coat and muffler and ran up the stairs and across the marble floor.

"Where the hell do you think you're going?" Langby shouted to me. I couldn't see him.

"I have to save Enola," I said, and my voice echoed in the dark sanctuary. "They're going to bomb Marble Arch."

"You can't leave now," he shouted after me, standing where the firewatch stone would be. "The tide's out. You dirty . . ."

I didn't hear the rest of it. I had already flung myself down the steps and into a taxi. It took almost all the money I had, the money I had so carefully hoarded for the trip back to St. John's Wood. Shelling started while we were still in Oxford Street, and the driver refused to go any farther. He let me out into pitch blackness, and I saw I would never make it in time.

Blast. Enola crumpled on the stairway down to the tube, her open-toed shoes still on her feet, not a mark on her. And when I try to lift her, jelly under the skin. I would have to wrap her in the muffler she gave me, because I was too late. I had gone back a hundred years to be too late to save her.

I ran the last blocks, guided by the gun emplacement that had to be in Hyde Park, and skidded down the steps into Marble Arch. The woman in the ticket booth took my last shilling for a ticket to St. Paul's Station. I stuck it in my pocket and raced toward the stairs.

"No running," she said placidly. "To your left, please." The door to the right was blocked off by wooden barricades, the metal gates beyond pulled to and chained. The board with names on it for the stations was X-ed with tape, and a new sign that read, "All trains," was nailed to the barricade, pointing left.

Enola was not on the stopped escalators or sitting against the wall in the hallway. I came to the first stairway and could not get through. A family had set out, just where I wanted to step, a communal tea of bread and butter, a little pot of jam sealed with waxed paper, and a kettle on a ring like the one Langby and I had rescued out of the rubble, all of it spread on a cloth embroidered at the corners with flowers. I stood staring down at the layered tea, spread like a waterfall down the steps.

"I . . . Marble Arch . . ." I said. Another twenty killed by flying tiles. "You shouldn't be here."

"We've as much right as anyone," the man said belligerently, "and who are you to tell us to move on?"

A woman lifting saucers out of a cardboard box looked up at me, frightened. The kettle began to whistle.

"It's you that should move on," the man said. "Go on then." He stood off to one side so I could pass. I edged past the embroidered cloth apologetically.

"I'm sorry," I said. "I'm looking for someone. On the platform."

"You'll never find her in there, mate," the man said, thumbing in that direction. I hurried past him, nearly stepping on the teacloth, and rounded the corner into hell.

It was not hell. Shopgirls folded coats and leaned back against them, cheerful or sullen or disagreeable, but certainly not damned. Two boys scuffled for a shilling and lost it on the tracks. They bent over the edge, debating whether to go after it, and the station guard yelled to them to back away. A train rumbled through, full of people. A mosquito landed on the guard's hand and he reached out to slap it and missed. The boys laughed. And behind and before them, stretching in all directions down the deadly tile curves of the tunnel like casualties, backed into the entrance-ways and onto the stairs, were people. Hundreds and hundreds of people.

I stumbled back into the hall, knocking over a teacup. It spilled like a flood across the cloth.

"I told you, mate," the man said cheerfully. "It's Hell in there, ain't it? And worse below."

"Hell," I said. "Yes." I would never find her. I would never save her. I looked at the woman mopping up the tea, and it came to me that I could not save her either. Enola or the cat or any of them, lost here in the endless stairways and cul-de-sacs of time. They were already dead a hundred years, past saving. The past is beyond saving. Surely that was the lesson the history department sent me all this way to learn. Well, fine, I've learned it. Can I go home now?

Of course not, dear boy. You have foolishly spent all your money on taxicabs and brandy, and tonight is the night the Germans burn the City. (Now it is too late, I remember it all. Twenty-eight incendiaries on the roofs.) Langby must have his chance, and you must learn the hardest lesson of all and the one you should have known from the beginning. You cannot save St. Paul's.

I went back out onto the platform and stood behind the yellow line until a train pulled up. I took my ticket out and held it in my hand all the way to St. Paul's Station. When I got there, smoke billowed toward me like an easy spray of water. I could not see St. Paul's.

"The tide's out," a woman said in a voice devoid of hope, and I went down in a snake pit of limp cloth hoses. My hands came up covered with rank-smelling mud, and I understood finally (and too late) the significance of the tide. There was no water to fight the fires.

A policeman barred my way and I stood helplessly before him with no idea what to say. "No civilians allowed up there," he said. "St. Paul's is for it." The smoke billowed like a thundercloud alive with sparks, and the dome rose golden above it.

"I'm fire watch," I said, and his arm fell away, and then I was on the roofs.

My endorphin levels must have been going up and down like an air raid siren. I do not have any short-term from then on, just moments that do not fit together: the people in the church when we brought Langby down, huddled in a corner playing cards, the whirlwind of burning scraps of wood in the dome, the ambulance driver who wore open-toed shoes like Enola and smeared salve on my burned hands. And in the center, the one clear moment when I went after Langby on a rope and saved his life

I stood by the dome, blinking against the smoke. The City was on fire and it seemed as if St. Paul's would ignite from the heat, would crumble from the noise alone. Bence-Jones was by the northwest tower, hitting at an incendiary with a spade. Langby was too close to the patched place where the bomb had gone through, looking toward me. An incendiary clattered behind him. I turned to grab a shovel, and when I turned back, he was gone.

"Langby!" I shouted, and could not hear my own voice. He had fallen into the chasm and nobody saw him or the incendiary. Except me. I do not remember how I got across the roof. I think I called for a rope. I got a rope. I tied it around my waist, gave the ends of it into the hands of the fire watch, and went over the side. The fires lit the walls of the hole almost all the way to the bottom. Below me I could see a pile of whitish rubble. He's under there, I thought, and jumped free of the wall. The space was so narrow there was nowhere to throw the rubble. I was afraid I would inadvertently stone him, and I tried to toss the pieces of planking and plaster over my shoulder, but there was barely room to turn. For one awful moment I thought he might not be there at all, that the pieces of splintered wood would brush away to reveal empty pavement, as they had in the crypt.

I was numbed by the indignity of crawling over him. If he was dead I did not think I could bear the shame of stepping on his helpless body. Then his hand came up like a ghost's and grabbed my ankle, and within seconds I had whirled and had his head free.

He was the ghastly white that no longer frightens me. "I put the bomb out," he said. I stared at him, so overwhelmed with relief I could not speak. For one hysterical moment I thought I would even laugh, I was so glad to see him. I finally realized what it was I was supposed to say.

"Are you all right?" I said.

"Yes," he said, and tried to raise himself on one elbow. "So much the worse for you."

He could not get up. He grunted with pain when he tried to shift his weight to his right side and lay back, the uneven rubble crunching sickeningly under him. I tried to lift him gently so I could see where he was hurt. He must have fallen on something.

"It's no use," he said, breathing hard. "I put it out."

I spared him a startled glance, afraid that he was delirious, and went back to rolling him onto his side.

"I know you were counting on this one," he went on, not

resisting me at all. "It was bound to happen sooner or later with all these roofs. Only I went after it. What'll you tell your friends?"

His asbestos coat was torn down the back in a long gash. Under it his back was charred and smoking. He had fallen on the incendiary. "Oh, my God," I said, trying frantically to see how badly he was burned without touching him. I had no way of knowing how deep the burns went, but they seemed to extend only in the narrow space where the coat had torn. I tried to pull the bomb out from under him, but the casing was as hot as a stove. It was not melting, though. My sand and Langby's body had smothered it. I had no idea if it would start up again when it was exposed to air. I looked around, a little wildly, for the bucket and stirrup pump Langby must have dropped when he fell.

"Looking for a weapon?" Langby said, so clearly it was hard to believe he was hurt at all. "Why not just leave me here? A bit of overexposure and I'd be done for by morning. Or would you rather do your dirty work in private?"

I stood up and yelled to the men on the roof above us. One of them shone a pocket torch down at us, but its light didn't reach.

"Is he dead?" somebody shouted down to me.

"Send for an ambulance," I said. "He's been burned."

I helped Langby up, trying to support his back without touching the burn. He staggered a little and then leaned against the wall, watching me as I tried to bury the incendiary, using a piece of the planking as a scoop. The rope came down and I tied Langby to it. He had not spoken since I helped him up. He let me tie the rope around his waist, still looking steadily at me. "I should have let you smother in the crypt," he said.

He stood leaning easily, almost relaxed against the wood supports, his hands holding him up. I put his hands on the slack rope and wrapped it once around them for the grip I knew he didn't have. "I've been onto you since that day in the Gallery. I knew you weren't afraid of heights. You came down here without any fear of heights when you thought I'd ruined your precious plans. What was it? An attack of conscience? Kneeling there like a baby, whining, 'What have we done? What have we done!' You made me sick. But you know what gave you away first? The cat. Everybody knows cats hate water. Everybody but a dirty Nazi spy."

There was a tug on the rope. "Come ahead," I said, and the rope tautened.

"That WVS tart? Was she a spy, too? Supposed to meet you in Marble Arch? Telling me it was going to be bombed. You're a rotten spy, Bartholomew. Your friends already blew it up in September. It's open again."

The rope jerked suddenly and began to lift Langby. He twisted his hands to get a better grip. His right shoulder scraped the wall. I put up my hands and pushed him gently so that his left side was to the wall. "You're making a big mistake, you know," he said. "You should have killed me. I'll tell."

I stood in the darkness, waiting for the rope. Langby was unconscious when he reached the roof. I walked past the fire watch to the dome and down to the crypt.

This morning the letter from my uncle came and with it a ten-pound note.

DECEMBER 31—Two of Dunworthy's flunkies met me in St. John's Wood to tell me I was late for my exams. I did not even protest. I shuffled obediently after them without even considering how unfair it was to give an exam to one of the walking dead. I had not slept in—how long? Since yesterday when I went to find Enola. I had not slept in a hundred years.

Dunworthy was at his desk, blinking at me. One of the flunkies handed me a test paper and the other one called time. I turned the paper over and left an oily smudge from the ointment on my burns. I stared uncomprehendingly at them. I had grabbed at the incendiary when I turned Langby over, but these burns were on the backs of my hands. The answer came to me suddenly in Langby's unyielding voice. "They're rope burns, you fool. Don't they teach you Nazi spies the proper way to come up a rope?"

I looked down at the test. It read, "Number of incendiaries that fell on St. Paul's. Number of land mines. Number of high explosive bombs. Method most commonly used for extinguishing incendiaries. Land mines. High explosive bombs. Number of volunteers on first watch. Second watch. Casualties. Fatalities." The questions made no sense. There was only a short space, long enough for the writing of a number, after any of the questions. Method most commonly used for extinguishing incendiaries. How would I ever fit what I knew into that narrow space? Where were the questions about Enola and Langby and the cat?

I went up to Dunworthy's desk. "St. Paul's almost burned down last night," I said. "What kind of questions are these?"

"You should be answering questions, Mr. Bartholomew, not asking them."

"There aren't any questions about the people," I said. The outer casing of my anger began to melt.

"Of course there are," Dunworthy said, flipping to the second page of the test. "Number of casualties, 1940. Blast, shrapnel, other."

"Other?" I said. At any moment the roof would collapse on me in a shower of plaster dust and fury. "Other? Langby put out a fire with his own body. Enola has a cold that keeps getting worse. The cat . . ." I snatched the paper back from him and scrawled "one cat" in the narrow space next to "blast." "Don't you care about them at all?"

"They're important from a statistical point of view," he said, "but as individuals, they are hardly relevant to the course of history."

My reflexes were shot. It was amazing to me that Dunworthy's were almost as slow. I grazed the side of his jaw and knocked his glasses off. "Of course they're relevant!" I shouted. "They *are* the history, not all these bloody numbers!"

The reflexes of the flunkies were very fast. They did not let me start another swing at him before they had me by both arms and were hauling me out of the room.

"They're back there in the past with nobody to save them. They can't see their hands in front of their faces and there are bombs falling down on them and you tell me they aren't important? You call that being an historian?"

The flunkies dragged me out the door and down the hall. "Langby saved St. Paul's. How much more important can a person get? You're no historian! You're nothing but a . . ." I wanted to call him a terrible name, but the only curses I could summon up were Langby's. "You're nothing but a dirty Nazi spy!" I bellowed. "You're nothing but a lazy bourgeois tart!"

They dumped me on my hands and knees outside the door and slammed it in my face. "I wouldn't be an historian if you paid me!" I shouted, and went to see the firewatch stone.

DECEMBER 31—I am having to write this in bits and pieces. My hands are in pretty bad shape, and Dunworthy's boys didn't help matters much. Kivrin comes in periodically, wearing her St. Joan look, and smears so much salve on my hands that I can't hold a pencil.

St. Paul's Station is not there, of course, so I got out at Holborn and walked, thinking about my last meeting with Dean Matthews on the morning after the burning of the City. This morning.

"I understand you saved Langby's life," he said. "I also understand that between you, you saved St. Paul's last night."

I showed him the letter from my uncle and he stared at it as if he could not think what it was. "Nothing stays saved forever," he said, and for a terrible moment I thought he was going to tell me Langby had died. "We shall have to keep on saving St. Paul's until Hitler decides to bomb the country-side."

The raids on London are almost over, I wanted to tell him. He'll start bombing the countryside in a matter of weeks. Canterbury, Bath, aiming always at the cathedrals. You and St. Paul's will both outlast the war and live to dedicate the firewatch stone.

"I am hopeful, though," he said. "I think the worst is over."

"Yes, sir." I thought of the stone, its letters still readable after all this time. No, sir, the worst is not over.

I managed to keep my bearings almost to the top of Ludgate Hill. Then I lost my way completely, wandering about like a man in a graveyard. I had not remembered that the rubble looked so much like the white plaster dust Langby had tried to dig me out of. I could not find the stone anywhere. In the end I nearly fell over it, jumping back as if I had stepped on a grave.

It is all that's left. Hiroshima is supposed to have had a handful of untouched trees at ground zero, Denver the capitol steps. Neither of them says, "Remember the men and women of St. Paul's Watch who by the grace of God saved this cathedral." The grace of God.

Part of the stone is sheared off. Historians argue there was another line that said, "for all time," but I do not believe that, not if Dean Matthews had anything to do with it. And none of the watch it was dedicated to would have believed it for a minute. We saved St. Paul's every time we put out an incendiary, and only until the next one fell. Keeping watch on the danger spots, putting out the little fires with sand and stirrup pumps, the big ones with our bodies, in order to keep the whole vast complex structure from burning down. Which sounds to me like a course description for History Practicum 401. What a fine time to discover what historians are for when I have tossed my chance for being one out the windows as easily as they tossed the pinpoint bomb in! No, sir, the worst is not over.

There are flash burns on the stone, where legend says the Dean of St. Paul's was kneeling when the bomb went off. Totally apocryphal, of course, since the front door is hardly an appropriate place for prayers. It is more likely the shadow of a tourist who wandered in to ask the whereabouts of the Windmill Theatre, or the imprint of a girl bringing a volunteer his muffler. Or a cat.

Nothing is saved forever, Dean Matthews; and I knew that when I walked in the west doors that first day, blinking into the gloom, but it is pretty bad nevertheless. Standing here knee-deep in rubble out of which I will not be able to dig any folding chairs or friends, knowing that Langby died thinking I was a Nazi spy, knowing that Enola came one day and I wasn't there. It's pretty bad.

But it is not as bad as it could be. They are both dead, and Dean Matthews too; but they died without knowing what I knew all along, what sent me to my knees in the Whispering Gallery, sick with grief and guilt: that in the end none of us saved St. Paul's. And Langby cannot turn to me, stunned and sick at heart, and say, "Who did this? Your friends the Nazis?" And I would have to say, "No. The Communists." That would be the worst.

I have come back to the room and let Kivrin smear more salve on my hands. She wants me to get some sleep. I know I should pack and get gone. It will be humiliating to have them come and throw me out, but I do not have the strength to fight her. She looks so much like Enola.

JANUARY 1—I have apparently slept not only through the night, but through the morning mail drop as well. When I woke up just now, I found Kivrin sitting on the end of the bed holding an envelope. "Your grades came," she said.

I put my arm over my eyes. "They can be marvelously efficient when they want to, can't they?"

"Yes," Kivrin said.

"Well, let's see it," I said, sitting up. "How long do I have before they come and throw me out?"

She handed the flimsy computer envelope to me. I tore it along the perforation. "Wait," she said. "Before you open it, I want to say something." She put her hand gently on my burns. "You're wrong about the history department. They're very good."

It was not exactly what I expected her to say. "Good is not the word I'd use to describe Dunworthy," I said and yanked the inside slip free.

Kivrin's look did not change, not even when I sat there with the printout on my knees where she could surely see it.

"Well," I said.

The slip was hand-signed by the esteemed Dunworthy. I have taken a first. With honors.

JANUARY 2—Two things came in the mail today. One was Kivrin's assignment. The history department thinks of everything—even to keeping her here long enough to nurse-maid me, even to coming up with a prefabricated trial by fire to send their history majors through.

I think I wanted to believe that was what they had done, Enola and Langby only hired actors, the cat a clever android with its clockwork innards taken out for the final effect, not so much because I wanted to believe Dunworthy was not good at all, but because then I would not have this nagging pain at not knowing what had happened to them.

"You said your practicum was England in 1300?" I said, watching her as suspiciously as I had watched Langby.

"1349," she said, and her face went slack with memory. "The plague year."

"My God," I said. "How could they do that? The plague's a ten."

"I have a natural immunity," she said, and looked at her hands.

Because I could not think of anything to say, I opened the other piece of mail. It was a report on Enola. Computer-printed, facts and dates and statistics, all the numbers the history department so dearly loves, but it told me what I thought I would have to go without knowing: that she had gotten over her cold and survived the Blitz. Young Tom had been killed in the Baedaker raids on Bath, but Enola had lived until 2006, the year before they blew up St. Paul's.

I don't know whether I believe the report or not, but it does not matter. It is, like Langby's reading aloud to the old man, a simple act of human kindness. They think of everything.

Not quite. They did not tell me what happened to Langby. But I find as I write this that I already know: I saved his life. It does not seem to matter that he might have died in the hospital the next day; and I find, in spite of all the hard lessons the history department has tried to teach me, I do not quite believe this one: that nothing is saved forever. It seems to me that perhaps Langby is.

JANUARY 3—I went to see Dunworthy today. I don't know what I intended to say—some pompous drivel about my willingness to serve in the firewatch of history, standing guard against the falling incendiaries of the human heart, silent and saintly.

But he blinked at me nearsightedly across his desk, and it seemed to me that he was blinking at that last bright image of St. Paul's in sunlight before it was gone forever and that he knew better than anyone that the past cannot be saved, and I said instead, "I'm sorry that I broke your glasses, sir."

"How did you like St. Paul's?" he said, and like my first meeting with Enola, I felt I must be somehow reading the signals all wrong, that he was not feeling loss, but something quite different.

"I loved it, sir," I said.

"Yes," he said. "So do I."

Dean Matthews is wrong. I have fought with memory my whole practicum only to find that it is not the enemy at all, and being an historian is not some saintly burden after all. Because Dunworthy is not blinking against the fatal sunlight of the last morning, but into the gloom of that first afternoon, looking in the great west doors of St. Paul's at what is, like Langby, like all of it, every moment, in us, saved forever.

THE WOOING OF SLOWBOAT SADIE

O. Niemand

*"O. Niemand" is a pseudonym—"niemand"
means "nobody" in German—used in this case
to disguise the author of this remarkably
effective story in the manner of O. Henry.
"Niemand" is actually a well-known sf writer
who is writing a series of science fiction stories,
all set in the same background, as they might
have been written by famous non-sf writers; to
avoid preconceptions on the part of readers, the
author chooses a different penname for each
story. The present tale is very true to the spirit of
O. Henry ("O. Henry" was a penname too,
remember) in style, characterization and plot,
and would have been a worthy inclusion in the
O. Henry canon. In a sense, it's an
alternative-world story: what if O. Henry had
written science fiction?*

IF YOU AWOKE ONE LUGUBRIOUS AND BLEARY-eyed morning to the dreadful knowledge that you had, in some manner yet only hazily recollected, lost the person of the wealthiest and most powerful man ever to visit the domed city of Springfield, what would you do about it? Would you inform your superior, the overworked Captain Helfmuhn, fully prepared to listen to his fine collection of oaths and curses? Would you explain to him that you hadn't truly lost the Beshta Shon, that you had merely misplaced him? Would you have the nerve?

You may weep joyful tears, for you have committed no such blunder. But save a salty drop or two for Officer Onayly, who did that very thing. And now you may search along with the kindly officer, who must find the Beshta Shon before lunchtime or be assigned to a new beat out on the airless side of the great green dome.

Officer Onayly needed to think about his problem, and when he needed to think he always went to Thragan's for a beer. If you don't mind having one with him so early in the day, take a place at the bar between Thragan's regulars and the honest cop. Then you and he may begin the day's adventure refreshed.

"Now, Onayly," said the surprised Thragan himself, "what brings you into me place so early? I'd be thinkin' your head was too big to be mindful of your duties this mornin'. Would you care for a short beer?"

Onayly rubbed his temples and uttered a groan of despair.

"Yes, thank you," he said. "My head feels like I rented it out all night to a pair of midget prospectors. But tell me, Thragan, how did you know my skull ached?"

"When you left here last night," laughed Thragan, "it was plain you'd be forfeitin' to the divil for the time you had." He placed a mug of sunny, foam-topped beer on the bar.

Slowly in an agony of regret to the barkeep's smiling face the copper raised his eyes. "I was in here last night, was I?" he asked.

"Aye, sure," said Thragan, "wid that little pal of yours. Don't you remember? Why, by all the saints, you must not have gone straight home like I told you."

"We saw you in the Sazerac at midnight," said a blowzy red-haired girl.

Officer Onayly was glad that he had found a clue. This was a beginning at least, even if it did come from sources that were often not wholly reliable on other matters.

"Pearl," he asked, hopefully, "when you saw me in the Sazerac, was my little friend there too?"

"Yes," she said, "that's why I followed you there. That little man knows how to spend his money. I wanted to let him know it was my birthday, but he wouldn't let me get near. He kept asking for some other dame."

"Thank you, Pearl," said the relieved minion of the law, "I owe you a favor." He gulped down the last of his beer and walked out of the bar with all the steadiness and dignity expected of a defender of public decency. His next call would be the Sazerac, a place of danger and notoriety and black intrigue, and consequently a popular little club among both hoodlums and young businessmen of great promise.

Molly, the barmaid at the Sazerac, called out to the policeman. "Onayly, I didn't expect to see you again for a week! Are you out to give your megrims the fresh air?"

"When I waked this morning, Molly, I was sorry I did. Say, tell me what happened last night. And set up a small one for me too."

Molly drew a beer on the house and put it in front of the penitent cop. "We got pig knuckles on the free lunch today, Onayly."

The officer's eyes bulged and his skin took on the color of pale jade. "No, thank you, Molly," he said, through clenched jaws.

"Who was that sawed-off little fellow?"

"Didn't I introduce you? That was the Beshta Shon himself. He came here to Springfield on a little holiday."

"What is a Beshta Shon?"

Onayly swallowed some cold beer. If I told you what Cap'n Helfmuhn said to me, you wouldn't believe it. I myself didn't believe it when I heard it. Where he comes from, the Beshta Shon ain't just the richest man in the world, he *owns* the world, every building, every sorry stick, every square inch in the place."

Molly stared down at the polished wooden bar. "It must be grand to be that rich," she said, dreamily.

"Well, this little fellow is lonely. He comes here once a year for a bit of a party."

"And you were supposed to keep him out of trouble? They assigned *you*, Onayly? What happened, did you lose him?"

The cop nodded his head miserably. "I just got to find him," he said.

"Well, you were headin' for Slowboat Sadie's when you left here last night. That's who he was askin' for. I don't know if you made it there or not. He was attractin' attention, throwin' money around like it was last week's newspaper. I hope nothin' happened to the gentleman."

"If he was robbed," said Onayly, scowling, "I'd just as well sign myself aboard a prison ship and be done with it. But I'll find him. Thank you for the drink and the information." He finished the beer and walked out of the Sazerac, turning up the street toward Slowboat Sadie's. When he stepped inside that venerable hostelry, the bartender raised an eyebrow.

"You had some skate on last night, Onayly," Dusty Jack greeted the cop.

"So I've been informed," said Onayly. "Please, if you're after helping out an old friend, let me wet my whistle on a tittle of beer. I'm looking for my little pal."

Dusty Jack filled a frosted glass with golden ale and set it in front of Onayly. "Your pal with all the money?" he asked.

"Yep." The cop swallowed half of the beer in one great, thirsty gulp.

A tall blonde woman sitting at a table across the dimly lighted room said: "Well, say, I know where he is." This was Slowboat Sadie herself. She was the proprietor of the establishment and a friend to all her customers, most particularly the crewmen of the long-haul freighters, whence her euphonious soubriquet. Now, when Onayly turned to observe the speaker, Slowboat Sadie appeared the same as she always did. She was a striking woman, let no one remark otherwise, and she had a certain grace about her that was at least half natural, the remainder consisting of conscious effort aided by generous doses of juniper liquor, administered on the quarter hour. The blondness of her hair was only mildly encouraged by some commercial preparation, a gilding of a rare lily on this desolate asteroid. But let us not judge her vanity harshly: it betrays a refreshing modesty, a blindness to her own true charm. Yes, Slowboat Sadie was no longer so young as the girls who worked in her establishment; and, yes, perhaps it was only the dim light that flattered her so immoderately. But it was Slowboat Sadie whom the Beshta Shon came to visit, and would you be the one to tell such a man he had erred in his choice of sweethearts?

"Perhaps, Sadie," said Officer Onayly, in a casual manner, "you have had dealings with Cap'n Helfmuhn."

"Sure, and he's an old bucket of mud."

"That is as may be. But the old bucket of mud will have my shield and my head unless I find the Beshta Shon and return him safely."

Slowboat Sadie exhaled a pale cloud of cigarette smoke and took counsel with herself for a little while. She shrugged her shoulders.

"Well," she said, "it's nothing to me, but I guess I'll tell you where he is."

The grateful cop raised a hand. "Let me finish my beer first." And he tilted the glass and drained it dry with another long, deep swallow. All the while he regarded Slowboat Sadie and wondered why the Beshta Shon, with all his money and power, had come to this seedy little dive, when he could have gone to any of the posh luxurious spots that Onayly imagined must exist for the wealthy.

"You're some chaperone, Onayly," said Dusty Jack. "If ever they send a copper after me, I hope they send you. I promise we wouldn't sober up until the angels come to get us."

"Aw, climb a rope, Jack," said Onayly, in a dangerous tone.

The eponymous owner of the house left her table and came to the bar. She seated herself on the stool beside the policeman. It seemed to Onayly that she had failed to bring some of her girlish comeliness with her from the shadows.

"The Beshta Shon is safe enough," she said. "He's sleeping it off in the alley behind the building."

The cop gazed at her in wonder. "Do you know who he is? He's one of the greatest men in the—"

"I know better than you who he is," said Slowboat Sadie. She waved a hand in a bored way, dismissing Onayly.

The officer muttered a few words too low for the woman or her nosy tapster to hear. Onayly went out of the barroom through a door in the rear and found himself in a narrow alley that smelled of many awful things well past their prime. Rotten cabbage leaves, egg shells, and coffee grounds the cop saw at first glance, the effluvious sweepings and outscourings that made a simple pallet for the magnificent Beshta Shon.

"Sir," said the officer, "perhaps you should wake up now. Let me escort you back."

There was no response from the sleeping man, unless you are capable of reading meaning in the open-mouthed snores of the gloriously squiffed. Onayly had not this talent.

"Sir," he said, nervously, "we can't let anyone find you like this. Please, sir." And timorously he shook the grimy shoulder of the Beshta Shon.

The little potentate stirred in his sodden dreams. "Wha," he declared. He opened one eye; it was the color of brick dust.

"Would you like me to help you sit up, sir?" asked Onayly.

The Beshta Shon nodded his head and immediately regretted the motion. "I was potted," he said, in a furry voice.

"Yes, sir. That's it, sit up. We must get you back before anyone sees you this way."

The Beshta Shon opened his other eye and squinted the first. He turned his head one way and another until he focused on the policeman.

"Who are you?" he asked.

"I'm Officer Onayly, sir. Don't you remember me? I was with you last night."

"Last night—I don't recall last night. What am I doing here?"

Onayly didn't have the answer to that. He decided to let the question slip away into the bright afternoon. "Let's try standing now, sir," he said. He helped the small man to his feet.

"I'm fine now, officer. I'm very grateful to you for looking out for me. Yes, I'd better be getting back. I need to take a bath and put on some clean clothes."

The great Beshta Shon, proprietor of a rich industrial world, possessor of a fortune beyond the limited imagination of a poor man like Officer Onayly, staggered just a bit as he tested his legs. In no more time than it takes a newborn wildebeest to learn the same trick, the Beshta Shon had once again mastered the art of walking. The cop gave him encouragement in a soft friendly voice. Together they made their way down the odoriferous alley.

"I shall call a car, sir," said Onayly.

"Thank you, officer."

A few minutes later, in the car, the Beshta Shon began to feel as if he might recover, after all. He sat back in the seat and uttered a long, weary sigh.

"I must apologize if I caused you any concern, officer," he said.

"No, sir, not at all."

"I have been coming to Springfield for a long time, and I always visit Sadie," smiled the Beshta Shon. "I'm in love with her, you know."

A large, fat fish falling from the sky into Officer Onayly's lap would not have puzzled him more. "But, sir, Sadie is—"

The gentleman stopped him with a gesture. "You do not need to tell me what you think of her, officer. You see only her brassy appearance. I have learned to love the beauty and gentleness that dwell beneath. Tell me, officer, do you know what this means?" A golden chain hung around his neck; on it was fixed a small golden pendant with the numerals 154 inlaid in lapis. The cop's eyes opened wider.

"You are one of the Thousand, sir," said Onayly, awestruck.

A daunting barrier rose between the two men that no amount of shared adventure could ever overcome. The Beshta Shon had paid three years of his life and a vast amount of money, and he had become immortal. The Thousand would live virtually forever, their bodies incorruptible, their minds inviolate. When Springfield itself was no more, when Onayly and all his progeny were forgotten, the Beshta

Shon and the others of the Thousand would still be alive.

"You hate me now, don't you?" asked the Beshta Shon.

"No, sir." But an uneasy feeling aggravated the officer's complacency. It was the envy of one who knows he will not also live forever.

"I know what you are thinking—I have heard it often enough since I acquired this number. I have searched endlessly for someone with whom to share the lonely centuries. Whenever I found a woman whom I admired and respected, I learned that it was only my fortune she loved. Disappointment piled upon disappointment. I felt doomed to an eternity of loneliness. Then I met Sadie. She seems to be a—what would you call her? A common wench? But she is so much more than that, officer. She is the only truly honest person I have ever known. She gives everyone just the measure of respect he deserves, no more and no less. She is far more than what she looks, my friend."

"Still, she doesn't care anything for you. Perhaps if you told her—"

"I will win her in my own way," smiled the Beshta Shon. "I believe that I have already almost succeeded."

"Very well," said Onayly, dubiously. "It isn't any business of mine to begin with."

The car came to a stop before a palatial marble edifice, surrounded by gardens and fountains. A uniformed attendant helped the Beshta Shon from the vehicle.

"I want to thank you again," said the little man.

"Please, sir," objected the cop, "it was all in the line of duty. It was my privilege."

"I will return next year. Perhaps you will accompany me on my little fling again." The very notion caused a shudder in Onayly's robust, able form. The Beshta Shon reached into a pocket and pulled out a handful of crumpled bills. He chose one at random and dropped it through the window, into Onayly's lap.

"I can't accept—" protested the cop.

"Please," said the Beshta Shon. And then he turned with a bemused smile on his face and started up the long flight of marble stairs.

The officer looked at the wadded-up money. "If it's a five or a ten," he muttered, "I guess I may keep it. If it's a twenty, I will have to report it to Cap'n Helfmuhn. I'm sure he'll know a good use for it." The cop smoothed out the bill on his knee and stared at it: in the corner was the number 1000. Onayly whistled softly.

A few minutes later the driver let him out of the car at Slowboat Sadie's. Onayly felt he owed the gentleman something. Inside the barroom everything was the same: Dusty Jack was serving up beer, Sadie herself had retreated to the table in the dusky corner, the customers were bickering fiercely about nothing vital. The officer went straight to Sadie.

"I trust you found him well," said Slowboat Sadie.

"I did. He will be leaving Springfield soon."

"We will see him again next year." The woman covered a yawn with her long graceful fingers.

"Sadie," cried the cop, "how can you treat him this way? The man loves you, you know. He has true feelings. He isn't just another drunken lout for you to boot into the alley. And he has so much to offer you, if you would only listen."

Sadie smiled a sad smile. "Does he, indeed?" From within her shimmering blouse she pulled a golden chain. Inlaid upon the golden pendant was the figure 838.

"Great bloomin' ducks, Sadie!"

"This is what he gave me twenty years ago, Onayly. Now think on this. To live forever is fine for a man like him, who has wealth and power and an empire to manage. But what of me? Shall I spend forever in this horrible place? This life is all I know, and the only escape from it is death. Your little friend stole that escape from me."

The policeman shook his head mournfully. "If you learned to love him, you could share all that he has, as well. But you must hate him a great deal."

Onayly thought he saw a modest flush suffuse the cheeks of Slowboat Sadie—her face glowed the charming color of the palest pink crepe myrtle blossoms.

"I do not hate him," she said, softly. "I love him very much."

"But then—"

Sadie laughed. "Because, you slow-witted excuse for a cop, he has been begging me to marry him for thirty years. And if I did marry him today, what would the two of us do for the rest of forever? There are enough days for all of that. Let him come back next year, and maybe I will be sweet to him. Or if not next year, the year after. Or the year after that. I love him too much to let it go stale so soon."

Onayly looked at the woman for a moment and realized that the Beshta Shon had been perfectly correct: Sadie *was* beautiful. The cop was surprised he had never noticed it before. He went out of the establishment and headed back to the station; Captain Helfmuhn would be greatly pleased at the turn of events. As he walked, Onayly thought over what he had discovered that day. A little scrap of old, old poetry kept passing through his mind. "Had we but world enough and time," he recited, "This coyness, lady, were no crime." He repeated the lines to himself and smiled. Then he laughed out loud. As he strolled along, the stalwart officer twirled his nightstick in the way that made him the envy of all the rookies, and he whistled away the last bit of hangover from the night before.

WITH THE ORIGINAL CAST

Nancy Kress

The title of this story is more literal than it seems, for it refers to a production of a play about Joan of Arc that features a young woman who is the reincarnation of Jeanne d'Arc herself. This might seem like a director's dream come true, especially since the play can be altered to present the facts of history as the heroine herself experienced them—but there are different orders of truth in art.

Nancy Kress is the author of the fine first novel The Prince of Morning Bells.

IN THE SUMMER OF 1998 GREGORY WHITTEN was rehearsing a seventy-fifth-year revival of George Bernard Shaw's *Saint Joan,* and Barbara Bishop abruptly called to ask me to fly back from Denver and attend a few rehearsals with her. She was playing Shaw's magnificent teen-aged fanatic, a role she had not done for twenty years and never on Broadway. Still, it was an extraordinary request; she had never specifically asked for my presence before, and I wound up my business for Gorer-Redding Solar and caught the next shuttle with uncharacteristic hope. At noon I landed in New York and coptered directly to the theater. Barbara met me in the lobby.

"Austin! You came!"

"Did you doubt it?" I kissed her, and she laughed softly.

"It was so splendid of you to drop everything and rush home."

"Well—I didn't exactly drop it. Lay it down gently, perhaps."

"Could Carl spare you? Did you succeed in blocking that coalition, or can they still stop Carl from installing the new Battery?"

"They have one chance in a billion," I said lightly. Barbara always asks; she manages to sound as interested in Gorer-Redding Solar as in Shakespeare and ESIR, although I don't suppose she really is. Of late neither am I, although Carl Gorer is my brother and the speculative risks of finance, including Gorer-Redding, is my profession. It was a certain faint boredom with seriously behaved money that had driven me in the first place to take wildcat risks backing legitimate theater. In the beginning Gorer-Redding Solar was itself a wildcat risk: one chance in a hundred that solar energy could be made cheap and plentiful enough to replace the exhausted petrofields. But that was years ago. Now solar prosperity is a reality; speculations lie elsewhere.

"I do appreciate your coming, you know," Barbara said. She tilted her head to one side, and a curve of shining dark hair, still without gray, slanted across one cheek.

"All appreciation gratefully accepted. Is there something wrong with the play?"

"No, of course not. What could be wrong with Shaw? Oh, Gregory's a little edgy, but then you know Gregory."

"Then you called me back solely to marry me."

"Austin, not again," she said, without coyness. "Not now."

"Then something *is* wrong."

She pulled a little away from me, shaking her head. "Only the usual new-play nerves."

"Rue-day nerves."

"Through-the-day swerves."

"Your point," I said. "But, Barbara, you've played Joan of Arc before."

"Twenty years ago," she said, and I glimpsed the strain on her face a second before it vanished under her publicity-photo smile, luminous and cool as polished crystal. Then the smile disappeared, and she put her cheek next to mine and whispered, "I do thank you for coming. And you look so splendid," and she was yet another Barbara, the Barbara I saw only in glimpses through her self-contained poise, despite having pursued her for half a year now with my marriage proposals, all gracefully rejected. I, Austin Gorer, who until now had never ever pursued anything very fast or very far. Nor ever had to.

"Nervous, love?"

"Terrified," she said lightly, the very lightness turning the word into a denial of itself, a delicate stage mockery.

"I don't believe it."

"That's half your charm. You never believe me."

"Your Joan was a wild success."

"My God, that was even before ESIR, can you believe it?"

"I believe it."

"So do I," she said, laughing, and began to relate anecdotes about casting that play, then this one, jumping between the two with witty, effortless bridges, her famous voice rising and falling with the melodious control that was as much a part of the public's image of her as the shining helmet of dark hair and the cool grace.

She has never had good press. She is too much of a paradox to reduce easily to tabloid slogans, and the stupider journalists have called her mannered and artificial. She is neither. Eager animation and conscious taste are two qualities the press usually holds to be opposites, patronizing the first and feeling defensive in the presence of the second. But in Barbara Bishop, animation and control have melded into a grace that owes nothing to nature and everything to a civilized respect for willed illusion. When she walks across a stage or through a bedroom, when she speaks Shaw's words or her own, when she hands Macbeth a dagger or a dinner guest a glass of wine, every movement is both free of artifice and perfectly controlled. Because she will not rage at press conferences, or wail colorfully at lost roles, or wrinkle her nose in professional cuteness, the press has decided that she is cold and lacks spontaneity. But for Barbara, what is spontaneous *is* control. She was born with it. She'll always have it.

"—and so now Gregory's *still* casting for the crowd scenes. He's tested what has to be every ESIR actor in New York, and now he's scraping up fledglings straight out of the hospital. Their scalp scars are barely healed and the ink on their historian's certificate is still wet. We're two weeks behind already, and rehearsals have barely begun, would you believe it? He can't find enough actors with an ESIR in fifteenth-century France, and he's not willing to go even fifty years off on either side."

"Then *you* must have been French in Joan's time," I said, "or he wouldn't have cast you? Even you?"

"Quite right. Even me." She moved away from me toward the theater doors. Again I sensed in her some unusual strain. An actor is always reluctant to discuss his ESIR with an outsider (bad form), but this was something more.

"As it happens," Barbara continued, "I was not only French, I was even in Rouen when Joan was burned at the stake in 1431. I didn't see the burning, and I never laid eyes on her—I was only a barmaid in a country tavern—but, still, it's rather an interesting coincidence."

"Yes."

"One chance in a million," she said, smiling. "Or, no—what would be the odds, Austin? That's really your field."

I didn't know. It would depend, of course, on just how many people in the world had undergone ESIR. There were very few. Electronically Stimulated Incarnation Recall involves painful, repeated electrochemical jolts through the cortex, through the limbic brain, directly into the R-Complex, containing racial and genetic memory. Biological shields are ripped away; defense mechanisms designed to aid survival by streamlining the vast load of memory are deliberately torn. The long-term effects are not yet known. ESIR is risky, confusing, morally disorienting, painful, and expensive. Most people want nothing to do with it. Those who do are mostly historians, scientists, freaks, mystics, poets—or actors, who must be a little of each. A stage full of players who believe totally that they *are* in Hamlet's Denmark or Sir Thomas More's England or Blanche DuBois's South because they *have* been there and feel it in every gesture, every cadence, every authentic cast of mind—such a stage is out of time entirely. It can seduce even a philistine financier. Since ESIR, the glamour of the theater has risen, the number of would-be actors has dropped, and only the history departments of the world's universities have been so in love with historically authentic style.

"Forget the odds," I said. "Who hasn't been cast yet?"

"Well, we need to see," she said, ticking off roles on her fingers. I recognized the parody instantly: Gregory Whitten himself. Her very face seemed to lengthen into the horse-faced scowl so beloved by Sunday-supplement caricaturists. "We must have two royal ladies—no, they must absolutely look royal, *royal*. And DeStogumber, I need a marvelous DeStogumber! How can anyone expect me to direct without an absolutely wonderful DeStogumber—"

The theater doors opened. "We are ready for you onstage, Miss Bishop."

"Thank you." The parody of Whitten had vanished instantly; in this public of one stagehand she was again Barbara Bishop, controlled and cool.

I settled into a seat in the first row, nodding vaguely at the other hangers-on scattered throughout the orchestra and mezzanine. No one nodded back. There was an absurd public fiction that we, who contributed nothing to the play but large sums of money, were like air: necessary but invisible. I didn't mind. I enjoyed seeing the cast ease into their roles, pulling them up from somewhere inside and mentally shaking each fold around their own gestures and voices and glances. I had not always known how to see that. It had taken me, from such a different set of signals, a long time to notice the tiny adjustments that go, rehearsal by rehearsal, to create the illusion of reality. Perhaps I was slow. But now it seemed to me that I could spot the precise moment when an actor has achieved that precarious balance between his neocortical knowledge of the script and his older, ESIR knowledge of the feel of his character's epoch, and so is neither himself nor the playwright's creation but some third, subtler force that transcends both.

Barbara, I could see, had not yet reached that moment.

Whitten, pacing the side of the stage, was directing the early scene in which the seventeen-year-old Joan, a determined peasant, comes to Captain Robert de Baudricourt to demand a horse and armor to lead the French to victory over the English. De Baudricourt was being played by Jason Kellig, a semisuccessful actor whom I had met before and not particularly liked. No one else was onstage, although I had that sensation one always has during a rehearsal of hordes of other people just out of sight in the wings, eyeing the action critically and shushing one another. Moths fluttering nervously just outside the charmed circle of light.

"No squire!" Barbara said. "God is very merciful, and the blessed saints Catherine and Margaret, who speak to me every day, will intercede for you. You will go to paradise, and your name will be remembered forever as my first helper."

It was subtly wrong: too poised for the peasant Joan, too graceful. At the same time, an occasional gesture—an outflinging of her elbow, a sour smile—was too brash, and I guessed that these had belonged to the Rouen barmaid in Joan's ESIR. It was very rough, and I could see Whitten's famous temper, never long in check, begin to mount.

"No, no, no—Barbara, you're supposed to be an *innocent*. Shaw says that Joan answers 'with muffled sweetness.' You sound too surly. Absolutely too surly. You must do it again. Jason, cue her."

"Well, I am damned," Kellig said.

"No, squire! God is very merciful, and the blessed saints

Catherine and Margaret, who speak to me every day, will
intercede for you. You will go to paradise—"

"Again," Whitten said.

"Well, I am damned."

"No, squire! God is very merciful, and the blessed saints
Catherine and Margaret, who speak to me every—"

"No! Now you sound like you're sparring with him! This
is not some damned eighteenth-century drawing-room repar-
tee! Joan absolutely *means* it! The voices are absolutely real
to her. You must do it again, Barbara. You must tap into the
religious atmosphere of your ESIR. You are not trying! Do it
again!"

Barbara bit her lip. I saw Kellig glance from her to
Whitten, and I suddenly had the impression—I don't know
why—that they had all been at one another earlier, before I
had arrived. Something beyond the usual rehearsal frustration was going on here. Tension, unmistakable as the smell
of smoke, rose from the three of them.

"Well, I am damned."

"No, squire! God is very merciful, and the blessed saints
Catherine and Margaret, who speak to me every day, will
intercede for you. You will go to paradise, and your name
will be remembered forever as my first helper."

"Again," Whitten said.

"Well, I am damned."

"No, squire! God is—"

"Again."

"Really, Gregory," Barbara began icily, "how you think
you can judge after four words of—"

"I need to hear only *one* word when it's as bad as that!
And what in absolute hell is that little flick of the wrist
supposed to be? Joan is not a discus thrower. She must
be—" Whitten stopped dead, staring offstage.

At first, unsure of why he had cut himself off or turned so
red, I thought he was having an attack of some kind. The
color in his face was high, almost hectic. But he held himself
taut and erect, and then I heard the siren coming closer,
landing on the roof, trailing off. It had come from the
direction of Larrimer—which was, I suddenly remembered,
the only hospital in New York that would do ESIR.

A very young man in a white coat hurried across the stage.

"Mr. Whitten, Dr. Metz says could you come up to the
copter right away?"

"What is it? No, don't hold back, damn it, you absolutely must tell me now! *Is* it?"

On the young technician's face professional restraint battled with self-importance. The latter won, helped perhaps by Whitten's seizing the boy by the shoulders. For a second I actually thought Whitten would shake him.

"It's her, sir. It really is. We were looking for fifteenth-century ESIR, like you said, and we tried the neos for upper class for the ladies in waiting, and all we were getting were peasants or non-Europeans or early childhood deaths, and then Dr. Metz asked—" He was clearly enjoying this, dragging it out as much as possible. Whitten waited with a patience that surprised me until I realized that he was holding his breath. "—this neo to concentrate on the pictures Dr. Metz would show her of buildings and dresses and bowls and stuff to clear her mind. She looked dazed and in pain like they do, and then she suddenly remembered who she was, and Dr. Metz asked her lots of questions—that's his period anyway, you know; he's the foremost American historian on medieval France—and then he said she was."

Whitten let out his breath, a long, explosive sigh. Kellig leaned forward and said, "Was . . ."

"Joan," the boy said simply. "Joan of Arc."

It was as if he had shouted, although of course he had not. But the name hung in the dusty silence of the empty theater, circled and underlined by everything there: the heavy velvet curtains, the dust motes in the air, the waiting strobes, the clouds of mothlike actors, or memories of actors, in the wings. They all existed to lend weight and probability to what had neither. One in a million, one in a billion.

"Is Dr. Metz sure?" Whitten demanded. He looked suddenly violent, capable of disassembling the technician if the historian were not sure.

"He's sure!"

"Where is she? In the copter?"

"Yes."

"Have Dr. Metz bring her down here. No, I'll go up there. No, bring her here. Is she still weak?"

"Yes, sir," the boy said.

"Well, go! I told Dr. Metz I wanted her here as soon as he was absolutely sure!"

The boy went.

So Whitten had been informed of the possibility earlier. I

looked at Barbara, suddenly understanding the tension on stage. She stood smiling, her chin raised a little, her body very straight. She looked pale. Some trick of lighting, some motionless tautness in her shoulders, made me think for an instant that she was going to faint, but of course she did not. She behaved exactly as I knew she must have been willing herself to, waiting quietly through the interminable time until Joan of Arc should appear. Whitten fidgeted; Kellig lounged, his eyelids lowered halfway. Neither of them looked at Barbara.

The technician and the historian walked out onto the stage, each with a hand under either elbow of a young girl whose head was bandaged. Even now I feel a little ashamed when I remember rising halfway in my seat, as for an exalted presence. But the girl was not an exalted presence, was not Joan of Arc; she was an awkward, skinny, plain-faced girl who had once *been* Joan of Arc and now wanted to be an extra in the background of a seventy-five-year-old play. No one else seemed to be remembering the distinction.

"You were Joan of Arc?" Whitten asked. He sounded curiously formal, as out of character as the girl.

"Yes, I . . . I remember Joan. Being Joan." The girl frowned, and I thought I knew why: She was wondering why she didn't *feel* like Joan. But ESIR, Barbara has told me, doesn't work like that. Other lives are like remembering someone you have known, not like experiencing the flesh and bone of this one—unless this one is psychotic. Otherwise, it usually takes time and effort to draw on the memory of a previous incarnation, and this child had been Joan of Arc only for a few days. Suddenly I felt very sorry for her.

"What's your first name?" Whitten said.

"Ann. Ann Jasmine."

Whitten winced. "A stage name?"

"Yes. Isn't it pretty?"

"You must absolutely use your real name. What acting have you done?"

The girl shifted her weight, spreading her feet slightly apart and starting to count off on her fingers. Her voice was stronger now and cockier. "Well, let's just see: In high school I played Portia in *The Merchant of Venice,* and in the Country-Time Players—that's community theater—I was Goat's Sister in *The Robber Bridegroom* and Arla in *Moondust.* And then I came to New York, and I've done—oh, small stuff, mostly. A few commercials." She smiled at Whitten, then looked past him at Kellig and winked. He stared back at her as if she were a dead fish.

"What," said Kellig slowly, "*is* your real name?"

"Does it matter?" The girl's smile vanished, and she pouted.

"Yes."

"Ann Friedland," she said sulkily, and I knew where the "few commercials, mostly" as well as the expensive ESIR audition had come from. Trevor Friedland, of Friedland Computers, was a theater backer for his own amusement, much as I was. He was not, however, a co-backer in this one. Not yet.

At the Friedland name, Kellig whistled, a low, impudent note that made Whitten glance at him in annoyance. Barbara still had not moved. She watched them intently.

"Forget your name," Whitten said. "Absolutely forget it. Now I know this play is new to you, but you must read for me. Just read cold; don't be nervous. Take my script and start there. No—there. Jason, cue her."

"You want me to read Joan? The part of *Joan?*" the girl said. All her assumed sophistication was gone; her face was as alive as a seven-year-old's at Christmas, and I looked away, not wanting to like her.

"Oh, really, Greg," Kellig said. Whitten ignored him.

"Just look over Shaw's description there, and then start. I know you're cold. Just start."

"Good morning, captain squire," she began shakily, but stopped when Barbara crossed the stage to sit on a bench near the wings. She was still smiling, a small frozen smile. Ann glanced at her nervously, then began over.

"Good morning, captain squire. Captain, you are to give me a horse . . ." Again she stopped. A puzzled look came over her face; she skimmed a few pages and then closed her eyes. Immediately I thought of the real Joan, listening to voices. But this *was* the real Joan. For a moment the stage seemed to float in front of me, a meaningless collection of lines and angles.

"It wasn't like that," Ann Friedland said slowly.

"Like what?" Whitten said. "What wasn't like what?"

"Joan. Me. She didn't charge in like that at all to ask de Baudricourt for horse and armor. It wasn't at all . . . she was more . . . insane, I think. What he has written here, Shaw . . ." She looked at each of us in turn, frowning. No one moved. I don't know how long we stayed that way, staring at the thin girl onstage.

"Saint Catherine," she said finally. "Saint Margaret." Her slight figure jerked as if shocked, and she threw back her head and howled like a dog. "But Orléans was not even my idea! The commander, my father, the commander, my father . . . oh, my God, my dear God, he made her do it, he told me—they all *promised*—"

She stumbled, nearly falling to her knees. The historian leaped forward and caught her. I don't think any of us could have borne it if that pitiful, demented figure had knelt and begun to pray.

The next moment, however, though visibly fighting to control herself, she knew where—and who—she was.

"Doctor, don't, I'm all right now, it's not—I'm all right. Mr. Whitten, I'm sorry, let me start the scene over!"

"No, don't start the scene over. Tell me what you were going to say. Where is Shaw wrong? What happened? Try to feel it again."

Ann's eyes held Whitten's. They were beyond all of us, already negotiating with every inflection of every word.

"I don't have to feel it again. I remember what happened. That wave of . . . I won't do that again. It was just when it all came rushing back. But now I remember it, I have it, I can *control* it. It didn't happen like Shaw's play. She—I—was used. She did hear voices, she was mad, but the whole idea to use her to persuade the Dauphin to fight against the English didn't come from the voices. The priests insisted on what they said the voices meant, and the commander made her a sort of mascot to get the soldiers to kill . . . I was *used*. A victim." A complicated expression passed over her face, perhaps the most extraordinary expression I have ever seen on a face so young: regret and shame and loss and an angry, wondering despair for events long beyond the possibility of change. Then the expression vanished, and she was wholly a young woman coolly engaged in the bargaining of history.

"I know it all, Mr. Whitten—all that *really* happened. And it happened to me. The real Joan of Arc."

"Cosgriff," Whitten said, and I saw Kellig start. Lawrence Cosgriff had won the Pulitzer Prize for drama the last two years in a row. He wrote powerful, despairing plays about the loss of individual morality in an institutionalized world.

"My dear Gregory," Kellig said, "one does not simply commission Lawrence Cosgriff to write one a play. He's not some hack you can—"

Whitten looked at him, and he was quiet. I understood why; Whitten was on fire, and exalted with his daring idea as the original Joan must have been with hers. But no, of course, she hadn't been exalted, that was the whole point. She had been a dupe, not a heroine. Young Miss Friedland, fighting for her name in lights, most certainly considered Joan the Heroine to be an expendable casualty. One of the expendable casualties. I stood up and began to make my way to the stage.

"I'm the real thing," Ann said. "The *real* thing. I'll play Joan, of course."

"Of course," Kellig drawled. He was already looking at her with dislike, and I could see what their rehearsals would be: the chance upstart and the bit player who had paid largely fruitless dues for twenty years. The commander and the Dauphin would still be the male leads; Kellig's part could only grow smaller under Ann's real thing.

"I'll play Joan," she said again, a little more loudly.

Whitten, flushed with his vision, stopped his ecstatic pacing and scowled. "Of course you must play Joan!"

"Oh," Ann said, "I was afraid—"

"Afraid? What is this? You *are* Joan."

"Yes," she said slowly, "yes, I am." She frowned, sincerely, and then a second later replaced the frown with a smile all calculation and relief. "Yes, of course I am!"

"Then I'll absolutely reach Cosgriff's agent today. He'll jump at it. You will need to work with him, of course. We can open in six months, with any luck. You *do* live in town? Cosgriff can tape you. No, someone else can do that before he even—Austin!"

"You're forgetting something, aren't you, Gregory, in this sudden great vision? You have a contract to do Shaw."

"Of course I'm not forgetting the contract. But you absolutely must want to continue, for this new play . . . Cosgriff . . ." He stopped, and I knew the jumble of things that must be in his mind: deadlines, backing (Friedland Comput-

ers!), contracts, schedules, the percentage of my commitment, and, belatedly, Barbara.

She still sat on the bench at stage left, half in shadow. Her
back was very straight, her chin high, but in the subdued
light her face with its faint smile looked older, not haggard
but set, inelastic. I walked over to her and turned to face
Whitten.

"I will not back this new play, even if you do get Cosgriff
to write it. Which I rather doubt. Shaw's drama is an artistic
masterpiece. What you are planning is a trendy exploitation
of some flashy technology. Look elsewhere for your
money."

Silence. Whitten began to turn red. Kellig snickered—at
whom was not clear: In the silence the historian, Dr. Metz,
began timidly, "I'm sure Miss Friedland's information
would be welcomed warmly by any academic—"

The girl cried loudly, "But I'm the real thing!" and she
started to sob.

Barbara had risen to take my arm. Now she dropped it and
walked over to Ann. Her voice was steady. "I know you are.
And I wish you all luck as an actress. It's a brilliant opportunity, and I'm sure you'll do splendidly with it."

They faced each other, the sniveling girl who had at least
the grace to look embarrassed and the smiling, humiliated
woman. It was a public performance, of course, an illusion
that all Barbara felt was a selfless, graceful warmth, but it
was also more than that. It was as gallant an act of style as I
have ever seen.

Ann muttered "Thank you" and flushed a mottled ma-
roon. Barbara took my arm, and we walked down the side
aisle and out of the theater. She walked carefully, choosing
her steps, her head high and lips together and solemn, like a
woman on her way to a public burning.

I wish I could say that my quixotic gesture had an immediate and disastrous effect on Whitten's plans, that he came to
his artistic senses—and went back to Shaw's *Saint Joan*.
But of course he did no such thing. Other financial backing
than mine proved to be readily available. Contracts were
rewritten, agents placated, lawsuits avoided. Cosgriff did
indeed consent to write the script, and *Variety* became
distressingly eager to report any tidbit connected with what
was being billed as *JOAN OF ARC: WITH THE ORIGINAL*

CAST! It was a dull theater season in New York. Nothing currently running gripped the public imagination like this as-yet-unwritten play. Whitten, adroitly fanning the flames, gave out very few factual details.

Barbara remained silent on the whole subject. Business was keeping me away from New York a great deal. Gorer-Redding Solar was installing a new plant in Bogotá, and I would spend whole weeks trying to untangle the lush foliage of bribes, kickbacks, nepotism, pride, religion, and mañana that is business in South America. But whenever I was in New York, I spent time with Barbara. She would not discuss Whitten's play, warning me away from the subject with the tactful withdrawal of an estate owner discouraging trespassing without hurting local feelings. I admired her tact and her refusal to whine, but at the same time I felt vaguely impatient. She was keeping me at arm's length. She was doing it beautifully, but arm's length was not where I wanted to be.

I do not assume that intimacy must be based on a mutual display of sores. I applaud the public illusion of control and well-being as a civilized achievement. However, I knew Barbara well enough to know that under her illusion of well-being she must be hurt and a little afraid. No decent scripts had been offered her, and the columnists had not been kind over the loss of *Saint Joan*. Barbara had been too aloof, too self-possessed for them to show any compassion now. Press sympathy for a humiliated celebrity is in direct proportion to the anguished copy previously supplied.

Then one hot night in August I arrived at Barbara's apartment for dinner. Lying on a hall table was a script:

A MAID OF DOMREMY
by
Lawrence Cosgriff

Incredulous, I picked it up and leafed through it. When I looked up, Barbara was standing in the doorway, holding two goblets of wine.

"Hello, Austin. Did you have a good flight?"

"Barbara—what is this?" I asked, stupidly.

She crossed the hall and handed me one of the goblets. "It's Lawrence's play about Joan of Arc."

"I see that. But what is it doing here?"

She didn't answer me immediately. She looked beautiful, every illusion seeming completely natural: the straight, heavy silk of her artfully cut gown, the flawless makeup, the hair cut in precise lines to curve over one cheek. Without warning, I was irritated by all of it. Illusions. Arm's length.

"Austin, why don't you reconsider backing Gregory's play?"

"Why on earth should I?"

"Because you really could make quite a lot of money on it."

"I could make quite a lot of money backing auto gladiators. I don't do that, either."

She smiled, acknowledging the thrust. I still did not know how the conversation had become a duel.

"Are you hungry? There are canapés in the living room. Dinner won't be ready for a while yet."

"I'm not hungry. Barbara, why do you want me to back Whitten's play?"

"I don't want you to, if you don't wish to. Come in and sit down. *I'm* hungry. I only thought you might want to back the play. It's splendid." She looked at me steadily over the rim of her goblet. "It's the best new script I've seen in years. It's subtle, complex, moving—much better even than his last two. It's going to replace Shaw's play as the best we have about Joan. And on the subject of victimization by a world the main character doesn't understand, it's better than *Streetcar* or *Joy Ride*. A hundred years from now this play will still be performed regularly, and well."

"It's not like you to be so extravagant with your praise."

"No, it's not."

"And you want me to finance the play for the reflected glory?"

"For the satisfaction. And," she added quietly, but firmly, "because I've accepted a bit part in it."

I stared at her. Last week a major columnist had headlined: FALLEN STAR LANDS ON HER PRIDE.

"It's a very small role. Yolande of Aragon, the Dauphin's mother-in-law. She intrigued on the Dauphin's behalf when he was struggling to be crowned. I have only one scene, but it has possibilities."

"For you? What does it have possibilities of—being smirked at by that little schemer in *your* role? Did you read how much her agent is holding Whitten up for? No wonder he could use more backers."

"You would get it back. But that's not the question, Austin, is it? Why do you object to my taking this part? It's not like you to object to my choice of roles."

"I'm upset because I don't want you to be hurt, and I think you are. I think you'll be hurt even more if you play this Yolande with Miss Ann Friedland as Joan, and I don't want to see it, because I love you."

"I know you do, Austin." She smiled warmly and touched my cheek. It was a perfect Barbara Bishop gesture: sincere, graceful, and complete in itself—so complete that it promised nothing more than what it was, led on to nothing else. It cut off communication as effectively as a blow—or, rather, more effectively, since a blow can be answered in kind. I slammed my glass on the table and stood up. Once up, however, I had nothing to say and so stood there feeling ridiculous. What *did* I want to say? What did I want from her that I did not already have?

"I wish," I said slowly, "that you were not always acting."

She looked at me steadily. I knew the look. She was waiting: for retraction or amendment or amplification. And of course she was right to expect any, or all, of those things. What I had said was inaccurate. She was not acting. What she did was something subtly different. She behaved with the gestures and attitudes and behaviors of the world as she believed it ought to be, a place of generous and rational individuals with enough sheer style to create events in their own image. That people's behavior was in fact often uncivilized, cowardly, and petty she of course knew; she was not stupid. Hers was a deliberate, controlled choice: to ignore the pettiness and to grant to all of us—actors, audience, press, Whitten, Ann Friedland, me, herself—the illusion of having the most admirable motives conceivable.

It seemed to me that this was praiseworthy, even "civilized," in the best sense of that much-abused word.

Why, then, did it make me feel so lonely?

Barbara was still waiting. "Forgive me; I misspoke. I don't mean that you are always acting. I mean—I mean that I'm concerned for you. Standing for a curtain call at the back of the stage while that girl, that chance reincarnation . . ." Suddenly a new idea occurred to me. "Or do you think that she won't be able to do the part and you will be asked to take over for her?"

"No!"

"But if Ann Friedland can't—"

"No! I will never play Joan in *A Maid of Domrémy!*"

"Why not?"

She finished her wine. Under the expensive gown her breasts heaved. "I had no business even taking the part in Shaw's *Joan*. I am forty-five years old, and Joan is seventeen. But at least there—at least Shaw's Joan was not really a victim. I will not play her as a pitiful victim."

"Come on, Barbara. You've played Blanche DuBois, and Ophelia, and Jessie Kane. They're all victims."

"I won't play Joan in *A Maid of Domrémy!*"

I saw that she meant it, that even while she admired the play, she was repelled by it in some fundamental way I did not understand. I sat down again on the sofa and put my arms around her. Instantly she was Barbara Bishop again, smiling with rueful mockery at both her own violence and my melodrama, drawing us together in a covenant too generous for quarreling.

"Look at us, Austin—actually discussing that tired old cliché, the understudy who goes on for the fading star. But I'm not her understudy, and she can hardly fade before she's even bloomed! Really, we're too ridiculous. I'm sorry, love, I didn't mean to snap at you like that. Shall we have dinner now?"

I stood up and pulled her next to me. She came gracefully, still smiling, the light sliding over her dark hair, and followed me to her bedroom. The sex was very good, as it always was. But afterward, lying with her head warm on my shoulder, I was still baffled by something in her I could not understand. Was it because of ESIR? I had thought that before. What was it like to have knowledge of those hundreds of other lives you had once lived? I would never know. Were the exotic types I met in the theater so different, so less easily understood, because they had "creative temperament" (whatever that was) or because of ESIR? I would probably never know that, either, nor how much of Barbara was what she was here, now, and how much was subtle reaction to all the other things she knew she had been. I wasn't sure I wanted to know.

Long after Barbara fell asleep, I lay awake in the soft

darkness, listening to the night sounds of New York beyond the window and to something else beyond those, some large silence where my own ESIR memories might have been.

Whitten banned everyone but actors and tech crew from rehearsals of *A Maid of Domrémy:* press, relatives, backers, irate friends. Only because the play had seized the imagination of the public—or at least that small portion of the public that goes to the theater—could his move succeed. The financial angels went along cheerfully with their own banning, secure in the presale ticket figures that the play would make money even without their personal supervision.

Another director, casting for a production of *Hamlet,* suddenly claimed to have discovered the reincarnation of Shakespeare. For a week Broadway was a laser of rumors and speculations. Then the credentials of the two historians verifying the ESIR were discovered by a gleeful press to have been faked. The director, producer, historians, and ersatz Shakespeare were instantly unavailable for comment.

The central computer of the AMA was tapped into. For two days executives with private face-lifts and politicians with private accident records and teachers with private drug-abuse histories held their collective breaths, cursing softly under them. The AMA issued a statement that only ESIR records had been pirated, and the scandal was generally forgotten in the central part of the country and generally intensified on both coasts. Wild reports were issued, contradicted, confirmed, and disproved, all in a few hours. An actor who remembered being King Arthur had been discovered and was gong to star in the true story of the Round Table. Euripides was living in Boston and would appear there in his own play *Medea.* The computer verified that ESIR actually *had* uncovered Helen of Troy, and the press stampeded out to Bowling Green, Ohio, where it was discovered that the person who remembered being Helen of Troy was a male, bald, sixty-eight-year-old professor emeritus in the history department. He was writing a massive scholarly study of the Trojan War, and he bitterly resented the "cheap publicity of the popular press."

"The whole thing is becoming a circus," Barbara grumbled. Her shirt was loose at the breasts, and her pants gaped at the waist. She had lost weight and color.

"And this, too, shall pass," I told her. "Think of when

ESIR was first introduced. A few years of wild quakes all over society, and then everyone adjusted. This is just the aftershock on the theater."

"I don't especially like standing directly on the fault line."

"How are rehearsals going?"

"About the same," she said, her eyes hooded. Since she never spoke of the play at all, I didn't know what "about the same" would be the same as.

"Barbara, what are you waiting for?"

"Waiting for?"

"Constantly now you have that look of waiting, frowning to yourself, looking as if you're scrutinizing something. Something only you can see."

"Austin, how ridiculous! What I'm looking at is all *too* public: opening night for the play."

"And what do you see?"

She was silent for a long time. "I don't know."

"What don't you know, love?"

"I don't know." She laughed, an abrupt opaque sound like the sudden drawing of a curtain. "It's silly, isn't it? Not knowing what I don't know. A tautology, almost."

"Barbara, marry me. We'll go away for a weekend and get married, like two children. This weekend."

"I thought you had to fly back to Bogotá this weekend."

"I do. But you could come with me. There *is* a world outside New York, you know. It isn't simply all one vast out-of-town tryout."

"I do thank you, Austin, you know that. But I can't leave right now; I do have to work on my part. There are still things I don't trust."

"Such as what?"

"Me," she said lightly, and would say no more.

Meanwhile the hoopla went on. A professor of history at Berkeley who had just finished a—now probably erroneous—dissertation on Joan of Arc tried various legal ploys to sue Ann Friedland on the grounds that she "undercut his means of livelihood." A group called the Catholic Coalition to Clear the Inquisition published in four major newspapers an appeal to Ann Friedland to come forward and declare the fairness of the church at Joan of Arc's heresy trial. Each of the ads cost a fantastic sum. But Ann did not reply; she was preserving to the press a silence as complete as Barbara's to me. I think this is why I didn't press Barbara more closely about her rehearsals. I wanted to appear as different from the rest of the world as possible—an analogy probably no one made except me. Men in love are ludicrous.

Interest in Ann Friedland was not dispelled by her silence. People merely claiming to be a notable figure from the past was growing stale. For years people had been claiming to be Jesus Christ or Muhammad or Judas; all had been disproved, and the glamour evaporated. But now a famous name had not only been verified, it was going to be showcased in an enterprise that carried the risk of losing huge sums of money, several professional reputations, and months of secret work. The public was delighted. Ann Friedland quickly became a household name.

She was going to marry the widowed King Charles of England. She was going to lead a revival of Catholicism and was being considered for the position of first female pope. She was a drug addict, a Mormon, pregnant, mad, in love, clairvoyant, ten years old, extraterrestrial. She was refusing to go on opening night. Gregory Whitten was going to let her improvise the part opening night. Rehearsals were a disaster, and Barbara Bishop would play the part opening night.

Not even to this last did Barbara offer a comment. Also silent were the reputable papers, the serious theater critics, the men and women who control the money that controls Broadway. They, too, were waiting.

We all waited.

The week that *A Maid of Domrémy* was to open in New York I was still in Bogotá. I had come down with a low-grade fever, which in the press of work I chose to ignore. By Saturday I had a temperature of one hundred four degrees and a headache no medication could touch. I saw everything through slow, pastel-colored swirls. My arms and legs felt lit with a dry, papery fire that danced up and down from shoulder to wrist, ankle to hip, up and down, wrist to shoulder. I knew I should go to a hospital, but I did not. The opening was that night.

On the plane to New York I slept, dreaming of Barbara in the middle of a vast solar battery. I circled the outside, calling to her desperately. Unaware, she sat reading a script amid the circuits and storage cells, until the fires of the sun burst out all around her and people she had known from other lives danced maniacally in the flames.

At my apartment I took more pills and a cold shower, then tried to phone Barbara. She had already left for makeup call. I dressed and caught a copter to the theater, sleeping fitfully on the short trip, and then I was in the theater, surrounded by first-nighters who did not know I was breathing contagion on all of them, and who floated around me like pale cutouts in diamonds, furs, and nauseating perfume. I could not remember walking from the copter, producing my ticket, or being escorted to my seat. The curtain swirled sickeningly, and I closed my eyes until I realized that it was not my fever that caused the swirls: The curtain was rising. Had the house lights dimmed? I couldn't remember anything. Dry fire danced over me, shoulder to wrist, ankle to hip.

Barbara, cloaked, entered stage left. I had not realized that her scene opened the play. She carried a massive candle across the stage, bent over a wooden table, and lit two more candles from the large one, all with the taut, economical movements of great anger held fiercely in check. Before the audience heard her speak, before they clearly saw her face, they had been told that Yolande was furious, not used to being so, and fully capable of controlling her own anger.

"Mary! Where are you sulking now, Mary?" Barbara said. She straightened and drew back her hood. Her voice was low, yet every woman named Mary in the audience started guiltily. Onstage Mary of Anjou, consort of the uncrowned Dauphin of France, crept sullenly from behind a tapestry, facing her mother like a whipped dog.

"Here I am, for all the good it will do you, or anyone," she whined, looking at her own feet. Barbara's motionless silence was eloquent with contempt; Mary burst out with her first impassioned monologue against the Dauphin and Joan; the play was launched. It was a strong, smooth beginning, fueled by the conviction of Barbara's portrait of the terrifying Yolande. As the scene unfolded, the portrait became even stronger, so that I forgot both my feverish limbs and my concern for Barbara. There were no limbs, no Barbara, no theater. There was only a room in fifteenth-century France, sticky with blood shed for what to us were illusions: absolute good and absolute evil. Cosgriff was exploring the capacities in such illusions for heroism, for degradation, for nobility beyond what the audience's beliefs, saner and more temperate, could allow. Yolande and Mary and the Dauphin loved and hated and gambled and killed with every fiber of their elemental beings, and not a sound rose from the audience until Barbara delivered her final speech and exited stage right. For a moment the audience sat still, bewildered—not by what had happened onstage, but by the unwelcome remembrance that they were not a part of it, but instead were sitting on narrow hard seats in a wooden box in New York, a foreign country because it was not medieval France. Then the applause started.

The Dauphin and his consort, still onstage, did not break character. He waited until the long applause was over, then continued bullying his wife. Shortly afterward two guards entered, dragging between them the confused, weeping Joan. The audience leaned forward eagerly. They were primed by the wonderful first scene and eager for more miracles.

"Is *this* the slut?" the Dauphin asked, and Mary, seeing a woman even more abused and wretched than herself, smiled with secret, sticky joy. The guards let Joan go, and she stumbled forward, caught herself, and staggered upward, raising her eyes to the Dauphin's.

"In the name of Saint Catherine—" She choked and started to weep. It was stormy weeping, vigorous, but without the chilling pain of true hysteria. The audience shuffled a little.

"I will do whatever you want, I swear it in the name of God, if you will only tell me what it is!" On the last word her voice rose; she might have been demanding that a fractious child cease lying to her.

I leaned my head sideways against one shoulder. Waves of fever and nausea beat through me, and for the the first time since I had become ill I was aware of labored breathing. My heart beat, skipped, beat twice, skipped. Each breath sounded swampy and rasping. People in the row ahead began to turn and glare. Wadding my handkerchief into a ball, I held it in front of my mouth and tried to watch the play.

Lines slipped in and out of my hearing; actors swirled in fiery paper-dry pastels. Once Joan seemed to turn into Barbara, and I gasped and half-rose in my seat, but then the figure onstage was Ann Friedland, and I sat down again to glares from those around me. It was Ann Friedland; I had been a fool to doubt it. It was not Joan of Arc. The girl onstage hesitated, changed tone too often, looked nervously across the footlights, moved a second too late. Once she even stammered.

Around me the audience began to murmur discreetly. Just before the first act curtain, in a moment of clarity, Joan finally sees how she is being used and makes an inept, wrenchingly pathetic attempt to manipulate the users by manufacturing instructions she says come from her voices. It is a crucial point in the play, throwing into dramatic focus the victim who agrees to her own corruption by a misplaced attempt at control. Ann played it nervously, with an exaggerated grab at pathos that was actually embarrassing. Nothing of that brief glimpse of personal power she had shown at her audition, so many weeks ago, was present now. Between waves of fever, I tried to picture the fit Whitten must be having backstage.

"Christ," said a man in the row ahead of me, "can you believe that?"

"What an absolute travesty," said the woman next to him. Her voice hummed with satisfaction. "Poor Lawrence."

"He was ripe for it. Smug."

"Oh, yes. Still."

"Smug," the man said.

"It doesn't matter to me what you do with her," said Mary of Anjou, onstage. "Why should it? Only for a moment she seemed . . . different. Did you remark it?" Ann Friedland, who had not seemed different, grimaced weakly, and the first-act curtain fell. People were getting to their feet, excited by the magnitude of the disaster. The house lights went up. Just as I stood, the curtains onstage parted and there was some commotion, but the theater leaped in a single nauseous lurch, blinding and hot, and then nothing.

"Austin," a voice said softly. "Austin."

My head throbbed, but from a distance, as if it were not my head at all.

"Austin," the voice said far above me. "Are you there?"

I opened my eyes. Yolande of Aragon, her face framed in a wool hood, gazed down at me and turned into Barbara. She was still in costume and makeup, the heavy, high color garish under too-bright lights. I groaned and closed my eyes.

"Austin. Are you there? Do you know me?"

"Barbara?"

"You are there! Oh, that's splendid. How do you feel? No,

don't talk. You've been delirious, love, you had such a fever
. . . this is the hospital. Larrimer. They've given you medication; you're going to be fine."

"Barbara."

"I'm here, Austin, I'm right here."

I opened my eyes slowly, accustoming them to the light. I
lay in a small private room; beyond the window the sky was
dark. I was aware that my body hurt, but aware in the
detached, abstract way characteristic of EL painkillers, that
miracle of modern science. The dose must have been massive. My body felt as if it belonged to someone else, a friend
for whom I felt comradely simulations of pain, but not the
real thing.

"What do I have?"

"Some tropical bug. What did you drink in Bogotá? The
doctor says it could have been dangerous, but they flushed
out your whole system and pumped you full of antibiotics,
and you'll be fine. Your fever's down almost to normal. But
you must rest."

"I don't want to rest."

"You don't have any choice." She took my hand. The
touch felt distant, as if the hand were wrapped in layers of
padding.

"What time is it?"

"Five A.M."

"The play—"

"Is long since over."

"What happened?"

She bit her lip. "A lot happened. When precisely do you
mean? I wasn't there for the second act, you know. When
the ambulance came for you, one of the ushers recognized
you and came backstage to tell me. I rode here in the
ambulance with you. I didn't have another scene anyway."

I was confused. If Barbara had missed the entire last act,
how could "a lot have happened"? I looked at her closely,
and this time I saw what only the EL's could have made me
miss before, the signs of great repressed strain. Tendons
stood out in Barbara's neck; under the cracked and sagging
makeup her eyes darted around the room. I felt myself
suddenly alert, and a fragment of memory poked at me, a
fragment half-glimpsed in the hot swirl of the theater just
before I blacked out.

"She ran out on the stage," I said slowly. "Ann Friedland.

In front of the curtain. She ran out and yelled something . . ." It was gone. I shook my head. "On the *stage.*"

"Yes." Barbara let go of my hand and began to pace. Her long train dragged behind her; when she turned, it tangled around her legs and she stumbled. The action was so uncharacteristic, it was shocking.

"You saw what the first act was. A catastrophe. She was trying—"

"The whole first act wasn't bad, love. Your scene was wonderful. Wait—the reviews on your role will be very good."

"Yes," she said distractedly. I saw that she had hardly heard me. There was something she had to do, had to say. The best way to help was to let her do it. Words tore from her like a gale.

"She tried to do the whole play reaching back into her ESIR Joan. She tried to just feel it, and let Lawrence's words—her words—be animated by the remembered feeling. But without the conscious balancing . . . no, it isn't even balancing. It's more like imagining what you already know, and to do that, you have to *forget* what you know and at the same time remember every tiny nuance . . . I can't explain it. Nobody ever really was a major historical figure before, in a play composed of his own words. Gregory was so excited over the concept, and then when rehearsals began . . . but by that time he was committed, and the terrible hype just bound him further. When Ann ruined the first act like that, he was just beside himself. I've never seen him like that. I've never seen anybody like that. He was raging, just completely out of control. And onstage Anne was coming apart, and I could see that he was going to completely destroy her, and we had a whole act to go, damn it! A whole fucking act!"

I stared at her. She didn't notice. She lighted a cigarette; it went out; she flung the match and cigarette on the floor. I could see her hand trembling.

"I knew that if Gregory got at her, she was done. She wouldn't even go back out after intermission. Of course the play was a flop already, but not to even *finish* the damn thing . . . I wasn't thinking straight. All I could see was that he would destroy her, all of us. So I hit him."

"You what?"

"I hit him. With Yolande's candlestick. I took him behind

a flat to try to calm him down, and instead I hit him. *Without knowing I was going to*. Something strange went through me, and I picked up my arm and hit him. Without knowing I was going to!"

She wrapped her arms around herself and shuddered. I saw what had driven her to this unbearable strain. *Without knowing I was going to*.

"His face became very surprised, and he fell forward. No one saw me. Gregory lay there, breathing as if he were just asleep, and I found a phone and called an ambulance. Then I told the stage manager that Mr. Whitten had had a bad fall and hit his head and was unconscious. I went around to the wings and waited for Ann. When the curtain came down and she saw me waiting for her, she turned white, and then red, and started shouting at me that she was Joan of Arc and I was an aging bitch who wanted to steal her role."

I tried to picture it—the abusive girl, the appalled, demoralized cast, the director lying hidden, bashed with a candlestick—*without knowing I was going to!*—and, out front, the polite chatter, the great gray critics from the *Times* and the *New Yorker,* the dressed-up suburbanites from Scarsdale squeezing genially down the aisles for an entr'acte drink and a smoke.

"She went on and on," Barbara said. "She told me *I* was the reason she couldn't play the role, that I deliberately undermined her by standing around like I knew everything, and she knew everybody was expecting me to go on as Joan after she failed. Then suddenly she darted away from me and went through the curtains onto the stage. The house lights were up; half the audience had left. She spread out her arms and *yelled* at them."

Barbara stopped and put her hands over her face. I reached up and pulled them away. She looked calmer now, although there was still an underlying tautness in her voice. "Oh, it's just too ridiculous, Austin. She made an absolute fool of herself, of Lawrence, of all of us, but it wasn't her fault. She's an inexperienced child without talent. Gregory should have known better, but his egomania got all tangled up in his ridiculous illusion that he was going to revitalize the theater, take the next historical step for American drama. God, what the papers will say . . ." She laughed weakly, with pain. "And I was no better, hitting poor Gregory."

"Barbara . . ."

"Do you know what Ann yelled at them, at the audience? She stood on that stage, flung her arms wide like some martyr . . ."

"What did she say? What, love?"

"She said, 'But I'm the *real thing!*' "

We were quiet for a moment. From outside the window rose blurred traffic noises: therealthingtherealthingtherealthing.

"You're right," I said. "The whole thing was an egomaniacal ride for Whitten, and the press turned it into a carnival. Cosgriff should have known better. The real thing—that's not what you want in the theater. Illusion, magic, imagination. What should have happened, not what did. Reality doesn't make good theater."

"No, you still don't understand!" Barbara cried. "You've missed it all! How can you think it's that easy, that Gregory's mistake was to use Ann's reality instead of Shaw's illusion!"

"I don't understand what you—"

"It's not that clear!" she cried. "Don't you think I wish it were? My God!"

I didn't know what she meant, or why under the cracked makeup her eyes glittered with feverish, exhausted panic. Even as I reached out my arm, completely confused, she was backing away from me.

"Illusion and reality," she said. "My God. Watch."

She crossed the room to the door, closed it, and pressed the dimmer on the lights. The room faded to a cool gloom. She stood with her back to me, her head bowed. Then she turned slowly and raised her eyes to a point in the air a head above her.

"In the name of Saint Catherine—" she began, choked, and started to weep. The weeping was terrifying, shot through with that threat of open hysteria that keeps a listener on the edge of panic in case the weeper should lose control entirely, and also keeps him fascinated for the same reason. "I will do whatever you want, I swear it in the name of God, if you will only tell me what it is." On the last word her voice fell, making the plea into a prayer to her captors, and so the first blasphemy. I caught my breath. Barbara looked young, terrified, pale. How could she look pale when a second ago I had been so conscious of all that garish makeup? There was no chance to wonder. She plunged on, through that first scene and the next and all of Joan's scenes. She went from hysterical fear to inept manipulation to the bruised, stupid hatred of a victim, to finally, a kind of negative dignity that comes not from accomplishment but from the clear-eyed vision of the lack of it, and so she died, Cosgriff's vision of the best that institutionalized man could hope for. But she was not Cosgriff's vision; she was a seventeen-year-old girl. Her figure was slight to the point of emaciation. Her face was young—I saw its youth, felt its fragile boniness in the marrow of my own bones. She moved with the gaudy, unpredictable quickness of the mad, now here, now darting a room's length away, now still with a terrible catatonic stillness that excluded her trapped eyes. Her desperation made me catch my breath, try to look away and fail, feeling that cold grab at my innards: It happened. And it could happen again. It could happen to me.

Her terror gave off a smell, sickly and sour. I wanted to escape the room before that smell could spread to me. I was helpless. Neither she nor I could escape. I did not want to help her, this mad skinny victim. I wanted to destroy her so that what was being done to her would not exist any longer in the world and I would be safe from it. But I could not destroy her. I could only watch, loathing Joan for forcing me to know, until she rose to her brief, sane dignity. In the sight of that dignity, shame that I had ever wanted to smash her washed over me. I was guilty, as guilty as all those others who had wanted to smash her. Her sanity bound me with them, as earlier her terror had unwillingly drawn me to her. I was victim and victimizer, and when Joan stood at the stake and condemned me in a grotesque parody of Christ's forgiving on the cross, I wanted only for her to burn and so be quiet, so release me. I would have lighted the fire. I would have shouted with the crowd, "Burn! Burn!" already despairing that no fire could sear away what she, I, all of us had done. From the flames Joan looked at me, stretched out her hand, came toward me. I thrust out my arm to ward her off. Almost I cried out. My heart pounded in my chest.

"Austin," she said.

In an instant Joan was gone.

Barbara came toward me. It was Barbara. She had grown three inches, put on twenty pounds and thirty years. Her face was tired and lined under gaudy, peeling makeup. Confusedly I blinked at her. I don't think she even saw the confusion; her eyes had lost their strained panic, and she was smiling, a smile that was a peaceful answer to some question of her own.

"That was the reality," she said, and stooped to lay her head on my chest. Through the fall of her hair I barely heard her when she said she would marry me whenever I wanted.

Barbara and I have been married for nearly a year. I still don't know precisely why she decided to marry me, and she can't tell me; she doesn't know herself. But I speculate that the night *A Maid of Domrémy* failed, something broke in her, some illusion that she could control, if not the world, then at least herself. When she struck Whitten with the candlestick, she turned herself into both victim and victimizer as easily as Lawrence Cosgriff had rewritten Shaw's *Joan*. Barbara has never played the part again. (Gregory Whitten, no less flamboyantly insensitive for his bashing with a candlestick, actually asked her.) She has adamantly refused both Joans, Shaw's heroine and Cosgriff's victim. I was the last person to witness her performance.

Was her performance that night in my hospital room really as good as I remember? I was drugged; emotion had been running high; I loved her. Any or all of that could have colored my reactions. But I don't think so. I think that night Barbara Bishop *was* Joan, in some effort of will and need that went beyond both the illusions of a good actress and the reality of what ESIR could give to her, or to Ann Friedland, or to anyone. ESIR only unlocks the individual genetic memories in the brain's R-Complex. But what other identities, shared across time and space, might still be closed in there beyond our present reach?

All of this is speculation.

Next week I will be hospitalized for my own ESIR. Knowing what I have been before may yield only more speculation, more illusions, more multiple realities. It may yield nothing. But I want to know, on the chance that the yield will be understandable, will be valuable in untangling the endless skein of waking visions.

Even if the chance is one in a million.

WHEN THE FATHERS GO

≈≈≈≈≈≈≈≈≈≈≈≈≈≈≈≈≈≈≈≈≈≈≈≈≈≈≈

Bruce McAllister

Women whose husbands are voyagers, seamen, explorers, have always had to deal with long periods of separation, and often radical changes in the personalities of their husbands when they do return. In the future, when people travel to other star-systems and encounter strange and alien experiences, travelers may return with incredible stories . . . and if one should bring back his "son" born of an alien woman, what should his wife think? What can she do? Especially if she finds that she loves the child?

Bruce McAllister, who has directed the writing program at the University of Redlands in Southern California since 1974, has written such superior stories as "Victor" and "Their Immortal Hearts," and the novel Humanity Prime.

WHEN HE TOLD ME HE HAD FATHERED A CHILD
Out There, I felt sure he was lying. I thought of the five years
I'd been awake, the five years since his return, the five years
I'd been pleading with him for a child, and I thought of all his
lies. (They *all* come back lying.)

I was sure he was lying.

It was night in the skyroom. We were naked and wet from
another warm programmed rain, and were again pawing at
each other in good-natured frustration, laughing because the
paper-thin energy field between us wouldn't let us touch.

The frustration was important.

Soon one of us would tell the room's computer to activate
a stencil, a brand-new pattern for our hands to explore
blindly, seeking the holes through which we might reach
each other.

The frustration was so important.

Before long—if everything went right—we would be moving against the field like animals, two starved bodies no
longer willing to accept the constraints so good-naturedly.

It was all a *karezza,* a game I suspected Jory liked, though
I could never be sure. The only things I was sure of were the
hallucinogens and the pheromas. These I knew he liked.
Only these.

He might pull away suddenly from the stencil, stare at me,
and walk off into the night.

And if he stayed, if he indeed stayed long enough for it to
happen, it would be an event as unrelated to me as any dim
nova in a distant galaxy. I would see it in his eyes: he would
be somewhere else. His moment would belong to him and
him alone—Out There.

I blame the hallucinogens as much as the rest. I am jealous

of the Moonlight, the Starmen, Schwarzchild's Love, and Winkinblinkins. They are his real lovers.

When he spoke, I assumed it was to the room's computer. But his voice went on—the amplified stars twinkling madly through the electronic glass, the moonlight falling on our naked shoulders like a cold blue robe. He was talking to *me*.

"I'm sorry, Dorothea," he was saying. "I am, as a long-lost poet once put it, a man adrift from his duties, a man awash in his world. I should have told you long before now, but did not. Why? Because it's horrible as well as beautiful."

He paused, so emotional, so crucified by remorse, and then: "When I was Out There, Dorothea, when I had the starlocks at my back and the universe at my feet, when I'd abandoned my home world as surely as if I'd died, I took an alien lover, Dorothea, and she bore me a son. I can't believe it myself, but it is true, and the time has come."

He was histrionic. He was heroic. He was playing to some great audience I couldn't see.

And he was lying.

They say the ones who go Out There—the *diplos, greeters,* and *runners*—come back liars because of what they've seen, because of the starlock sleep, because of what they dream as they make their painful slow way through the concentric rings of sequential tokamaks, super-pinches, marriages of light-cones, and miracles of winkholes. It is a sleep (the rumors say) filled with visions of eternal parallel universes, of all possible alternative worlds—where Hitler did and didn't, where Christ was and wasn't, where the Nile never flowed, where Jory never left, or if he did, I never went to sleep for him.

They are changed by it. They come back seeing what isn't but what might have been, what isn't but *is*—somewhere. And because they come back liars to a world fifteen years older, there will always be jobs for any man or woman willing to be a *diplo* or *greeter* or *runner*. They are the lambs. They are sacrificed in our names.

Whether Jory's lies are universes he indeed perceives, or simply the handiwork of a pathology, I do not know. I do know that there are times when I enter his lies with him and times when I do not. There are even times when I love his lies, though it embarrasses me to say so. When we lie together on the little stretch of sand below our house and make a simpler love—the roll of the waves mercifully drowning out the sucking of the great factory pipes so nearby—I want those lies, ask for them in my own way, and he gives them to me:

"Dorothea, my love, I have known women, insatiable women, women from a satyr's wildest dreams. I have known them in every port of the Empire—from Dandanek II to Miladen-Poy, from Gloster's Alley to Blackie's Hole, from the great silicon-methane bays of Torsion to the antigravity Steppes of Heart—and none of them can compare with the softest touch of your skin, with the simplest caress of your breath."

There are no ports like these. Not yet. No swashbuckling spacelanes, no pirates of the Hypervoid, no Empire. No romantic Frontier for the sowing of the human seed throughout galaxies so vast and wondrous that their glory must catch in your throat. It is, after all, a simpler, more mundane universe we inhabit.

But when he speaks to me like this, my world is suddenly grand, the ports as real as San Francisco, the women as lusty as legends, and I, a Helen of New Troy with a strange and beautiful apple in my hand.

I could have answered him with "What was she like, Jory?" I could have entered that lie, too, and said, "Did you ever see your son, Jory?"

But this one hurt. It hurt too much.

"What do you mean, the time has come?" I asked, sighing.

He was turning away, toward the darkness of the hills behind our house.

"He is coming to live with us," he said.

I closed my eyes. "Your son?"

"Of course, Dorothea."

I hate him for it.

He knows how it hurts. He knows why.

We have encountered three races Out There. The first two—the nearest us in light-years—are indeed humanoid, offering (for some, at least) clear proof of the "seeding" theory of mankind's presence in this solar system. The third race, the mysterious Climagos, is so alien that instead of animosity and avarice we find in it a disturbing generosity—

gifts like the energy fields, crystalline sleep, and the starlocks. In return, it has asked nothing but goodwill. We do not understand this. We do not understand it at all.

We have (we have decided) nothing to learn, nothing to gain, from the two humanoid species, the little Debolites and stolid Oteans. We ignore them, and are jealous of the attention the Climagos pay them. We are, it would seem, afraid of what these two humanoid species might eventually do with the Climagos' gifts. After all, we know well what it means to be "human."

"You haven't asked, but I will tell you anyway," he says.

He has followed me down to the tidepools, where I am trying to count the species of neogastropods and landlocked sculpins, to compare them against those listed in a wood-pulp book printed fifty years ago.

He seems sober, matter-of-fact. This means nothing.

Oblivious to the chugging of the factory behind him, he looks wistfully out to sea and says:

"She was Otean, of course. Her thighs like tree trunks, her body a muscular fist. The sable-smooth hair that covered her glinted like gold in the sunset of their star. She was a child by their standards, but twice as old as I, and her wide dark eyes were as full of dreams as mine. That is how it happened: we both were dreamers. I'd been away too long."

It is a moving tale, in its own way convincing. Otus is indeed a heavy world, the atmosphere thick, the surface touched by less light than Earth. In turn, Otean eyes are more photosensitive, their bodies stockier, their lungs accustomed to richer oxygen. And although they are much more like us than the little Debolites are, they hate Terra; they cannot stand to be here even for a day, even in lightweight breathing gear. (Some say it is a photophobia; others believe it is a peculiarity of the inner ear; still others, a vascularization vertigo.)

"I was drunk on the oxygen mix of that world," Jory is saying now, "and never did smell the lipid alienness of her. My poor blind passion never stumbled the whole long night."

I remember something else that gives credence: the marks—the dozen of tiny toothlike marks on his chest, on the inside of his arms. They've been there since I can remember, though I've never asked about them, assuming, as I did, that they'd been left by the medical instruments that prepared him for his journey.

Abruptly, somberly, Jory says, "No, I never saw the boy. I left Otus long before he was born."

It is almost convincing. But not quite.

1. Humans and Oteans are able to copulate, but fertilization is impossible; the Otean secretions are toxic. And were a sperm cell to survive, it would not penetrate the ovum; and were it to penetrate, the chromosomes would fail to align themselves on the spindle.
2. Jory was never on Otus.

One day not long after he returned and I awoke, Jory said to me: "What does a man gain by winning the universe, if by doing so he loses himself? He can never buy it back once it is bartered away." He was quoting someone, I felt sure. But I didn't ask and he didn't explain.

He was quiet for a while, and then, voice hoarse with sorrow, he whispered, "They lied to me, Dorothea, just as they lie to us all," and he began to weep. I took him in my arms and held him. I did not let go.

That was the man I knew. I have not seen him since.

I have located four species of rock shell, but it has taken nearly five hours. According to the wood-pulp book, fifty years ago I'd have found four times as many, and in half the time.

The factory has been here for thirty-five, yet it denies its pipes have ever dumped oxygen-depleting wastes into the delicate littoral zone.

The liars are so nearby, Jory.

I recall something else now, too.

Four years ago, not long after we had the addition built, Jory received a tape in the mail. He never offered an explanation; I never asked for one. That is our way. But one day I heard it, and saw it.

I was passing his new room, the one he'd built for privacy. I'd never stopped before, but this time I did because I heard a voice.

It sounded innocuous enough—mechanical and skewed to

the treble like a cheap computer voice. But when I tried to understand it, I realized that it wasn't a simvoice at all, that the language I was hearing was not of Earth.

When I reached the doorway, I stepped quietly inside and stopped.

Jory was seated at the screen, his back to me, and by the way he was staring I felt sure the screen held a face, a face belonging to the voice.

I took one step and saw the screen.

There was no face. Instead, an alien landscape filled the screen, violet crags and crimson gorges bathed by an unearthly light, the entire vision quivering like a bright, solarized rag.

The voice chattered on. Jory remained hypnotized. I left quickly, shivering.

That evening I pleaded with him again. All I could think of was the gorges, the eerie light, the quivering screen. I still believed that a child, however it came, would be able to banish such strangeness from the heart and soul of the man I loved, the man I thought I knew.

Despite the Climagos' greatest gift, very few humans have traveled Out There. As our technocrats learned long ago, the exploration of space is handled best by machines, not by flesh and blood liabilities.

There is one matter, though, that cannot be handled by mechanical surrogates—not, that is, without risk of diplomatic insult. That matter is Business—the political and economic business between sentient races and their worlds.

The leaders of Business understand the risks, and in turn, the *diplos* of interstellar politics, the *greeters* and *runners* of interstellar trade, and the occasional *scope* of interstellar R&D are all common men and women. All contract for the money (so they claim); all are commissioned with instant diplomatic or corporate rank in the departments of state, MNCs, and global cartels that hire them; and all have little computers implanted in their skulls.

To make them what they are not.

To make them what those back on Earth so need them to be.

"She was a Debolite, Dorothea." His agony is profound, his confession sincere, tortured. "Forgive me, please. I know few women would, but I ask it of you because you, more than most, should be able to understand." The pause is a meaningful one. "I shared a meal—skinned *rodentia* of some kind and a fermented drink made from indigenous leaves—with a committee of seven provincial demipharaohs. She was their courier. Later that night, she visited me in my quarters with an urgent—and I might add, laudatory—message from the Pharaohess Herself. I was intoxicated from their infernal *tulpai,* Dorothea. Otherwise, I'd never have been able to do what I did—to touch a body like that, so small and fragile, the face a clown's, the skin like taut parchment except where the slick algae grows."

He puts his head in his hands. He slumps forward. The scar is no longer red.

He says: "I saw the boy two years later. I could barely stand the sight of him."

He seems to collapse. "Dear God," he whispers. Quietly he begins to sob.

I get up. He is probably sincere. He probably believes what he is describing. Nevertheless, I blame him and with blame comes the hate.

1. Procreation is no more likely between humans and Debolites than it is between humans and sheep.
2. Jory was never on Debole.
3. Jory does not believe in the God whose name he takes in vain.

Debole is a small planet, and does not spin. Its inhabitants—fauna and flora alike—hug the twilight zone between eternal sun and endless night, and the thermal sanity which that zone provides. The Debolites are much smaller than humans, no larger in fact than the prosimians who scampered on Earth's riverbanks, forty million years ago, grist for the gullets of larger reptiles. The black algae that feeds on the secretions and excretions of their skin helps insulate them from the cold, as do the arrangements of fatty deposits around their vital organs, deposits which give them a lumpy, tumorous look. And the natural violet pigment of their dermis protects them from ultraviolet agony.

The Debolites are five thousand years away from their own natural space age. Because they are, mankind couldn't be less interested. But the Climagos are interested. This puzzles us. What do they see?

I've taken the pheroma capsules, and try not to complain. To keep our skin's bacterial succession intact, we have not bathed. Our exertions fill the air with a nightmarish brine, and I choke on it. The copulins are fiery ants behind my eyes, I am as nauseous as I've ever been in my life. (What was the dose this time? Which series did he use? Am I developing an allergy? Is there anyone who hates them as much as I do?)

We are squirming like blood-crazed chondrichthy. Jory's breathing is stertorous from the olfactory enhancement, the steroid bombardments, and I am doing my best to emulate his passion despite the threat of peristalsis.

Suddenly, in the voice of a stranger, Jory says:

"You'll choose not to believe me, as always. That is your right, Dorothea. But I must try to prepare you."

I shudder, shudder again. The room is warm, sickeningly so, but Jory's body has stopped moving. What will it be this time?

"She was a Climago, Dorothea. I use the term 'she' to help you—to help us both—understand what happened. Don't bother insisting that such a thing is impossible, because it *is* possible—it *indeed* happened. The Climagos are a compassionate race. They gave humanity the starlock secret; they gave humanity crystalline sleep and energy fields. And they gave one lone man—me, Jory Coryiner—another gift as well."

He pauses, mouth open, his jaw struggling.

"I don't need to tell you what they look like. You know."

I say nothing, the nausea unending.

How could I possibly know? Those who come back with descriptions are liars, and there isn't a government on Earth that appears interested in dispelling the mysteries. Even the commedia claim they can't get stills or tapes—not even of those Climagos who visit Earth. (Are they so shy? Are they so archetypally terrible to behold that the teeming masses of Terra, were they to find out, would riot, destroy their own cities, demand an instant end to diplomatic relations?)

But like everyone else, I've collected the descriptions—dozens and dozens of them. Chambered nautili with radioactive tendrils? Arachnoids cobalt-blue or fuchsia, or striped like archaic barber poles? Bifurcated flying brains? Systolic muscles with "gyroscope" metabolisms? Silicon ghosts? Colonial pelecypods looking more like death's-head skulls than clams? Which do *you* prefer, Jory?

"And you know, I'm sure," he is saying now, "how they've managed to survive on their hostile world for two hundred million years. I'm sure you know."

Perhaps I do. Perhaps I do not. I have heard the stories— and chosen to believe them—about those miracles of symbiosis, the Climagos. How their world is a litany of would-be predators, of knife-blade mandibles, deadly integuments, extruded stomachs that should have consumed every Climago on the planet a million times over—and would have were it not for the one trait that makes them not unlike us: a talent for adaptation, for cooperation, for helping and being helped.

It isn't simply cortical convolutions, though Climagos are certainly as intelligent as Terran cetaceans and pachiderms and *Homo erectus,* whatever "intelligence" may mean. It is the myriad ways in which they have learned to cooperate— to co-opt and thereby to best every other species on their home planet. The apelike things (so the stories go) who for eons lent them their prehensile hands. The great saurians who provided them with locomotion and "gross environmental-manipulation capability." The mindless coelenterates who shared their nutrient flesh with them during drought and famine. And the endless others. The helpers, and the helped.

In return, the Climagos—telepathic, patient—provided the sensory information needed to lead the day-blind lizards to new species of prey, to keep the feathery simians one step ahead of their growing enemies, to help the eternal jellyfish foresee the impending changes in the great tidal inlets of the world.

"You can understand why it happened. She was a greeter, too—one of theirs—and I was a lone human. As a devout student of humanity, she understood what my solitude meant; she understood that in their social needs humans are not at all Climagos, who do not fear loneliness, but are instead like the bottle-nosed dolphins of Earth, who suffer horribly when removed from their own kind."

He pauses now, averts his eyes and sighs. I smell half-digested food. I smell my own bile. The world swims.

"There was an eon of need within her," he is saying, "the need to help, the need to cooperate, the need to court a creature who, under other circumstances, might have been a predator. And within me, there was an eon of need as well—the need to find kin, a creature I would recognize by the most primitive of means."

I am still on my hands and knees, unable to move, the sickness darkening with a dread. Above me, Jory's eyes are the true purple of space, and the metallic breath of nausea moves through me like a toxic tide. It is the pheromas, yes, and the sweat, the androstenol, and all the others, but it is what I see too. Whether he knows it or not, I can indeed see his Climago greeter clearly. It is the version most often described. The horrible consensus.

I see a man so lonely, so crazy from his years of inhuman sleep, so twisted in his pent-up libidinal soul, that he can bring himself to touch it—a worm, a slug, its rolls of fat accordioned on a cartilaginous spine, its face (do I dare call it that?) a lamprey's, the abrasive bony plates, the hundreds of tiny sucking holes pulling the blood gently—like honey—from his chest, from the insides of his arms and thighs and—

Somehow I get up. I stumble. I rush from the room.

The footsteps behind me are heartbeats.

When I reach the bathroom, the sickness comes out. The pheromas make it the odor of death.

Behind me, a voice, disembodied:

"It wasn't like that at all," he whines. "Why can't you try to understand?"

I have started to cry.

"It was *beautiful*," he says, faithful that words can change it. "She *made* it beautiful. They are an incredibly beautiful people, Dorothea."

A moment ago, it was tears. Now, it is laughter. Here I am, kneeling in my own ambergris, as though worshipping a sunken bathtub, as though believing his most outrageous lie yet. The teeth marks, the rapture. Perhaps that, yes. But not the other.

Not a child.

I turn to him savagely. "And who carried the fetus for her? Some obliging surrogate, some Otean bound by diplomatic duty? If that strikes your fancy, Jory, just nod once and we'll tape it. But I'm puzzled, Jory. How will he reach us? The locks are far too slow. Is he coming in a taterchip can with tiny retrorockets? Or an FTL attaché case? Climagos are small, you know."

He looks at me in amazement, his eyes like a child's. I could kill him and he doesn't even know it. And I would kill him, I'm sure, were there anything near me sharper than a dryer or a toothcan. This man—this man who for five years has shown so little interest in the woman he lives with, who has heard none of my pleas—now offers me lies for a moment's absolution.

He steps toward me, takes my arm. I twist my head in a snarl, but I do not pull away.

The look is still there. He shakes his head, horribly hurt. "There's a son, yes, Dorothea, and, yes, he's very small—as you surmised. He's more Climago than human—an *alien*, yes—but he's intelligent and caring and he has the capacity to love us. Can't you at least—"

"Stop it!" I scream, hands over my ears, the smell of my own body like dung.

He goes dreamy now. He turns slowly, stares at the closed windows. I will scream again; I cannot bear what he will say.

"There's a son, yes," he begins anew. "He isn't small at all. He's a mutant, Dorothea, barely alive, and he may not make it through the starlocks. He's a pitiful thing, and he deserves our compassion. He has a human head, a nudibranch's body; he whimpers like a human child, but chokes on his own excrement if held the wrong way. Climago scientists have been studying him for years, but I want him with me now, and his mother—decent soul that she is—agrees. The child is allergic to so many things there; perhaps he will fare better here. *If* he survives the trip. *If* we can love hi—"

I hit him. I hit him on the temple, over the scar, feeling the metallic edge of the thing the corporation put there. The thing that has helped make him what he is.

The skin splits at the metal. He flinches, grabs my wrist. The blood begins to ooze.

I'm screaming something now that neither of us understands.

He says calmly, "Accept it, Dorothea. He'll be arriving soon."

He leaves me in the bathroom, where I continue to cry.
I do not see him for days.

I was a pale girl and still haven't lost it. No amount of
UV—no matter how graduated—can change that, with all
the Irish and English I have in my genes. I've got big bones,
too—big country-girl hands, pronounced veins and tendons,
and hipbones that bruise loves. "Daughter of a meatless
tribe," as my father used to put it.

I wonder how I first looked to Jory.

He was the darkest man I'd ever met, as dark as an
"olive" complexion can get—the curse (as he put it later) of
some rather thoughtless BlackAm, Amerind, and Hmong-
refugee ancestors.

His face, when he turned it to profile, was a hatchet from
an ancient dream, and he frightened me at first.

I was raised on one of the last megafarms of the American
Midwest. No, that's wrong. I was raised as the daughter of
the senior administrator of one of the last megafarms of the
American Midwest. There *is* a difference. Our house was a
big plasticoated three-story Victorian in Cedar Falls, an
hour's helirun from The Farm. No one ever really grew up
on a farm like that.

Jory, though, was a son of the Detroit Glory Ghettos—
those Recessional projects begun by a cornered liberal ad-
ministration two decades before his birth. Every minute of
his life had been subsidized by citizens who, at their noblest,
were full of self-congratulating "concern"; at their worst,
rationalized bigotry; and for 1439 minutes of every day,
apathy and indifference. He knew this. He'd grown up
knowing it—1440 minutes of every day.

For years I dreamed of a career somehow related to the
magical sciences of megafarming. What I really wanted, of
course, was a way never to leave home—a career to protect
my narrow affections, first loves, prized childhood memories of a mother and father who worked happily for The
Farm. My father, the loud, proud administrator; my mother,
the taciturn gene-splicer whose love of her work showed
clearly in her quiet eyes.

The last time I saw The Farm was the eve of Jory's
departure. I was twenty-eight years old. The machines were
still incredible—the immense nuclear combines, the comput-
erized "octopus pickers" and "dancing diggers." The land

was just as awesome—the dark pH-perfect soil stretching from horizon to horizon. But it was boring now. How could this be the world I'd romanticized for so long?

The career I finally chose to pursue—at the clear-thinking age of fourteen—was veterinary medicine. Not the anthropomorphic-pet kind (which I knew was glutted with practitioners), but the animal-husbandry kind (about which I knew absolutely nothing).

I made it as far as my fourth year of undergraduate studies, and then the world changed. I discovered people, and the dream of veterinary medicine began to fade.

One day I discovered a young man named Jory Coryiner and never dreamed the dream again.

I met him at one of the dinners my parents gave for the Huddleston Industries trainees. There were twelve this time—the usual fifty-fifty split of women and men—and Jory was impossible to miss: dark, cocky, intimidating, haloed with heroic rumors—in all, the most magnetically masculine thing I'd ever encountered in my cloistered Iowan life.

He disliked me intensely at first, I know that now. And with good reason. He knew who I was, and dreaded the inevitable patronizing. I persisted. Here was a young man all were talking about, a young man who'd won a fertboss traineeship not through federally imposed quota-tokenism but through his own impressive record, and for some reason I felt chosen, destined to understand him—his obvious need for a wall, tough carapace, calciferous shell, to hide behind.

How it happened, I can't say. After an hour's efforts, he softened. By the end of that hour, I felt I had glimpsed what few others had—the real reason for his chitinous ways: he was the son of a "welfare gloryhole" and he believed he wore that stigma for all to see in the melanin of his skin.

He was wrong, of course. To most men and women, his complexion was charismatic, magical, superior to their own. My own parents certainly never thought twice about my seeing him. But he never understood this. He still doesn't, and now, it is too late.

I should have seen it. I should have realized that the son of two mothers and two fathers—a boy shuttled back and forth from "step'nt" to "step'nt" throughout childhood—might perceive families in a different way. That a man from a Glory Ghetto who had struggled to escape the dark badge of its dependency might never stop struggling. That the moat might never dry up, the walls never crumble, the carapace never see a shedding no matter how much love fell upon it.

Were there alternative worlds in your eyes even then, Jory—places where Hiroshima never rose toward heaven, where the Jurassic Sea never dried, where the Visigoths held Italy for over five centuries?

I do not know. I lied to myself then, too.

When you told me you had contracted as a runner for Quanta, you took two hours to explain it. When you were through, you did not want to hear any of my questions. *Fait accompli.* You wanted no chinks, no soft underbelly through which your resolution might be undermined.

You said you were doing it because of your great boredom—and because of the money, the fortune you'd have when you returned. The fertboss position was driving you crazy, you said. Even with the antidepressants The Farm's headmeds were giving you (I knew nothing of this), your days were leaden with despair, you said.

You said, too, that you'd talked it over thoroughly with three who'd just come back. Two greeters and a diplo—three men. They were colorful talkers, yes, even a little strange at times, but, they weren't crazy, not at all. And they were very happy they'd gone.

Willi, who was eight then, said the only thing he could have: he didn't want to leave. He didn't want to give up his school, his teams, his clubs, his counselor, his center, his world. I had no choice. I had to respect it. He would not be our son fifteen years later when Jory returned and I awoke, but it was Willi's life, too, and to take him with us to a future where he would have only the two of us was all wrong. I believe that still. I do.

My mother was ill. She probably would be for the rest of her life. He could not stay with them. It was Clara and Bo, our friends from Cedar Falls, who at last agreed to take him. He would live with them during the school year until he was eighteen; he would spend summers with Jory's sister in Missoula or my parents in Cedar Falls. Whichever he preferred.

That was the best I could do, and as I did it, I wept.

You signed your contract. Quanta responded, depositing fifteen years of executive salary with the Citibank trustees.

While you slept in the starlocks and did your business on Climago, the capital earned. When you finally returned, you were (like the others) a millionaire and (like the others) so happy.

I slept for you, Jory, because that was my adventure, an adventure I believed was as noble as yours. All around us men and women were doing such things for their departing lovers, and I knew we would meet again—you and I—in a distant, idyllic future, to begin life anew like a modern Adam and Eve.

I slept for you, and my sad but loving parents paid for the suspension care without complaint, though they knew they were burying me.

I've seen my father only once since I awoke. Mother is dead. He had nothing to say.

I will not do that to him again.

Time marries. Time reconciles. "It is a recombiner like no other," as my mother used to say quietly. It has only been two weeks since Jory's announcement, and I have already begun to believe, to accept what I know cannot be true.

I must be prepared. I cannot afford not to be. If what Jory claims is true, if indeed we are about to have a visitor, I must begin to prepare this house physically—and myself psychologically—for its arrival. Whatever *it* may be.

After all, the notion of a visitor is, in its own way, appealing. Anything that makes the days feel different is, in its own way, appealing.

I give it the better part of each day. I give it so much that the headaches are excruciating. But they are a small price to pay for being prepared.

1. I'm actually quite qualified to receive the creature, whatever it may be. I received a decent formal training in biology, zoology, and physiology, and I've educated myself in recent years in invertebrate and marine biology, malacology, conchology. Jory would be the first to admit this, I'm sure.
2. If the creature is indeed intelligent, I cannot afford to make it feel unwanted. Jory will insist, I am sure, that it remain with us indefinitely, and I will have to abide by that as graciously as possible.

If the creature is intelligent and feeling—*if* it is indeed from a race driven by an eon-spanning need to help, to cooperate, to "care"—there is reason, is there not, to assume that some day I will be able to feel something resembling affection for it?

If it survives, of course.

I cannot guess his exact needs. I can only prepare for a variety of contingencies. I know, for example, that Climagos do not need daily intakes of atmosphere, that their integumentary system is "closed," that they require infusions of oxygen, nitrogen, hydrogen, and other elements only occasionally—once a week, say. And though the notion doesn't reconcile easily with hemophagia, their nutritional needs (according to the one reference tape I've been able to locate) follow a similar periodicity.

I will order the appropriate compressed gas tanks from San Francisco, and I will have a marine construction firm in Fort Bragg build a self-sterilizing, air-tight room. But I need to do more homework on the nutrion. Perhaps through supplements of some kind—say, a concentrated mineral/protein mixture tailored to blood profiles on Climago—we may be able to circumvent the need for volumes and volumes of blood-bearing tissue.

I've gone ahead and phoned three exobiologists in the Bay Area and in Houston, and have extracted all the information I can without jeopardizing our secret. We just can't let people—scientists, doctors and commedia folk—know what is about to happen here. Were the word to get out, our lives would be a hell of ruptured privacy. And if the child is as fragile as Jory claims it is, such a commotion might endanger its life.

But the exobs are willing to part with more information than either the transnational corporations or national governments seem to be, and I have unearthed the following: a Climago should be able to exist comfortably on a mixture of oxygenated, hydrogenated, and proteinized Na, K, Ca, Mg, Cl, and various iron- and copper-based transport pigments taken from Terran mammals and accessible through a durable membrane, natural or synthetic.

*   *   *

I haven't seen Jory in days; I have, in fact, seen him only two or three times in the past few weeks. It is as though his announcement that day—his "gift" to me—was at last able to liberate him.

Which is what he has wanted for five years.

When he visited me at the hospital just after I awoke, he said he wanted a house on this desolate coast. I thought I knew why. I imagined the harshness and solitude would be his way of bringing us together again.

I was lying to myself then.

It was the gray sea, the cold crags, the solitude itself that he wanted, not a marriage of lives. It was the inhumanity of it all that he wanted, and he wanted it more than anything else.

There are times—those rare moments when we embrace without the need to consummate—when I feel in his body the rhythms, the suckings and chuggings of the factory itself, of the great pipes that pull their material from the far seabed, of the dark engines that do to it what they do.

"Why is he coming?" I ask gently, wondering if gentleness can prevent a lie.

"His mother is dead," Jory says. "He is too human to live out the rest of his life there."

"No, Jory," I say. *"Why is he coming?"*

He looks at me sadly, cocks his head like a dog, and tries again: "Because he has a terrible congenital disorder and has very few years to life. He wants to be with his father, his cold mad feary father, before he dies."

"Please. Why is he coming?"

The smile flashes like a knife. The cruel eyes transfix me.

"Because I'm sick and tired of your nagging, your slop pails of complaint, Dorothea. I am giving you what you want and need. It's a better career than the aborted one, isn't it?"

All I can think to say is, "I see."

In a softer voice, he tells me, "Because I asked him to, Dorothea."

"Oh," I say. "And when was that?"

He looks away. "A few years ago. I've missed him so."

"Jory, a lockgram come-go takes two or three years."

"Yes, it does, but their telepathy is a very special kind. That's their survival secret, Dorothea. I can think a message to my beloved son across the whole galaxy and he can hear me. Hemispherical space is no obstacle for a love that—"

I turn. I leave him.

I am sure of it now: Jory invited his "child" to live with us before he left Climago.

Only one explanation is possible: the Climagos are immeasurably more advanced than we are in genetic engineering. They are able, through computer modeling and analog translation, to convert human genetic message into Climago genetic code. They are able to replicate human morphological and physiological capabilities in Climagoan cellular arrangements. But they made a mistake this time. The translation failed. The resulting organism: a hybrid mess, a congenitally doomed anomaly. What Jory has described.

Why they would attempt such a thing, I do not know. They are aliens, and perhaps we should not expect to understand them.

I heard voices as I came down the cedar stairs from the helipad yesterday. One was raised, almost violent; and I should have recognized it.

The other was softer, though not conciliatory.

"I can assure you," the softer voice was saying, "that we do not look sympathetically on visas for them, let alone immigration."

"And I can assure *you*"—it was Jory's voice; I recognized it now—"that if any government tries to block this, you people will know more trouble than you've ever known in your puny functionary lives. I've accommodated you and your bigoted quarantine laws; now you will accommodate me. If you do not, I can promise you I will spend what funds I have on the loudest, most public litigation this nation has ever seen. The diplomatic repercussions will not be negligible. Official prejudice is never negligible."

The softer voice said something and Jory screamed, "That's xenophobic bullshit and you know it! How in God's name can an organism that must replenish itself once a week with available equipment, that hibernates for two months of the year, that can move no faster than a walk be dangerous? A creature like that is considerably less dangerous than most federal bureaucrats, Mr. Creighton-Mark."

There was a silence. I stepped into the room.

The violence seemed to recede from Jory's eyes, which twinkled suddenly in a smile. But the violence was still there; it was there in the rippling muscle of his jaw.

"This is my spou, Mr. Creighton-Mark," he said. "Dorothea, this is the BIN—or at least a representative of it." To the official, he said, "May I assume her feelings are admissible?"

The man ignored me and said, "She knows what's at stake here?"

"Of course." The anger glowed in Jory's eyes again, the scar livid. "But why ask *me?* She's only a meter from you, and I'm sure she'd answer a question put to her. She might even thank you for the courtesy of it."

The man ignored the sarcasm. He looked at me at last, and waited.

Helpless, I looked at Jory, found eyes burning with a passion I did not recognize. If love, love for what? If hatred, toward whom?

I nodded, found myself saying, "Of course," and then repeating it. "Yes, of course."

Again the violence receded from his eyes, only to be replaced by a distance I knew all too well, as he said:

"We are childless, Mr. Creighton-Mark, I was gone for fifteen years. My spou suspended for me. Our one pre-contract child is now twenty-nine. He's a courteous young man, but he doesn't know us, and couldn't care less. Who could blame him? We abandoned him, did we not? We want to try again now—to be a family."

My face burned. I could not look at either of them. How could Jory use me like this—against this man? How could he claim feelings he'd just never had!

When I finally did look at the visitor, I could not understand what I saw. His eyes were on Jory; his expression was chaos—as though nothing Jory had said had made any sense to him, as though Jory's entire speech was the last thing he had expected to hear.

It was the look, I would realize later, of a man stunned by insanity, by the look of it, by the sound of it.

"I see," the visitor said at last, expression fading, words full of a relinquishing fatigue.

It was over. Jory had somehow won. Parting amenities

were exchanged, and as he left the official offered a platitude about government's debt to those who serve its diplomatic and economic interest at great sacrifice. He stressed it—the word "great."

The autonomous room was finished two weeks ago. The shipment of blood components arrived yesterday. I still have questions, dozens of basic ones, but there's nothing to be done about it. I've used every possible tape available through interlibrary banks and manufacturer listings, and I will not risk further exposure by contacting more "experts."

These remaining questions would worry me if Jory seemed at all anxious. But he is calm. He must feel we're prepared.

We argued today about who should copter in to SFO to get him. I insisted that both of us should, but Jory said no, that would be unfair to both "the boy" and me. I did not understand this, and I said so. Jory said only, "I need some time to prepare him."

I resent it, being excluded. Am I jealous already?

Jory took the copter to SFO this morning. I've been spending the day putting finishing touches on the special room, and on the refrigeration units with their blood substitutes and pharmaceutical stocks, all of which should allow us to control any Terran disease to which the poor thing might be susceptible. (I've done my homework. I've mustered up enough courage to phone two more exos—both at UC San Diego—to get the chemoprophylactic information we need. And I did it without making them suspicious, I am sure.)

They're here and I never heard them arrive! I've been too involved in last-minute scurrying.

I try the covered patio first, expecting Jory's voice, but I hear nothing. I start to turn, to head back toward the south patio, imagining that Jory has perhaps carried him down the cedar stairs toward our bedroom.

I see something, and stop.

A figure—it is in shadows under the patio beams. I cannot see it clearly, and what I do see makes no sense. It is too small to be Jory; it is *not* Jory. Yet I know it is too big for what he described. It is standing upright, and that is wrong too.

I walk toward it slowly, stopping at last.

My mouth opens.

I cannot speak; I cannot scream. I cannot even cry out in terror or joy.

It is a *boy*. A very real, very human boy.

He is thin, a little too thin, and he has Jory's hatchet face. He has Jory's blue-black hair.

He is, I know suddenly, more Jory than our Willi ever could have been.

I feel the tears beginning to come, and with them, the understanding. It is the kind of lie I never foresaw. There was no alien lover, no. Instead, it was a woman, an honest-to-god woman. On the lock shuttles perhaps. Or on Climago itself. A greeter, or diplo, or runner just like Jory.

This boy, this very real boy, is theirs. The truth is wonderful!

Why Jory felt he had to lie, I cannot say. I would have accepted the boy so easily, so gratefully, without it.

I take another step toward the boy, and he smiles. He is beautiful! (Don't be vain. You don't *really* care whether there's a chromosome of yours in him, do you?)

A voice intrudes suddenly, and I stop breathing.

"Amazing, isn't it, Dorothea. Can you guess how they did it?"

I turn to Jory, a plea in my eyes: *Don't ruin it. Please don't ruin it.*

"Don't worry," he says. "I've talked it over with the boy and everything is fine. He grew up with the truth and is proud of it. As he should be." He turns to the boy, winks, and smiles. "Isn't that so, August? You know a lot more about it than your dad does, right?"

The boy nods, grinning back. The grin is beautiful.

Jory is grinning too, saying, "Take a guess, Dorothea. It's nothing us human beings couldn't have done ourselves."

I look at the boy. The world is spinning. Everything I have ever known or accepted is about to become a lie.

"I don't know, Jory," I whisper.

No one says a thing, and suddenly Jory shouts:

"Cloning! Simple cloning! Nothing fancier than that. Are you surprised?"

There is nothing I can say.

"On our second night together," Jory is saying, "she put it so well. 'It's the least we can do,' she told me. 'A living symbol,' she said, 'of our refusal to accept passion's ephemeral insubstance.' "

"He's all me, Dorothea!" Jory exclaims, laughing, glowing.

I look at the boy again.

"I'm going to leave you two alone," Jory says cheerfully, "let you get to know each other better. Our copter is in dire need of a cleaning!"

The father smiles paternally. The father smiles bountifully.

I want to believe him. I so want to believe that this is, at last, the truth.

When I look into his brown eyes, I see a real boy. When I take his hand in mine, I feel one. He is human. He is Jory, and no one else. I am able, yes, to believe that no mother's chromosomes are in him; I am able to believe what Jory claims.

We start by talking about his trip through the starlocks. My voice shakes for a time, but that is all right. He, too, with his strange, halting English, is unsure of himself. We must help each other overcome the fears. We cooperate; we allow the other to help.

As we say good night, he whispers to me, "I love you, Mother, I do," and kisses me. It catches me off guard; I laugh nervously, wondering if his father told him to say it, or if it is just the boy's own sensitivity.

He looks hurt, and I know now I shouldn't have laughed.

"I'm sorry, August." I say it as brightly as I can, taking his warm hand. "I wasn't laughing at *you;* I'd never do that. Sometimes people laugh when something surprises them, especially when it's something nice."

I squeeze his hand. He squeezes back, and I am filled with emotions I haven't felt in a long long time.

Jory is with me in bed tonight, the first time in a long time.

"August was in the starlocks?" I say, afraid to ruin the magic, but haunted by a thought.

Jory gets up on one elbow and looks at me sleepily. "Yes, he was. Why?"

"He told me he loved me, and I was wondering—"

His face lights up with a grin. "Hey, that's wonderful!"

"He's been through the starlocks," I begin again. "Would he lie to me, Jory? Would he even *know* he was lying to me?"

The cheerfulness dies. He stares at me for the longest time.

"August never lies," he says finally.

I have been awake in the darkness for hours, thinking to myself, thinking about men and boys, fathers and sons, about a man—a liar—who swears to his wife that their son is not a liar. It is a joke of sorts, a riddle. It cannot be solved.

The strange thing is, I wouldn't mind it if August did lie to me that way.

I could come to love his lies so easily.

Jory is gone again. From the house. From my life. Back to the woods, the beach, the Winkinblinkins and Starmen, the endless worlds spinning within him.

I don't mind.

I have August. I have the child who in only five days has changed my life completely. We've picnicked on the peninsula where the remaining seals sun themselves like lazy tourists. We've tramped the tidepool reefs to identify *mollusca* and to make the Kirlian photographs of their fairylike "souls." We've chartered an oceanographic trawler from Mendocino, and spent the day oohing and ahing over the dredgings. We've even found time to attend a fair in Westchester, that ugly, charming little town whose streets are lined with the slick red manzanita boles washed down by the Gualala at its meanest.

Wherever we go, I feel alive, I feel proud, I feel loved. The way people look at us can only be envy. And why not? It should be clear to anyone that August, handsome and devoted son that he is, does enjoy being with me.

It happened five hours ago. I am still shaking. I should move from this chair, but I am afraid to, afraid that if I do I will lose my mind.

August came to us a week ago.

Today he asked to use the special room.

To *use* it.

I stared at him, unable to speak, and he asked me again.

As I took him to it, I did my best not to look at him, afraid of what I might see.

At the gasketed doorway, he looked back at me tenderly and said, "I'm sorry, Mother, but I must shut the door. I think you know why."

Yes. I do.

It is not just because of the gases.

It is because of what I might see when he attends to his body, to his needs, and forgets me.

He shut the door gently, and as he did he asked me to set the food and air controls for him. He could not do this himself, he said. (Yes. I remember now. He did not hold the cameras at the tidepools. He did not remove anything from the dredgings of the trawler. He did not pay for anything with his own hand. He did not open doors. He did not prepare food. He ate little, and I never saw it enter his mouth. He was simply a vision—present and loving.)

He has been in there with his proper mix of gases and his nutritive membrane for five hours. The last thing he said to me was: "Don't worry, Mother. I used a room just like this in quarantine for sixteen months. It really wasn't so bad."

How to accept it all? How to accept it without screaming? That August is no clone, that he is not human, that he is not what I see.

That he is but a projection, the gift of illusion, a lie.

That something else entirely lives and thinks there behind the loving face.

As the truth sinks in, I begin to see what the books and tapes dared not explain, what governments must take pains not to reveal, what in my own unwillingness to expose our lives to public scrutiny I kept five experts from telling me.

I begin to understand what the word "telemanifestor" means—the word heard only once, a single tape, a passing reference buried among information I assumed was much more important. I thought I knew what "tele" meant, in all its forms.

Will I be able to live with this? When I touch his arm and feel the pulse just under the skin, what do I really touch? When he kisses me and says, "I love you, Mother, I do," what is it that really presses itself against my lips? Bony plate, accordion of fat—how can I not see them?

The scream that first rose in my throat has faded. The August-thing will soon be leaving his special room; I must try to pretend that everything is all right. It will see through the pretense, of course, but I must try anyway. As a gesture. It is intelligent, after all. It has feelings. It is a guest in my house. And I, a representative of humanity, must act accordingly. That is all I can do.

It is clear now. It is clear how the Climagos convinced the jaws and talons and eversible stomachs of their world not merely to ignore them, but to help them build a civilization on its way to the stars:

The Climagos are liars too. They have survived for two hundred million years because of the terrible beauty of their lives.

I awoke this morning to an empty, familiar bed.

It was easier than usual. A sound had awakened me, I knew.

I listened and soon heard it again.

In the next room, on a small foam mattress, I found it. It stopped its crying as soon as I appeared, and like a fool I spent the first half hour inspecting it.

The "evidence" was there of course. Even neonatal physiognomy couldn't mute that nose. The eyes would darken, yes, but the complexion would remain the same—only slightly lighter than its father's.

I changed his Dryper and took him to the garden. Soon, he was cooing and chuckling and pulling up the flowers I'd planted only yesterday. He liked the big red zinnias most, of course, bright suns that they are, and in the end the only thing able to distract him was the sight of a cypress silhouetted against a pale morning sky. (I remembered how Willi loved such things staring for hours at a high-contrast print or a striped toy animal.)

We had played for over two hours when suddenly I remembered my appointment. August and I were going to Gualala for crabs! I'd been promising it to him for days.

What to do? (What would *August* want me to do?)

It came to me then like a breeze, a waking dream, in a voice that was indeed August's. It was *so* simple.

I rose. I took the baby to the little mattress, kissed it, and left the room without looking back. It did not cry.

Ten minutes later, just as I finished the replanting of the flowers, August appeared. *So* simple.

He was very striking in his navy-blue one-piece, hailing me from the top of the cedar stairs like a sea captain from centuries ago. I felt frumpy and told him so, but he insisted I looked beautiful, even in my earth-stained shorts.

We had a wonderful time. "Helluva season!" the erudite crabseller crowed, and we took the crabs home for a delicious salad under amplified stars.

The baby is in bed with me tonight. I know what it is, but it doesn't matter.

August is with me, too, though I cannot see him.

And Jory is wherever he wishes to be.

It has been another day of magic. Jory and I went to a mixer in Fort Bragg this evening, for the first time in years. He was all wit, wisdom, and charisma, free with his engaging tales of Climago and the exciting chases of interplanetary Business.

When we got back to the house, he stopped me and put his hands on my shoulders. I could feel their weight. "I've been insensitive as hell, Dorothea," he said. "I know that. This time, no pheromas!" He laughed, and I couldn't help but smile. "And no damned sling field or *son y lumière* either!" Face in a mocking leer, he added, "Unless, of course, you'd like to try some Everslip oil, just to keep things from being too easy."

"No, no, not the oil!" I cried in mock horror. Then, softly, I said, "I've always wanted it easy, always."

And it was. We made love—miracle of miracles!—in our very own unadorned hoverbed, the opaque ceiling above us wonderfully boring, the unsynched music quaint, the steady lamplight charming, and no stencils to frustrate us.

The new Jory sleeps beside me, and I lie awake, happy. I can hear the sounds, yes. The footsteps, the chairs slithering, the sighs. I hear them in the den, in the distant kitchen— but they do not bother me. A faint voice within me whispers, "That is the *real* Jory; those are his sounds." But I answer: "It is only a stranger, a stranger in our house. He does not bother us, we do not bother him. He is really no more than a memory, a dim figure from a fading past, a man who once said to you, 'My son is coming to live with us,' when he didn't mean that at all, when he meant instead, 'It is my lover who is coming. . . .' "

In the morning, the tiny holes on my chest and arms will ooze for the briefest time. I will touch them lovingly. They are a small price to pay.

In a house like this one, but in a universe far far away, a stranger once said as he wept, "In the end, Dorothea, in the end all of our windows are mirrors, and we see only ourselves."

Or did he say, "In the end, Dorothea, all that matters to mankind is mankind, world without end, amen"?

Or perhaps he said nothing at all.

Perhaps I was the one who said it.

Or perhaps neither of us said a thing, and no lie was ever spoken.

THE SCIENCE FICTION YEAR

Charles N. Brown

The New York Times HARDCOVER BESTSELLER list for January 2, 1983, has science fiction or fantasy books in seven of the top nine places. Arthur C. Clarke and Isaac Asimov challenge a quasi-sf novel by James Michener for first place. Douglas Adams's "Hitchhiker" trilogy makes the hardcover and paperback lists simultaneously with volumes three and two. Volume one, out for over a year in paperback, makes the list again.

Cut to Hollywood where George Lucas congratulates Steven Spielberg on *E.T.* becoming one of the top money-making movies of all time. The others? *Star Wars, The Empire Strikes Back, Jaws* and *Raiders of the Lost Ark*. Four of the five are sf; all are produced or directed by the same two men. Nearly all the top grossing films of the year are also sf or fantasy; besides *E.T.*, there was *Poltergeist, Blade Runner, Star Trek II, Tron*, etc.

It sounds like a science fiction fan's wildest dreams. Ten years ago, it would have been. Now, it's just a picture of the 1982 science fiction field.

It was a year of merger for the paperback book trade: Ballantine swallowed Fawcett, Berkley took over Ace and Playboy, Warner got Popular Library, and Tower and Leisure went out of business. Most general publishers also had poorer sales and smaller profits. On the other hand, few of the science fiction leaders were complaining. DAW had an excellent year; Del Rey had some huge bestsellers and outperformed its parent company, Ballantine; Pocket and Berkley did well with sf; Bantam and Tor have announced 1983 expansions. For the fifth year in a row, over 1,000 sf and fantasy books were published, with a majority of them new and original. The prices went up again. Lead titles are now $2.75 to $2.95, with $3.50 for bestsellers such as Heinlein and Donaldson. The bookstore chains and, I hope, the audience have been resisting prices of $3.50 for mass market sf books. Some publishers have been forced to limit themselves to thinner books to keep them priced under $3.00. Hardcover prices went up and there were more trade paperbacks. An original novel even by a major writer may now come out as a trade paperback.

In major editorial changes, Susan Allison moved to Berkley (and then took over her old Ace line when Berkley bought it), Lou Aronica became sf editor at Bantam, George Scithers moved to *Amazing* and Shawna McCarthy eventually became editor of *Isaac Asimov's SF Magazine.* Ben Bova left *Omni* for full-time writing.

Heinlein, Asimov, Clarke, Herbert, Donaldson and Anthony had new novels on the general bestseller lists. *Helliconia Spring,* a magnificent worldbuilding novel by Brian Aldiss, hit the top of the British list and sold out its American first edition. Clarke's *2001: A Space Odyssey* sequel, *2010: Odyssey Two,* was even better than the original book. There were a quarter million hardcover copies in print within a month of publication. *The Sword of the Lictor,* the third volume in Gene Wolfe's excellent "Book of the New Sun" tetralogy, appeared to almost universal praise. The writing is superb. C. J. Cherryh turned out *The Pride of Chanur,* an excellent space opera with sympathetic aliens. Asimov's *Foundation's Edge* was a fitting continuation of the popular series. Frederik Pohl, surely one of our best writers, produced *Starburst,* an expansion of his award-winning novella, "The Gold at the Starbow's End." *Friday* was Heinlein's best novel since *The Moon is a Harsh Mistress,* and *Hawkmistress!* by Marion Zimmer Bradley was a fine addition to the Darkover series. Other science fiction novels I both enjoyed and can recommend included *Merchanter's Luck* by C. J. Cherryh, *Courtship Rite* by Donald Kingsbury (a first novel), *Crystal Singer* by Anne McCaffrey, *A Rose for Armageddon* by Hilbert Schenck, *Roderick* by John Sladek, and *Coils* by Roger Zelazny and Fred Saberhagen. Two first novels which are fantasy, not sf, *The Red Magician* by Lisa Goldstein and *God Stalk* by P. C. Hodgell, are also on my recommended list.

The Compass Rose by Ursula K. Le Guin was easily the best collection of the year, with *The Complete Robot* by

Isaac Asimov, *The Robot Who Looked Like Me* by Robert Sheckley, and *Majipoor Chronicles* by Robert Silverberg as distinguished runners-up.

Outstanding anthologies were *The Road to Science Fiction #4: From Here to Forever* edited by James Gunn, and *The Eureka Years* edited by Annette Peltz McComas. Both are historical surveys with historical commentary on the sf field.

Science Fiction Writers: Critical Studies of the Major Authors From the Early Nineteenth Century to the Present Day edited by E. F. Bleiler is the best of the three author encyclopedias to appear so far, and the best non-fiction sf book of the year. It covers seventy-six authors and has some excellent critical articles. For an entertaining, individual, and iconoclastic view of science fiction, try *The Engines of the Night* by Barry Malzberg.

Frank Herbert signed a $1.5 million contract for another "Dune" novel; on the other hand, Stephen King accepted a $1.00 advance for his new novel, *Christine*. "They earn out anyway, and I don't need the money," he said. In another unusual move, King refused to sell reprint rights to his limited-edition book *The Dark Tower: The Gunslinger* because it's an early, different work which might mislead his readers who expect "a regular Stephen King book." Isaac Asimov got $1 million for reprint rights to the four "Foundation" books. Anne McCaffrey signed to do another "Dragon" novel.

An unpublished "Little Fuzzy" novel was discovered among the papers of the late H. Beam Piper, who died in 1964. Harlan Ellison helped the Los Angeles police solve a series of bookstore burglaries. He also resold *The Last Dangerous Visions* to still another publisher.

It wasn't the best year for sf magazines but it wasn't the worst either. There were fewer titles (seven) but more issues (sixty-one) than in 1981. It would have cost you $102.90 to buy the pure fiction ones on the newsstand, and $30.00 to add *Omni* with its two stories per issue. *Amazing* achieved the lowest circulation of its long career (11,500) before being sold to TSR Hobbies, the manufacturers of "Dungeons & Dragons." George Scithers was installed as editor, raised rates and page count, and did a complete interior redesign. I hope the magazine isn't past saving and can bounce back. *Analog* had a good year and brought its circulation back up to 100,000. *Fantasy and Science Fiction* was, as usual, the best in terms of good fiction. It lost newsstand circulation but made it up in subscriptions. For the first time in nearly a decade, there were four monthly (or better!) magazines. Alas, it didn't last; *Twilight Zone* went bi-monthly at the end of the year. The two 1981 pocket-size magazines, *Destinies* and *Weird Tales*, did not come out for the 1982 round. *Science Fiction Digest* died after its fourth issue. No actual figures are available, but it probably sold under 60,000 copies. I didn't like the idea of an "excerpt" magazine and I guess the readership agreed.

Two British magazines which fall into that nebulous area between semi-pro and professional appeared. One of them, *Extro*, died before the end of the year. *Interzone*, a "co-operatively produced" magazine in the style of *New Worlds*, is still hanging by a thread.

In Australia, an *Omni*-style slick magazine titled *Omega Science Digest* that was founded in 1981 produced six bi-monthly issues in 1982 filled mostly with popular-science articles plus two science fiction stories per issue. The stories, most of them written by writers new to sf, weren't very good, but if the magazine can draw more on the talents of experienced Australian sf writers, it could become an interesting contribution to the field.

There was a surprising amount of sf interest in the Soviet Union and in China last year; many fans and writers toured both countries and met with foreign authors. Arthur C. Clarke received VIP treatment on his recent Russian tour and Robert A. Heinlein was feted in China. I went to the Soviet Union as part of a science fiction tour and was very well treated. Can science fiction be considered the pingpong of the eighties?

Philip K. Dick, one of the great writers of science fiction, died on March 2, 1982, after a series of strokes. In many ways, Dick was one of the most important authors of our time. His work affected other writers even more than it did readers, and his influence has been and will continue to be felt. It was particularly ironic that he died just as *Blade Runner*, the movie version of one of his best books, was about to appear and he had at last achieved some financial independence. His last novel, *The Transmigration of Timothy Archer*, appeared two months after his death. A Philip K. Dick Memorial Award for best original paperback has been proposed. The 1983 judges will be Thomas M. Disch, Ursula K. Le Guin and Norman Spinrad.

Hubert Rogers, 83, whose artwork in the thirties, forties and fifties in *Astounding* helped set the John W. Campbell "style" and affected a whole generation of sf artists, died of heart failure on May 12, 1982.

Stanton A. Coblentz, 86, a writer who was generally ahead of his time when he combined satire, social commentary and science fiction in a series of novels published in the pulps in the twenties and thirties, including *The Sunken World* (1928), *After 12,000 Years* (1930) and *In Caverns Below* (1935) and was once offered the editorship of *Science Wonder Stories* by Hugo Gernsback, died September 6, 1982, after a stroke.

Other deaths reported in 1982 included Harry Bates, 80, the first editor of *Astounding;* Edmund Cooper, 55, author of many books including *The Cloud Walker* (1973); Ayn Rand, 77, whose *Atlas Shrugged* (1957) briefly caused an objectivist vogue in sf; Kendell Foster Crossen, 71, a well-known pulp writer; Joan Hunter Holly, 50, author of thirteen sf novels; and D. F. Jones, 66, author of the "Colossus" series.

The 1981 Nebula Awards were presented at the seventeenth annual Nebula banquet, held this year at the Claremont Hotel in Berkeley, California, on April 24, 1982. The winners were: Best Novel, *The Claw of the Conciliator* by Gene Wolfe; Best Novella, "The Saturn Game" by Poul Anderson; Best Novelette, "The Quickening" by Michael Bishop; Best Short Story, "The Bone Flute" by Lisa Tuttle. Tuttle attempted to refuse the award but received it anyway because she announced her withdrawal too late.

The 1982 *Locus* Awards were announced in San Francisco on July 18, 1982. Winners were: Best Science Fiction Novel, *The Many-Colored Land* by Julian May; Best Fantasy Novel, *The Claw of the Conciliator* by Gene Wolfe; Best First Novel, *Starship & Haiku* by Somtow Sucharitkul; Best Novella, "Blue Champagne" by John Varley; Best Novelette, "Guardians" by George R. R. Martin; Best Short Story, "The Pusher" by John Varley; Best Anthology, *Shadows of Sanctuary* edited by Robert Lynn Asprin; Best Single Author Collection, *Sandkings* by George R. R. Martin; Best Related Non-Fiction Book, *Danse Macabre* by Stephen King; Best Artist, Michael Whelan; Best Magazine, *The Magazine of Fantasy and Science Fiction;* Best Publisher: Pocket/Timescape. The twelfth annual *Locus* Awards received 834 nominating ballots—more than the Hugo and Nebula Awards combined.

The tenth annual John W. Campbell Award for best novel of the year was given to *Riddley Walker* by Russell Hoban at a July 10 banquet in Lawrence, Kansas.

The 1982 Hugo Awards were presented in Chicago on September 5, 1982. Winners were: Best Novel, *Downbelow Station* by C. J. Cherryh; Best Novella, "The Saturn Game" by Poul Anderson; Best Novelette, "Unicorn Variation" by Roger Zelazny; Best Short Story, "The Pusher" by John Varley; Best Non-Fiction Book, *Danse Macabre* by Stephen King; Best Professional Editor, Edward L. Ferman; Best Professional Artist, Michael Whelan; Best Dramatic Presentation, *Raiders of the Lost Ark;* Best Fanzine, *Locus* edited by Charles N. Brown; Best Fan Writer, Richard E. Geis; Best Fan Artist, Victoria Poyser. The John W. Campbell Award (not a Hugo Award) went to Alexis Gilliland.

Chicon IV, the fortieth World Science Fiction Convention, held September 2nd to 6th, 1982, in Chicago, Illinois, drew an attendance of 4300. It was smaller than expected and more relaxed, but the parties actually started the Monday before and ended the Friday after. The two-week convention seems to have finally arrived. The Hyatt Regency Hotel was big enough for the entire convention. Guests of Honor A. Bertram Chandler, Lee Hoffman and Frank Kelly Freas were duly feted. Highpoints included the masquerade, art show and dealers' room; a special hall masquerade, the flight of a balloon-powered scale model of the space shuttle in the hotel atrium lobby, trying to get from one tower to the other, an embarrassed Bob Tucker, Toaster Marta Randall dressed in a slinky evening gown and an aardvark mask and four tracks of nonstop programming with more than enough of everything for everybody.

The forty-first World Science Fiction Convention will be held in Baltimore, Maryland, September 1–5, 1983. Guests of honor are John Brunner and David Kyle with Jack Chalker as Toastmaster. For information on membership, write Constellation, Box 1046, Baltimore, MD 21203.

The forty-second World Science Fiction Convention will be held in Anaheim, California, August 30–September 3, 1984. Guests of honor will be Gordon Dickson and Dick Eney with Jerry Pournelle and Robert Bloch as Toastmasters. For information on membership, write LA Con, Box 8442, Van Nuys, CA 91409.

Charles N. Brown is the editor of Locus, *the newspaper of the science fiction field. Individual copies are $1.95 each postpaid from the publisher. Subscriptions in the United States are $18.00 for twelve issues, $34.00 for twenty-four issues via second-class mail. First-class subscriptions in the U.S. or Canada are $25.00 for twelve issues, $48.00 for twenty-four issues. Overseas subscriptions are $20.00 for twelve issues, $38.00 for twenty-four issues by sea mail. Airmail overseas subscriptions are $32.00 for twelve issues, $60.00 for twenty-four issues. Locus is published monthly. All subscriptions are payable only in U.S. funds to* Locus Publications, *P.O. Box 13305, Oakland, CA 94661.*

RECOMMENDED READING—1982

Terry Carr

PAULINE ASHWELL: "Rats in the Moon." *Analog,* November 1982.

DAVID BRIN: "The Postman." *Isaac Asimov's Science Fiction Magazine,* November 1982.

DAMIEN BRODERICK: "The Magi." *Perpetual Light.*

RAY BROWN: "Looking for the Celestial Master." *Analog,* September 1982.

JOSEPH H. DELANEY: "Brainchild." *Analog,* June 1982.

LEIGH KENNEDY: "Helen, Whose Face Launched Twenty-eight Conestoga Hovercraft." *Universe 12.*

GARRY KILWORTH: "The Invisible Foe." *Isaac Asimov's Science Fiction Magazine,* January 18, 1982.

MICHAEL P. KUBE-MC DOWELL: "The Garden of the Cognoscenti." *Analog,* June 1982.

BRAD LINAWEAVER: "Moon of Ice." *Amazing,* March 1982.

DAVID REDD: "The House on Hollow Mountain." *Fantasy and Science Fiction,* May 1982.

KIM STANLEY ROBINSON: "To Leave a Mark." *Fantasy and Science Fiction,* November 1982.

JOANNA RUSS: "The Mystery of the Young Gentleman." *Speculations.*

WARREN SALOMON: "Time on My Hands." *Isaac Asimov's Science Fiction Magazine,* October 1982.

ROBERT SILVERBERG: "Gianni." *Playboy,* February 1982.

SOMTOW SUCHARITKUL: "Aquila." *Isaac Asimov's Science Fiction Magazine,* January 18, 1982.

GEORGE TURNER: "A Pursuit of Miracles." *Universe 12.*

ROBERT F. YOUNG: "The Moon of Advanced Learning." *Isaac Asimov's Science Fiction Magazine,* October 1982.